The Pearl

of

Ruby City

For John & Loma

The Pearl

OF

Ruby City

*May Thanks for may
years of friendship*

Jana Harris

*Jana Harris
10/11/98*

ST. MARTIN'S PRESS 〰 NEW YORK

Design by Victoria Kuskowski

Library of Congress Cataloging-in-Publication Data

Harris, Jana.
The pearl of Ruby City / Jana Harris. — 1st ed.
p. cm.
ISBN 0-312-19315-7
I. Title.
PS3558.A6462P4   1998   98-23932
                                                      CIP

First Edition: October 1998

10   9   8   7   6   5   4   3   2   1

IN MEMORY OF
my horse, Vera, a pearl without price.

AND FOR
my horse-girlfriend, DeAnna Woolston,
who never failed us.

ACKNOWLEDGMENTS

For their endless readings of this manuscript, their encouragement, insight, comments, their contributions or furthering of my research or their computer genius, I owe a tremendous debt to the following: Kelley Ragland, Robin Straus, Kathy Ellingson, Irene Wanner, Cindy Lord, Valerie Miner, Mark Bothwell, the Okanogan Historical Society, Gary Landreth, Laura Jolley, the Idaho State Historical Society, the University of Washington's Allen Library, and the Washington State Library system. I would also like to thank Raymond Smith, Joyce Carol Oates, and the Ontario Review Press for publishing my book of poems, *Oh How Can I Keep on Singing? Voices of Pioneer Women*, which was the progenitor of this novel.

The Pearl

of

Ruby City

CHAPTER ONE

Ruby City, Washington
April 16, 1893

Poisoned. That was my diagnosis.

Though I told people I hoped to become a nurse someday, what I really wanted to be was a doctor. In fact, I'd secretly applied for admission to medical college. In the meantime, I kept notes on all my "patients"—the lads who came to me to have a finger wrapped when they cut it chopping wood or to have a fever mopped. (That is to say, they'd come to me if Doc was busy tending casualties at a mine cave-in and the nurse was miles away delivering a baby.) I took notes on Mayor "Shaky" Pat McDonald, too, and wasn't at all convinced that his symptoms were those of typhoid fever. But who was I to disagree? A hundred-pound laundress, age twenty-one years, not wanting to call attention to herself for fear of the warrants sworn out against her. If anyone asked me, and nobody did, I'd say Mayor Shaky Pat's liver had ceased its willingness to thrive—which can happen from consuming too much bad liquor or any one of several toxic substances listed in my *U.S. Cavalry Frontier Medical Guide*.

Hiding in the chaparral behind the livery stable, I nervously tried to bury a pail of whitewash and a paintbrush. Almost dusk, and the sage made long, witchy shadows across the brick-colored sand. My nerves turned to rags as I huddled next to the damp ground, the tie-strings of my bonnet beating my face in the relentless Cascade wind. But even though I was up to the devil's handiwork and my teeth chattered so hard from fright that they made my tongue sore, I couldn't keep my mind off of Shaky Pat. While mentally reviewing the symptoms surrounding our mayor's sudden decline in health, I noticed that whitewash stained my arms and apron. Frantically, I tried to scratch the incriminating evidence off with a stick. Then, afraid to move, I peered through the scrub pine at my labor scrawled across the livery stable: "AVARICE" glowed in the late afternoon sun, the letters at least a yard high. Fueled by this meager act of revenge, my teeth stopped rattling and my heart burned brightly.

Again I thought of the mayor. Accompanying Doc on his rounds yesterday, I'd seen no evidence of what he diagnosed as typhoid—no red rash on Shaky's chest, and his stomach didn't pooch. Though Salmon Creek had been fouled enough to cause an epidemic, our mayor hadn't had occasion to sample the water in this silver-mining camp. I'd never seen man or beast fail as fast as he did, except perhaps for one of Doc's horses after it had grazed in a field of poison jimsonweed.

Several men gathered in front of the livery, gazing at the A and the even larger V, but I couldn't see who they were. Then a string of curses rang out over the river valley below our tiny tent town, and I clearly saw the bearish towheaded body of the livery owner, Jake Pardee. As his arms waved like the sails of a windmill, I noticed he'd torn out the elbows of a shirt I'd washed and mended just last week. He disappeared around the corner under the building's false front and returned with a bucket, dashing water against the side of his building. The V elongated into a Y and the C bled a little, but the message remained clear.

A hunchbacked Scotsman in a white plug hat and black woolly chaps began beating the sagebrush next to the livery with a crooked stick. Hunting rattlers? It was early spring and too cold yet for a snake to awaken from his winter sleep.

He yelled to Pardee, "Diamondbacks! Get away, mon. Nothing brings them out faster than the glow of the setting sun on something white!"

I cringed. "Diamondbacks" reminded me of the stolen necklace and what could eventually happen to me if I were found out for this bit of vandalism.

" 'Ware serpent!" I recognized Doc Stringfellow and watched as he beat the sage with a shillelagh. The crowd of men stepped away, none wanting to be a hungry rattler's first meal of the year. I imagined that the idea of a snakebite might pale even our livery owner's ruddy complexion. Supposedly he'd survived a near fatal bite by tying a chicken carcass to the fang marks on his foot, then downed a quart of whiskey every day for a week. Fact or fiction, I had it on good account that Jake never took his boots off when he climbed between the sheets. But I doubted that it was for fear of snakes. A cunning thief like Pardee would find it to his advantage to sleep fully clothed and shod.

"Get back, mon!" yelled Doc, his burr thicker than usual. He stepped toward me, furiously swinging his cane against rock and root. Had he partaken of an overdose of his newest concoction, Stringfellow's Chocolated Cure? I crouched down, hoping my tattered calico dress would blend in with the thicket. After burying the pail of whitewash and the paintbrush, I rubbed sand across my arm, hoping to scour off the white, my mind racing for excuses in case one of Jake's men uncovered my hiding place. Lord help me if Pardee ever ferreted out my true identity.

"Their venom's especially toxic in early spring." The heavy roll in Doc's r's echoed against the log walls of the trading post across the street.

Thinking of the lizardy scales of snakes made my teeth commence their violent chatter. Last summer I'd killed no fewer than a hundred rattlers outside the door of my establishment, the Laundry by the Lake. The meat had the color and taste of hare, so the old-timers said. I'd been in Ruby a full year now hiding from the law and, God be praised, roasted serpent had not passed my lips.

Doc moved toward me, thrashing harder. I rolled myself into the smallest ball, tucking my head between my knees. Excuses galloped through my head like Indian ponies, all as lame as Jake Pardee's livery horses: A crow stole an unmentionable off my clothesline and dropped it somewhere near here. . . . My motives seemed as transparent as well water, and I began to regret my actions as this time I was certain to be discovered.

Though the last chill of winter leadened the air, I broke out in a sweat. Doc stood so close that his white plug hat loomed in front of me like the relentless August sun. I could smell his chaps made from a freshly tanned hide. Doc had broad shoulders and almost no neck; his head, accentuated by his hat, sat on his chest like a giant egg.

Wa-whunk, his shillelagh came down on the sagebrush next to me, breaking the poor skeleton of a bush in half.

Popping my head up an inch, I put a finger emphatically to my lips in a "shhh."

"Well," whispered Doc, "if it isn't the wee Pearl of Ruby City." He gave me a cynical glance. "Back, back, get back," he yelled in the direction of Jake's livery.

I cowered. "Yes, 'tis Mrs. Pearl Ryan you're about to slay." My voice pleaded for mercy in the humblest tone, though I'd never been much good at beseeching authority. As my stepmother used to admonish: Someday my mouth would be the death of me.

4

"I thought you might be at the bottom of this, lass," he whispered, waving his cudgel. "A poor excuse of a Florence Nightingale you've turned into! Now look here, ye might blame our livery owner for your life's sorrows, but if he finds you out, you're horsemeat. I'll distract Pardee and his blacksmith. You lope up the brae to Mayor Shaky Pat's diggings. He's almost gone and wants to thank ye for your kindness. Go on, lass, there's not much time. You'll need the luck of your Irish father to get out of this stew."

My stomach felt as if it had filled with mud. Shaky was the spitting image of my dear old da, may he rest in peace. Again I considered the circumstances of the mayor's ill health and wondered who would want to poison him.

Doc bent down, rubbing his shirt cuff across my chin. "Better scrub that white off your face, Mrs. Ryan." He turned quickly away and tramped back to the street, shouting threats to the sleeping diamondbacks and waving his stick at the darkening heavens.

What an infantile thing to have done—writing nasty messages on the sides of buildings. Doc should have taken me across his knee and spanked me. But I couldn't help myself. Pardee caused the extinction of my childhood, and my jaw locked as if I was afflicted with tetanus every time I heard his name. Jake Pardee had once been my father's business partner. He'd robbed Da blind, driving him into the workhouse where he'd perished. That had been a long time ago. Still, when I brooded on the fact that Jake was alive and well and had never been brought to justice on any account, every fiber of my being craved revenge.

Hand over hand, I crawled uphill through saltwort toward the Laundry by the Lake. Not a lake really, but a ravine dividing North Ruby from South. My hands got pricked by thorns, and my knees bruised on the rocks. It seemed as difficult a trek as when I'd traversed the continent! On this journey—as then—I made it undetected. When the roof of my laundry tent came within view, the sight of it recalled the first time I laid eyes on Ruby Camp. My only thought had been: There's no describing this place.

As if my journey west hadn't already been remarkable enough. After arriving in Spokane Falls on the iron trail from New York City, I had set out by stage one hundred miles through dry coulees to Ruby City, where I knew I would be able to escape the law as well as find the infamous Jake Pardee. It took a week of eating alkali dust to reach the Okanogan River, where Indians—the first I had ever seen—ferried me across. The natives had copper skin and copper eyes and dressed in tattered clothing. On the west side of the river, they pointed the way to Loop Loop Canyon trail, where I walked for two more days alongside a wagon that had a tree tied to the back of it for a brake.

"Ruby City, One Mile" read a crude sign made from a shingle. Scratched below it was the addendum, "One mile to Hell." Ruby, aka Mudtown, West Babylon, Opium Alley, and a number of other names I shan't repeat. No water, no lights except tallow dip barely making darkness visible—a far cry from Manhattan. I counted eight saloons, Little Ella's Boarding House, a livery, bank, faro tent, jailhouse, trading post, justice of the peace, and an assayer better at sampling spirits than ore. The town hall and courtroom convened at the mayor's saloon. The living quarters consisted mainly of tents or log cabins that lined Main Street, where plank sidewalks traversed a mountainside plagued by snow slide.

"What's the difference between North Ruby and South?" I had asked at the trading post. The log mercantile buzzed with ragged miners and cowmen in high-heeled boots and squaw-embroidered gauntlets. The miners' clothing and facial features were so ingrained with dirt and smoke that it would take Mr. Charles Dickens himself to do them the justice of a description—except to say that bathing had fallen completely out of fashion. To make a long story short, North Ruby was founded by Mayor Shaky Pat, who staked the Ruby Mine, which he later sold for an unheard-of sum to Blackman Forrester, Sr., an East Coast tycoon of my acquaintance. South Ruby was founded by "Hot Ziggety" Johnson when he took a bullet over a boundary dispute. South Ruby, which lay just beyond my present establishment, was occupied by row upon row of grave mounds.

<hr />

My apron tore and my stockings hung in tatters, but, as I slithered up the final ledge, I began to breathe easier. And there caught in a briar was my excuse for crawling on my hands and knees through the wilderness should I need one: a pair of red satin drawers, which had escaped my clothesline last week. Clutching the unmentionable, which belonged to a soiled dove who boarded at Little Ella's, I stood dusting off my skirt with my free hand. Picking the burrs from my stockings, I walked toward what looked like—and was—a canvas tent attached to a piano crate.

I called to my assistant, "Mary Reddawn, Mary? Are you here?" Among other things, Indian Mary brought me wood while her husband, Chin Lu, hauled water up from Salmon Creek to my wash cauldron for two cents a bucket.

"Mare-ry?"

The front door was a blanket, which I pulled aside. My little tent-crate home appeared empty, but still warm, indicating that Mary had left a short time ago. Folding the satin undergarment, I placed it on a pile of clean laundry, my eyes skating over the enormous stack of dirty wash in the corner and several buckets, strategically placed under ceiling leaks, where pairs of miners' trousers soaked in dark water rimmed with anemic-looking suds. Quickly stirring the coals in the small black stove, I lit a candle and checked my face in the shard of mirror propped up on the nail keg I used as a vanity.

In front of me appeared the likeness of Ivan the Terrible in his youth. My carrot hair fell to my waist like tangled bed-springs, and my freckled skin was scratched and streaked by grime. An exhausted sigh forced its way through my colorless lips. Not long ago, Davy, the boy I was betrothed to, had called me Fairy Queen and wrote a sonnet to my moss-green eyes, porcelain complexion, and strawberry lips. Now, after a year on the lam, I looked as coarse as a charwoman. "Aye, best not to dwell on the past," I said out loud, mimicking Doc. "Getting on with me life," was Doc's creed and should be mine also, in his opinion. After a quick scrub I couldn't see even a hint of the whitewash that would give me away as the ghost writer who had been scrawling pointed messages to Jake Pardee on the sides and roof of the largest building in Ruby City.

I took a deep breath, which put my jangled nerves to right. Securing my front door by placing a rock on the end of the blanket that dragged on the ground, I ran uphill toward Shaky's digs at the Gem Saloon. It had rained torrents that morning, and muck oozed from under my too-big boots as I slipped back-ward in the street, the hem of my skirt and the bottom of my bloomers splattered with manure. The first candles of evening lit our little glowworm village, the brightest of which emitted from the porch of the Gem.

Shaky's quarters were in the back, a room consisting of a wooden frame and board sides with a huge tent drawn over it. From within, lantern light the color of butter filtered out through the grimy canvas. Even before I entered, breathless from my hurried climb up the steep street, I could see that the room was cram-jammed to popping.

Amid a crowd of people, the invalid lay on a narrow cot covered with blankets not six inches from the stove. It must have been a hundred and ten degrees in there, hotter than my laundry tent at the end of a long summer day of ironing. Any delight I felt concerning my little revenge of an hour before im-mediately faded. I ran to the mayor, fell to the splintery floor, and took hold of his weak wrist, not wanting to admit the truth:

If Shaky were an ox in such condition, you'd want to put him out of his torment with all possible haste. His jellied blue eyes slid toward me, and I heard him whisper, "Pearly, I'm so cold. Couldja get me closer to the fire?" Like his skin, his eye whites had turned yellow, and the tremens that spawned his name had ceased. What to do?

"He's been away; you've brought him back," said Carolina Bitterroot, the nurse-schoolteacher. Her high forehead and aquiline nose loomed above me.

"Where's he been?" I asked stupidly. Fever can take a man most anyplace.

"On *der* banks of the Missouri," boomed a voice from the foot of the cot. "Ve collected buffalo bones and loaded them onto *ein* riverboat for *der* lime kiln," said Dutch Wilhelm, Shaky's ex-partner. "Vas how ve grubstaked our vay vest." Dutch, an immense man with a nose that sprawled across his face, stood teary-eyed. Shaky had been the best partner he'd ever had. For once Dutch fell silent about his gods, Engels and Marx.

"Ah, Pet," I said to the patient, "would you like a little of my hot pitcher plant tea? I could be back in a minute with a cup full."

Doc ordered a drop more of his Stringfellow's Liver Purger mixed with brandy.

"Let me give it to him," said Dutch, "he only vants me to do for him. *Ja*, he said this *morgen*, 'Let Herr Dutch do for me. He knows vhat I like.' " Dutch's beefy hand automatically slid across his empty hip holster checking for his gun, then gripped the bottle, pouring brown liquid into an unwashed shot glass. Six months ago, Shaky had decided that his shooting arm wasn't what it used to be and gave one of his twin pearl-handled six-shooters to Dutch and one to me. I kept mine under my pillow while Dutch wore his on his hip. Today I noticed that the socialist's holster was empty.

"That'll do him more harm than good," protested the nurse

with authority. Carolina was married to the mine foreman and thought of as the town's first lady. The only certified school-teacher within a hundred miles and the editor of the *Carry Nation Temperance News*, she was the keeper of good health and morals as well as good grammar. Not yet thirty and despite her classic beauty, she seemed old beyond her years. "What he needs for typhoid is to be dosed with calomel. If only he could swallow more than a sip . . ." She looked pityingly at the patient.

Doc raised a heavy gray brow, then took a swig of liver purger to brace himself.

"He's suffering delirium," Carolina Bitterroot added. "Give him drink and you'll bring on choke, even pneumonia."

"He's not delirious," I said, though I knew perfectly well that he was. I wanted to shout, He's been poisoned, can't you see? But Carolina, Doc, and I had argued about that yesterday and everyone pooh-poohed my theory. It made me sick at heart to see Shaky in such a state—a once tall timber of a man, now thin and bent as marsh grass. Only last Friday his smile lit up the street with a loud "Hell-o, Pearly."

He muttered something. I pressed my ear to his lips, dry as the grasshopper shells that littered the sagebrush in summer. His voice sounded like what passes for the muffled roll of the sea when you hold your ear to a conch.

"Pearly, when I'm gone I want you to have the Glory Hole Mine," he whispered.

"Let's have no talk like that," I told him. "You'll be up and about in no time."

At this came cheers from the crowd in the little room, which included the sheriff, the justice of the peace, and Little Ella—a bulky woman who must have weighed close to three hundred pounds. Ella pressed a handkerchief to her one good eye, then drew a foot-length of hemp from the folds of her billowing purple dress. "I brought this to him for luck," she said, waving the rope in her dimpled hand. "Was from the noose they used to hang that thievin' Injin."

Shortly before I arrived in camp, an Indian boy accused of stealing cattle was lynched by vigilantes outraged at the flavor of justice visited on another Indian whose name, loosely translated, meant Wild Coyote. Wild Coyote was called Pokamiakin in the Siwash tongue and purportedly was a notorious horse thief who always hired a lawyer and went free on bail. The day I arrived in Ruby City, Jake Pardee was selling pieces of the poor Indian boy's noose for a dollar a lucky souvenir.

Tears poured down my cheeks. I stroked Shaky's face; his yellow parchment skin felt as loose as an ox's days on the trail without water. He definitely needed pitcher plant tea, which, in addition to being the best antitoxin I knew of, would bring down his fever.

Behind me Carolina bickered with Doc. "Maybe some spirits *would* make his going easier," she relented.

I cast our physician an indignant look. What if Shaky heard? When I became a doctor, my motto would be: Never give up. Not as long as there was breath left in 'em.

"A little tea will warm you up, Pet." I mopped Shaky's brow with a rag soaked in a bowl of ice brought down from the caves in Three Devils Mountain. His forehead felt as hot as a stovetop, and his eyes had a dim, faraway stare.

As Dutch lifted the invalid into his arms and pressed the glass of spirits to his cracked lips, I recalled the kindnesses that Shaky had showered upon me. I might have frozen to death last winter if he hadn't found me the piano crate. And for no reason other than the fact that I washed his clothes! His most recent present was a gift of udder balm that had saved my hands from ruin. None but the Lord knew where he'd gotten it—even necessities took months to arrive here. If only he would show a hint of a smile, flashing the glitter of his new gold and hippopotamus ivory dental plates.

Just then the tent door flew open, and the night wind ran into the room. Someone shouted, "For God's sake, man, shut the door." Who should stand in front of me, but the devil incarnate, his receding blond window's peak, pink-as-a-pig-scrubbed-for-slaughter skin, and dung-colored eyes burned into my memory since I was a child of ten.

"Come to say your good-byes, Jake?" Carolina asked icily. Everyone in the room took a step back. There wasn't a soul among us who didn't give Jake Pardee wide berth. Carolina Bitterroot, however, was the only person in Ruby City who had ever dared to stand up to him, face to face.

Please, don't speak like that, my eyes flashed at Carolina in disapproval.

"Your hat, Jake," Carolina reminded the intruder. And saints preserve us, if Jake didn't remove his battered felt hat, clutching it to his proud chest with his two filthy bear paws. Trembling, I stared at the floor, fearful he could sniff out my guilt, but he looked through me as if I was air. Not a trace of his recent indignity clouded his face.

"It's about that loan," he began meekly addressing the patient.

Doc and I exchanged glances. No one had ever seen Jake humble himself before.

Pardee produced a crisp folded document. "I've written it all down on here. Just Shaky's signature—or his X—will do." The liveryman lowered his tawny eyes to the floor.

"Vhat's this?" asked Dutch.

Ella stopped blubbering. The justice of the peace made nervous washing motions with his hands. All heads turned toward Jake.

Pardee handed the paper to Dutch, who unfolded it and studied the contents. Then Jake drew a pen and ink from somewhere inside his great sheepskin jacket. "If you could just hold his hand around this, then put pen to paper . . ."

Carolina touched the amanita-white document with thumb and forefinger.

"Zhaky borrowed money from you, Herr Jake?" Dutch asked, his red face flushing crimson. "Zhaky," Dutch addressed his ex-partner, "didja take a loan from Herr Jake?"

I grasped the invalid's hand. He babbled something inaudible, then spoke quite clearly and with vigor: "Steamer's comin', Dutch. Feel the stern wheel's vibrations in the water? Must be beyond the next bend. . . . You know what them preachers say, any river might be Jordan. I'll be waitin' at the river for you."

Doc Stringfellow said, "My good mon, this is no time to trouble the patient about paying back a pittance of silver."

Carolina grabbed the paper away as if it were an illicit note passed by one of her scholars. She had the highest cheekbones I'd ever seen on a white woman, and her complexion had the texture of rose petals. "Jake," she addressed the intruder after studying the text, "why would a man who sold the Ruby Mine for enough money to buy every Siwash woman in the county a coffeepot have need of borrowing money?"

We waited for his reply.

Jake shrugged his wide shoulders, pursing his lips. "Don't know, mum." His bear paw hands kneaded his hat, which he continued to press to his chest. "Don't know."

There was a violent thrust of blankets. The invalid convulsed and spat up blood. His pale lips turned purple and his gums went blue.

"No, please," I begged. As Shaky gasped, I tried to help him sit up. Now I knew for certain that he'd been poisoned. With the convulsions, the bloody vomit, and that blue line on his gums (where had I seen that before?), I felt positive that the offending substance wasn't washtub liquor, but lead.

In a fury, Carolina pointed her long schoolteacher's finger toward the door and with all the authority of Queen Victoria commanded, "Jake, get out!"

Everyone in the room mumbled in agreement. Shaky fell limp into my arms. Dutch rushed forward to take him from me, the socialist's breath smelling of sauerkraut.

Doc felt for a pulse. "Still with us," he said, his gaze meeting mine in reassurance. The iris of each chestnut eye was all pupil because of his lost spectacles. Doc had an odd way of looking at me as if he were expecting to see someone else.

As soon as Jake left, I asked, "Doc? I've warming stones under my stove. I could go home and get them to comfort his chest. And I could bring the tea . . ."

Both Doc and Carolina nodded. "Better hurry," Carolina added. Doc took another swig of liver purger.

As I pushed past everyone and out the door of the tent, I watched Jake's lantern bob down the street, rising and falling to the rhythm of his ursine gait. Having failed to collect on a bogus loan, he was no doubt on his way to reap payment from some poor lad to whom he'd extended credit at the faro hall— and to sell him a jug of the rotgut he manufactured in his livery's feed room at the same time.

When my eyes adjusted to the blackness of the evening, I caught sight of a mixed-blood woman, her hair hanging in a rope down her back. Next to her, waiting near the corner of the Gem Saloon, stood a Chinese man with an even longer braid.

"Come on," I said, not pausing to give them an update on Shaky's condition. We ran through the brittle night, down the steep muddy side street, really just a trail. "Chin," I turned toward the small Asian man, his face the color and shape of an onion, "Shaky needs pitcher plant tea." Mary, who was tall and leather-faced with slight ax-shaped features, ran ahead like a deer. Chin, who walked with the abbreviated steps of a man once shackled to a railroad chain gang, fell behind.

Bursting into my tent, I poked up the coals in the stove, checking the stones for warmth. From somewhere inside her blankets, Mary produced a forearm's length of wood. Indian Mary had a way with fire and could coax even the greenest log into a blaze. As she worked the stove, Chin measured herbs from the shelf above my ironing board and put them in a tin cup. Pouring water from the copper kettle over it, he set the cup on the stove. Where Chin got his bits of Venus's-flytrap, no one knew. I often asked about his potions, but though he understood English, he spoke only Chinook, so I never found out much about his remedies. His wife sometimes helped translate. She spoke trapper's English if she spoke at all. Usually Mary pretended to be mute around whites.

"Hurry," I commanded the tea, then tested it. As the drop went down my throat, my mouth filled with a prickly feeling and my nose cleared.

A rap on the side of the piano crate startled me. Jake Pardee strutted in, his large blond features filling up every nook and cranny of my tent. Without being asked, he sat down on one of the two crates pulled up to my little table and put his muddy boots on the other, leaning back against the canvas wall.

"I come for my clothes," he said, chewing on a pine twig. His sheepskin jacket fell open, exposing a vast shirtless torso. The heaviness in my stomach churned. "At fifty cents a shirt, the least a man could get is prompt service," he growled. "Whatcha do with all your money, anyway?"

I stirred the tea. The tension in the air felt as thick as bread dough. Surely he must be on to me.

"Cat got your tongue, Pearly?"

"I've been called to tend the sick and finished no work today," I told him in my most polite but frozen voice. "They're still soaking, as you can see," I motioned to the buckets of laundry next to the stove.

"My ma used to say that a scrub board 'n' elbow grease worked wonders."

"You'll have to be patient," I answered.

"Just tryin' to help. Soaking's no way to get a job done." He leaned back farther, as if he planned to stay all night. Jake was an expert on everything, even woman's work.

Chin melted into the corner where I kept my potatoes. Mary split bits of kindling with the hatchet she always carried in her belt. With each ring of her little blade, I imagined her dismembering a piece of the livery owner.

"I don't know why Carolina does me that way," he said, chewing thoughtfully. "I like ladies to behave as ladies, not talk you blind with questions."

What was he referring to? Carolina had but few words for Jake, though she'd had several run-ins with him like the one I'd witnessed at Shaky's bedside.

"Her and her haughty ways," Jake said, stretching out, putting his hands behind his head. But you, Pearly . . . I could watch you write in your notebook all day. I'll bet that's what you was doing instead of my shirts. But I'm a broad-minded soul. I could watch your hand like a finch flying across them pages for hours."

Jake was speaking of my medical journal, I supposed. "I've been tending Shaky, as I said." I put an extra bite into my words, hoping to cover my lie.

"What sense in that? He's near gone and I'm in need of my flannels."

"Don't speak that way, please." I wished I was the hot-headed murdering sort redheads are supposed to be. I wouldn't give this man time to say his prayers.

He eyed Shaky's potion brewing on the stove. "If there's anyone who needs tending to, it's me. I could use a little warm tea. I've had a hard day what with some swine playing dirty tricks on me." He whined like a child, and his jowls drooped in a pout.

I raised my brow in mock confusion.

"I'll find out who done it—I got ways. He took the stick he'd been chewing and broke it like the neck of a rabbit. "*Avarice,*" he spat mockingly.

I didn't like the look in his eye. My hands busied themselves, clanking pots. He hadn't a shred of evidence against me, but I feared he suspected I was the culprit. Guilt breeds suspicion, and that's probably why I began to wonder if sneaky, conniving Jake didn't have something to do with Shaky's sudden decline.

Jake drew his crate closer to me. "I try to help you out," he said, lowering his voice. "I make a special trip here to get my clothes so your tiny feet won't have to tramp up the ravine to bring me my laundry. But instead of washin', you're writin' all day, or up at Three Devils workin' your Lost Cause Mine."

"Last Chance," I corrected him.

He continued undaunted, "I tell you, Pearly, my fortune's made. You'd do well to say a kind word to me. Why, I'd marry you any day over that nose-in-the-air Carolina."

I could not help but raise my voice. "I'm already married, as are you. It's Mrs. Ryan, you might recall."

"So you say, but I ain't seen any sign of a husband."

I did not reply. The strength drained from my hands, and my arms dropped as if to prevent my wounded heart from falling out of my chest. In front of me pulsed the image of the dark-haired man I'd married in a hasty ceremony. Behind him appeared the auburn head of another, whom I'd loved since girlhood.

My imaginings dissolved when Jake rose to his feet and muscled his way through the doorway. He turned to Mary as if he'd just noticed her, "Well, if it ain't my favorite hangs-around-the-town half-breed." And with that he fled my establishment.

His departure was followed by a heave of relief from all of us. As Mary gathered the stones in a warmed pot and covered it with a blanket, I heard her mutter, "Pokamiakin *mamaloose* Stinktail someday."

Chin nodded, speaking in shrill Chinese monosyllables.

Mamaloose, I learned soon after arriving in Ruby, was Chinook for "to make dead." "Stinktail" was trapper talk for "skunk" and the Indians' name for Jake Pardee. Pokamiakin was Mary's cousin and not the only man, white or copper, who'd sworn to get even with Jake. Pokamiakin could also be translated as Rabid Coyote or shortened to Poka Mika, meaning anything from, "I fight you," to "I poke you," to words that shall not be mentioned. Whites thought him a desperado; Indians considered him an underchief. In any case, he had crossed blood-shot eyes and was the most frightening-looking Siwash I'd ever met though he always favored me due to the fire color of my hair.

Putting a lid on the tin teacup, Mary Reddawn, Chin, and I headed uphill to Shaky. Above us pinprick stars dotted the sky. There was no moon, and we could barely see. Indian Mary had not only the gait of a doe but also a doe's night eyes, and she plunged ahead. I followed the rustle of her blankets as they brushed against her leather leggings worn as protection against cold in winter and snakes in summer. Chin fell in behind, his small muscular feet thrashing the mud like birds' wings. My calves ached and my feet were cold even though I wore two pairs of knit socks as well as a pair of socks on my hands instead of mittens, which I hadn't had time to crochet nor could I afford to buy. All my laundry profits went into the Last Chance Mine, and all the money I took out of my claim I saved for medical college. Socks served just as well as gloves.

Though weariness bore down on me, I felt suddenly fired up by my little revenge on Jake. He relished a practical joke. One of his favorite boasts concerned the time he'd rearranged the entryway to his livery so that when Carolina Bitterroot sent her blind son to bring home their horse from the blacksmith, the boy thought he'd found the wrong establishment and lost his way. That must be why I decided to give Jake a taste of his own lamb stew. I could only hope that he hadn't any notion I was Seamus O'Sullivan's only surviving child and that my name, Pearl Ryan, didn't give me away. I'd a new last name, and my da had always called me Pinky. Still . . . every so often I seized up with fear that he knew all about me and was only waiting to corner me in some dark alley.

Shaky's digs came into view, and from them rang a sober verse of the mayor's favorite hymn. Carolina's bell-like soprano pierced the frost that glazed the saloon windows. Mary quickened her stride. As we came within reach of the door, I heard voices, Doc's baritone more voluminous than the rest. Funny how a corner of your brain grasps the meaning of something and secrets it away. When he said, "We'll take him down to little Pearly's tent in the morning," I thought, At last they've come to their senses and realized he's been poisoned. They're bringing him to me to be dosed with antidote.

Just then the tent's flap door opened. Doc's black woolly chaps appeared against the yellow lantern light inside. Holding something metallic in his hand, he cleared his throat a good long time. "It's all over, lass," he said, lowering his eyes to the crate that served as a step into Shaky's room. "He's gone." Doc looked as if he might break down. "Our mayor wanted you to have this." Pushing past me, he thrust a cold disk into my palm—Shaky's gold watch with the picture of his mother inside.

I stood in the entry. My shoulders drooped. It wasn't as if I had never lost someone I loved. You would think I'd learn to bear it better each time, but it felt as if all of life's sorrows revisited me. I stared at Shaky's motionless body. Silently I prayed that he was warm at last. The others sat around on feed sacks, crates, a pile of hides.

I entered along with Chin and Mary to sit up all night with the remains, which would be brought down to my laundry for preparations, as was the custom in western towns where there was no undertaker. Kneeling next to Shaky's cot, I felt both exhausted and angry. He'd been poisoned, I was positive. Glancing around the room, I saw that the sheriff was too moribund to chew tobacco. Ella, weeping into her immense bosom, still held onto the length of hanging rope. Which one of them would have wanted to kill Shaky Pat McDonald?

Dutch spoke first. "Be sure to save *ein* lock of his hair for his mutter," he told me. Dutch's ruddy face was wet, "Zhaky vas the most uncomplaining man I ever met."

"Amen to that," said several at once.

I breathed heavily. Rage coursed through my veins. Something felt amiss, I could smell it. Shaky hadn't responded to any of my cures or to anyone else's. He had begun failing two nights ago and continued unchecked on a downward slide. My dear old da hadn't died as suddenly, but hadn't he lost his health in a similar manner? That blue line on Shaky's gums, hadn't Da complained of a like affliction? No doubt Doc's autopsy would shed light on the tale. And of course you know what was going on in the back of my head: Somehow Jake Pardee was at the root of this. But what possible motive could he have had? Then and there I vowed to discover if a murder had been committed—even if it meant jeopardizing my safety.

The terrible truth was that when I made a mental list of the person or persons who would profit most from Shaky's death, the finger pointed directly at me.

CHAPTER TWO

April 17

The next day dawned with a seamless pewter sky that let not one ray of sun leak through. My spirits felt as gray as the weather. I had Shaky inside on my ironing table in preparation for laying out the body, but I didn't want to heat up the tent. So until our jack-of-all-trades moved Shaky outside where it was easier to take measurements for the coffin, I thought I'd build a fire in my front yard and finish the laundry out there.

Did one wash a body before an autopsy? I'd made a list for Doc. I wanted Shaky's liver carefully examined. If he'd been poisoned, it might be enlarged to twice normal size. Lead was one of the heaviest of all elements, so that organ would weigh noticeably more. And Doc would have to look carefully at the contents of the mayor's stomach and intestines for any suspicious bluish-gray metallic substances. But who was I to tell a man of science what to do? Where would he want to commence his cutting, inside or out? And where would I go? I'd always wanted to assist an autopsy, but not this one. Doc, no matter how bad his sight or how painful the war wound made his shoulder, would have to stitch Shaky back up again without my help. I hadn't the stomach for butchering such a kindhearted man.

After putting two silver dollars on the mayor's eyes to keep them closed, I hauled wash outside to the cauldron. While carrying a tub of Jake's trousers, I considered how I might fill out Shaky's cheeks: using two fistfuls of quarters—the money to come from the baking soda tin I'd buried in my vegetable garden. I'd hidden all the tips Shaky'd ever given me there. Why not keep my money in the Ruby First National? Who knew when a flash flood might rage down the narrow canyon and carry the safe away as it had in Salmon City, the next camp to the north. To this day that safe has never been found.

Soundlessly, Mary appeared draped in cavalry blankets, carrying a bundle of sticks the size of a small horse. A long-handled ax protruded from one side like a tail, her burden so heavy she bent almost to the ground. As was the Indian way, she said not one word of greeting. Helping her break twigs, I caught sight of the top of Chin's black silk scarf tied like a scull cap around his head. Carrying two buckets of water balanced on a wooden yoke, he labored up the ravine.

"Ollo, ollo," he called to me, bowing his head. Hello, hello was the only word of English Chin ever spoke, and he employed it for all purposes. Unlike Mary, whose face always remained expressionless, Chin never stopped smiling and bowing. In these parts, Chinamen were often the object of vicious pranks and threatened hangings. Chin's theory was that the more he kept everyone laughing, the less likely they'd be to turn on him.

After Mary and I positioned the cauldron on top of a pyre of logs and sticks, Chin filled it with water, then added dried rhubarb leaves. In Canton, Chin Lu had been an herbalist. From him I'd learned that rhubarb softened the hard mountain water.

I took a handful of gooey lye soap from a lard bucket and dropped it in, stirring the contents with an enormous wooden

n't give to get Ella's sheets a
'one with work."

"It'll be just my luck," I said
dom conversed with white
time for a spring snow. I

is wife, who remained

ner ax against a rock. "I'm

I thought, Thank God. The wash, if
, would dry fast and without a crease. Of
ed her sheets ironed to a satiny sheen. I imagined
raisin eyes would glare out from her pulpy face when
e saw that her linen wasn't done to perfection. My shoulders crumpled at the thought of the critical clucking of her tongue. Burying my face in my hands, I dropped my stirring stick. I thought I'd cried my eyes out last night, but tears still flowed for Shaky Pat.

Then it struck me. I'd put those silver dollars on the mayor's eyes with the liberty lady faceup and the eagle facedown. Shaky would have wanted it the other way around with the lady caressing his eyelids and the American eagle facing skyward and forever vigilant. As I turned to go inside and correct my error, Mute Mary commenced shrieking.

At first I thought she was mourning the mayor in the Indian fashion. Shaky was one of the few white men the Indians revered. The day he sold the Ruby Mine, he went directly to our postmistress, Jake's wife, "Windy" Pardee, and ordered every Siwash woman in the county a coffeepot from the Sears Roebuck catalog. He wanted the squaws to be gainfully employed making miners' coffee instead of selling themselves. Most native women used their pots to store dried olalla berries. Though some learned to make miners' coffee, the problem of removing the grounds became a sore point.

Mary continued to scream. She wasn't
singing her laundry song: "trousers hung, sa
was a sail to Mary). I'd caught my skirt on fire
to swat it, the wind gusted and I caught a flying
sleeve. The terrible smell of burning hair wafted i
and I thought, Oh, Joseph, Mary and Jesus, not only
to meet my maker before I get Shaky decent for his
but I'll never know if he died from natural causes or fou

The next thing I knew, Chin felled me to the ground.
kicked gritty soda-tasting mud onto my head. Chin emptie
bucket of laundry and laundry water on me, then ran to th
cauldron for more. After almost drowning under Ella's wet
flour-sack pillowcases, Mary smothered me in a blanket. I could
no more raise myself up than I could raise the dead. Tears
poured out of me in a fit of loss and and self-pity. I owned only
two dresses other than my wedding gown, and now I was down
to one. My singed hair felt considerably shorter on one side
and my fingertips blistered. With yesterday's work on top of me
dirtier than before I'd begun, sobbing my lungs out was all I
could do.

Any minute Jake Pardee would appear demanding his
clothes and threatening to dock my pay due to tardiness. He'd
taken a dollar out of my wages the last time I'd done his wash
because, he said, I owed him extra on my livery bill: something
about him having to hold my pony—which I had foolishly
boarded at his establishment over the winter months—when
the blacksmith shod him. I'd never ordered Tillicum shod! He
was an Indian cayuse and used to going barefoot. How his little roan soul must have shuddered when he'd had a hot shoe
held to his hoof and smelled the horn burning. I'd been furious!
Going directly to Ruby Livery, I'd removed the horse that
Mary's cousin, Wild Coyote, had given me in trade for making
him a Bibleman coat and trousers. From then on I tethered
Tillicum amid the grave mounds in South Ruby or corralled
him behind the surgery at the other end of town. In exchange

for oats, Doc rode him when his big black gelding, President Lincoln, was all played out.

In fact, Doc was using my cayuse at this very hour. The physician had been called away from our group of Shaky's watchers in the wee hours to tend a woman in childbed. Rumor was that her husband, our stage driver, had ridden the length of the Okanogan River looking for a doctor. The first physician he encountered was too drunk to stand, the second out politicking for state legislature and without his medical bag. The stage driver had gone back to the house of the first who, though inebriated, at least had his bag. But alas, the drunken doctor, who practiced over on the reservation, had no chloroform, which was what was needed for the laboring mother-to-be. Finally, Doc was located.

Along with all my prayers for Shaky, I said a prayer for Doc to ride back into town ahead of the weather. From where I lay, I had a clear view of the iron-hard fields of heaven. It looked more and more like snow. Which made me bawl all the harder.

Chin and Mary cowered at the sight of me, then exchanged a few words in Chinook, Mary speaking mainly in sign. The skin around her slanted eyes and angular nose tightened into the frightened face of a sparrow. Chin drew his hands up into his tunic, his high yellow brow wrinkling into the black scarf, then reached down and helped me up. From a pocket in his dark pajamalike trousers, he produced a pinch of powder. "Ollo, ollo," he said, gesturing to his mouth. With his double-jointed fingers he gently placed a small measure of dust on my tongue. Whatever it was (pennyroyal and cayenne pepper?), it cleared my head and nasal passages for a year into the future. Inside, Mary helped me into a clean wool shirt and jeans, which some miner had left and never picked up, then put me to bed. Without a word, she went outside and began to stir the laundry, singing softly, "Cut some wood, Use the ax, There is no saw, Make fire, Boil water, Wash dishes, Tomorrow I pay you a quarter dollar."

As I curled into the fetal position and listened to her sorrowful a cappella, my eyes felt pulled toward the ironing table where Shaky lay. It had been a long time since I'd been this sick at heart, not since girlhood when I'd seen my own dear da sprawled out in the same condition on the dining room table. Children have a keen sense of justice, and at the time I had accused, tried, and found Da's business partner Jake Pardee guilty of driving my father to his grave. Was the past clouding my powers of analysis concerning the queer death of Pat McDonald? Try as I would, I could not shake off my suspicions concerning Jake's hand in the mayor's demise.

Drawing the covers over my head, I nestled into my mattress of feed sacks filled with willow leaves, then plumped my pillow made from a sugar sack filled with cattail fluff. Methodically, I felt for the reassuring hardness of Shaky's pearl-handled six-shooter, which I kept hidden underneath. Since the mayor hadn't an enemy in the world, what possible motive could Jake have had for poisoning him?

I imagined myself wandering up Main Street looking for suspects. Considering the proprietor of each establishment, I began with one of my best customers, Little Ella. If she had a last name or was Miss or Mrs., I never knew. Most Rubyites often dropped their surnames along with huge chunks of the past. And who was I to be critical? If I wanted to stay out of jail, my past was best left undisturbed.

When I first came to town, I'd applied at Ella's for a room. She suffered terrible bouts of rheumatic pain, which made walking difficult. Though Doc's Chocolated Cure brought her some relief, I thought I could be useful to her. Discovering that Ella boarded only calico come-ons, I'd blushed from my chin clear up into my bonnet and made some excuse to flee up the plank sidewalk, chased by the spotted pig that lived under her larder. Other than the madam's rolls of doughy flesh and henna-dyed hair, the most striking thing about Ella when I met her was that she had one brown eye and one blue and wore a garish necklace that reminded me of an imitation of the gems I had been accused of stealing. Her blue eye never closed. It had been Shaky who'd discovered a jeweler who manufactured a little brown raisin to match Ella's good one and paid for it to boot. From the day that false eye arrived, Ella held her head up a foot higher. On her birthday, Shaky ordered the tail of the livery's gray horse dyed the beet color of Ella's hair and paraded them up Main with Ella decked out like royalty in that gaudy necklace and an ermine coat.

There was no possible reason for Ella to have poisoned the mayor. Though she certainly could have dropped a pinch of paint pigment or some other lead malignity into a bottle of Chocolated Cure and passed it to Shaky when he begged a swig as he often did.

I pulled the Hudson Bay blanket tighter over my shoulders and continued my imaginary walk up Main to the faro hall owned by Jake Pardee. He catered to miners with their pockets full of silver and their blood thinned by liquor. I always crossed the muddy thoroughfare when I passed the gambling tent, stepping around God knows what: broken wagon wheels, the decaying head of a dead ox, even a miner who'd decided it was a fine day to prospect in the streets. It wasn't the lecher's hand I feared, nor the aroma of the "four-seater" (not a proper necessary house, just a stand of four pines behind the circus-sized tent), but running into the mine owner's son, Blackman Forrester, Jr. He was the one person in town other than Jake (who hadn't seen me since I was a child) who might recognize me from my former life as a char girl in Manhattan and who might also remember the "unpleasantness" concerning my sudden departure from service.

"Forr," who'd become Jake's partner upon arrival, had a face as long and thin as a cucumber and eyes narrowly spaced. His father—often a guest in the Fifth Avenue house in which I served—sent him west to learn the silver business. Forr was not one to soil his dealing hand in the mine fields, however. He was my former employer's godson, and it was through his letters that I had discovered—in this smallest of worlds—the present whereabouts of one Jake Ezekial Pardee, a fact, combined with other circumstances, that set my flight to Ruby in motion. Forr had often chased me through the upstairs rooms of his god-mother's mansion, whispering the joys of spring in my ear. Just wanted to console me after my parents' death, he'd said. The situation had caused me no end of displeasure. However, in this silver-mining camp on the other side of the continent, his face blazed with another fever, and (though I couldn't be completely certain) he seemed not to recognize me in my present disguise as a laundress.

I'll never forget the day I first laid eyes on Forrester Jr. here in Ruby. I had been walking past the gambling tent and, glanc-ing in, fixed my gaze on his familiar face. Freezing in my tracks, I prepared myself for the sheriff to grab me by the neck, waving those arrest warrants in my face. But Forr's lecherous stare re-mained nailed to the filthy cards in his hand as if in a trance. Finally, he took the jack of hearts and itched the nit scabs on his neck. The lack of a manicurist and barber had utterly trans-formed him.

Though Forr possessed a weak intellect and an even weaker character, I decided that he wasn't the murdering sort. He wasn't smart enough to poison anyone, not by design. (I seemed to re-call that he'd once accidentally poisoned himself by drinking a bottle of Valet's Hoof Polish on a bet.) On the other hand . . . Shaky was a popular man, capable of channeling town senti-ment this way or that, and wouldn't someone with such power pose a danger to a mine owner?

Dozing, my toes curled around the warming stones Mary had put in my bed. I imagined the next establishment on my walk: the mud-chinked walls of the trading post where Jake's wife Windy presided over the PO. Here Dutch Wilhelm could also be found as well as a never-ending stream of town folk come to hunt for their mail or to enjoy the camaraderie and warmth of the stove. Windy always set the contents of the weekly mail bag in a lard bucket on her threshold, so that the populace could sort out their correspondence while she read Marshall Field's catalogs undisturbed. A flirty, baby-faced woman with a head of straw-colored curls, Windy talked about nothing but hats.

Dutch, calling for a strike at the mine while pontificating on the plight of the worker, spoke over her in gravely High German *ich, iches*, engaging anyone present in a feisty exchange of political rhetoric. Whenever I stopped in to hunt my mail and didn't find Dutch in residence, I got a lecture from Windy about how a new hat could improve my appearance: "Now see," she'd say, pointing to a catalog, "this one's rolling brim'd highlight your tiny eyes and not draw attention to the nappiness of your hair. When your husband arrives, he'll think you're the prettiest thing." Her criticism often blew me right out of the trading post, no matter how badly I needed lye for making soap.

Windy had no reason that I could fathom for wanting Shaky dead. Though, through her mercantile, she had access to every kind of toxin imaginable, including lead arsenate for killing rodents and quicksilver for mining ore.

But as I plumped my pillow, I wondered about Dutch. A seemingly good-hearted man, he possessed a fiery temper. His huge rawboned frame towered over everyone in camp. Hadn't he and Shaky had some falling out over the sale of the Ruby Mine? The transaction took place before I arrived here. Still, every so often I heard a whisper of discord. Something about Dutch wanting it in the sales agreement that the miners be allowed to organize. Which was illegal, so of course it hadn't transpired that way. All the same, Dutch had taken away a kernel of discontent. But the idea that Dutch bore Shaky even the slightest ill went against anything I'd ever witnessed. Still . . . I considered Dutch's temper: worse than a bobcat disturbed at supper, especially when he'd been bending his elbow at the Gem, which he did more often as the discomfort of his smoker's throat worsened. And those pewter pots he made his sauerkraut in—didn't he once tell me that each batch had to be thrown away at the end of winter for fear of lead poisoning?

Reaching under the covers, I took hold of one of the warming stones and pressed it to my chest. Something concerning Dutch began to nag at me. It was only a hair's breadth of an idea, but at the moment that was all I had to go on. As I drifted into sleep, it stuck me as odd that Shaky had left me his pet dig, the Glory Hole Mine. Why hadn't he left it to his faithful friend and former partner, Dutch Wilhelm?

CHAPTER THREE

Noon, the same day

I awoke from my nap to a hammering. Thunder was my first thought. But it turned out to be a coach and six, the weekly stage with Cranky Frank driving in the mail and payroll. Why was he roaring down the Ruby grade at such a clip? Then I noticed another, fainter noise, as if someone was throwing shelled corn against my tent.

"Mary?" Laundry hung from every tent pole, a *drip-drip* drumming lightly on the floor. Mary and Chin hovered near the stove, carrying on a fierce conversation in sign. Standing so close together, they barely took up the space of one person.

"Where's Shaky?" my voice cracked like a rusty well handle that hadn't been primed since the winter freeze. The mayor and my ironing table were gone.

Mary's dark thin arm pointed to the door. Chin patted the canvas wall of the tent, "Ollo, ollo."

"Outside? You put him outside?" In the cold? I stopped myself before I said it. The *ping-ping-ping* against the tent wall and roof got louder.

"*Cole snass,*" Chin said, his amber fingers pointing to the roof.

"It's snowing?" I got up and made for the door. The hammering of hooves beat louder. We heard a fierce "gee-ha," the unmistakable deep-throated voice of Cranky Frank Belknap. Pulling the blanket door aside, sleet cut my cheeks to the quick.

As the stage passed, spraying me with ice pellets, Mary and Chin ran to it like children. I shielded my face, unable to see anything but the glint of steel horseshoes.

Back inside we secured the door with an extra rock. The narrow planes of Mary's sparrow face fluttered.

"Frank *tenas hehe,*" she said in wonder, pulling her blankets closer to her body. Her robes were the usual army-green cavalry rugs. Around the hem and sleeves, Siwash symbols had been painted in black tar.

"Cranky Frank was laughing?" He must be deep into his cups. Word had it that he often polished off his first quart before mid-forenoon. Maybe the new baby—the one Doc had gone to help deliver just after Shaky died—had arrived and that was what had finally brought a smile to Frank's lips.

Mary repeated herself, nodding. I thought, My girl, the snow has blinded your vision. Cranky Frank hadn't come by his sobriquet casually. His usual bad humor and ghoulish scowl discouraged even the most aggressive highwayman. Frank Belknap was the only stage driver in the state of Washington never to have been robbed.

We listened to the clatter of the mail stage as it skidded down the grade and onto Main Street with Frank screaming something unintelligible as he went.

Snow pellets rained harder against the canvas walls and roof, and I began to worry about Doc getting caught in the storm on his way back from delivering Frank's wife. The laundry dripped. Chin poked the fire, and the three of us shared a cup of swamp weed tea. How would we get Shaky safely into the ground? There'd be no shovel that could penetrate the stone orchard of South Ruby if the world froze up with snow.

At high noon it was so dark that the oil lamp had to be lit. I dipped into my stores for some potato starch for Ella's sheets and pillowcases. And what was I going to iron them on with Mr. McDonald lounging outside on my ironing board? It was a sad day in my life, but with Mary and Chin talking in high-pitched Chinese and Chinook about Frank's never-seen-before smile (he'd shown both sets of gums, upper and lower!), who wouldn't break into comic relief? Perhaps his wife had delivered twins.

"How could you see his expression through the bedspread of white outside? Surely you're mistaken." Adding a dipper of water to the potato starch, I stirred vigorously.

As if in answer to my question, there was a banging on the door frame. The leather hinges that attached the blanket to one side of the entry fell open.

Doc appeared covered in winter's dust, the wind having struck him squarely in the face for so long that his nose was the color of rhubarb jam. I hadn't eaten since yesterday, and the thought brought to mind that, oh, I sure was hungry. Doc staggered in. Before I shut the door I noticed a familiar form standing out in the road. My little cayuse, Tillicum, had snow covering his back and icicles in his mane and whiskers; even his tail was weighted down with ice.

Immediately I upended the washtub for Doc to sit down on and pulled off his gloves, which were stiff as bones. Strange to say, his hands hadn't frozen. I took off his boots, put his feet in a pot of warm laundry water already filled with trousers, and clasped his hands around a hot tin cup of swamp weed tea.

All he said was, "God bless you, Pearly, but ye'd better see to the horse."

I pulled the blanket from my bed and the top sheet from a stack of fresh linen and braved the outside. Poor Tillicum. He stood head hanging, his haunches brought up under him, shivering uncontrollably.

"Chin, Mary, come help before he takes a chill." The two had a way with horses.

No one answered. I glanced into the house, then strained my eyes to see through the blizzarding snow. Gone. As was the Siwash custom, they never said hello or good-bye, a situation most whites found infuriating. My helpers had left with no time to spare if they wanted to reach their teepee before the trails became impassable.

Nothing for me to do now but run around the side of the piano crate and cover the mayor with a sheet to keep the snow off him and then bring Tillicum into the house. So stiff and cold, my horse had to be coaxed to move, then swatted on the rump to get him through the narrow door. Backing him into a corner, I corralled my cayuse between two rows of hanging laundry. Then uncinching the girth, I pulled off the saddle and upended a wooden box I used as a chair, filling it with dry grass pulled from the walls of the piano crate. I'd employed hay as insulation and might as well make use of it before it molded. Pouring hot water over the feed, I put it under the grateful pony's nose. Though he steamed from beneath his blanket, he ceased shivering and chewed methodically. My father had been head groom at Brooklyn Downs Racetrack, and his words echoed in my ears: Horse before rider. It was the eleventh commandment.

I glanced over at Doc. His knees knocked. "Could I get you something to eat?"

"What's that soup cooking on the stove, lass? It sure smells gud."

It was potato starch for the laundry, but I wasn't going to tell on myself. I'd become famous in Ruby for my "potato soup," though I couldn't bear to bring it to my own lips. Add a little onion and dried sage from the trail, and my customers swallowed it without complaint, never suspecting it was the same stuff that made their collars stiff.

"I've been in the saddle eight hours," said Doc, "of what's usually half a morning's ride. All I could think of was building a fire and now so much heat makes me faint." His Humpty Dumpty head teetered above his buffalo hump, then toppled onto the table.

I propped him up and put a tin cup of potato soup to his mouth.

"Did Cranky Frank pass you on the road?" I asked.

"Didn't see a glimmer of him," Doc answered. "Nor any other living soul."

I thought that odd. Wouldn't a new father forced out on the road before his wife delivered want news? I didn't say as much and not just because it was none of my business: I didn't like the white pasty tinge to Doc's cheeks, and his pupils were so small that his eyes were almost entirely iris, the color of rotting leaves. Doc would go blind if his new glasses didn't arrive soon.

His head sprang up. Clearing his throat and puffing his chest out in a professional posture, he asked, "Have ye prepared the body?"

"I thought it best to wait until the autopsy," I answered, sitting down on the heap of Doc's saddle and pads. Remembering that I was wearing miner's gear several sizes too big, I thought about how peculiar I must look. My charred dress hung in a corner, dripping in time with the sheets. Tillicum dozed—a horse can sleep standing up, it's a wonder. Melting ice fell from his tail, adding another rhythm to the drip beat. Soon there'd be as much mud in here as out on the wagon road.

Doc's eyes didn't meet mine. "Pearly," he said, "I've no feeling in my hons, and I'm dead on my feet. I don't see how it can be done."

"Please, Doc," I implored. The mire in my stomach churned.

He took a long breath of laundry air. "We know why he died, lass."

"But no one else has come down with typhoid," I said beseechingly.

"None that we know of. Shaky Pat McDonald pickled himself over time, and the fever finally pushed him across the brig." A white beard of potato soup rimmed Doc's thin blue lips. His large head began to sit more squarely between his shoulders, and the hump on his back seemed to shrink. Drawing a brown bottle from his pocket, he unscrewed the top and took a bracing swig of Stringfellow's Wizard Remedy.

"You saw his chest," I countered. "There was no rose rash. And his stomach didn't pooch out. When someone dies of typhoid, the stomach always pooches."

"You're clever for such a wee lass, Pearly, but I saw a thousand of these cases during the War Between the States. The telltale symptoms aren't always acute."

"I've got a strong suspicion," I said, lowering my voice, though I didn't know why. No one could hear us but Tillicum. "Shaky never rallied, not once. Like when your cavalry mare got poisoned. Even a man with cholera will rally. But Shaky got sick quite suddenly on Sunday and sank like a stone."

At this Doc laughed, the color returning to his face. Even his pupils were starting to seem a normal size. "Poisoned with drink, Gud love him."

"Yes and no." I thought about the most logical way to present my case. "I think it might have been from that rotgut Jake sells."

At this Doc absolutely roared. "Shaky never touched Jake's brew. Mayor Patrick McDonald sold only first-class spirits at the Gem."

"He did and he didn't," I corrected him, still whispering. Maybe it was Shaky who I thought would hear me telling the town his secrets.

Now that Tillicum had stopped steaming, I got up, took the blanket off of him, and hung it from the only vacant tent pole.

I continued, "Sometimes Cranky Frank ran late with a load, or drank most of it on his way. You know what a kind heart the mayor had. He couldn't let the boys go without. Just so he'd have some in reserve, he often bought a keg from Jake and mixed it with his first-class stock or drank it himself, so the boys would be sure to have plenty on payday."

Doc studied me with interest. His brow was as broad as a wheat field, and great furrows appeared when he wrinkled it up into his gray, short-mown hair. "That doesn't prove anything. Those gambling tables at Jake's faro tent never sleep. All there is for refreshment is Jake's corn brew after the Gem closes up at night. Not one of the boys has missed more than a day of card playing from a hangover, not to mention dyspepsia brought on by bad booze. No, Pearly, I'd say that our mayor's made history: He's the first in Ruby to die of natural causes since Hot Ziggety Johnson founded the cemetery."

"That's just it," I said. "Jake doesn't make his booze from corn anymore. He used up every bushel the army meant for the Indians, the molasses too. He's been making it out of old seed potatoes. Jake's a genius and can make spirits from nearly anything, weeds even, my da used to say. You forget, Pardee and I go way back. . . ." Doc was the only person in town with whom I'd trusted my secret, or part of it, anyway.

Doc gulped soup, then looked at me sternly. "Yes, lass, and you ought to burn your grudges. You're no match for that mon when he gets his hackles up. And pray he never finds out it was ye who painted those notes across his livery. Ella told me he paid one of her little tarnished lilies a ten-dollar gold piece to keep her ear to the ground."

My breath caught in my throat.

"Jake wouldn't feel safe if he didn't have a tasty bit of in-

formation on most of the solid citizens. I hear he ruffled the justice of the peace's feathers pretty good. Jake's rattled everyone's
cage trying to discover how that 'ghost writing' got on his wall."

Except for my last endeavor, I'd done most of my writing by
night, thus the description. I sucked my lower lip, wondering if
I'd gone too far in trying publicly to humiliate Jake Pardee. As
Doc had said, if he found me out, I'd be horsemeat.

"And just what were you doing up at Little Ella's?" I asked.
I'd never known Doc to have any romantic inclinations, not
since his wife died on the Overland Trail years ago, and I
couldn't help but take note of the endearing way he said "tarnished lily."

His eyes glazed over with the frozen look of a just-slain deer.

"Sorry, didn't mean to pry." The less said about affairs of the
heart, Doc's or mine, the better. Again the mirage of my dark-
haired husband flanked by another, the bronze head of the lad
who'd been the light of my life, appeared in front of me, then
vanished.

Other than Doc Stringfellow, only Mary and Chin knew of
my hatred for Jake. My plan had been to get him run out of
town or, better yet, draw the attention of a federal marshal.
The only problem was that if Mr. Pardee ever discovered my
true identity, he'd uncover the warrants issued against me and
have me arrested—or worse.

"It's not so much what Jake put in his rotgut booze that did
Shaky in. I think it was in the new apparatus. He sold the mayor
a keg of the first run out of a new still he'd invented. New stills
are always a danger due to the impurities in the pipe." It was
amazing what I remembered from some of Da's less savory racetrack cronies.

Cocking his head, Doc lowered his lids halfway over his
eyes.

"I know, I was there when Jake popped in and made the
sale." I put both hands around my cup of tea as if holding the
lines of a coach and six, steering the conversation back to my

theory. Doc pulled on a clean pair of socks and his boots, then placed his head on the sugar sack and his feet in the flour barrel. All the better that he get comfortable. The sooner the feeling came back to his hands and the pain in his war-wounded shoulder subsided, the sooner he could get to work. I was bent on having Shaky autopsied.

"I've been reading up on it," I said, pointing to a leatherbound book on the shelf above the stove. It was a medical manual the cavalry had left behind following the threat of an uprising after that Indian boy was hanged.

"What?" Doc asked. Was he going to fall asleep?

"Poisons," I said. "My theory is that lead killed Shaky, because Jake was too cheap to use copper pipe in the apparatus and used lead instead. That's how the drink got contaminated." Operating an unlawful still was common fare in the Okanogan. There were so many guilty parties that it would have been senseless to zero in on just one of them. Selling adulterated spirits, however, was a much more serious offense and usually punishable by "miner's justice," aka lynch mob. "It was a long time ago, but I swear my da was afflicted by a blue line below his teeth when he started to lose his health, just like the blue line on the mayor's gums. Now I'm wondering if Jake didn't . . ."

Doc pursed his lips, which were no longer purple but a powdery pink. "Ruby's water supply is so polluted it's just inviting trouble," he said. "It was typhoid."

"But he never tasted the water!"

Doc grimaced. Placing his hand to his right shoulder, he groaned as he began to massage his upper arm through his Shetland wool sweater. Whenever he wore his gorgeous green cable knit, I always scanned it for moth holes or snags.

I cleared my throat. "The manual says to measure and weigh the liver. If it's larger and heavier than average, that's some proof, isn't it? If it was typhoid, then the spleen will be enlarged and the gallbladder enflamed."

"Lass, I know Shaky was like a father to ye, but you've got

to bury your dead." Doc's cheeks sagged with exhaustion. "Even if we did an autopsy and it turned out as you say, where's the motive? And how could you prove Jake intended to kill the mayor?"

"But Doc, I've got such a strong feeling! Besides, does one need a motive for an incorrigible like Jake?"

"You've got no motive, no proof, and only women's intuition to go on. And let me remind ye, while Jake has a lot of enemies, he's a lot of chums up at his faro tent. People don't always stay in town long enough to see his dark side. It would be your word against theirs, and despite the fact there's hardly a mon or woman in the county Jake hasn't cheated, his chums are growing in numbers. Young Forrester's come with enough of his father's silver to buy everyone's vote—if his fast pal Jake were to put the notion in his head that he should run for office to replace Shaky Pat."

I sunk my chin into my palms. Maybe Jake wanted Shaky dead so that he could pocket the mayorship for one of his pawns.

"You've got more sense than all the lasses I've known put together. But your inborn feminine weakness has got the best of ye this time. I don't think Jake had a hand in Shaky's death. I say that as your friend—you know I've no fondness for the gent."

I sighed. Tillicum dumped the empty feed box over with his muzzle, then defecated. Immediately, I removed the pile.

"You don't know what it was like," I said, still hoping to persuade Doc. I'd tried reason and failed, now I would try sympathy.

"What *what* was like?" he asked irritably.

"My childhood, how Jake ruined all our lives."

"Lass, you're not making sense, and I'm so spent I'm afraid the candlewick inside me head has been snuffed out."

I felt frustrated to tears. "I've never told you but half the story. I'm not sure how Da met Jake. I think they were privates together in the infantry that marched on Atlanta just after Da immigrated. Years after the war they ran into each other at a racetrack pub. Jake was down on his luck, so of course Da gave him a job at the Downs. Then they went into partnership on several horses. Somehow Jake convinced Da to put up the mortgage money so they could buy just one more promising two-year-old, Minstrel's Song."

Doc's eyes burned with new light. "The famous flat racer?"

"The same," I said.

"But he ran under Cornelius Vanderbilt's colors."

"I'm getting to that," I said. "Oh, he was a marvelous piece of horseflesh. In the sun, his coat shown as red as battle, a true-blood bay. Da and Jake bought him at the spring auctions. But the Jockey Club registration papers were made out in Jake's name only. Da said it was just an oversight, that Jake would have the club put it right. But when Mr. Vanderbilt bought Minstrel, well, Da never saw his share of the money."

It rained saliva as Doc tisk-tisked. " 'Tis a sad but familiar story."

"We lived near the Downs, me, Da, my stepmother, my younger sister, and the twin baby boys—my natural mother having died when my sister was born. Da had bought us a little plot of land amid the mansions of Flatbush Avenue near Prospect Park—"

"Aye, so you've told me many a time, lass," interrupted Doc.

"I haven't told you everything," I continued. "It didn't have a regular dwelling, just a carriage house, which once belonged to the Pratts. We were living there until Da's ship came in and we could build my stepmother's dream house. A sunny lot and in the spring you wouldn't believe how butterflies flocked to our hydrangeas. Us kids trapped them in jars, and when we got a fair number, Da made a fancy cherrywood case. I never will forget it. Our collection looked like a work of art embroidered in silk thread."

Clearing my throat, I got up and stirred the soup. Potato broth was the smell of my childhood.

Doc eyed me wearily as I began again. "The coach house had a footman's quarters where we ate, but the sleeping area where carriages had once been parked was cold and drafty, and we children were always sick. We knew better than to complain, though, even when my sister Mary-Terese came down with scarlet fever. Doctor calls ate at the money my stepmother put aside for the house and made her scowl for days. The baby boys had been born with diseased lungs, so we always had piles of bills."

"Got to nip infant consumption in the bud," said Doc, helping himself to seconds of soup. "Best to move to a dry climate. 'Tis why so many homesteaders have taken up claims down below in the valley." He held the cup to his lips as if it were stout.

"Stepmother wouldn't hear of moving," I recalled. "She was in love with the idea of having a house on fashionable Flatbush. Mary-Terese and I slept on one side of the grand black buggy, and our parents and the babies slept on the other, closer to the coal stove in the groom's quarters. Da had bought the phaeton for my stepmother as a wedding gift. We hadn't a team, but after a win when Da had doubled his earnings by wager, he hired a pair of fancy bay standardbreds and took us for a drive in the park.

"Money from the sale of Minstrel's Song would have built us a house, but Jake disappeared after the horse was sold. We lost everything since the mortgage money was gone. Da, stepmother, and the younger ones went to the workhouse. I went into service. . . ." My voice faded as if all those dreams had melted away only yesterday, not a dozen years ago. "You know what those places were like. They didn't last long."

Doc sat up and punched the sugar bag, then laid his head back down. " 'Tis a tragedy, Pearly," he said. "And Jake is one of Lucifer's own, but I'm going to have to rule Shaky's death by natural causes. No proof or evidence otherwise."

He must have seen my eyes well up with tears, because he added, "But if your heart's set on an autopsy, there's only one thing to be done."

I jumped at the opportunity, "You'll do it?"

"Me shoulder's acting up something fierce, but if you'll do the cutting . . ."

My stomach turned into a butter churn with sour curd rising into my throat.

Outside, the heavens ceased dumping snow. From the north I heard the sounds of Ruby coming back to life. I stared at the leaves in the bottom of my teacup. The liquid had gone tepid, and I began to think of it as typhoid water.

I took a long breath. "Okay," I said, though my hand had no strength. The tin cup fell from my grasp, peat-colored water falling into the dirt floor.

Pale sunlight began to seep through the cloth walls. For a moment I considered changing my mind—a woman's prerogative, as Doc always said. But since I wanted to attend medical college, I would have to be well skilled even before I'd be considered for admission. I fought back my revulsion at the thought of disemboweling the mayor.

"Just give me another forty winks," said Doc, "to gear myself up. By then the sun will be at its brightest and the storm well past. We'll need the best light possible. Ye might make a note of that in your journal." He was always poking fun at my note taking. "We'd be well advised to do it outside in natural light, but if the wind doesn't die down, we'll have to do it in here. No sense carrying Shaky through all those drifts to my surgery. I have the necessary instruments with me." Doc glanced around. "Suppose we could use your laundry scale to weigh the organs."

I thought I would regurgitate the tea.

Doc drew a small, dark bottle from his breast pocket. "Take this to reenforce yourself," he instructed. "A first autopsy is always the hardest."

Usually I declined Doc's potions, because they adversely affected my vision. This time I pressed the bottle to my lips, taking a swig of the thick brown liquid, which tasted of sugared pine tar. Doc did the same. And like Doc, I put my head down on the table and nodded off into a deep sleep filled with strange dreams. What woke me? The squeak of Doc's chair as he rose, slapping his cheeks as if he were applying shaving lather? Rolling my head to the side, I listened to the icicle clink of his instruments as he laid them out. Opening my eyes, the brightness of the afternoon sun near blinded me. And, oh God, it shed light into every dusty nook of my little home. With the wash still dripping onto the muddied floor and Tillicum's scent permeating everything, Doc must think me the world's worst housekeeper.

He'd set up the laundry scale on my nail-keg vanity and lined the shallow dishes of the balance with writing paper. The thought of Shaky's liver sitting there like a pile of washrags sent a knife stabbing through my chest.

"Let's bring in His Honor," the r's of Doc's burr rolled out behind him.

I twisted my hair into a coil and tied it in a knot, before pushing up my sleeves. Outside, the unobscured blue sky showed not a hint of a storm cloud, and the sun flooded the drift-covered town with so much glaring white I feared it would damage my sight. The brisk Chinook wind, which was sure to dry my canvas walls in no time, blew sandy grains of snow in a fine dust, caking my shoes and trouser legs.

Doc was first to round the corner of the tent, springing backward like a shying horse almost into my lap. Then I saw the trouble. The mayor had fallen from the ironing board, and the sheet I'd covered him with was torn and colored with blood.

Doc bent down, rolling over the frozen corpse. My hand

flew to my mouth to stifle a gasp as I stared at the gaping wound in Shaky's abdomen. A rope of veiny white intestine rolled out before Doc could secure it back in the cavity.

"Great Julius Caesar!"

"What's happened?" I pleaded, sure that Jake Pardee was at the root of it.

"Not enough innards left to autopsy," he said, spitting tobacco juice on the snow.

CHAPTER FOUR

S top blubbering," commanded Doc, though not unkindly. Late-day sun seared the canvas walls of my laundry, shining so brightly that it hurt to keep my eyes open. But as Doc and I leaned over Shaky, our shadows fell black and solid across his corpse.

We'd finally gotten the disemboweled body back inside. Wanting to do the best stitching job possible, I'd used the last of my white thread, when what did it matter? The melting blood from the gaping hole in the mayor's stomach stained the sutures brown. I tied one of Windy Pardee's lace handkerchiefs around the mayor's stubbly chin and up over his head of matted gray curls to keep his jaw closed, praying that once he unfroze, he'd stiffen up that way.

"You're sure it was wolves?" I wasn't convinced.

"Lucky we got to him when we did," said Doc. "Seen worse cases. Up at Ragtown, they've a one-armed grave digger—he's a Civil War vet, so I don't want to speak against the mon. But he puts 'em down only a foot. During a bad winter, there's often nothing left but polished bones after the wolves and coyotes finish their task."

Shaky Pat's clothes had been shredded, so we'd draped a

new sheet around his frail form. The sutures in his abdomen made a winding path from the mossy hair of his privates up to his protruding sternum as if we'd sketched a miniature railroad track across him. I'd found only one of the silver dollars that kept his eyes closed. Doc donated several coppers for the other.

Pulling a second handkerchief from a stack of clean laundry, I wiped my nose. "Shouldn't we use dimes instead?" I asked, fishing around in my apron pocket. I hit on something heavy and round (the lost dollar?) and drew out Shaky's gold watch. Holding it by its fine Viennese chain, I studied the intricate ivy leaves engraved on the cover. What a handsome treasure, finer than anything I'd ever owned. I'd have to guard it with my life, if I expected to hang on to it in Ruby City. The price of this jewel would put me through a year of medical college. But this was one keepsake I'd never sell.

"Pennies aren't good enough?" he said, the thrifty Scot in him showing through.

"Indians don't value dimes. They want silver dollars or coppers."

"No Indian did this, my lass," he said.

"But this gash, couldn't it have been done by a blunt knife?" I held a flap of open flesh between thumb and forefinger, imagining the sharpened rib bones Indians used to scrape hair from deer hides. Why hadn't I begun the autopsy the minute Doc arrived?

"An Indian would have taken both silver plugs," argued Doc, as he measured out the last piece of thread for me. "No, lass, this is the work of timber wolf greed 'n' hunger. There're even doglike gray hairs left in the cavity. Feel," he held up an invisible fiber.

I raised my hand to shield my eyes, not wanting to hear or see any more.

Tillicum stomped his foot, heaving a sigh. Though his thick

roan coat had dried down to the skin, I was afraid to turn him out into the drifts for fear he'd break his leg. Pulling more insulating hay from the wall of the piano crate, I refilled his feed box.

"Wouldn't we have heard a wolf?" I asked. "We were right here. It was all so soundless. And tracks. Wouldn't there have been tracks in the snow?"

"Indeed," said Doc. "Whatever prints there were, were erased, blown clean as a school slate by the Chinook gale. That wind's a wolf's best friend. Their coat's too thick to be pierced by it, and the noise makes their work all the more silent."

"But I've never heard tell of a wolf attacking a dead man in town," I countered, watching Doc lift another helping of potato soup to his lips. I felt so famished I could almost eat the wretched stuff myself.

"I've got to have a bite," I said, putting down my needle. "What I wouldn't give for a gingersnap or a lemon biscuit." Mary had swapped me a red ribbon for a basket of wapatoos and sunflower shoots, which I chewed like celery. Indians believed that red objects contained special powers, and Mary had thought she'd gotten the better of the trade.

"Aye," said Doc. "Most of your undertaking clients reeked of whiskey even in death and, before they were brought to you, were laid out behind the faro hall near the latrine. No varmint would venture there. The smell of urine and liquor repels 'em."

I felt suddenly better after eating, and my lips cracked a smile at the thought of the instincts I shared with wolves.

"It's a sad thing about old Shaky and getting sadder, but lass, you've got to put the idea that he was poisoned to rest." Doc straightened his perpetually stooped shoulders as much as his buffalo hump would allow. "A man dies in Ruby on an average of once a week, most from gunshot wound and it's seldom self-inflicted. There's arrests—the sheriff has to quell the mob—but never a conviction . . . unless it's an Indian."

"I suppose you're right." Like whites, there were good Indians and bad Indians. But when a red man got arrested, it was usually the one on the slowest horse.

I knotted the thread, don't ask me why. Shaky wasn't going to raise himself up and break out his sutures.

After a moment, Doc said, "I believe we're done and not a moment before he unfreezes. Have you got some rags to sop up this blood? We wouldn't want the beasts of the forest returning to eat the laundress."

Doc was kind to try to lighten my mood. But ghosts continued to nag me. "Why'd Shaky leave me his pet dig?" I asked. "Why didn't he leave it to Dutch?"

Doc's coal eyes studied the floor. "Those two had strong ideological differences, to be sure. Dutch wanted to organize a strike at Forrester's mine, and Shaky was against it. But the real reason Shaky left his claim to you, I fear, is because ol' Dutch isn't long for this world. Smoker's throat," he said after a moment. "Not as lethal as smoker's lip, but . . ." He shook his head, then his expression turned into a bemused smile. "And because His Honor felt awfully guilty on your behalf." He laughed and moved the tobacco plug he chewed whenever he was overly tired to the other side of his mouth.

"Guilty? Go on with you." What was he talking about?

Doc helped me prepare a vinegar wash for the body. "Remember when Shaky Pat and I introduced ourselves at the trading post?" he asked.

"My first day in town, certainly I remember. A room crowded with bewhiskered, smelly gents, one with great tufts of hair coming out of his nose, another with the drooping eyelids of an opium eater, and Windy Pardee trying to sell me a hat!"

Doc slapped his knee. "Well, Shaky thought that, judging by the way you were looking at the lads, you must be the new professional woman in town. . . ."

My chest filled with not-so-mock indignation. "I judged

their garments, assessing the need for a laundress . . . and a barber." I seldom barbered anymore—too many head lice.

"He just thought by the way you were looking the boys over . . ."

"Good Lord!" I began sponging Shaky's head and then his sunken chest, which was dusted with a few lonely gray hairs that all spiraled clockwise.

Spitting his plug on the floor, he took a soapstone pipe from his pant pocket, lighting it with a piece of kindling held to the slag at the bottom of the stove. "The mon felt terrible about his mistake in judgment," he went on.

Tillicum sighed, resigning himself to the heat of the tent. My poor pony looked dehydrated. The cold was taxing, but the raging wind had taken even more out of him.

"Say what you might about Ruby's state of lawlessness," said Doc, "a virtuous woman is sacred here."

Yes, I thought, and the Prince of Wales is my father.

He continued. "Shaky brought drinks all around when he found out all you wanted was the piano crate and an empty whiskey cask for washing laundry. We took a pledge that when your husband arrived, we'd all swear to him concerning your honor."

"My husband? Oh, well . . ." I stammered. The image of a man with ashy skin and tar black hair flashed in front of me. "I've no judgment when it comes to men. I'm better at assessing horseflesh." I gave Tillicum's red, velvety nose a pat. "Just like my da. I appreciate the gesture, but I'd better be making my own way in life . . . and not as a laundress, I hope. I've about worn my fingers raw." I blew on the cracks between my thumb and forefinger to relieve the vinegar sting.

"What will ye do with the Glory Hole claim?" Doc asked. He puffed a cloud of smoke from the pipe's bowl. Tobacco juice is something I can live without, but a pipe is not a bad thing as far as man smells go.

"Don't know. I couldn't possibly afford to develop it."

"Sell it to the Forresters," said Doc. "Day before yesterday Forr bought two Dutch filed on. A bird in the hand, that's my advice. The money will more than buy you a seat at medical college, though I don't know why ye wouldn't want to nurse. You're born to the task. I guess contrariness is just a part of your nature."

"I can't sell it to the Forresters," I said, ignoring his comment.

Doc knitted his brow.

"It's my own wrong life caught up with me."

Jake hadn't recognized me. I was a child when he last laid eyes on me. He didn't pay attention to children or women, unless it was with regard to his animal instincts. But God only knew why Forr hadn't recognized my face. As I said, it was through his letters to my former employer that I first learned of Ruby's existence and Jake's residence here. Asleep in my narrow attic room of the Fifth Avenue mansion, I had ached for nothing but going west and avenging my father's death.

"I'd make myself a handsome sum and get put in the clink all at once." My voice trailed away. "As it is, I can barely spare a day to pick for pay ore at the Last Chance, let alone work two claims. Suppose I could stake someone to half the profits of the Glory Hole, but who in Ruby wouldn't rob their own brother blind?"

Then I thought of Chin. He'd been a miner before he was kidnapped by a railroad contractor. Maybe I could employ him to work my claim.

"What makes you so sure young Forr would recognize you?" Doc asked.

"If he didn't, then his father is sure to," I said. "I was in service in Forr's godmother's house for ten years."

"And left under a cloud, I presume?" he prompted.

"Left accused of theft," I replied flatly. "Mrs. Ritters had a good heart, but her wits were scattered. She took me in when I could have very well gone to the workhouse with the rest of my family. Her husband owned Brooklyn Downs, and when Da lost his job due to drink, they took pity on me. I owe her my life. Still, when her heirloom diamond necklace disappeared, no one believed my innocence, not even my fiancé."

"Then you're not married?" He asked raising his brow.

"That fiancé isn't the man I married." My voice cracked like an egg against a fry pan. "Please, Doc, don't ask. The whole sordid mess is too confusing even for me." Clearing my throat, I refreshed the sponge in the pail of vinegar water. Wiping Shaky's biceps, I combed the hair on his arm as if it were a doll's.

After a silence I began again. "I was Mrs. Ritters's lady's maid. Laced her into her corset and tied her shoes because she couldn't bend down strapped in with baleen. On Saturdays, I aired her clothes. Her only son drowned just before I joined the staff, and she was prone to fits of crying. Her son and Forr had been friends since their cradle days."

Closing my eyes, I imagined the dining room of the Fifth Avenue mansion. "Every Monday we'd count the Limoges, examining it for chips. The idea of the slightest additional loss was untenable to Mrs. Ritters. Tuesday we cleaned her jewelry. I knew that diamond necklace like the back of my hand. Such a gaudy collection of grapes and vines, just like a tart's finery. Why would I steal it after ten years of honest labor?"

"Did you?" asked Doc.

"Certainly not!" I stomped my foot so hard it splashed mud on Doc's trousers. "Sorry." My floor had turned to soup.

"So why'd they suspect ye?"

"Jealousy raged through that house. I was Mrs. Ritters's favorite, because I was Protestant Irish, not Catholic like the rest. The others never taunted me in front of Madam. But once, when I complained, they really got me," I said, letting memory run.

Reaching under the tent wall, Doc dumped the vinegar water into the melting snow. Then he drew out a straight razor, sharpening it on a leather strop.

I began mixing shaving cream in a wooden bowl. "I was eleven at the time, been in service almost a year," I said. "Mrs. Ritters had me down on my knees on the Oriental rug in the withdrawing room examining a cigar burn. Kathleen, the head kitchen maid, came in with a message: My father was in the servants' dining hall waiting for me! I nearly had an attack of vapors from the joy of it. What did I care about Mrs. Ritters's sour expression? My father had come to take me away, *tra la*. Dancing a jig right there on the priceless carpet, I could almost hear Seamus O'Sullivan's Friday night fiddle. My father was an inspired man when it came to caressing a bow and strings."

I beat the shaving cream into a lather, then continued. "Running into the servants' kitchen where Kathleen and her staff sat drinking tea and eating buttered bread heels from a piece of newspaper, I caught only a hint of their conversation— something about the principal color of liquor. Their words went dead when I asked, 'Is it true? Is Da here?' 'The ol' boyo's in the servants' hall,' Kathleen said flatly. The fat laundress didn't meet my eye. Father Cormac, Kathleen's brother, had such terrible palsy in his hands that he clanked his cup down so hard the spoon shot off the saucer. I flew past them, through the heavy swinging doors of the unheated dining room.

"There was Da, once the Ritterses' head groom, lying dead on the table."

Doc's lower jaw dropped. " 'Tis the cruelest joke I've ever heard."

I raised my shoulders to my neck in a shrug, hoping to dispel the past. "But I haven't finished about the necklace," I said, frosting the mayor's face with shaving cream.

It was important that Doc believed my innocence.

Sighing, I said, "After Da died—the rest of my family had

passed over as well by this time—I latched on to Davy, the groundskeeper's son. In hindsight, I think he had his way with most of the servant girls, but I was the one he intended to marry, which made his mother furious. Sometimes I think that's why he proposed—as an act of rebellion. Davy had peach-colored hair, shining eyes, and buckets of charm, the light of his mama's eye. We'd gone to school together ever since I'd been at the Ritterses'.

"I'd always done better in my lessons, though he was older," I said as Doc tested the razor for sharpness and then handed it to me. "That made his mother even more angry. I couldn't help love him—everyone did. His family was Protestant like mine, and his was the only sunny face in that sober house. Despite his mother, we planned to marry. I would write Davy's arithmetic tables, while he explained our escape to Oregon. Later, Mrs. Ritters began reading me letters from her godson who'd been sent out west—or, rather, I read them to her. Her eyes were always inflamed from tears." I drew the straight razor across Shaky's cheek like a violin bow and began plucking at his sideburns.

"Forr made Ruby City sound like paradise," I continued. "I got it in my mind that that's where we'd go. I couldn't believe my eyes when I saw the name Jake Pardee penned in one of Forr's letters."

My cutting hand dropped to my side at the memory of it. Doc took the razor from me, running it over the strop a few more times.

"I smelled destiny on the stationery on which his letters were written. Davy and I would go to the Okanogan. I'd have a family again and settle the score with Jake Pardee all at the same time. When your life has direction, your sorrows pale. Not even my attic room mattered—I had to sleep submerged under blankets, even in the stifling heat of summer, because rodents ran over me after dark."

"The necklace?" Doc prompted.

Lifting the handkerchief that tied Shaky's jaw closed, I began shaving his cheek. "Yes, well, I was the last one to see it. After cleaning each setting with baking soda, checking the clasp, and replacing the diamonds in Mrs. Ritters's armoire, I reminded Madam to lock it up. Two nights later when she went to put the necklace on, it was gone. Every finger pointed at me—the servants, Davy's mother. Which came as no surprise. What hurt most was Davy turning his back on me. My blood still boils when I think of it. Even he thought I'd done it! But I didn't steal it, I swear."

I gripped the razor with murder in my hand. My breath came so hard and quick I couldn't speak. Doc snatched the straightedge from me and began cleaning it. "How could he doubt me?" I beat my fist on the ironing table. "I'd never told a lie, not even to save myself from getting a lashing."

Doc steadied the tabletop so that the mayor wouldn't slide off.

"That night every servant in the house petitioned Mrs. Ritters concerning my bad character. Madam had always held me up as an example, saying that I would rise above my lot and make something of myself. She hated Catholics, you see, and thought Davy a rake, though she put up with him because of his father. The servants and Davy's mother went for me like hawks to prey. I felt so betrayed I left that night, just walked out of the house with nothing." I swallowed a swell of saliva. "Leaving my dreams behind me, I felt like I'd torn the fingers off my hand."

Doc's face elongated in sympathy. "You're not alone, lass. Most in Ruby have a past they've buried, and few as honorable as yours. You're a woman of substance, I'll vouch for that, and so would he." Doc motioned toward the body, and we both laughed.

"You're a good hand at barbering," Doc added, admiring

my work. "His head may shrivel before the funeral, in which case you may have to shave him again."

From outside came noises of shovels pitching snow. I began to worry about an avalanche roaring down over Main Street as it had the winter before I arrived.

Doc looked puzzled. "So, if ye didn't marry Davy, then who's your husband?"

Footsteps—heavy boots—crunched the white coverlet in an irregular cadence, a left, right, left, accompanied by a shuffle as if one of the marchers had a limp. I caught the harsh consonants of Dutch Wilhelm's German accent as he spoke to another whose voice I also recognized. Dutch and General George Washington Jones, an ex-slave who served as Ruby's jack-of-all-trades, had arrived to measure Shaky for his coffin.

Tillicum kicked at an imagined fly. The stove burned low and orange. I poked it up, wondering where they would find enough milled lumber for Shaky's casket. No one wanted our mayor to be buried in a steamer trunk.

Dutch began yelling, "Frau Ryan, Frau Ryan," even before the pair got to my door.

"In here," I called. They entered breathless, as if they'd run all the way.

The nostrils on Dutch's sprawling nose flared, and even from where I sat, I could see purple veins scribbled across his face, so constricted were his blood vessels from the cold. General Jones stood in back of him, his mittenless black hands dangling from his too-short sleeves like venison hams. I wondered that he didn't get frostbite.

Doc bid his fellow Union army veterans a hello with their special salute.

"Have ya heard the news?" Dutch asked.

"Frank Belknap brought h'm in on da stage," said Jones, staring at his feet. He was almost six feet tall and spider thin, his skin the color of burnt taffy.

"I'm a trail-weary mon," Doc said. "What's happened?

Who's hurt?" He began to replace his instruments in his battered black bag tattooed with scuff marks.

Dutch spoke loud and fast, his accent thick with excitement. My heart thumped. It sounded like, "Jake Pardee's been found dead vith a bullet through his brow."

CHAPTER FIVE

That night

No one grieved. In fact, if you were to have happened upon Ruby, Washington, that night, you might have thought it was the Fourth of July had it not been for the bone-piercing dampness of melting snow. How did I feel? I didn't believe a word of Jake's demise and was sure he would appear at my door with a demon's grin, saying that his "death" had been nothing but a prank.

No one else shared my skepticism. Gambling was serious business in Ruby City, and bets were placed as to the murderer of Jake Ezekial Pardee. Jake's root cellar was liberated and quarts of Sanford's Jamaica Ginger handed out on the sidewalk. Quickly emptied and the bottles smashed, a rich glitter soon paved the narrow spaces between buildings. A pyre blazed in front of the Ruby First National where the spotted sow was butchered and roasted. Every washtub became a drum. Before long strains of "Comin' Through the Rye" and "Foggy Foggy Dew" drowned in war whoops and Rebel yells.

As Doc and I sat inside my tent, listening to rifle shots and savage screams, a dark, burly man with a face as flat as a dinner plate entered without knocking.

"Pleases, Misses, I gotta have your washboard, it's the only thing I can play," said the blacksmith. When he saw Doc sitting there, he left in haste.

I shivered in my doorway, watching the smith's progress up the steep incline of Ruby's main thoroughfare to the Gem Saloon high on the ridge. Outside the tavern, Indians stood with faces pressed to the frosted glass of the barroom, their tattered clothing silhouetted against the orange of the bonfire. I strained my eyes, searching for Pokamiakin, but could not find the tall, sturdy Indian.

Doc followed my gaze. "Siwash hoping for *melican*," he said. *Melican*, the native word for whiskey, was the same term employed for "medicine," thus its derivation.

Black powder exploded from the mine shafts in the ragged mountains behind our village. Back inside, I placed my broom in front of the door as a barrier to a drunken midnight intruder, then went over to my bed to feel for the reassurance of Shaky's pearl-handled revolver hidden beneath the pillow.

We'd finished preparing the body and placed it outside, hoping the chill of night would keep it from changing. The vinegar smell, Doc assured me, would keep the wolves and coyotes away until morning when the corpse would be soaked in spirits of camphor. Measurements for the coffin taken, Dutch had left promising to return with his best silk shirt for Shaky's burial. Doc slept with his head down on my wee table as I began ironing, but soon I abandoned the effort.

Had my thoughts killed Jake Pardee?

Keep busy, I told myself and started unpinning dried laundry from the tent poles, folding it into piles. Tillicum tensed at every powder blast. Doc stirred, then reached into his breast pocket for a swig of Stringfellow's Wizard Remedy. What I wouldn't give for a sweet. But the confectionery was a day's ride away.

Screwing the cap on the brown bottle, Doc rose and began throwing the instruments he used on Shaky's repair work into the fire to sterilize them. I took my scorched dress down from where it hung and put my sewing basket at my feet. If it hadn't been my warmest gingham, I'd have given it to Mary and her sister to braid into a rug.

"Doc, who do you think killed Pardee?"

Doc yawned and stretched. "Puzzlement," he said. "From what I gather, Cranky Frank found Jake just before noon when he passed by the ice caves at the foot of Three Devils Peak. Pardee was sprawled under his wagon with a bullet in the back of his head. The body was still warm and nothing stolen, not even Jake's revolver!"

"So it's true that his hat was nearby with a hole in it?"

Doc nodded.

"Where'd they take him?"

"Sheriff's," he said. "As coroner, I'm obliged to have a look at the wound that did the trick. A nasty one, according to Frank." Doc wet his lips with his tongue.

My entire body shuddered. Much as I disliked Jake, I hadn't the slightest need to view him in his present state; though, of course, I would have to prepare him for burial.

Doc put an arm wearily into the sleeve of his coat and picked up his bag. "Better get back to me surgery. I'm bound to be needed before the night's through. Think I'll stop in at the Gem. Might be interesting to know who's betting on whom as the culprit. Stay inside, lass, and don't brood too much on the death of Mr. Patrick McDonald," Doc advised. "He was sorely afflicted, even before he was struck down."

Sighing, I waved good-bye. I knew darn well Shaky hadn't died from typhoid, but how could I prove it? And what good would it do? As Doc pointed out, countless Rubyites had been tried for murder. In Ruby the guilty party either bribed the justice of the peace or escaped the territory. What nagged at me now was that the murders of Shaky and Jake had transpired within twelve hours of each other, and I felt certain this was no coincidence.

My little horse seemed to watch me take a tuck in the waist of my dress to camouflage a burn hole. "Haven't I just inherited one of the most valuable claims in the country?" I asked him. "If it's discovered I'm the ghost writer, it won't take a genius to deduce that I had a grudge against Pardee. Next thing you know, I'll be accused of his murder by someone hungry for my claim." My hand shook so much that, for a moment, I had to put down my sewing, but soon I attributed my imagined peril to a guilty conscience.

I lit the lamp—just a rag in a plate of tallow—and held up my handiwork for inspection. "What a sight. Like wearing a crazy quilt." My pony shook himself.

After shoving a log into the fire, I walked to the window, pulling aside the sheepskin covering. Crisp evening air danced on my face. As I stared out at the stone orchard of South Ruby, piles of cobbles resembling sugar lumps lay under a tablecloth of snow.

The most recent grave, that one over there under the leafless cottonwood, belonged to Gimpy French Pete. Ella had gunned the poor Frog down on the porch of her bawdy house during his second visit. Our sheriff, who had spent the night at Ella's, tripped over the body when he left the next morning. The story was that the soiled dove French Pete fancied wasn't partial to his advances. During his first visit, she'd shot him while he struggled with his belt buckle. That time Pete escaped with his life and an addendum to his sobriquet. I know all about his wounds, because Doc got me out of bed in the middle of the coldest night of the year in order to assist. "Good thing you're a married lady," he'd said, "because this is a delicate matter." Sewing basket in hand, I trudged across town to Doc's surgery. The mercury had plunged to thirty below—thank the Lord there wasn't a hint of a breeze. Doc dosed Pete with chloroform, then prostrated the patient on his bed and tied his legs to the footboard, straddling his chest. I tried my best to sew up what looked like a butchered prairie chicken's neck and giblets. Pete came to, shrieking louder than a woman in childbirth. As I finished, Doc searched in vain for his vial of iodoform crystals. He ended up spitting tobacco juice on the wound the way cowmen do at round-up time after castrating a calf.

French Pete spent several days tanking himself at the Gem, then paid Ella a second visit. It took him until almost dawn to find her door. Ella was not a woman to be disturbed from her beauty sleep—I'm told she wakes up swinging if caused to rise before noon. But Pete made his demands and paid dearly.

Upon tripping over the body, the sheriff felt obliged to take Pete's remains into custody as evidence. Meanwhile Ella boarded Cranky Frank's stage for Spokane Falls in order to enjoy a sudden reunion with her sister. They brought Pete to me to prepare while two deputies dug a hole in South Ruby. As I sponged him down, I had to fight off my rage. I hadn't sewn this gent up in the dead (if you'll excuse the expression) of the coldest night in a decade just so someone could punch a hole in him a week later! Before I had the deceased fully laid out, the deputies picked him up like a rolled carpet and dumped him in his new address without a coffin or even a burial cloth, which the county—always without funds—would have had to pay for. Then, while Gimpy French Pete's shameful demise was heatedly discussed, a new scandal involving Jake Pardee arose.

I glanced at Jake's just-washed khaki trousers, feeling a pang of sadness for his wife. It must pain her deeply that their empty cuffs should never caress Mr. Pardee's stout legs again. A black thought suddenly seized me. "Tillicum, what about Windy? If she discovers I'm the ghost writer, mightn't she accuse me of her husband's murder?" I slapped my cheek. My guilty conscience again.

Looking back out the window, I remembered that the day after French Pete was buried, some cattlemen down in the valley accused Jake of being in possession of several of their branded horses, insinuating that he actually hired the men who'd done the thieving and not just accidentally purchased stolen livestock. After Pokamiakin (or Poka Mika as the ranchers called him) examined Jake's stock pen, horses with Siwash brands were also discovered, so the Indians became involved. Copper skins and cowmen banding together was unheard of. This was serious, even by Ruby's standards.

In the Okanogan, horses were priceless. The ranchers organized a lynching party and waited on the wagon road to the river, hoping to seize the nefarious liveryman on his fortnightly ride to the steamboat dock. Jake, as I've mentioned, knew better than most how to play both ends against the middle. He often treated a prospector down on his luck to a free game of faro, so the miners, who had an inbred hatred of the ranchers, took offense at the cattlemen's insinuations.

Then our justice of the peace pointed out that, since the horses had disappeared, the cattlemen and Indians didn't have any solid evidence. After Jake promised to be more discerning about inspecting for brands, the cattlemen's vigilance committee went away in disgust. That night a blizzard drove the miners back to their digs. By this time the populace had forgotten about French Pete's death. Temperatures plummeted, the snow crusted to hard pack. Two days later when the ice melted and the smell of spring grass blew in on the Chinook, Mayor Shaky Pat was suddenly stricken.

After securing the sheepskin back over the window hole, I put the dress away and drew out a pen, ink pot, and paper in order to write Shaky's mother the sad news. In addition to being thought of as one of the few women of virtue in Ruby, I was one of the few people of either sex who could read or write.

"Unflinchingly he faced his end without a tremor," I wrote

in my best hand, "passing on in a peaceful sleep, a fitting close for a well-spent life." I had just finished the last sentence and was thinking about going outside and snipping a lock of the mayor's wavy gray hair to enclose in the letter when I heard footsteps. Doc thrust the blanket aside, struggling against the broom handle, almost breaking it.

"Bad news travels fast," he said more to himself than to me. As he entered, he rubbed his chill-reddened hands together nervously, warming them in front of the stove.

A lynching party? But who, even in the Okanogan, would want to hang the murderer of Jake Pardee?

"The widow's staked a reward," he said.

I bit my lip. Rewards were bad medicine in Ruby Camp.

"A thousand dollars."

My eyebrows flew up my forehead in surprise. "An unheard-of sum!"

"Rumor has it Forr Jr. helped her out. He doesn't take kindly to having his *partner* murdered," Doc said with brogue-flavored cynicism.

"And now there's also the federal marshal to answer to." He gave a long exhale as if he could have blown out all sixty-one candles on his birthday cake.

"What marshal?" I blotted the sorrowful letter to Shaky's mother and put it in a safe place until I could take up a collection for the price of a stamp.

"The marshal's office feels indebted to Jake. Wants a full accounting of the case. Word just came in from Spokane Falls on the telegraph down at the steamboat landing."

My jaw sprang open. If there had been mosquitoes about, my mouth would have been full of them. "Surely there's a mistake."

Doc sat down on a crate leaning into the wet canvas wall. Water from the melting snow had pooled on the roof and dripped through the greased sailcloth. I got up and poked the puddles with the broom handle, spilling the dark water over the side of the tent.

"It's like this: When Jake left his post as Indian agent—"

"He was run out," I interrupted. "He sold every provision the government sent for the Salish in return for taking their land."

Doc leaned forward. "True enough. But before he departed his post for the more prosperous Ruby Camp, he informed on several no-good white whiskey peddlers like himself. Big Belly Tribly for one—still in the penitentiary. The marshal feels it his duty to buttonhole this murderer, and if he isn't satisfied . . . he'll come to investigate himself," Doc finished.

Feverishly, I ran my fingers through a red coil of singed hair. My hands began to shake as I thought about those New York warrants. Burying my face in my apron, I hoped to blacken the imagined interior of a women's prison. "But any one of fifty people in Ruby might have murdered him . . . including myself," I added slowly.

Doc hammered the little table with his clenched fist. "No one wants a federal marshal here. The news has flown through every tavern in town. Not only that, but Brownie Bitterroot, our esteemed mine foreman, got a letter yesterday. The mine owner, Forrester Sr., is on his way here for an inspection."

Jumping to my feet so fast my wind rustled the tent walls, I demanded, "Why didn't you tell me?" The image of the cold stone walls of a women's prison threatened. Surely my former employer's dearest friend would recognize me.

Doc sputtered, "I, I, lass, I had Shaky knocking on heaven's gate all afternoon."

I walked to my bed and collapsed in a heap. "It's God's will," I said. "I came here for revenge and got it, though not the way I imagined." Outside the blasting abated, then renewed itself with cannon shots that sounded like an avalanche.

Doc sprang to his feet. "Get hold of yourself, woman!" He rubbed his palms across this woolly chaps. "You were hell-bent on investigating Shaky's death a minute ago. Why not take on Jake's? I wouldn't want to lose the best assistant I ever had. You're a clever lass, while our sheriff is inexperienced and new to these parts. Just between us, what say ye do a little scratching around on your own to help him out? Justice is a rare commodity in Ruby, but we don't want it to become extinct altogether."

I stared at the floor.

Doc clenched my shoulders. "The mon hasn't a prayer of discovering the true culprit," he went on. I felt like a china figurine about to shatter. "You've the perfect cover. No one would think it odd if you gossiped with your customers about Jake's demise when you delivered laundry. Every woman's a natural gossip. Let's put it to practical use."

Tears welled in my eyes. Doc grazed my hand with his to comfort me. Why had I ever come west? I should have stuck to my guns in the Ritterses' house and defended my reputation. Too late now. The trip back would eat all my savings for medical college.

I pulled myself to my feet. Taking my writing tablet from the shelf in order to list possible suspects, "Where do we start?" I asked, jabbing the turkey quill into the ink pot. My hand filled with strength as if I, Pearl O'Sullivan Ryan, were reviewing the evidence.

A look of relief passed across Doc's brow. "Up at the gambling hall, the odds are two to one it was Windy herself."

"You mean the widow who just put up the reward?"

"There's been rumors about her for some time," Doc said, refusing to elaborate. According to him, most tavern talk was unfit for a lady's ears. "The reward could very well be a ploy. Being married to Jake was surely no picnic. And Jake died a wealthy mon. Windy's sure to profit from his untimely demise."

I jotted her name down. "Two to one against whom?"

"Little Ella," he said. "Seems she owed Jake money. She's killed before and without remorse. It adds up."

I scribbled her name. "But it was from her girls that Jake bought information about the lads. When a lonely gent spilled his heart to a tarnished lily, Ella and her girls were all ears. You told me so yourself. Why would she kill the golden goose?" My mental faculties galloped ahead of my writing hand like runaway horses.

"Perhaps Ella paid off her debt to Jake with the girls' information," mused Doc. "Don't know, lass. That's where your sleuthing would come in handy."

My thoughts ricocheted through the night. "You said that while Jake was searching out the ghost writer, he rattled the justice of the peace's cage pretty good. Jake mined everyone's past for paydirt, and if we do the same maybe we'll uncover something. What's the local lawyer got to hide?" I considered Arizona Charley, our JP, with his propensity for always washing his hands. He was the cleanest gent in Ruby. A curious situation, considering that his office was always in a state of complete disarray.

Doc pressed his fleshy hand to his temples. "Horse stealing. In Oregon . . . no, no, Idaho, the Coeur d'Alenes." Doc studied my expression of disbelief and rushed to explain, "You know Charley, he's a solid citizen when sober, but after a pint, he can't tell one horse from another. Rode out of town on the wrong bay colt, as I understand it. Happened to be the railroad owner's best breeding stallion."

"Who else?" I prompted.

Doc's brow furrowed in thought.

"And yourself, Doctor Stringfellow? You were none too fond of the deceased. What about when he broke your glasses?"

"A barroom fight," said Doc.

"What was the argument about?" I'd never before thought to ask.

"A horse."

Was there anyone in Ruby who had not argued with Jake over a horse? I put down my pen, trying to wipe the ink off my hand with some dried leaves from the kindling bin.

Doc screwed up his mouth, setting his heavy jaw. "I'd bet my last silver dollar that ol' Jake had something on the Bitterroots, though I don't know what."

"Carolina?" I jerked forward. "Mother Superior herself?"

"Her husband, mainly," said Doc.

"How do you know?" I prodded.

"Observation," he lectured. "A physician's most trusty tool. Here was Jake, a mon of the worst sort, who'd threatened Bitterroot's wife with a gun, demanding her school record books and telling her that because she was a woman, she was ineligible for the office of superintendent of instruction—all because he wanted to build a schoolhouse–cum–'social hall,' as he politely called it, with federal dollars and she wasn't about to let him."

"Was that when she told him she'd stand her ground until God or the Supreme Court directed otherwise?" I smiled at the thought of Carolina's pluck and regretted that she had shown so little interest in being a friend to me.

"Aye, and most of the town was behind her, though few would admit it. Then a week later Bitterroot is yes-sirring and no-sirring Jake as if he were Jake's footman." Doc rubbed the barnacley growth on his chin. "Might be something amiss at the mine. I never did learn why Forrester Sr. was making an unprecedented trip."

"Carolina Bitterroot hasn't even committed the sin of bad grammar. I can't imagine she has any dirty linen for Jake to air." I had never known a word of gossip to pass her lips. She remained aloof and kept her own counsel.

"She was the first person Jake accused when the ghost writing began to appear. It made sense. She could write, and she certainly had a bone to pick with him. She set him straight about her innocence. Then he knew it was you, lass—a simple processes of elimination. He just didn't know who'd put you up to it."

I dropped my pen. "He knew?" Ink splattered everywhere. My hands went numb.

"You've distinctive writing. It wasn't difficult to figure. What he wanted to know was who'd paid you."

I shouted, "I don't believe you!" Tillicum's head jerked up from sleep and his ears flew backward, pinned to his neck.

"Yesterday when I walked past the livery? Do you remember when you were hiding in the thicket, burying your paint and brush?"

I nodded.

"Jake knew I was hunting you for Mayor Pat. 'Doc,' he says, 'Pearly's in the sage, been up to one of her tricks. You better get her out of my sight before I wring her neck.' "

"Why didn't you tell me he knew?"

"I, I . . . didn't I warn you not to tread on Jake Pardee or you'd be horsemeat?" Doc tried to deflect my anger with a severe expression. "Had to placate the man somehow, didn't I? He threatened to wreck my surgery if I let on that he knew."

I was so irked I could have broken the pen in half.

Seeing murder in my eyes, Doc spoke rapidly, "Now I'm starting to wonder if my horse was poisoned accidentally, that maybe Jake . . ."

"Good God, why didn't you tell him no one paid me?"

"For two good reasons." Doc gulped air. "One, he thought that you did it to get his attention, a schoolgirl lark, you know . . . because you were in love with him. . . ."

"In love with—" I threw my ink-spotted writing pad on the muddy floor in a fit of fury. "That arrogant swine."

"He didn't believe for a minute that you were married," Doc said flatly, as if he didn't believe me either. "Telling the mon you were acting on your own would have only reinforced his theory."

Now I felt truly vexed. "I certainly am married, to Mr.

Paddy Ryan from Dublin, Ireland." I folded my arms in front of my apron and raised my chin to the ceiling.

An amused smile spread across Doc's narrow lips. "Lass, you couldn't possibly weigh more than a hundred pounds wet with your pockets filled with silver dollars. But when you have that look on your face, you're as formidable as a woman weighing fifteen stone. Ye must be telling the truth."

I looked at the floor. "The truth is, I am married to him, though I didn't know him but for a day," I confessed, reaching down to retrieve my writing pad.

Suddenly I felt the need to unburden myself. "Just before Mrs. Ritters's diamond necklace turned up missing, a man came to the servants' entrance asking for Pinky O'Sullivan. Only my da called me Pinky, and when I'd gone into service, Mrs. Ritters had dropped the O' of my name, so no one had heard of such a person. Kathleen was just turning the man away when I walked in. His name was Paddy and, except for a sallow complexion, he was a pleasant looking lad with a dark mane of hair—what they call black Irish—whose father had been a school chum of my da's.

"Well, this younger Ryan was just off the boat when he'd been arrested for being in league with union organizers. He needed an American wife, in name only, to avoid deportation. He'd no friends in this country. Did I know any lass who could oblige him?

"I did not. Furthermore, I'd just been on a stroll with Davy, window-shopping in the diamond district for a wedding ring, and my mind was a complete flutter. Paddy said there'd be a hundred dollars in it for some 'lucky girl' and bid me good-bye, his eyes shimmering like the Hudson River in summer. He went away, and I never thought of him again. Then a week later, the ax fell. Everyone in the household turned against me over the theft of the necklace, including my fiancé. I walked out of the Ritterses' house forever, thinking, I will find that Mr. Ryan, marry him, and head west with a hundred dollars."

I averted my eyes, adding, "Which is why my *husband* has not joined me here in Ruby City. My *marriage* was merely a business transaction and never consummated."

Doc asked kindly, "Do ye still seize up with melancholia when ye think of him?"

"Davy?" I asked, staring at the floor. I nodded, feeling over-whelmed by a wave of self-pity: how sad my life had become. Oh, how I longed for a letter from medical college. Why didn't I just leave this place? Surely I would do better somewhere else.

"Your little secret's safe with me, Pearly." He took a tin of snuff from his breast pocket and laid a pinch in the corner of his mouth. "There's another reason I didn't let on to Jake that you were acting under your own volition."

"What's that?"

"Someone confessed to paying you to write those messages."

"Confessed!? Who would do such a thing?"

"Mr. Patrick McDonald, of course. He hoped it would calm the mon down."

For a moment I was speechless. "What reason did Shaky give Jake?"

"None. He fell into delirium." The tobacco plug bulged out Doc's cheek and made me wonder, Should I bury Shaky with a chaw in his mouth, he enjoyed it so? "Our mayor was awfully fond of you," Doc said. "It irked him to no end that Jake thought you were in love with him and trying to get his atten-tion by writing insults on walls."

"Only the most egocentric man in the world would think such a thing." I balled my fists, studying the ink stains on my calluses.

" 'Tis true, lass."

Outside the noise of snowmelt dripped from every eave and gutter. After a moment I added, "I wouldn't blame his wife for murdering him."

A queer feeling rose like bread dough from the pit of my stomach. I knew in my marrow that the death of our mayor and the death of Jake Pardee were connected. Worse, I sensed the bony hand of the grim reaper clawing at my tent's door. You're letting your imagination run away with you, I said to my-self. But was I?

CHAPTER SIX

April 18

I began my investigations the next morning promptly at eight. As you can see, inheriting Shaky's watch changed my life. Now and then I'd hold it to my ear. The faint little ticktock whispered, "Pearl-y, Pearl-y," in Shaky's breathy smoker's voice.

Putting the pot to boil, Mary Reddawn noted the time. As I peeled potatoes for soup and starch, Mary held up ten fingers— ten minutes before heat bubbles began to form. Less than a minute to check that the mayor's remains had been undisturbed during the night. Twelve minutes to tether Tillicum to a log on the slopes of South Ruby. The same for Chin to carry water up from Salmon Creek. I checked everyone's pulse, including my cayuse's, which was normal at thirty-six. And I couldn't wait to begin clocking how long it took for pitcher plant tea to reduce a fever. Tying my bonnet strings beneath my chin, I calculated the minutes it would take us to walk to Windy Pardee's trading post.

The instant I hoisted the postmistress's laundry parcel over my shoulder, it began to rain in torrents. Clouds the color of cast iron pots trailed across a colorless sky, and a southeasterly cut at me from behind, pounding against the back of my head. But the Chinook wind was warm. Most of the snow had melted, and everywhere freshets raced down to the swollen banks of Salmon Creek.

Mary never minded getting wet, but Chin carried a tattered umbrella with several broken ribs, a contraption resembling a decaying bird. They followed as I darted from doorway to awning in the hopes that the shower wouldn't take all the starch out of my bonnet. There's nothing more uncomfortable than a soggy bonnet bill sagging in front of your face, and nothing more unbecoming, either. I would have done what I did on a rainy day when working up at my Last Chance Mine—wind a rag around my head—but that would have begged even a mourning Windy Pardee to sell me the latest cartwheel hat.

Men and dogs lay sleeping in doorways. Some gents reeked of alcohol, others of the opium den. The smell of wet horseflesh and manure made inroads to my lungs. Everywhere shards of broken liquor bottles littered the alleys. Stepping over a sleeping gent's denim legs, I thought, This one looks just like my Davy, same rippling auburn hair . . . My face cracked like a dropped teacup and I almost started bawling. I had to stop right there in front of the assayer's office and give myself a lecture.

Leaping the sleeping miner, my mud-stained hem brushed his cap away from his waxy face. The boy had a jagged blue scar across his forehead, very much the way I imagined the crack in my heart. Turning away, I rushed up the plank sidewalk toward the PO, where I hoped to find a letter from the Willamette Institute of Medicine. I watched Mary and Chin dart behind buildings while gathering trinkets—bits of broken glass, a thrown horseshoe—left behind by last night's cheer. Given the local prejudice against Indians and Chinamen, it was safer for them to travel as stealthily as possible.

The canvas door to the faro tent was tied open. Next to

it, in the alley, the remains of the head of the spotted pig roasted the night before lay eyeless and with one ear missing. Inside the circus-sized tent a barker took wagers as to the murderer of the gambling parlor's owner. "Five dollars on the mistress of the bawdy house," called a man at the back table. "Poka Mika," yelled a second, "that Injin hated Jake's axle feathers." "Five bits on his old woman," said the partner of the first. A cold sweat beaded my brow. I wondered if anyone would wager that I'd done the deed.

The mine owner's son sat so that the entryway illuminated his poker hand. Forr scrutinized his cards the same way he used to scrutinize my bodice. Afraid he'd recognize me and have me sent back to Manhattan, I yanked my bonnet down over my face.

"I'll raise you ten," Forr said, tossing a tiny muslin bag of gold dust into the center of the table. He never lifted his watermelon seed eyes from his cards. Unshaven, his face appeared thinner than usual, his pale, lifeless hair hanging down to his shoulders.

Before stepping into the trading post, I had to pause to steady my nerves. Fixing a sympathetic expression on my face, I willed there to be a letter addressed to Pearl Ryan.

Across the street, the unpainted planks of Jake's livery were stained dark by rain. A group of men lingered inside the huge entrance. Hands in their pockets, they leaned against the support posts, a marooned, confused look on each face.

"Bullet blew the hat clean off his head," said one as several others called out to me, did I know where Doc was?

"Out tending last night's casualties." I wondered at whose digs.

"Are you ill? Is it an emergency?" I asked one gent with an ashy complexion.

"No. Just wanted him to look at my horse's swollen leg." I nodded. Doc was as good at treating livestock as he was at doctoring people.

Like two frail saplings, Mary and Chin huddled together watching. I heard them whispering about the afterlife to which Jake's spirit had fled.

"*Kalakala kuitan*," flying horses, Chin said in Chinook.

"*Moosum nanaitch kuitan*," dream horses, breathed Mary.

I smiled at their expressionless faces. Perhaps Jake Pardee had gone to the place of flying dream horses and not to hell.

But as I opened the trading post door—not a makeshift split log barricade but a real door with brass hinges—I heard the ring of cheerful laughter and was dismayed by the gaiety within. Windy stood behind a counter spread with catalogs. She hadn't dressed in black, but in a sky blue cotton wrapper and a crisp white apron. On top of her curly blond hair sat a wide-brimmed straw hat trimmed with silk sweet peas that crowned her dimpled face like a halo.

The fire in the potbellied stove blazed. As usual Dutch sat on his cider barrel, and by the expression on his face I knew I'd just interrupted a meeting of the miners' strike committee. Our jack-of-all trades, the ex-slave General George Washington Jones, straddled a nail keg. His arms were lost inside his too-big shirt, his skinny ankles dangled beyond his too-short pants. Arizona Charley, our justice of the peace, occupied the only real chair. In his lap lay a sheaf of legal papers, which he shuffled like cards.

A tower of individually bundled burial shrouds hovered in the corner. Crates of hammerheads and nails were stacked next to cases of ammunition. A basket of withered apples was the only fresh produce. From the rafters hung plow and ax handles; by the door stood picks, pans, and assorted miners' gear. A few letters and small parcels lingered at the bottom of the lard pail next to the counter where our bald-headed sheriff searched for his mail and, finding none, departed. For a few moments I enjoyed the summery air inside the trading post. Before I had time to check the pail's contents, everyone greeted me with a round of "Hello, Pearly."

Dutch took his heavy boot from the box where he rested his bum foot, stood, and tipped his navy cap, as did General Jones. Jones's head resembled a polished nut rimmed with steel wool. Once bunkmates at a Union Army infirmary where they were recovering from war wounds, the two had been reunited all these years later in Ruby City.

It was a familiar story. Most of the old-timers in camp, especially those with a limp or an arm missing, were vets. After the War Between the States, many soldiers who'd lost their roots turned to prospecting or Indian fighting. We had several members of the Kansas Seventh Cavalry and I don't know how many survivors of the Battle of Bull Run. You could tell by the color of a man's hat which side he'd fought on—a gray-capped miner never spoke to blue caps. Boundary and claim disputes might be the root of most of our homicides, but the North-South question spawned most of our late-night shootfests.

"*Ein* millinery shop?" asked Dutch. "Frau Pardee, couldn't you give a little to our miners' relief fund?"

"You've inherited quite a sum," said Charley, pulling on his lemon yellow gloves. Charley smoothed a dog-eared corner of one of the legal documents, then, as I shuffled through the remaining envelopes, began the motions of hand washing.

"Lookin' for a love letter from your husband?" Windy asked in a mocking tone, never lifting her eyes from her catalog. "Or have you finally decided to order that Marcello Misses chapeaux?" Her fragile white-gloved fingers romped from page to page. As patrons entered and left, dropping off mail and their condolences, she waved to each, wiped an invisible tear from her eye, then moved her hand in a puppetlike gesture almost singing, "good-bye-bye." The brightness of her eyes told me that she had a hard time containing herself.

"Ya know, Pearl," she said to me between customers, "with that Marcello Misses, we don't run the risk of trimmin' you in any reds or pinks, mottlin' your complexion. The Marcello comes in strictly peacock hues—a lifesaver for a girl with your coloring."

"Not today, thank you." Smiling meekly at the proprietress, I closed my eyes, took a deep breath, and plunged my hand to the bottom of the lard pail.

There was nothing addressed to Mrs. Pearl Ryan. Biting my lip in disappointment, I placed Windy's rain-speckled laundry on the counter. "Sorry about your loss, mum," I said in the voice I'd used as a servant in the Ritters household.

Her violet eyes did not meet mine, except to cut at me side-long with (did I imagine this?) a slightly triumphant cast. She said nothing.

"It's hoped the killer will be apprehended," I continued awkwardly. How could I fail to engage the town blabbermouth (she wasn't called "Windy" for nothing) in conversation? Perhaps I should order that hat, just to free up her lips. I was so struck by her gay mood and her thinly veiled hostility toward me that she suddenly became my first choice as a suspect.

Windy paused, holding up the catalog next to her face. "Looky here," she turned to Charley with a demure expression. "It says that a clever jeweler has devised a way to attach earrings 'effortlessly and painlessly,' " she quoted, "without making a cruel hole in my ear. Ain't that modern?"

"Very becoming," said Charley, his sandy hair falling into his aging yet boyishly freckled face. He stared at her adoringly.

"No mail for me," I said sorrowfully, hoping to get Windy's attention.

The door burst open, and the liquor-bellied blacksmith entered. His flat face had been shaved clean, and he bore no evidence of ill health due to last night's cheer. "Can I do anything for ya, Windy?" he asked, stepping in front of our justice of the peace. "Sure you're up to waiting on customers today?"

"No thank you, Dovie," she answered, turning the page. "Sweet of you to ask. My philosophy is: Whatever happens, don't stall out." She made a prodding motion with her tiny, size-two hand. "Get on, get on, life's short."

"I was wondering . . ." I began.

"No laundry today," she said, waving me away. It struck me that she wouldn't be wanting her late husband's wash, and I was now out the price of it. At the same time, her callous disregard for Jake's passing almost made me feel sorry for the man.

"Windy," I said, "Shaky's funeral is day after tomorrow and I—"

"I'll have *das* silk shirt over to ya this afternoon, Frau Ryan," interrupted Dutch. "And don't fret, Jones has a line on some milled lumber for *der* coffin. We'll have it to you by dusk. Isn't that right, Vorkman Jones?"

"Yessa, Massa," said General Jones, his voice stumbling. Try as he would, Dutch had not been able to break Jones of addressing every white man as "Master."

"Windy," I said, "would you have a flower for Shaky's breast? It's too early for spring blooms, but your hats, they've so many flowers. Could you spare one?"

Everyone waited for Windy's response. The postmistress pursed her lips into a heart, refusing to look me full in the face. Why wouldn't Windy meet my gaze?

The postmistress sighed heavily, stooped, and began rummaging under the counter among parcels. "Well, I suppose, if it's for the mayor . . ." she said reluctantly.

"It would be most generous of you, mum," I said. "And tonight after chores, some ladies are coming to help dress him and line the coffin. I could use a hand, if you're up to it." I wondered if I'd stuck my foot in my mouth by talking about Shaky's preparations as no services were planned for Jake.

Windy made an angry clatter in her search for a bouquet of artificial flowers.

Carefully I said to no one in particular, "You've heard about the federal marshal coming?" I thought I'd plant the seeds of doubt and fear so they could take root in Windy as strongly they'd taken root in me. But it was Charley's attention I knew I'd captured when I saw his eyes jerk away from his papers and stare at the wall of ax handles.

Dutch began again about the strike, "If *das* owner knew ve had some funds behind us . . ." His facial features softened as he gazed wistfully at Mrs. Pardee.

Pretending to be oblivious, I rattled on. "I was preparing the mayor at the time of Jake's . . ." I cleared my throat. "Poor Shaky, the wolves, it was terrible . . . Anyway, Doc says we must have our alibis. I'm a little worried, I've only Chin and Mary to vouch for me." In Ruby, the word of an Indian and a Chinaman counted for next to nothing at best.

Suddenly Windy turned on me. "Well, Dovie, I was right here distributin' the post as everyone in town can attest," her voice turned cold as Salmon Creek. "First mail pouch to come over the mountains from Seattle this spring. Poor mail carrier was on the trail for weeks, went snow blind 'n' got lost. He's sufferin' from frostbite somethin' terrible."

I took a step back from her as if pushed, she spoke with such vehemence. Windy appeared to have more sympathy for the beleaguered postman than her own husband.

"It's no good for *ein* rich man to sveat *die* bile out of four hundred poor ones!" Dutch's grainy voice gained volume.

"Here," she said, thrusting a bouquet of artificial violets at me. "He was a good man. This is for *Shaky*." The implication, I assumed, was that they were not for me. "And," she said, "I'll tell you another thing, missy. Don't flatter yourself by thinking you meant a thing to ol' Jake. You were nothing to him. Nothing." Her eyes narrowed as she turned her back and went on with her catalog reading.

My God, did she think I fancied her husband? I felt furious and couldn't control the blood rising in my cheeks. What vile gossip was flying about town with my name attached to it?

I was grateful when Dutch brought his cannonball-sized fist down on the top of a crate of ammunition. "If ve could present *ein* united front to Herr Forrester."

Charley remained uncharacteristically silent, his eyes welded to his papers.

"Massa, ya gonna break your hand and explode us all," said Jones, rubbing his twig fingers in front of the fire. His nails were yellow and thickened.

"Don't call me 'Massa,' " Dutch's gravelly voice boomed, then vanished like a gramophone when the needle scratches across the record. He coughed violently. "Think proud, walk proud, all vorkman of the vorld should valk proud."

Dutch reminded me of Mrs. Ritters in the way that my former employer had lectured me about raising myself up. It made my heart heavy to think of how I'd broken with her. I sighed, telling myself to get a grip. Still, I often thought of writing to her.

"Vith every stride, say to yourself, Herr Jones, 'Valk proud.' Maybe ve could get Frau Pearl to learn you *die* alphabet. I vant every man to sign *der* United Vorker's Vage petition to Herr Forrester—no making of X's. If the mine owner thinks ve can read, ve have more chances of raising our vages and getting safety down in the hole." Dutch bent over in a fit of coughing. "Otherwise: Strike!" he managed in a saliva-studded whisper. This time Dutch's rock-hard fist flung into a fifty-pound flour sack with such force that the stitched end burst open and white dust enveloped the room. I ran for the door as it rained down on everyone. Jones's black hands turned white, and Dutch's ruddy face looked as if he was drenched with wig powder.

Though covered in white, both Windy and Dutch Wilhelm remained undaunted. Before the door banged shut behind me, I heard a catalog page turn as Dutch's wet voice rose up, "Ve cannot forever sow for others to reap!"

Resting outside on the front step of the trading post, the crisp air made my skin tingle as I pounded flour from my dress. Like Shaky, Jake had been an active voice against a miners' strike. I couldn't help but wonder if their antistrike position didn't have something to do with both of their murders. Then it came to me. There was another common denominator between Shaky and Jake. It was assumed by some that I was in love with Jake and known by all that Shaky was sweet on me. How much longer before I was implicated in one or both of their deaths?

Run, said a voice inside my head as loud as the blacksmith's hammer, *run before you're accused of something else you didn't do.* But another voice quickly answered, *Stay and find the murderer.*

CHAPTER SEVEN

❦

When I stepped out into the street, the sun shone. Glancing down each alley, I hoped to see Mary's and Chin's stooped figures picking up pretty bits of broken bottles.

The crowd at Jake's livery had grown larger, and khaki-clad men milled in the manner of swarming bees. I asked everyone who passed if they'd seen Doc, feeling that I would burst if I didn't recount for him the scene that had just transpired at the trading post. All the way home, I conducted a conversation with myself. Perhaps the actuality of Jake's death hadn't hit Windy yet. No, no, the will had been executed within twenty-four hours, and she was already ordering supplies for a millinery shop. For whom was she going to make hats? The squaws? She didn't allow Indians inside her trading post. And how had Charley accomplished the legalities so swiftly?

Immediately I headed for the justice of the peace's office across from the Gem. Last winter it had miraculously escaped avalanche, but it had not escaped Charley, who, though fastidious in his personal habits, was not a good housekeeper. A "Closed" sign scratched into a shingle hung from the door. Cautiously, I peered into the window. His rolltop desk was heaped with papers yellow as sulfur, they'd lain there so long. Dust-covered legal volumes lined the walls of the narrow room. Piles of "Wanted" posters and bounty hunter handbills completely covered the floor. Odd, I muttered, heading in the direction of home. It didn't look as if Charley had been to work in months.

How Mary and Chin arrived at my establishment before I did, I'll never know. Mary had built a fire outside, and Chin had filled the black witch's cauldron with water. The minute he saw my bonnet's frill come over the rise, Chin ran toward me, the slack in his black pajama trousers beating against his legs like a sail against a mast, his yellow face glowing beneath his black skull cap. With childlike glee he plunged his hand into my apron pocket, grabbed the watch, and sprang the lid. "*Piah kloshe*," he said, pointing to the blaze, then gesturing to Mary. Indeed, she had built a "good fire" in record time.

In my absence Ella had dropped off her laundry, which lay in heaps on the driftwood I used as a front porch. A visit with the bawdy house mistress was next on my list of investigations— but mercy, I needed a cup of tea before tackling her and her wash.

The three of us sat around my kitchen table warming our hands on tin cups of pine needles steeped in hot water. Though the sun shined, the air felt as if the melted snow had left its spirit behind.

"The look on Charley's face as he gazed at Windy—he's deeply smitten," I said as the three of us recounted the events at the PO while sorting Little Ella's unmentionables. "And Jake's blacksmith stared at Windy with the same adoration."

"Jake *kalakala kuitan*." Chin spoke again of the afterlife.

I agreed. "Jake has to have gone to the land of flying horses, because hell wouldn't have him."

Chin laughed, and Mary's small dark eyes fixed on the wall as most Indians' did when they were deep in thought. "Jake's *kloochman* put Bostonman up to *mamaloose* Jake?" she asked as she pulled a camas bulb from her belt. Dividing it with her small hatchet, she offered us each a chunk. Sometimes I thought I'd starve if it weren't for Mary.

"I'd have bet my bottom dollar Windy put someone up to killing her husband, but it's all too obvious. Why would she have staked a reward?" I pondered.

"*Mesachie* or *no mesachie*," guilty or not guilty, said Chin, narrowing his hooded eyes. He took a finger full of bear grease from the rawhide pouch Mary offered. I refused. The smell nauseated me. Though I had to admit that it did wonders for my chapped hands.

"Guilty or crazy," I added, feeling something small and hard in one of Ella's pockets. I could see at a glance that Ella's white blouses had what Mrs. Ritters called "a sinful amount of silk decoration." It would take me hours to press the tiny scallops with the point of my iron—the best way I knew of to burn my fingers.

I held up the pocket's contents—a cheap ring that might have been a companion to her garish necklace. Examining the crystal dewdrop attached to several beads by silver wire, it crossed my mind that Ella was testing my honesty. Didn't Mrs. Ritters test the moral fiber of her housemaids by planting a silver dollar in the pocket of an about-to-be-laundered pair of pants? Now I had the perfect excuse for paying Ella a visit.

"What we've got to do is get hold of a bullet from Charley's gun and another from the blacksmith's," I said after securing the glass ring in my apron pocket. I picked up Ella's corset, which was so heavy and in such dire need of mending that it was more of a task for a harnessmaker than a seamstress.

Both Chin's and Mary's faces went as cloudy as the rising water in Salmon Creek.

"Then I'll get Doc to bring me Jake's hat," I explained. "We'll match the bullet to the hole in his Stetson. And remember, not a word about this to anyone."

Chin tilted his amber face sideways.

"As evidence goes, it's a little flimsy, but I don't know where else to start. If one or both of the bullets don't fit, then we'll know neither of them was the killer. The hole in Jake's hat will gauge the size of the bullet, and that will lead us to the gun that fired it."

I chewed my thumbnail. "The problem is getting a slug from each weapon."

Mary hummed as she sucked bear grease from her fingers the way a baby sometimes does. "Wood and *tumwata*," she said after swallowing.

I agreed excitedly. "Good idea! When one of you goes to deliver wood or drinking water, try to get a bullet. Charley usually keeps his Colt in his desk drawer. Can't remember where I've seen the blacksmith keep his."

Mary and Chin broke into the wild vowels of her Salish tongue augmented with Chinese—discussing strategy, I presumed—until Mary took a buckskin bag out from her belt and laid it on the table. I tugged at the string and looked inside: a hundred tiny pieces of colored glass carefully cleaned of street mud. Reverently, Mary drew out one shaped like a lightning bolt. This she would use as a charm, that she would give to her sister, another she would use to decorate a buckskin dress.

I turned back to the laundry. "A hat shop," I said, shaking my head and examining a pair of Ella's black stockings. Another corset, a pair of very grubby corset strings. The garment had been tied so tightly that the knot had worn a hole in the fabric.

Union suit, union suit, several pairs of silk gloves with the tips worn transparent, three sheets, and four linen pillowcases stained with face paint.

Chin was a waterboy and did not concern himself with laundry. Instead, he took up his whittling, carving a wooden spoon and fork from stove wood. "Friends of the knife," he called my new stirring sticks.

"We've our work cut out for us," I said, hunting up my scrub brushes.

Mary stroked one of Ella's skirts, examining the garment and measuring it against her frail body. "No good. Has to come down to here," she said pointing to the floor, "cover *shush*," by which she meant shoes. "Tyee de Rouge tell me so, Jesus tell me so." Her face screwed up in an expression of disapproval at Ella's mode of dress.

Mary and Chin missed Father de Rouge, the recently deceased Jesuit who ran the reservation mission. He had held his services in Chinook and converted all he said into a kind of poetry. The primitives cottoned to the Catholic priest who never condemned Mary because of her father, a sailor who had taken liberties with several squaws and not married any of them. Father de Rouge slept alongside the Siwash, ate their food, and preached under the sky, saying prayers with the use of glass beads, which mystified Chin and Mary and all of her kin. But then Father had died, and the new Jesuit blackgown was unable to capture the hearts of the Salish. In fact, a group of bucks lead by Pokamiakin purportedly overturned his canoe with homicidal intent. To make a long story short, soon after Father de Rouge departed this life, Mary and Chin moved their teepee away from the log mission and into the ragged hills behind Ruby, which had once been Mary's mother's tribe's hunting ground. Neither had shown an interest in *Tyee wawa*, God talk, again.

"Like this," Mary said, gesturing the shape of the dress Father de Rouge favored. It had to cover a squaw from head to heel and be wide enough for her to straddle a horse without her moccasins showing.

"Perhaps Ella's girls will order hats," I said, wondering out loud. Some of the well-to-do Indians, such as Pokamiakin (who, since the departure of Father de Rouge, had taken on two additional wives), would probably like to order ready-made bonnets, but, as I said, Windy would not allow them into her mercantile. "They enter without knockin' and after they've been in, the place needs a good airin'," she complained every time I brought Mary with me to the PO. Windy had allowed squaws into her trading post when she first married Jake and opened her establishment. But after she saw that the mothers allowed their children to pass water on her floor, that had been the end of that.

"Where was your cousin Poka Mika last night?" I asked Mary. "He didn't come to town with his fellows."

"Pokamiakin had first wife roast little buck elk," she said in the most perfect English I had ever heard her speak, "*Mucka-muck*—"

"Say *eat*," I corrected.

"Eat and *tanse* and *myeena*." Dance and sing. Copper skins, they never hid their feelings. I liked that.

"Good thing Jake was murdered near Three Devils," I mused. "Everyone knows an Indian won't come close to it."

"*Mesachie miitlite,*" bad place, said Chin shaking his head. The Indians believed that wicked spirits lived in the three-peaked mountain and never trespassed.

Chin rose to go outside and test the new stirring sticks in the cauldron. I called after him, "Could you check on Shaky? Perhaps we should move him to the shady side of the piano crate."

Better get Patrick McDonald into the ground before he started to look corpsy, which always happened within three days. But how would the lads manage to dig a grave? Yesterday I'd been fearful the ground would be frozen stone hard; today my concern was that the earth would be so soupy that a hole, much less a dry one, would be impossible. I couldn't bear the thought of putting the poor man into a soggy grave. Of course, I knew how to line it with willow branches, but lining it would keep it only so dry.

Jumping up to stir the potato soup before it burned, I added the sage leaves I'd pounded to powder with a mortar and pestle Mary had swapped me for English lessons. Stirring the thick white liquid, I brought a spoonful to my nose but could not bear to taste it. So many years of eating endless bowls of potato porridge when I lived in Brooklyn brought back painful memories. I couldn't countenance the grainy feel of potato gruel on my tongue no matter how my stomach gnawed. But Doc and Dutch and my other customers loved to take a bowl, so I always kept a pot ready.

I was planning my sewing strategy regarding Ella's corset when I remembered where I'd seen the blacksmith hide his gun—in a box of wagon hubs next to the water trough. But as I rose to go tell Chin, he began bleating like a sheep.

"*Latahm, kliminawhit!*"

Lying teeth? Mary and I exchanged confused glances. "Oh, false teeth," I said. "What's wrong with Shaky's dentures?"

Chin ran into the piano crate, his arms moving like a Ferris wheel. His broad face flushed and grimacing, he pointed frantically to his own teeth with his newly carved friend-of-the-knife in one hand and toward Shaky's body with the other. "*Chako halo,*" disappeared, he said, his brow so furrowed it looked as if a cultivator had run across it.

I held my head in my hands, fearful that it would come unattached from my body. Even if they had been fashioned of gold and ivory, who would stoop so low as to steal the false teeth out of a dead man's mouth?

Any one of a number of people in Ruby Camp.

CHAPTER EIGHT

12:30 P.M.

Course it's mine. Give it here," demanded Ella when I presented the ring.

"Nightingale, where's my lunch tray?" As her husky voice called through the canvas wall, her fleshy body shuddered and her immense bosom heaved great sighs beneath the pleated bodice of her purple dress. She offered me not one word of thanks.

"Shaky's choppers?" she said turning back to me. " 'Tis the most ungodly thing I've ever heard." Ella began swaying back and forth in a rocker made especially to accommodate her girth, pausing only to take a long swig from a bottle of Doc's Chocolated Cure. "My rheumatiz is painin' me, honey, and my nerves is in tatters," she said by way of apology, jamming the ring back on her finger. "Nightingale," she called. Nightingale was not the girl's real name, you can be sure of that. "Night-in-gale! Bring me my tray this instant!"

I studied the room for clues. We sat in Ella's parlor–bed

chamber, partitioned from the rest of the "hotel" by soiled red satin sheets. Two of the walls were rough boards papered with the pages of a penny dreadful novel while the floor was covered with a threadbare Turkish carpet. A stained silk dressing gown hung from a nail. We shared the room with the largest feather bed in the county, and on the footboard near Ella's shoulder perched Lorenzo, a black-and-red rooster. Newsprint was scattered beneath him, and one of Ella's girls, a harelip, darted in to exchange the dirtied paper for fresh.

"My tray, Nightingale? Where's it at?"

The rooster let out an ear-piercing crow, then tucked his head under his wing.

"Be here in a minute," said the girl, who looked about seventeen. "We're almost through bakin' the . . . er, recipe." She moved quickly and kept her eyes to the floor. Mary Reddawn once told me that when Nightingale's mother was pregnant, she must have eaten too much rabbit, thus bringing on the girl's deformity.

"Shaky's new dentures stolen right out of his mouth," I told Ella. "Who would have done such a thing?" I lowered my voice, "If Jake were alive, I'd swear it was him. No one else would have the cheek. Authentic African hippopotamus ivory, the poor man didn't have them but a few months. He paid a fortune for those clappers." The madam shook her head as a tear formed in the corner of her good eye.

"So, you here about a job? Had enough of undertakin'?" she asked, regaining herself. An odd odor permeated the house, wafting in from the kitchen. The sweetness of cocoa butter mixed with the sharp cedar incense of tannic acid made my nose itch.

"Ah, no, thank you. Just came to return the ring," I stammered. "His poor mouth, now it looks like a rotting peach, all sunken and wrinkled. How to fill out his cheeks?"

Ella took another swig, let out a tiny belch, and shuddered. Her doughy flesh hung from her bare upper arms in turkey wattles, and her double chin fell in crepey folds. "Don't stare at me, girl," she said.

"I wasn't, sorry. An hour ago, I'd have said that Ruby lost both her best and worst citizens in less than a day, but there's still a character lower than mud out there."

"Reckon it was one of them primitives come to town last night for the festivities."

I shook my head. "An Indian would have waited until Shaky was buried, then robbed his grave. Natives are scared of Spirit People, won't be alone with a fresh corpse. The Spirit People fly off once the body's put underground. At least a no-good Indian has scruples. I couldn't say the same for some of the no-good whites in these parts."

Ella's cool expression said she disagreed with me. "Sure you don't wanna job? A girl who can read 'n' write would be a comfort to a fancy ass gent far from home."

"Have you seen Doc?" I asked, changing the subject. "I've been hunting him all morning." I wanted to ask him an important question, not just if he would get me Jake's hat. Something was eating away at me, and I had to clear the air of it.

"Whatya want him for?" she scowled. "Was supposed to be here last night, fix up one of the girls. Hear he's tendin' the mail carrier who come over the mountains yesterday.

"Nightingale?" Ella called through a rooster crow. The bird stretched his glossy neck toward heaven in such a taut arc that I thought he might hang himself in thin air.

I could guess what she meant by "fix up." In fact, I supposed that the concoction baking in the kitchen was some kind of preventative suppository that often failed. Doc wasn't fond of that kind of work, but he said it was better than the girl putting knitting needles inside her to try to break up the womb. I shuddered at how often Doc was summoned here to perform the grisly task.

The aroma wafting in from the kitchen smelled nothing like Ella's lunch, which the harelip finally brought on a tray.

Nightingale was tall and gangly with anemic skin and limp hair. She had hazel eyes and a periwinkle nose—rather sweet faced, despite her disfigurement, which Doc said could be patched by surgeons in San Francisco, though Ella certainly wasn't about to spring for the fare or the operation. Like the other girls, she was meek and didn't seem to mind bawdy house work, so she stayed on hoping to meet a miner who would take her to Frisco where she could get her face fixed.

Ella attacked her cornstarch pudding like a starved coyote. Nightingale and I looked on as she swallowed the tin can of beef tea in one long gulp. Two brown rivulets ran down either side of her receding chin. "Stop starin', the both of ya," Ella commanded. "Ain't ya ever seen someone eatin' lunch before?" Stuffing fistfuls of hard biscuit into her mouth, she sounded like a pig cracking corn.

"Ella, I need you to come over tonight and help dress His Honor. And . . . I've been wondering," I hesitated. "I know you were fond of the mayor. I'm in need of some flounces to line his coffin. I thought, if you could spare a dress . . . He'd look so nice all laid out against a deep purple background."

Ella wiped her mouth with the back of her hand, then ran her tongue around her few remaining teeth. "Nightingale," she called sharply. She handed Nightingale the lunch tray and instructed her to fetch a garment from one of the steamer trunks out in the hall.

"Tell me, Ella," I said, settling back in the crude chair made of split logs, "did you find Shaky's death as much a puzzlement as I?"

"Some Injun brought him bad water . . . or maybe it was that dang Chinaman." She took another tug on the little brown bottle.

"He sank like a stone," I said. "Didn't seem like typhoid to me. Cholera's the only ailment that can take a man like that, and it certainly wasn't cholera."

She shook her head of hennaed hair, which was pinned up

in piles of tangled sausage curls meant to cover her bald spot. "Don't talk to me 'bout cholera. Took my mam and pap on the Overland when I was just a tyke. The wagonmaster gave me away to a carnival owner. Or maybe he sold me, I always wondered." The cords in her neck stuck out like the strings on a bass fiddle, and her complexion turned a dusky red.

"Doc thinks I'm all wrong, but I still wonder if the mayor was poisoned. It's probably a ludicrous idea, but . . . Do you know anyone who might have wanted him dead?"

"Well, Jake was plenty mad at the mayor for puttin' you up to ghost writin' messages to him." Ella leaned across her rocker and brought her pulpy face near mine.

I shrank back, my gaze dropping to the floor.

"I don't just hire any girl, ya know." I could be mistaken, but there might have been a victorious look in Ella's eye.

Better to let dead dogs lie, I told myself, moving on to my next question. "It was a surprise, Jake's death, wasn't it?"

Out in the hall, Nightingale shuffled the contents of several trunks, tipping their squeaky lids up and then banging them down again. She brought in a dress. "Not that one, stupid," Ella grumbled. The girl retreated, and I heard more banging and sighing.

"Who do you think killed Jake?" I asked.

"Poka Mika," she said without hesitation.

"Yeah, that's the one," she told Nightingale. "Bring it here."

"No Indian ever goes to Three Devils," I told Ella, touching the skirt of the orchid-colored garment. "You know that." I tried to soften my retort. The velvet dress had a thick pile and would put the most exquisite finishing touch on Shaky's coffin.

"Well, if you got all the answers, sweetie, then why ask me?" Her cheeks flushed.

I said, "A federal marshal is on his way here to investigate. Doc says we must all have our alibis in order."

This gave her pause. "None of my girls done it, I knowed that much," she said. "Jake came here often. I's acquainted with him since my carnival days, back when he was barker for a wild west show and I was called Lil' Aphrodite. Farmers used to pay dearly to see me, you can be sure of that. Course I was younger then."

I didn't have to ask if Lil' Aphrodite was the carnival's fat lady.

"There was a spell a year or two back when he was almost," she fumbled, "kindhearted. Then he turned ugly again. Any one of hundreds might have killed him. If it weren't that Injin, reckon it was one of those cattlemen down in the valley."

I nodded. "You say he was happy? What about? I guess he'd just gotten married again and . . . well, what man isn't happy on his honeymoon?"

"Yeah, he'd just married Windy, and he was sending for the child. You know, Pearl, you're a regular village busybody. Don't you got work to do?"

"Child?" I asked excitedly. "He had a child?"

"How should I know?" Ella's voice filled with agitation. She sat back wearily and began rocking. "Maybe a nephew—never knew if it was boy or girl. Something happened. The child was gonna come but didn't. When I asked him about it, he near talked my ear off—the ungratefulness of younguns these days, didn't know what hard times was all about, expected to be born with silver spoons in their mouths." Ella sat up, pointing a red fingernail at me. "There wasn't nothin' that gent wouldn't do for a dollar."

I could tell that Jake had shortchanged her as often as he had me.

"Tell me somethin'," she said after a pause. "Why'd Shaky hire you to write mean things about Jake on sides of buildings?"

I faltered. "I, I . . . I don't know. I needed the money," I said finally. I couldn't think of how else to extricate myself.

She nodded, looking satisfied. For a moment I forgot about sleuthing. All I could think was, My God, it's all over town about me being the ghost writer.

"Ella," I ventured, pretending to prepare to leave, "tell me, where were you yesterday morning when Jake was killed?"

"Oh my God, so now you're the sheriff's deputy, are you? First it was Doc's assistant, now you's our sheriff's little helper . . . If it's any of your beeswax, Pearly, I drove down to Pard Cummings's ferry at Okanogan City."

She'd just told me a bald-faced lie. At that moment, however, I glanced down at the bottom of the bedsheet wall to a small pair of blue satin feet. Ella followed my gaze and began swatting the wall violently. "Get on with ya, Nightingale," she yelled as if goading a mule. Soundlessly, the two slippers disappeared into the bowels of the house.

I'd noticed when I'd sorted Ella's laundry that there hadn't been a hint of the fine brick-colored mud that her hems would have been laden with if she'd driven to the ferry down in the valley. And how had she made it there and back through yesterday's terrible storm? My blood was up, but I had to be careful.

"The weather must have slowed you considerably," I said.

"Sure damned did," she replied.

"Must have been an important trip."

"My new dove was supposed to come in on the stage. Never showed up." Ella shrugged her heavy shoulders and took another swig of Chocolated Cure.

"Only a lunatic would go out in such a gale." I shouldn't have been so frank, and I tried to regain my ground. "Well, she'll probably be on next week's overland coach."

"That's what the gent said." Ella puffed her chest out like an angry turkey. "Damned well better. I'm in need of an extra hand around here. If you see Doc, you be sure and tell him to hightail it over here tonight."

"What gent?" I asked.

"The one who come on the ferry across the river. Only passenger. Never will forget him, nicest manners. Good-lookin'. Hair as shiny as Lorenzo's tail feathers. Was hunting a girl, same as me. Told him to be sure and stop in if he ever came to Ruby."

My mouth was a question mark.

"Oh, I never will forget him. Tall fella, well dressed, had some kinda eastern accent. A little like yours," she added accusatively. "Thought he might be the mine owner's—Mr. Forrester's—secretary, so's I went up and introduced myself. But he weren't. Had a very fancy-looking gold tooth in the front of his mouth."

I could feel perspiration beading on my brow. "Who was he looking for?"

"A Miss O'Somethin'. How should I know? I've always been one to mind my own business." My pulse quickened when she added, "Oh, now I 'member, her name was Pearl, same as yours."

I felt as if someone had just thrown a pail of cold water on my head. The breath caught in my throat as the blow traveled down my spine to the soles of my feet.

"Course I told him he was wasting his time," Ella said, twirling the ring around her finger. "I know every single girl near and far, ain't no Pearl O'Somthin' in these parts."

The image of a familiar well-turned-out man with a gold-toothed smile danced in front of me. Then my heart slammed against my ribs, and my teeth began to chatter so hard I thought they'd loosen.

CHAPTER NINE

Inside my laundry hut, I sat with my head down on my kitchen table. By this time tomorrow the man at the ferry would probably have located me and had me locked up. I couldn't find Chin or Mary anywhere. Probably they'd taken their harvest of broken glass back to their teepee for safekeeping. When Doc walked in, he stared at the crying woman seated at the table as if he didn't know me. My face felt hot as a kettle and something like "Jabberwocky" came out of my mouth. I didn't know where to begin: with the man at the ferry, Windy's gay behavior, the blacksmith's and the justice of the peace's solicitousness of the new widow, Ella's alibi, or my need of Jake's hat to size the bullets. What did finding Jake's killer matter now?

For a moment Doc looked as if he'd walked into the wrong house and was about to make a hasty retreat. His large head sank into his buffalo hump as his fingers swam through his mother-of-pearl-colored hair. Then he opened his bag, drew out a green bottle of Stringfellow's Mentholated Physicking Cure, and held it to my lips.

"Pearly, what's happened, lass?" I exhibited every symptom of melancholia. "Here, drink it down. It'll help ye get hold of yeself."

I didn't want to, but it was easier to comply, so I drank the foul-tasting stuff. Then Doc held a vial of ammonia salts to my nose, which cleared my head.

"Did ye recognize the description of this mon?" Doc asked.

Nervously I toyed with a strand of hair. Red coils fell down my back like balls of unraveling yarn. "Mrs. Ritters's husband."

"In hopes of recovering the necklace or to apologize for his household's behavior?" Wasn't it just like Doc to always look for a silver lining.

"The former," I replied soberly.

Leaning back on my crate, an odd calm washed over me.

"I've been hunting you and so has Ella. On my way back from Windy's trading post, half the town asked if I'd seen you." I tried not to sound reproachful. "And, Doc, I've got to have Jake's hat from the sheriff's."

He said that it was as good as done, then sat down and helped himself to a bowl of soup. A thin scum had grown across the top of the liquid. It embarrassed me that he should have nothing to eat but cold potato water, but he didn't seem to mind.

Feeling better, I noticed that the bags under Doc's eyes had darkened and his pupils were tiny as pinpricks. He'd been working all night again. "The mail carrier," he said. "Frostbite. Had to take off a few toes. Thank Gud I had enough chloroform."

"You should have sent for me," I said, feeling guilty.

"He used language unfit for a lady, married or not. It wasn't as if it were a leg or an arm—one of the easier ones I've done, to be sure."

There was no one better or quicker at an amputation that Doc Stringfellow. He once told me that at the Battle of Missionary Ridge he'd done fifty in one afternoon without anesthetic or assistance, except for an itinerant embalmer who looked over his shoulder waiting for customers. Such frightful work, I was glad Doc hadn't called me.

"What am I going to do?" Getting up, I went to the pail and splashed cold water on my tear-stained face, but I felt strangely light-headed. "I'd clear out of town, but I've not gotten Shaky buried yet."

"Pearl O'Something doesn't necessarily mean Pearl O'Sullivan, lass."

I sucked on a strand of my hair. "Who else would it be?"

"You've a different last name now and, no offense intended, but he's unlikely to recognize your present appearance, not at first glance."

Didn't I look like a worn-out charwoman? It almost made me laugh.

"I've a suggestion," he said. "Back in sixty-two, when the Army of Northern Virginia marched on Gettysburg, the Pennsylvania Dutch lasses painted their cheeks with red dots to mimic the pox, so no Rebel would be tempted to take indecent liberties."

"Smallpox? Wouldn't that really be calling attention to myself?" I was struck with irony by the contrast between the white race and the natives. Mary Reddawn once told me that when an Indian woman wanted a husband, she painted her face with red dots and bars to attract a young buck.

"Well, ye might smear a little dirt on your face and powder your hair with ash. Puts ten years on your life."

By now the Mentholated Physicking Cure had smoothed my frayed nerves to silk, and my concerns hung out in front of me like laundry on a line. A queer sensation, but I much preferred it to feeling like I dangled over a cliff. I decided that the possibility of Mr. Ritters—if, indeed, the man at the ferry was Mr. Ritters—coming to Ruby was slim but not impossible. All the more reason why I'd better get on the trail of Jake's murderer. Should a federal marshal take me into custody for theft of the necklace, it would be in keeping with Ruby's flavor of justice to saddle me with Jake's murder as well. I sat down again, taking up the threads of Jake's case very much as I would my sewing.

"Doc, do you know anything about Jake having a child?" I asked.

"Never heard him mention a relative. But it could be why the current Mrs. Pardee was so enthusiastic about the will being executed with all possible haste."

Doc finished his soup. My light-headedness eased, my fright replaced by exhaustion. When I told him about Shaky's stolen teeth, the news caused his eyes to roll like out-of-control bowling balls and his mouth to beseech the Lord for answers.

Outside, swallows sang in the bare trees. As I chewed sunflower root, I thought I heard labored footsteps coming down the ravine. The air smelled of warm canvas, and the early-afternoon sun filled my tent with white light. I fumbled for words. Just as I was about to pose a delicate question to Doc, two familiar voices interrupted my thoughts.

It was Dutch and General George Washington Jones bearing the coffin. They were an oddly matched team: Jones, long and thin as a shadow, took great strides as he held up the broader end of the carrot-shaped box, while immense, florid-faced Dutch walked backward, dragging his bum foot, carrying the narrower.

I asked excitedly, "Wherever did you get the milled lumber?" Jones had nailed brass tacks into the lid in the shape of *P. McD.* The two men turned the coffin sideways and sidled it first this way and then that to get the box through the door. Then more machinations were necessary to set it down with one end on the flour barrel and the other on my nail-keg vanity. There was barely room to move.

"Had to take apart *ein* necessary closet," whispered Dutch.

"Whose outhouse?" I wanted to know, unable to suppress a giggle.

But both men remained mute, except for a mischievous smile that spread across Dutch's thick lips like a snake sunning itself. Despite the lack of space, each man found a place to settle in and helped himself to a bowl of soup.

I showed them the purple flounces Ella had given me. All agreed: Our mayor would look his best laid out against a background the color of a winter sunset. Dutch and Jones had seen the violets Windy contributed, but Doc hadn't, so I showed them off. Each flower's tiny yellow center looked so lifelike I could almost smell it, and the green silk leaves looked astonishingly real next to the whiteness of Shaky's bloodless hands.

Doc said, "I reckon there's a dove at Ella's who'd lend ye a drop of violet scent."

"The perfect final touch. You're a clever man, Doctor Stringfellow." Why hadn't I thought of that?

When I told Dutch and General Jones about the missing teeth, there was a round of wild cursing and head shaking. Then Dutch turned the conversation from Shaky's preparations, clean past Jake's murder, to the impending visit of Blackman Forrester, Sr., and *strike, strike, strike.*

"Vhen I first come to *Amerika* I vorked as *ein* lint head," he said. "Jones's people picked *der* cotton and I vorked in *die* mill."

General Jones's dark olalla-berry eyes darted furtively into each corner of my hut. After the two men brought Shaky inside and laid him next to the coffin to make sure of a perfect fit, I sensed Jones's discomfort at being in the same room as a corpse. The ex-slave sat in a corner, stiff and appearing eager to leave.

"Den I got Jesus," said Dutch, pacing across what floor there was free of wash and funeral preparations. His right hand jiggled the nuggets in his pants pocket. "Jesus was *ein* seer, *ja*, but his followers vere no-seers. Me, I couldn't not see *kinder* losing fingers in spinning machines; armies of unemployed in *die* streets, their breath reeking of rum. I saw var coming. *Der* bosses needed var to make even more money. It vas no better for the common man here than in Frankfurt. Except that in this country I could preach. I could get ten men together and try to make them into seers. Rise up, I tell 'em. Stick together. Twenty thousand of you to every one of them. Here there is no divine right of kings. According to *die* Constitution, *der* bosses vere born no better than you. Education is destiny. Learn yourself to read. It's vhat the bosses have that you do not."

Dutch waved his fists like the pistons of a steam engine with a loose gear, almost punching a hole through the canvas wall. Now and then he stopped to clear his afflicted throat, coating it with a swig of whiskey. Fate was in the knotted joints of his misshapen knuckles and every time he laid a hand on my shoulder, I said to myself, Yes, the meek *shall* inherit the earth. How could I have ever thought that he'd poisoned Shaky?

"When Herr Forrester arrives ve must present *ein* united front. Better vages, safety in *die* hole, schools for *die kinder*. Ve are villing to vork in the Forrester hard-rock mine to grubstake our own claims, but Herr Forrester must share with his brother. He *is* his brother's keeper. Frau Ryan," he said, turning to me. "Vhat vill you do with *der* claim Zhaky left to you?"

I shrugged. "I've barely time to work the Last Chance," I said, imagining the steep climb to Torment Creek.

"Tell you vhat," Dutch said enthusiastically, though his words came out no louder than a breeze. "You team up with Jones here, and Chin; start a company of your own. Not to sell the mine to Herr Forrester. Cooperative partnership vould give *die* mine owner something to sleep on, vouldn't it?" His eyes blazed. Again he brought the flask of whiskey to his lips, kneading his throat like a cylinder of pastry dough.

"Have ye tried talking to young Forrester Jr.?" Doc asked Dutch.

Dutch shook his head. Gravel instead of words came out of his mouth, and we had to strain our ears to understand him. "He's too much in demand at *das* faro hall. Is *die* only thing Herr Mine Foreman Bitterroot and I agree on."

"Massa," said Jones, shifting uneasily.

"Don't call me dat!" At this point Dutch remembered something. He rose, opened the coffin, and produced a white silk shirt.

"Praise be," I said, fingering the elegant garment. "Shaky'll certainly look his best day after tomorrow. Some of the ladies are coming over this evening to help dress him."

"Be sure to save a lock of hair for his dear old *mutter*," said Dutch.

Again I promised that I would.

"General," Doc asked, turning to the ex-slave, "did you hear anything at the trading post? Any news about who might have killed Jake?"

Jones didn't answer. He sat on the floor, leaning against Tillicum's saddle. Shifting his bony shoulders, he continued to stare at his feet. Jones being rude to a white man? No doubt about it, Shaky's corpse had upset him something fierce.

Doc posed his question a second time.

Jones said grudgingly, "Sheriff was up at Three Devils this mornin', measurin'."

"Measuring what?" I wanted to know.

"Heard the same at the Gem," said Doc, trying to make Jones feel at ease. "Seems Cranky Frank remembered there were lots of hoofprints near the scene. Sheriff went up to have a look, see if anything was left after the storm."

"Be very distorted if they vas," said Dutch. His voice wasn't back to normal, but we could understand him now without thinking about each word.

"Then all he's got to go on is Cranky Frank's memory?" I asked.

Doc put in, "Other than the culprit's, there'll be the tracks of Frank's team and Jake's. With all the snow and wind, should be quite a challenge."

"Was the murderer's horse shod on all four feet or just the front?" I asked Jones.

"What direction did he come in from?" Doc wanted to know.

Jones moved his head as if dodging stones. "Sheriff come to de livery 'n' pull off de shoes of Jake's team," said Jones nervously. "And the shoes of Frank's mail coach team."

"So those prints—if they're any left—can be eliminated," said Doc.

Clearly, Jones was smarter than he let on. Like Chin, he feigned a childlike personality so as not to attract attention to himself. I knew the ex-slave could add in his head. I'd seen him counting gunny bags of ore up at Dutch's claim, calculating their weight. And I also suspected he could read but wanted to keep this talent to himself.

I dreaded asking Jones where he was when Jake had been killed. Mr. Pardee had taken special glee in ridiculing his livery's jack-of-all-trades for his seeming slow-wittedness, and I wouldn't have blamed the general for shooting Jake in a fit of rage.

"Was fixin' de runnin' gear on a wagon," the African replied. He shifted his position, bending his knees and stretching out his legs, which were almost as thin as my arms. From where I sat I could see that one of his lace-up boots had worn through the bottom, the pink of his foot sole poking out like the bald stomach of a newborn mouse.

"On that dratted Schuttler two-axle?" asked Doc. He fumbled inside his jacket pocket, then put a pinch of snuff in the back of his mouth, making his cheek bulge. He offered Jones a plug, but the ex-slave refused.

"Naw, Ella done took that wagon out," he replied reluctantly. My ears perked up. "Was de Studebaker that broke."

"Best wagon made," Doc jollied. "Never had a day's concern with mine."

"Ella had de other wagon this time," Jones repeated.

So Ella *had* gone to Pard Cummings's ferry.

"Dutch, where were you when Jake met his maker?" I asked. I already knew: warming himself in front of Windy Pardee's potbellied stove.

But Dutch surprised me. "Vent up to the ice caves early in *die morgen*. If I'd known a storm vas coming, I never vould have gone. Needed something to ice *die* vhiskey. If I pack it on my throat at night, sleep comes easier."

Every winter an ice-cutting crew was dispatched to the

Okanogan River five miles away to cut great chunks of ice. These were insulated in straw and taken by wagon to the caves above camp where, with luck, they kept through summer until the autumn frosts.

"And you didn't see Jake?" Doc asked eagerly.

"Not Jake. Not Cranky Frank. Only Ella," he said.

"Ella?!" Doc and I said at the same time.

"*Ja*, passed me galloping down the grade at *ein* dangerous clip. Didn't even vave. Figured you'd be fixing her vagon soon, Vorkman Jones, *die* vay she vas abusing it."

"You saw Ella at the ice caves *yesterday* morning, the day Jake died?" I asked.

He nodded, clutching his throat.

"Are you sure?" I said, looking eagerly into Dutch's face. Ella couldn't possibly have gone to the ferry and then to the ice caves in the same day.

Dutch said, "It vas Frau Ella. Haven't I got eyes? She had *ein* fierce mountain lion expression, and her crimson hair looked like a madwoman's.

"Not to offend your lovely red tresses," he said turning to me, his fleshy lips pinned up in a smile.

I demurred. "And you never saw Jake or Cranky Frank?"

"*Nein*," he said. "But I vasn't looking at anything but *die* sky. Once I got up there, *der* weather changed, and I vas vorried about getting back to my digs."

Maybe Ella had never gone to Pard Cummings's. Maybe she knew more about me than I thought, and the story about the man at the ferry was a complete fabrication to frighten me. Suddenly my backbone felt like jelly.

"Ella gone to de ferry the day before, the mornin' Shaky died," said Jones, letting down his guard at last. "Them wheels was so covered with grit that I had to take de hubs apart. That's why de runnin' gear on de Studebaker failed."

Then one of the doves must have forgotten to bring me that day's dirty laundry—it would be easy enough to check.

"You're sure," Doc asked, "about when Ella went to the ferry?" He smoothed the fur on his eyebrows with his hand. The soup had put a little pink into his gray cheeks, and his pupils had grown from pencil points to near normal.

"Yup. I 'membered dis-tinctly. When she brung de wagon in, she and Massa Pardee got to raisin' their voices."

"What about?" I wanted to know.

"Over what?" Doc asked, running over my question.

Jones shrugged his coat-hanger shoulders and feigned a lapse in memory the way black folks are trained to do when asked about a white man's business. "I mighta heard her say she didn't owe him one more red cent. Was just before Massa—"

"Vorkman Jones, I never vant to hear you say dat vord again!" rasped Dutch.

"Just before Jake saw de ghost writin' you done painted on a wall, Miss Pearly," said Jones sheepishly.

My face turned to fire. Did everyone in town know? Did they think I'd a grudge against Jake, or did they think I was in love with him?

CHAPTER TEN

Evening the same day

Along the ridge behind town, dark tips of lodgepole pines rose like arrowheads into the snowy caps of the Cascade Range. The sky was a cold azure, except for a yellow square that came from the window cut into my piano crate. Inside, stove fire shadows lapped against the canvas sides of my tent as Ella, Mary, Carolina, and I set about the task of Shaky's final preparation. Carolina's little blind son played underfoot.

"It's for a good cause," said Ella, covering her raisin-shaped eyes with her fleshy hands. She could not bear to watch me cut into her purple dress.

I'd made a pattern of the coffin from old newspapers and matched the skirt of Ella's gown to each pattern piece. Then I cut and stitched and glued the pieces into the inside of the splintery boards of Shaky's box. Mary busied herself filling the coffin's bed with rose branches, which gave the mayor's final resting place a clean, fresh smell.

"Pearl, deary, hand me your sewin' scissors," said Ella. Carefully, she trimmed Shaky's sideburns and forelock to show off his perfect widow's peak.

"*Illahee kalakala kuitan,*" I said as I admired her handiwork. "He's gone to the land of the flying horse." Though I spoke in Mary's tongue, the Indian woman never acknowledged that she'd heard me.

"Smells like rancid bear grease in here," Ella said, holding her nose in objection to Mary's presence. Carolina, who taught many mixed-blood children, said nothing.

Mary spoke not one word. The only reason she'd entered a house with a corpse was because we were here with her. According to Mary, the deceased's spirit was eager to have company in his new home. Though I cleared my throat again and again, she never looked at me. The sharp features of her sparrow face remained intent on her work.

Carolina's son had short-cropped blond hair, pallid blue eyes (which did not appear at all sightless), and milky skin. "Feel," he said, raising his right arm into the air.

I put a scrap of velvet fabric into his hand, which was the size and shape of a huckleberry leaf. He stroked the cloth, then put it to his cheek. A frail child of seven, he could amuse himself for hours stroking things between his index finger and thumb.

"Mommy, like the fur on Mrs. Brokenhorn's neck," he said, referring to the family cow. He had a voice like a little bell, especially the way he said "Mommy."

"Yes, Bill, that's right." Carolina was the only person in Ruby who did not call the boy Blindy. "Cow. Can you spell cow?"

He could and he did. He could see well enough to make out the words on a flour sack if he held it within two inches of his face in the clear light of day. But he couldn't identify his ABC's on a chalkboard unless they were written two feet high. It was disturbing to watch his mother's tortured expression as he struggled writing his letters. According to Doc, the Bitterroots had planned to send him to San Francisco to a private school, which taught Braille. However, when Jake had had Carolina relieved of her duties as school superintendent, their plans fell through for lack of tuition. As a mere schoolteacher, Carolina was paid in potatoes and sugar instead of currency.

"Why you doing that?" Ella grumbled at Mary. "Filling Mayor McDonald's box with sticks? He weren't no heathen. He was a God-fearin' gent, one of the few in Ruby."

Mary's gaze fell to the floor, and her shoulders drooped. As she continued with her task, I willed her to look at me, but she did not.

Ella made a face. She was preparing rouge and lampblack for painting His Honor's cheeks and eyes. The mayor had gone a corpy shade of gray, and I was hoping that a little dance hall paint would put some life into him. I was bound and determined that Shaky's layout would be my best ever.

Carolina employed one of my crate chairs as an ironing board, pressing creases into Shaky's formal trousers with a hot brick. She dusted his black hat with a damp rag, then blew on it to dry the silk.

"Feel?" said Blindy. Carolina bent down, letting him stroke the "fur" on the stovepipe's crown.

"President Lincoln," he said after he'd touched the hat all over.

"Very good," his mother said. "President Lincoln wore a hat like that." Carolina looked at her son and radiated the cool white light of the moon.

"Do we have cuff links?" I asked, baste-stitching Shaky's headrest, a purple satin pillow fringed with a French ruffle taken from the hem of Ella's skirt.

"Yes," Carolina said. Her delicate fingers held up a pair of gold nuggets fashioned into a set of men's wrist furnishings. Not even the harshness of life in Ruby had tarnished Carolina's beauty. Her perfect teeth were as white as lye soap. Not a strand of gray crowned her sable head. She always appeared in public well corseted with a fashionable wasp waist that even Windy Pardee must envy. She hadn't a single smile or frown line, because, I supposed, she seldom showed any emotion whatsoever. In fact she was so aloof that the populace seldom remarked on her beauty. Her haughty attitude and acid tongue had preceded her as far as our acquaintanceship was concerned. I'd expected a dour woman with an expression like the photos of Carrie Nation I'd seen in newspapers. The first time I'd met Carolina you could have scraped my jaw from the floor with a coal shovel.

Ella finished with the straight razor. I watched as she began applying lampblack to darken his brows and hair. "Shall we paint him a little mustache?" she asked.

"Certainly not," said Carolina definitively.

Ella rocked her immense shoulders back and forth, sucking in her flabby cheeks, mocking the nurse schoolteacher.

"Certainly not," echoed Blindy from the floor. I'd given him some chunks of wood and a little willow stick to play with. The wood chunks were cows and he was the buckaroo, herding his dogies by prodding them with the willow stick whip.

Carolina looked over Ella's shoulder. "I'm afraid that won't do at all," she said.

We all stared at Shaky. The cloud-white face powder, crimson lips and cheeks, and black brows brought tears to my eyes. He looked ridiculous. I'd filled his mouth with the silver coins from one of the baking soda tins I'd buried in the garden, plumping his cheeks out nicely. It was money I'd saved for medical college, but I didn't mind as I was sure to replenish my cache washing and ironing everyone's funeral wear. Tying a handkerchief around Shaky's chin and up over the top of his head had done the trick—he'd stiffened up with his jaw closed. And those dimes Doc had put on his eyes after the wolves attacked him had kept his eyelids down. His face's shape was all I could hope for considering the circumstances. His coloring, on the other hand, looked demonic.

"It's all wrong," said Carolina as if she were studying an arithmetic sum.

"Done me best," Ella pouted. Glaring at Carolina, Ella stood back, putting her hands on her hips, which were as wide as the elk antlers Mary used for a saddle.

"Can I have a drink of water, Mrs. Ryan?" Blindy asked.

I filled the water dipper and handed it to him, but not before Carolina inquired whether it had been boiled.

"We've already had one death this week from typhoid," she said pointedly.

I bit my tongue.

Mary held up a small buckskin bag. Motioning for me to look inside, she hung her head and would not meet my eye.

Ella walked over to the newly lined coffin. "It's all lumpy due to them sticks," she complained.

I turned to Carolina, "See, Mary's dyes. The ones she uses to color beads and porcupine quills for decorating gauntlets. Maybe they'd tone down Shaky's complexion."

Carolina studied the contents of the buckskin totes, nodding. Mary set about mixing the dust of a rotten birch stump with water, the pigment of which would make our mayor's skin color more lifelike. Putting a dab of powdered serviceberry on my palm, I thought it the exact color of natural lips. We set about mixing little pools of dye and painting them on Shaky's face.

Ella stood back and scowled, then with the greatness of her girth, pushed all three of us out of the way. "Le'me do this. I used to give china-paintin' lessons." Soon Shaky started to look as if he were having his portrait painted right over his own sweet face.

"I hope the man with the photographic equipment arrives on tomorrow's stage," I said. Tintypes of the dead laid out in all their finery were the rage. Unfortunately, it would be my only likeness of Shaky.

As Pat McDonald's body took on a more lifelike appearance, our conversation grew animated. Blindy, tired of driving his toy cattle, had fallen asleep on the floor.

"When's Jake's funeral?" Ella asked. "Not that I care. Don't bother asking me to come help lay *him* out."

"There's none planned," I answered. "His body has to be kept as evidence. Until the marshal comes, at least," I added, watching each of the ladies' reactions, but I saw none.

Doc had brought over Jake's hat for my inspection. Now it awaited the bullets Mary and Chin had promised to pilfer from the blacksmith and the justice of the peace.

I pinched Mary's arm, but she still wouldn't look me in the eye. Desperate, I said, "Mary, come outside with me for a moment. I want to have a word with you about these rose brambles." A satisfied expression passed over Ella's face. Meekly, Mary followed me out the doorway into the chill. Below us, the rising waters of Salmon Creek rushed down mountain. I cupped my hand to her ear so she could hear me above the grinding of boulders. "Get a bullet from Ella's gun. She keeps it in the deep pocket of her cape. Her cape's under Carolina's wrap, lying on my bed."

Mary nodded. Her expression never changed. Mary was a stealthy hunter, able to sneak up on a deer undetected, and her talents were invaluable to my sleuthing.

Back inside, there was only silence broken by stove-fire crackle and the *tisk-tisk* of Ella's critical tongue as Carolina sponged rouge from Shaky's lips in order to reapply a more realistic shade made from Mary's dye.

"I was afraid Windy might wanna have a double funeral, her husband and the mayor," said Ella. "And if'n that was the case, I was gonna go to her and say, 'Ain't no way Jake Pardee's goin' to crash the good mayor's send-off.' Besides, no one other than herself and that Yankee greenhorn would come to Jake's burial." She paused. "Except maybe for the ghost writer," she mused, smiling wryly.

I felt as if I'd just put my foot into a creek of mountain

water. "Greenhorn? You mean Forr?" I asked, ignoring her insinuation.

Carolina said nothing. Her expression remained as blank as slate.

"Yeah. If'n he could put down his cards long enough. Never saw no one stricken so fast 'n' hard with gamblin' fever as that boy."

I recalled Mrs. Ritters's distress when Forr had been sent down from school for wagering. If her son had lived, she said, the expulsion would never have occurred. Which I had doubted. Forr was easily led. Mrs. Ritters's son had drowned in the Long Island Sound after he'd bet Forr a hundred dollars that he could swim out to the rocks in front of the Ritterses' summer house during a storm—or so the servants told me—and had been the one who'd whetted Forr's appetite for gambling in the first place.

"When I called on Windy this morning, she already had a line of admirers," I said. "Arizona Charley and Hames the blacksmith." If Hames had a Christian name, no one in town seemed to know what it was.

Carolina remained silent. Not one word of gossip passed her lips.

"Who do you think killed Jake?" I asked. I wasn't sure Ella or the nurse-schoolteacher had heard me.

Mary began sweeping the coffin lid with rose switches.

Ella demanded of me, "Make her stop that." Then she said, "Don't know who did it and don't care." After a moment, she added, "Though I'm sure it was his wife, of course."

Relieved that Ella had decided against Pokamiakin, I wondered if she knew that this evening's odds at the faro hall favored her over Windy as Jake's murderer.

"Ella," I ventured, "when Dutch brought the coffin over this afternoon, he said he saw you up at the ice caves near Three Devils yesterday morning."

"Ah, what of it?" she snapped. "Did you ever find Doc?"

Ella reminded me of a recalcitrant horse, shying at nothing

in order to evade the commands of my spur and whip. "Yes, I found Doc. You told me you went to the ferry."

"So what? I did as I said I did."

"Can you prove it?" I said.

"Can you prove I didn't? Anyway, who says I gotta answer to you, missy?"

Mary waved a rose branch across the mayor's torso, singing in her Salish tongue.

"Quit," said Ella, pushing Mary aside with a swat of her arm. Mary fell back onto the coats folded on my flour sack bed. I gave my assistant an approving half smile. By tomorrow I'd have the bullets to three different guns to size in the dead man's hat. It occurred to me that I should get a bullet from Dutch's gun, so that I could eliminate him. After all, he'd been near the scene at the time and had a bone to pick with Jake: Jake was very disapproving of the idea of a miners' strike.

"His brow should be arched like this," said Carolina erasing Ella's makeup effort.

"I suppose a lady like you took sketchin' lessons," said Ella.

"I studied watercolor at seminary school," Carolina said.

"Seminary school, is it?" Ella's voice was contemptuous. "And I thought our ex-superintendent of schools had a hand-written certificate from the State Normal signed by the governor." Ella looked satisfied, having caught Carolina in a lie.

"Not exactly," said Carolina. She highlighted Shaky's cheek, making it look more three-dimensional. All the wear and tear on the corpse had flattened his features.

I thought she'd done a superb job. "Where'd you get your certificate?" I was becoming more and more curious about Carolina.

"At least you can eat off a china plate," said Ella. "China paintin's a useful art."

Mary was fitting a pair of newly polished boots on Shaky's feet.

"I took the normal course at Seattle Territorial University," she said. "Summers, I studied nursing at the military hospital attached to the fort where I grew up—Mother's idea. She always told me, 'Order is the first law of heaven; preparedness the second.' "

Why, I wondered, had a woman of her stature come to Ruby City? Local gossip had it that Carolina and her husband, Brownie, migrated here from an island in Puget Sound. "Where was your mother from?" I asked.

"The Carolinas," she said with a slight toss of her head. She was working on Shaky's upper lids. Mary pulled the mayor's cuff links through the holes in the wristbands of the white silk shirt donated by Dutch.

"That's where you got your name, then?"

For the first time that evening, Carolina smiled, " 'Namesake, keepsake,' Mother always said."

"How'd your parents get so far from home?" I ventured.

Ella stood by, arms folded across her watermelon-sized bosom. "His lips is gonna fall open. Gotta stitch em shut or put something inside em that looks like teeth."

I agreed but couldn't think of what.

Carolina paused to check on her sleeping child. "Came here on their honeymoon, to visit an uncle stationed at Port Townsend. When the rebellion between the states broke out, they got stranded." She put her hand thoughtfully to the corner of her mouth.

"Ever see the plantations where your parents grew up?" I asked.

"Oh no, the Yankees burned Palmetto and Old Holly Hill to the ground."

It didn't surprise me that Carolina had aristocratic roots.

"Mother'd finished at Virginia Seminary, so she was fully prepared to teach while father headed for the Caribou gold fields. I practically grew up in a schoolroom. Father died in a mine accident. I still remember throwing dirt over his box."

"They didn't put any straw on the lid to muffle the noise?" I asked.

"Nothing," she said. "I'll never forget the hollow sound of dirt striking a coffin. Cried myself to sleep every night for weeks, thinking I might have buried him alive." She shivered. "I've had a touch of claustrophobia ever since."

"You got straw for Shaky's lid?" asked Ella, glaring at me.

"You can have some of Mrs. Brokenhorn's," Carolina offered. "Anyway," she continued, "my stepfather sent me to boarding school—so he could have mother to himself." She averted her eyes as if regretting this statement. "When I finished at the university, mother got me a nursing job at the fort. . . ." She paused a moment. "Then I married Brownie. His family grew hops near Tacoma. When those vines came into flower, I thought I'd died and sailed to Corinth." She wiped her hands on a handkerchief, twisted it, and looked at the floor. "Blight struck, ruining the crop two years in a row. When the doctor told us that little Bill had consumption, we decided to come here for the dry climate. Then he took brain fever— that's what ruined his sight. We packed all our belongings and herded fifty cows over the pass, homesteading on the river north of Pard Cummings's. The next year the cattle-killing winter hit. . . ."

I sighed. Some years ago the snow and temperatures reached Arctic proportions. The entire town of Ruby was taken by avalanche. The only cattle that didn't perish were those settlers brought into their dugouts. Locals called the storm the Great Equalizer, because wealthy and small farmers were ruined alike, most near starving and heavily in debt. A few stayed on. Only a handful—like Carolina and Brownie Bitterroot— were lucky enough to find work to pay off their debts.

"Pig's teeth," said Carolina suddenly.

The other three of us looked puzzled.

Carolina explained. "The pig they butchered and roasted the night Jake died. We can use those teeth set in candle wax for Shaky."

"Don't talk to me about that pig," said Ella. "If that pig belonged to anyone, it was to one of my girls and should have gone to Shaky's wake."

"Do you know what happened to the sow's skull?" Carolina asked.

"Rotting in the alley beside the faro hall," I said.

"Don't look at me. I ain't pullin' out its teeth," retorted Ella.

"Yes," I said excitedly. "We can give the sow's teeth to Shaky!" All I needed was the front teeth, which looked so much like a human's that it was nearly impossible to tell the difference, so much so that traveling dentists used pig teeth when making dentures.

"I'll get them for you tomorrow," said Carolina agreeably,

At last, I thought, she's warming up to me. Maybe I can make a friend of her yet. Other than Mary, I had not one lady friend in Ruby. "I'll help," I said eagerly. "In the morning, I could come up and—"

"No thank you," she said, her face closing in on itself.

My heart sank a notch.

"I'll take care of it," she continued. "I've a lot to do tomorrow. Someone carted our necessary house away during the hoopla last night. A joke, I presume." For a moment her expression betrayed her vexation and annoyance, then her lips froze into a fixed half smile. The Bitterroots had the most civilized outhouse I'd seen in the West. Constructed of milled lumber and whitewashed with lime, it was topped by a cupola.

Carolina drew her upper lip tightly over her teeth, enumerating her tasks, "I'll have to put something primitive together for the time being, then help get the account books in order for the mine owner's visit, and there's new trousers to sew for Bill's trip."

"Where's the boy going?" both Ella and I asked together.

"To the California School for the Blind," she said flatly. I had never known the word "blind" to have passed Carolina's lips, not with regard to her son.

I wondered at the Bitterroots' sudden change in fortunes.

For the first time that evening, Mary met my eye. Now we knew where the wood for Shaky's coffin had come from and traded smiles.

"Carolina?" I asked. I'd finally got my nerve up. "Where were you at the time of Jake's death?"

"Yeah?" said Ella. "Why's the finger always pointin' at me? And Injin Mary," she said, turning to my assistant, "where was you, half-breed, when Jake got himself shot? It was your cousin who wanted him dead more'n anyone."

Mary made the motions of chopping wood with an ax.

"I can vouch for her," I said, perhaps too quickly.

"She vouches for you, you vouch for her. Ain't that just cozy." Ella was making a mold for Shaky's new candle-wax gums into which I'd fit the pig teeth. She'd had to remove the little eel skin sacks of money that filled out His Honor's mouth. "What are these things?" she said eyeing me inquisitively, "French safes?"

I gave Ella a sharp look. Elastic and waterproof, eels had a thousand practical uses, not the least of which was to protect my fingers from the tortures of lye soap.

"Where was you, Mrs. Bitterroot?" Ella flashed her nicotine-stained teeth.

"Delivering a baby," she said flatly, offering no added information.

All I could think was, Good thing she's well skilled in midwifery, because it was impossible for Doc to be in more than one place when two new mothers got themselves into a fix at the same time.

I pulled the last thread through the dusky purple fabric that lined Shaky's elegant-looking coffin. "Finished," I said.

Immediately Mary took up a rose switch and began sweeping it over the casket.

"Quit," yelled Ella. "Make her stop that fool Injin medicine," she demanded of me.

But I did not. Mary worried that Shaky's spirit still flew

around the room and continued to sweep the coffin. The thorns of the rose would keep Shaky in his world and the living in ours. She brushed my chest and shoulders. According to Mary Reddawn, the companion Shaky was most likely to take away with him to the next world was me. Usually I didn't give a fig about Indian superstitions, but as the rose bramble swept my hand I was suddenly seized by the idea that maybe she knew something I didn't.

That night after the ladies had gone, I sank into bed, exhausted but with a satisfied heart. The mayor was laid out in all possible splendor. As he slept with his hands crossed over his chest, crowned with silk violets, I almost wept at the sight of his complete peace. "Shaky Pat McDonald," I said, "you are my most perfect opus."

Plumping the cattail fluff in my pillow, I began a review of the day, starting with my visit to Windy's trading post. This was followed by a list of tomorrow's tasks, not to mention a worry over the mysterious man at the ferry, and making a mental list of all suspects, motives, alibis, and clues concerning Jake's murderer—the weight of which pushed me down into the waters of unconsciousness.

Illahee, land of, *kalakala kuitan*, flying horses. *Illahee*, land of, *moosumk nanaitch kuitan*, dream horses. Had Jake and Shaky both gone to primitives' land of the flying horse? Unlike whites, Siwash did not divide their afterlife into heaven and hell.

I don't know how long I'd slept, but it was deepest night when I sat bolt upright. Everything around me blackened. The fire in my cookstove had dwindled to embers, and the air felt heavy with frost. Outside, the forest and town were eerily quiet, not even a coyote howled, nor was any gun fired. No worldly noise had awakened me. Silence gripped my shoulders as my brow beaded with icy sweat. The muscles along the ridges of my spine pulled each vertebra tight as a bowstring.

I recalled what was now the previous day: Chin, Mary, and I standing outside the trading post, watching the men milling in front of Jake's livery. Neither Chin Lu nor Mary Reddawn had used the word *illahee*, which was Chinook for "land." What they had said was merely, "flying horse" and "dream horse," respectively. They hadn't been talking about Jake dying and going to another world. "Flying horse" and "dream horse" were the words used to describe the shape and outcome of something else entirely:

An opium pipe.

Why hadn't I seen the truth sooner? Not only was Jake the most infamous horse dealer in the county, he was also the local opium trader. Who would move in to take his place? Perhaps that someone had been Jake's murderer. Every muscle tightened. I felt as if I was walking over the frozen Okanogan River, wondering if my next step would make a jagged crack in the ice and cause me to plummet into the paralyzing water below.

CHAPTER ELEVEN

April 19

I rose at first light, rekindled the fire, set the pot to boil, and filled a poke with oats for Tillicum. Stepping outside, clouds the shape of stagecoaches trailed across the sky. Then the noise of the raging creek startled me. It had risen a yard, and the water had turned from milky white to muddy brown. No telling if it would reach into the graveyard before cresting.

Tillicum grazed on the very spot where the lads would soon be digging the mayor's grave. When he heard my boots scrape over a burial mound, my roan cayuse raised his velvety nose and whinnied. Though I had no near neighbors, I never felt lonely as long as I had the companionship of my little horse.

Giving him a good-bye pat on his red rump, I turned toward my tent, casting a sideways glance at the rising creek. The flood carried the bloated body of a prospector's mule and a tree trunk the size of a house—typhoid water if ever I'd seen any. Soon Shaky's death would be attributed as the first in the epidemic of '93, leaving me no hope of ever discovering if there'd been foul play.

Crossing the ravine, I saw Doc waiting for me at my door. As I called out, I noticed that he was dressed for a long ride, wearing high-heeled boots, the heels an extra measure of insurance that his feet wouldn't fall through the stirrups should he fall asleep in the saddle. Doc held his instrument bag in one hand and clutched several bottles to his chest, cradling them in the folds of his green Shetland sweater.

"Spirits of camphor, oh thanks so much. I'd completely forgotten!" I held the blanket doorway aside for him. "And wait'll you see His Honor," I said pridefully.

Impressed, Doc's head rolled to the side of his hump as he stared into the box.

By now the kettle was boiling, so I brewed us each a cup of coffee made from real beans, which I'd received in payment for sewing. I wasn't going to be able to put anything aside for medical college taking barter in payment instead of currency, but green coffee browned in a frypan with a hint of ham fat was more valuable than money.

"Camphor's a must with these warming temperatures, lass." Gratefully, Doc took the bowl of coffee, sat down at my table, and held it to his lips. "You douse his clothes with this and it'll keep him from wolves for six months."

"They'll dig the grave good 'n' deep, won't they?" I asked, as I studied Doc's sweater, looking for wear. It would be a good idea to darn the elbows before they broke through.

Doc's brow furrowed into a trail of wagon ruts. "Creeks are rising, lass. The lads won't be able to dig doon very far before they hit the water table." His eyes skidded away from mine. "Which is another thing I've come about. Mr. Lincoln's hoof got torn up pretty bad when he threw a shoe. Could I borrow ye horse? I want to get down to Pard Cummings's ferry for surgical supplies before high water prevents me."

"Surely," I replied, taking the last sip of delicious darkness. I lowered my voice, "Will you keep your ear to the ground about a man looking for a Pearl O'Sullivan?"

He nodded. "Did ye learn anything about Jake's murder from the ladies?"

I told him that Ella continued to insist she'd gone to the ferry on the morning of Jake's death. Mary'd gotten a bullet from Ella's gun, and just as soon as she got here with the other lead balls, I'd be able to size them. "It's a curious thing," I added. "Mr. and Mrs. Bitterroot are sending their son to a school for the blind. With all their debts, where do you think they got the funds? By the way," I cupped my hand around my mouth in the manner of a schoolgirl whispering a secret, "it was their out-house His Honor's coffin was made from. Carolina couldn't be more vexed. My theory is: Dutch didn't want Forrester Sr. to have any of the civilized advantages that the lads don't enjoy."

A smile spread across Doc's lips, exposing his yellow en-jammed teeth. Then his face again took on a sober expression. "The Bitterroots are no longer in hock to Jake, who obviously exacted a contribution from them every month. That's where they got the silver to send the bairn away to school."

"But what could Mr. and Mrs. Goody Two-shoes possibly have to hide?" Doc never minded my irreverence; in fact, I think he enjoyed it.

He shook his head slowly. "As I've said before, I canna say."

"Would it be reasonable to assume that, if Windy didn't have her husband killed, the murderer was someone Jake had by the purse strings?"

"Aye, lass." Doc took a long slurp of coffee. "And the next logical question is: What valuable information could Jake have had on Ella?"

Another question rested on the edge of my tongue, but I couldn't quite get it out. Instead I asked, "Can't Hames nail President Lincoln's shoe back on?"

"His mind's not on his labor. Since his employer's demise,

the mon's stuck two horses in the quick, lamed 'em good. With President Lincoln's hoof so ragged, I thought it best to let him grow a little horn before I took him in for repairs. In the meantime, maybe the mud will settle and the lost shoe will turn up."

Since I'd awakened last night in an icy sweat, I now had two pressing questions I needed to ask Doc. I swallowed. "Is it because Hames has a guilty conscience or . . . is Hames in need of a little 'flying horse'?"

Doc said nothing. I never knew when he was going to be overcome with a fit of silence. Finally he spoke, "And what would the likes of you be knowing about that?"

Unable to judge his humor, I forged ahead. "As you've often said, Doctor Angus Stringfellow, I'm a clever lass." The coffee not only lifted my spirits, it gave me courage.

A faint smile returned to his lips. " 'Tis true. There was nothing that freebooter Jake wouldn't sell. But these are matters too indelicate for feminine pursuit."

My blood boiled. "Doc, if I'm going to get to the bottom of the case, all the known cards have to be on the table. There's enough queer aces up God knows whose sleeve without the trump card being hidden from me. I may be of the female gender, but since I've come to Ruby, there's not much man's or beast's work I haven't done."

He nodded slowly as if handling a temperamental mare. " 'Tis a dirty business, filled with scoundrels. I wouldn't want to speak of you and them in the same breath, lass. Even if ye be a laundress, you're every inch a lady as much as Mrs. Bitterroot— sometimes I wonder if ye know it."

So, my night thoughts were right about Jake. I wondered what else Mary and Chin knew and weren't telling me.

"Well, thank you," I said, feeling my feathers puff out with pride. "And," I hesitated, "there's something else you've got to level with me about—"

Doc cut me off. "Before I forget, the sheriff did find tracks of a third party near the murder scene. According to him, the culprit's horse was unshod on all fours. Came up from the east and stopped twenty feet from the wagon road, then reared and leaped sideways downhill. After that the tracks disappeared up the sandy slope."

I was incredulous. "Didn't the gale and melting snow obliterate everything?"

Doc's head swiveled. "The mountain's volcanic ash worked like a plaster mold in this case. If it had been muddy grazing land it would have been a different story."

Putting his empty coffee bowl on the table, Doc got up to leave.

I blurted it out, "Doc, I've got to know. Was Jake taking payments from you?"

Doc gaped at the ground. He pulled on his buckskin gloves with the embroidered gauntlets, shifting his weight from one boot to another. "Yes, lass, he was." He put on his jacket and picked up his white plug hat, turning toward the door.

"Why?" I whispered.

He shook his head, and his manner turned cold. " 'Tis a painful subject and I've a long ride in front of me. I'll stop in this evening and lay it all out in front of ye." He did not look at me as he spoke; rather he addressed the blanketed door and was gone.

Or so I thought. He turned back. "Don't ye see?" he demanded harshly.

"See what?" I asked, feeling sorry I'd brought it up. The tension between us made me flash back to the day my intended, Davy, sided against me along with the rest of the Ritters household concerning the theft of Madam's necklace. Davy'd been my confidant, my confessor, and the light of my life one minute and then . . . Now the same impenetrable stone wall had suddenly gone up between Doc and me, and I wasn't sure why.

"Don't play stupid with me, lass. Surely you knew you were one of the few in town from whom Jake wasn't extorting money or treating to a tug on the opium pipe." His face turned to granite.

I felt as if I'd just been kicked by a horse. "No, I didn't know." After a moment, I said, "It was only a matter of time before Jake found me out as well, discovering my real name and that I was wanted for jewel theft." I mustered a smile as I handed Doc Tillicum's bridle, hoping his cheery air would return.

As he tipped his hat in a cool gesture of good-bye, his eyes fixed on me like the muzzles of two revolvers aimed at a traitor.

CHAPTER TWELVE

Whenever I felt low, I sank my hands into a tub of laundry. There's something about scrubbing out stain and returning a muddy work shirt to its original plaid that puts me right. Or I'd take a walk up to the Last Chance and pick ore. No time for either today. I poured myself another bowl of coffee and tried not to think about Doc's sudden chilly demeanor, though a thousand possible indiscretions ran through my head.

Waiting for Mary to arrive with the bullets, I made lists of things needing to be done for the funeral. Number one was chairs—it was a bring-your-own-to-the-gravesite situation. I pulled out Shaky's watch to judge the time spent on each task and took solace in the fact that though Shaky's heart had stopped, his watch ticked on. Never, never would I let it run down.

What had become of Mary? I hadn't much wood and needed her help today more than ever. Which wasn't the only reason I wanted her here now. I'd begun to worry. Doc said that, according to the sheriff's estimation, the murderer had ridden an unshod horse. Not a lot of people kept their horses barefoot, but of those who did, this group included all Siwash. Now it was certain that a finger would be pointed at her cousin, Pokamiakin.

Footsteps. I thought, Oh, she's finally here, then realized

that no Indian ever tread so heavily. In fact, like the creatures of the forest, one never heard their footfalls at all.

"Frau Ryan."

"Dutch," I called, "come in." I should have known it was he by the *thud-thunk* of his limp.

"*Sehr gut*," he said after ducking in and removing his Union cap. His voice sounded worse than gravel grinding along a miner's flume. "*Jawohl, sehr gut*," he said studying Shaky. Was I mistaken? As he mumbled, "*Ein bruder* to me," didn't he move his hand to his cheek, quickly wiping away a tear?

"Glad you stopped in." I bade him sit down and offered him a bowl of the precious coffee. "I wonder," I said, "could I borrow Shaky's pearl-handled six-shooter for the funeral procession? I want to display them on top of his coffin with their shafts crossed. It'll be the perfect touch."

Dutch's fleshy lips spread wide in indulgence, then turned down. "*Danke*," he clasped his hands around his neck, "but *kaffee* is like swallowing knives. Though I would take a cup of your potato soup."

"Oh, Dutch, I've not had time to peel or dice." Or even to set out laundry starch, which was what I'd served him. "Stop in later, I'm sure to have a pot."

He shook his head. "The gun, I'm sorry to say, I lost when I packed a load of ore down to *der* riverboat." His words rose into a frog-croak. Disappointed about the pistol, I considered how I was going to get a bullet from whatever firearm Dutch now used.

A moment later he regained himself. "I know a little secret," he said, sitting down on my crate chair. Taking a tin cup of mistletoe tea, which I'd given him as a painkiller, he drew it slowly into his mouth.

"What? By the way, have you seen Mary Reddawn or Chin?" I wanted to get busy picking willow to line the grave as well as making wreaths, not to mention searching for a nice piece of oak for a grave marker.

"You have a namesake," he said.

I shrugged. What was he talking about?

"At the Gem last night, one of *der* boys said that there is an-other Pearl up north in Nighthawk. And do you know what I said?"

"No." I felt as if the waters of Salmon Creek were inching around my ankles, chilling my entire body.

"I said, 'But Frau Ryan is *die* Pearl of Ruby City.' "

"Another Pearl, are you sure?"

"*Ja.* One of *der* boys said he won a hundred dollars in a card came with a man who was on his way to Nighthawk to see a Missy Pearl. So there is another bone of contention between Ruby City and our rival for county seat. Our Pearl versus their Pearl."

The blood ran to my feet. I wanted to ask more but didn't dare. "Thank you," I said, sitting down before my knees caved in. I suspected there was only one Pearl.

My mind turned to wool fuzz, and my nerves jangled. Out-side, the noise of the rising creek grew louder, and on top of everything else I began to worry that Shaky's funeral would be flooded out.

Dutch took a few sips of tea, which obviously revived his throat. He began on a long tirade about the criminal acts of mine owners and the impending visit of Mr. Blackman Forrester, Sr., every sentence punctuated by "taking industrial action" and "withdrawing our labors," ending with a fist-pounding, "Strike, strike, strike." He beat my table with his gavel of a fist so many times that I thought it would split apart like kindling. The raw meat of his lips turned purple. As I watched him mouth the words, all I could think of was flight. A voice said, *Go now, run, to Spokane Falls, Seattle, Portland. Go, before Mr. Ritters finds you, before Mr. Forrester arrives and recognizes you.* The voice flogged me like one flogs a balking horse. But how could I flee? Doc had my little cayuse, and Shaky wasn't safely in his grave.

"Dutch," I said, rising quickly and straightening my apron. "Stay and take another cup, if you like. But I've got to find Mary Reddawn." Dutch could not bear to be without an audience, so he departed, walking uphill to his digs in the minefields while I headed in the opposite direction, toward upper Main.

The warm desert air dried the nervous sweat that stippled my face. Every footstep screamed at me: *flee, flee*. But by the time I'd scrambled up the ravine to where the shops and saloons began to appear, the voice had been beaten down by my exhaustion and was less insistent. I glanced into the alley next to the faro hall to see if Mary was picking up pretty pieces of broken glass. From inside the gambling tent came the noise of wagers being taken, even at this early hour. Passing the canvas door, I pulled my shawl up over my head and kept my eyes down, fixed on the plank sidewalk.

Beyond the faro hall, Bald Barton, the new sheriff, who was also the town cobbler, stood holding an armload of gunny bags that he handed out, though not to everyone. As Nightingale passed, he held his ragged-edged sacks tightly to his chest. Ditto when Pokamiakin sauntered by like a hulking bear in moccasins, buckskin trousers, and without a shirt. Barton handed a sack to General George Washington Jones, mumbling inaudibly, then handed one to the assayer, the most skeletal man I'd ever seen. Sheriff Barton, a self-righteous individual who was always quoting the Bible, often bragged that he could repair your shoe sole and your immortal soul all in one fell swoop.

I watched as the two men flung their sacks over their shoulders and immediately headed to a rock pile down the alley behind the assayer's tin-roofed shop. "What's going on, Sheriff?" I asked hurriedly. I wanted to catch up with either Nightingale or Poka Mika, who might have seen Mary.

Bald Barton held tightly to his oakum-smelling sacks. "You'd be no help," he said as if I'd asked for one. He did his own laundry and had never offered me a message from our

Heavenly Father, so I'd not had much contact with him—which, considering my present situation, was a blessing.

"But what's going on?" I repeated.

"Flooding," the sheriff replied grudgingly. He had a sharp, angular face.

Men hurriedly filled the sacks with sand and gravel, passing the bags along a human chain to the riverbank where a miner, standing in muck that came over the tops of his gummed boots, stacked the sacks into a dike.

"No, it's not, I won't let it, not until after tomorrow. God would not be so cruel as to flood out Patrick McDonald's funeral."

Sheriff Bald Barton cocked his head, eyeing me suspiciously. Word had it that when the ghost writing first appeared, Jake thought the sheriff had defaced his building with messages from Jesus and roughed him up to the tune of two shiners and a sausage lip.

I thanked him for donating his horse and harness for the funeral hearse and hurried on, though the image of him pursing his lips stayed with me. My stepmother used to fix her mouth like that during a fit of pique—usually when the doctor (with his bloody high fees) had to be called to tend the sick twins. Though she was ten years dead, her voice still rang in my ears: "All they do, them physicians, is steal your money. We can't even buy shoes for all these kids." Well, I would not be a doctor like that.

Flee, the voice said, *or you'll rot in some jail and never amount to anything.*

I hurried on, hoping to overtake Nightingale, then at the justice of peace's office, I stopped short and ducked into the low-ceilinged room the size and shape of a railroad car. Arizona Charley sat at his rolltop desk, which was still heaped with legal papers, "Reward Offered" handbills, and unopened mail. How on earth had he gotten Jake's will executed on such short notice? His lined though boyishly freckled face looked up at me in astonished confusion as if I'd just awakened him from a dream.

"Yes? Do you have an appointment?"

"No. I just . . ."

Gathering himself up, he began wringing his hands as if he were washing them, then pulled on a pair of lemon-yellow gloves. "I was on my way out," he said.

I could guess where. "I wondered, have you seen Mary Reddawn or Chin?"

Before he could answer, a loud war whoop exploded from the direction of the livery, followed by the noise of a tin pail crashing against a wall. Hames, the blacksmith, had a short fuse, and when he came to the end of it, he often let fly at some poor nervous beast who wouldn't stand still for a "manicure."

Charley pointed a gloved finger to the wood stacked by his door. "She was here when I opened up," he said. I stared at the drawer where I knew his gun was kept and wondered if Mary'd managed to get a bullet.

"Funeral's tomorrow at two," I said. A look of relief came over his face as I bid him a prompt good-bye.

I caught up with Nightingale. When I touched her thin arm from the back, she froze, then whirled around at me with a fierce expression on her little rodent face, her harelip squinching up into her nose.

"Sorry," I said. I supposed she thought I was one of the lads hoping for a free sampling of her favors.

"Oh, it's you," she replied, relieved though not exactly friendly. She was hard to read. Nightingale had a good heart, but not only had she inherited a hare-shaped mouth but, I feared, a hare's brain as well. On several occasions I had tried to draw her out, but to no avail. The minute I became at all familiar, her eyes glazed over and her wits fled like a prairie hen running through the buck brush. The thing that made me doubt her stupidity was that she was an absolute genius at likenesses. Once in payment for her laundry, she'd given me a sketch of Tillicum, which I kept in my trunk, vowing to get it framed at the first opportunity.

"Have you seen Mary this morning? Did she bring you wood? Or Chin? I need water something terrible."

"No," Nightingale said flatly. "And Ella's cursing a hurricane. She's likely to brain Mary with a stick of her own kindling when she does show up."

"Thanks," I said, running up the walk. I wanted to catch Pokamiakin before he ducked into Windy's mercantile. Today I could not abide being told how a mail order hat would transform my red hair and other shortcomings into assets.

"Pearl, have you seen Doc?" Nightingale called after me. "Ella sent me out to hunt him up."

"Rode to Okanogan City for surgical supplies in case it floods," I called over my shoulder. Just then I caught my toe on an uneven plank, and the sidewalk rushed forward to meet my face. I heard the noise of hands slapping against wood as I reached out to brace myself. My flesh stung. Luckily nothing was torn or broken, but Jesus, Mary, and Joseph, hadn't I skinned my already chapped hands something fierce. And my poor elbow. I must look as if I'd been in a carriage wreck.

Men ran past me, down the alleys to dike the creek before it rose into the saloons. None stopped to help me up. So much for being a woman of virtue, I mused, dusting off the front of my once-white apron. Now it was printed with wet moss and lichen stains.

As I sped after Pokamiakin, I realized where Chin was. He certainly couldn't draw clean water out of the muddy banks of Salmon Creek. Ruby had few wells, due to boundary dispute— who would want to dig a thirty-foot hole if your claim was going to be taken over by another the minute your back was turned? Chin was probably out searching for spring water, and Mary was helping.

Finally I caught up with Poka Mika on the threshold of the trading post and PO.

" 'Morning," I said as he bent down to search the lard pail for a letter. He couldn't read, but he could recognize the letters that made his name. Pokamiakin's picture, he called it. Inside I heard Windy Pardee's little-girl voice talking to Hames about "a Newport suit with leg-o'-mutton sleeves, gored skirt, very full and wide . . ."

"*Kla-how-ya,*" Pokamiakin said by way of a greeting. It meant something like, "come in and get warm," a little out of place on the street, but never mind.

"Seen Mary Reddawn?" I asked. He was the tallest Indian I'd ever met, with skin the color of a cedar log and a shirtless chest as broad as a tree trunk. Poka Mika had cut his hair short after the fashion of the white man to please Father de Rouge, but when the little French priest died, the underchief returned to native custom. Now he wore his black hair pulled back in a long braid. The features of Pokamiakin's face were sharp, his nose and cheekbones jagged as the Cascade mountains, his heavy brow looming over them like an alpine ledge. The red man gave off a strong odor. Other than that, the thing I noticed most about him were his eyes, which were crossed and reddened to cinders by the irritation of campfire smoke and pinkeye.

"Livery," he said, pointing across the street. Of course, why hadn't I thought of that? The livery with its fuel-eating forge was one of Mary's biggest customers. "Need you to write me *pepah,*" he added after a silence.

"A letter to whom?" I asked. He'd sorted through the envelopes in the lard pail and, not finding any for himself, began to look again. I bent down, searching the envelopes with him, hoping for one from the medical college.

As a man stopped on the threshold of the trading post, the smell of cologne wafted into my nostrils. When his frock coat brushed my sleeve, I was overcome with a déjà vu that spoke of

Fifth Avenue, New York City. I turned and saw Arizona Charley entering Windy Pardee's establishment dressed to the nines.

"Spokane Falls lawyer man," Pokamiakin answered. I couldn't tell if he was looking at me or not. Crossed and with eye whites as bloodshot as a wound, he had a murderous stare. Though, since his eyes didn't track, it was impossible to say what or whom he was staring at.

Yes, I thought, you may need an attorney, and soon. "Go see him in person," I offered. "The snow's melted. The trail across the reservation will be clear all the way."

"Week's ride," he said, shrugging his massive shoulders disinterestedly. He seemed to feel no need to get out of town.

"Come to my laundry tomorrow, after Shaky's funeral. Then I'll have time to write you all the *pepahs* you want." I stared at each envelope, hoping that next one would be for me. "Do you think Salmon Creek will flood?" I asked. I began to worry not only about the funeral but also about Doc and Tillicum fording the high waters on their way home.

Pokamiakin held an odd-shaped letter upside down, examining the return address. "Much plenty water every Moon of Leaves," he said. "*Skookum Chuck*," Water Power, he added, looking in the direction of the creek and the men diking it. "What this?" he asked, pointing to the upside-down street number on the return address.

"Numbers," I replied. "That says 'five.'" I held up five fingers after righting the letter. Like most of the indigenous people, Pokamiakin counted by making knots on strings. Poka Mika loved jewelry, and, in addition to several brass bands on his wrist, he wore a buckaroo belt with a silver buckle. Tied to his belt were several yard-long rawhide strings with many knots in them. These were the equivalent of his account books, though what they tallied (the number of horses in his herd?) I didn't know.

I sighed. No letter for me. "I've got to find Mary," I said, bidding him good-bye and crossing the street to the livery.

The mud was so thick it almost sucked my lace-up boots from my feet. The air filled with the scent of horse, which had a mysterious way of soothing my nerves. Like my da, I found the presence of horseflesh reassuring.

"Got my shirts?" asked a voice.

I turned, looking squarely into the khaki belly of Hames the blacksmith. His flat face bore a defeated expression as he ran a filthy hand through his oily black hair. I imagined that the competition for Windy had been too fierce, and he had left her in the company of Arizona Charley, though not without a swear word or two for his rival. As I mentioned, Hames had a temper as hot as his forge.

"I, I, I've no water this morning," I said. My fingers pulsed with dread. "Chin's not come, and what with all the funeral preparations . . . It's scheduled for two o'clock tomorrow, did you know?" It completely slipped my mind that the poor man had brought me his shirts a week ago and I still hadn't washed them.

"Hey, you haven't seen Doc?" he asked as if he'd suddenly forgotten all about his laundry. "The mail carrier who came over the mountains is bunkin' with me. Kept me up all night callin' for Doc."

"Went to meet the incoming steamer," I explained, then said a silent prayer that Doc's new glasses would also be in this shipment. "Seen Mary Reddawn?" I asked.

"Chased her outta here not a half hour ago," the blacksmith answered, his defeated expression turning mean. "Threw a coal scuttle at her ugly mug and got her square between the eyes, the thievin' little half-breed louse."

Startled, my hand flew up to cover my open mouth. Poor man, my foot! "You threw a coal bucket at her? What for?"

"She come here, plunked down her wood, then started skulking around for somethin' to steal. You can always tell, Injins get real quiet when they're in a thievin' frame of mind."

"Is anything missing?" I asked, studying the vast interior of the barn, Ruby City's tallest building. The shake roof towered three stories above me, and the opening in the false front went from floor to loft like a huge mouth gaping open. Beasts whinnied from every stall, except, of course, the stall in the corner marked "Feed Room, Keep Out" and nailed shut. It had been where Jake distilled rotgut out of government-issue corn intended for the Indians. In the atrium, harnesses hung from rafters and ceiling joists. The foyer where I stood was strewn with wagon parts and horseshoeing supplies, and in the center blazed the forge. Hames gestured to the stack of wood Mary had brought him.

"Don't know what's missin'," he said. "But if I ever find out, I'll blacken more than her heathen eye."

My body stiffened. You shan't ever find out and you shan't blacken her eye. I sucked in my breath, already feeling guilty. I should have come myself and confiscated a bullet—it wasn't worth Mary taking a licking. "I'll have one of your shirts ready for the funeral and the rest the day following," I said with resolve. "Did you see which way Mary went? You know, she probably took nothing at all."

His sneer said, You're a newcomer, you'll learn differently. Hames picked up his hammer and brought it down against the anvil with the most piercing noise I'd ever heard. "If you're so smart, I shouldn't have to tell you where she's at. Though you might try the alley." He made an obscene gesture with a rapid motion of his monkeylike arm. As I turned to leave, he lowered his voice and added, "Gotta give you credit for raising Jake's hackles, Mrs. Ryan."

I didn't like the way he said Mrs.

Hames blocked my path, bringing his face directly down in front of mine. "Too bad someone put a bullet through his head before you could marry him." He opened his mouth in laughter, his front teeth resembling the sharpened pegs in a shark's mouth. The blacksmith's noxious breath smelled of gum disease, and I felt as if I might vomit.

"I beg your pardon," I said, mad as spit. "But I was certainly not in love with your employer."

"Sure you weren't," he said and laughed even louder.

My protests only made the situation worse, so I fled the establishment, my fists clenched as hard as the rocks I'd like to throw through Hame's window—if he had one.

⁕

I found Mary about half an hour later crouching under Ella's larder where the spotted pig had lived. She held a poultice of crushed earthworms to her slashed eyebrow and swollen shining eye.

Pulling her out into the light, I said, "Let me see that." The cut wasn't deep, but it bled profusely—a good thing, as a free flow of blood always cleansed a wound of tetanus. Her temple was swollen, and so pressure on the brain was a worry. Best to get her a cold pack. If she had any pain, Mary certainly didn't let on. She spoke not one word but remained staring dead ahead, barely acknowledging my presence.

We gathered up her ax and bundles of wood. Taking the shortcut to my place, we passed Nightingale, who nodded in my direction, then cast the injured woman a curious glance. When Ella's girl was out of hearing, I turned to my assistant. "Did you get the bullets?" Negotiating the ravine, I carefully wedged my foot between two granite boulders the color of an old donkey in order to brace myself and my load.

Mary smiled, though because of the swelling her expression was lopsided, a little grunt passing from her lips. She had the bullet from Arizona Charley's gun in the hem of the right sleeve of her buckskin dress together with some tiny brown pieces of a whiskey bottle found in the street near his office, and the bullet from the blacksmith's revolver in her belt with her camas bulbs.

"Good work," I said. Her back straightened a notch under my praise, or so I imagined. "I feel terrible that he hit you."

Mary carried her wood on her back; I carried mine in my arms like a baby. When we arrived, we found Chin waiting for us with two buckets of precious clear water. He'd spent all morning gathering it dipperful by dipperful from a spring near their teepee.

"Ollo, ollo." His wide grin faded when he saw his wife. Chin's black-scarfed head bobbed up and down as he examined her, his expression sober.

"*Pil-pil,*" he said over and over, red-red, the Chinook word for blood. Chin *humm*ed several times, speaking of "the water of the eyes."

In China he had been an herbalist, the equivalent of a doctor, and in addition to searching for water had spent the morning picking herbs. The pockets of his black pajama trousers bulged with skunk cabbage, cow parsnip, and lily of the valley— not to mention wild onion shoots of which I had seen no evidence. Judging by his breath, however, he must have been eating them.

The water Chin had brought felt glacier cold, so by wetting a sterile towel I was able to make a cold pack for Mary's face. I bade her to lie down on my bed while Chin and I tended to fitting the bullets into Jake's hat. Mary did not sleep in a bed and would not use mine. She much preferred the floor, where she sprawled among heaps of sorted laundry, reminding me again that my day was going to be a long one. I had to make sure every lad in town had a clean shirt to wear to Shaky's service tomorrow, which meant washing and ironing all night. And, oh God, I had forgotten about Ella's shirtwaist with the tatted collar, which needed to be bleached and starched and . . . My head spun from weariness—lucky I had a good supply of coffee beans.

I brought out Jake's gray felt Stetson and laid it on the coffin lid. Next to it, I placed the tin cup containing the bullet from Ella's pistol. From somewhere in his baggy clothes, Chin drew out a pair of tweezers.

"Where'd you get those?" I asked.

He shrugged. "Don't know" was a safe answer to most any question.

Delicately, Chin put Arizona Charley's bullet—together with a tiny glass shard for identification—in an enameled bowl. Then, with just as much care, his double-jointed fingers placed the tweezers around Hame's bullet, placing it with a slice of camas root on a plate next to Ella's bullet in the tin cup.

Ominous silence filled the tent. From where she lay holding the towel to her eye, Mary looked on intently. A serious expression affixed itself to Chin's face. I motioned for him to size the first bullet. "Try Ella's," I pointed to the metal cup, then held my breath. Chin plucked the lead slug from the cup; then, with one hand holding onto Jake's mud-stained hat, he placed the bullet in the round hole that bore only the slightest hint of a burn mark. Apparently the bullet had exited through Jake's face and left quite a charred crater in his jaw. Thinking of the wound, I shuddered.

The bullet was so small it fell completely through the hole onto the coffin lid. Obviously it had not been fired from the murder weapon.

"That's one suspect cleared," I said, though I wasn't convinced of Ella's innocence.

Next Chin picked up the bullet from the blacksmith's gun. The ball looked even smaller than the one from Ella's pistol. It made an eerie hollow sound as it fell on the coffin lid and rolled out of sight under the dish. "*Hyas tenas,*" too small, said Chin.

"Clearly it wasn't Hames's bullet that killed Jake." My lips twisted. I glanced at Mary's ruined face, recalling the blacksmith's temper and sewer-smelling breath.

Chin returned the slug to the dish and picked up the bullet Mary'd taken from Arizona Charley's gun. I thought, This is more like it. It's fat as a grub. My pulse quickened as I leaned over the gray felt hat. Chin held the bullet firmly between tweezer tongs. As he pushed it up against the hole, I stared at his fingernails—well manicured and cleaner than my own even after I'd had my hands in soap and bluing all day.

The bullet was far too big even to begin to enter the hole. "Let me see," I said, taking the slug between my thumb and forefinger. I didn't want to alter the evidence and spoil any further sizing, so I proceeded carefully. No, this bullet could never have made that pockmark. The slug from Charlie's gun would have blown the entire top off Jake's hat, and I did not want to imagine what it would have done to the head beneath it.

"So none fits," I said disappointedly

Both Chin and Mary sat silently, gazing off into space as if they were waiting for a stage that wasn't due for hours. Clearly another gun had been involved. Ruby was armed to the teeth, and at this rate I'd never find the murder weapon. There had to be another angle to work. The only thing I could think of were the tracks left at the murder scene. I would ask Doc to get a description and start looking at the bottom of every hoof in Ruby.

Mary drew a camas bulb from her belt and broke it up, handing a piece to Chin and me. I offered the beginning of potato soup, which would more accurately have been called potato water, but both refused. Mary did not eat white man's food or sleep in a white man's house. Actually, the idea of a house frightened her terribly, and it was only reluctantly that she ever entered mine. Bad air, she said, the smell of white men's houses had *Cultus Skookum*, Evil Power.

Abruptly, the pair got up and prepared to leave. They seemed disappointed and (was I wrong?) a bit angry at me because none of the bullets had fit. Sometimes it was impossible to interpret their emotions. As the army blanket Mary used for a shawl brushed across my toe, I offered her another cold towel. She hesitated for a moment, then refused. Her eyes searched the room, falling upon the beginning of a crazy quilt I was making from clothing too ruined to mend. "Color," she said.

"What?" I asked, then remembered that "color" was the Indian word for "quilt."

It represented hours of work, but I guess I owed that much to Mary. I folded the swatch of crazy quilt, dipped it in cold water, and handed it to her. I'd forgotten that she was suspicious of the color white and much preferred something with red in it—I'd used a red chain stitch to sew the oddly shaped pieces to one another. She accepted it, smiling, the solemn atmosphere broken by the couple's sudden high-voweled chatter.

"Tick-tick?" asked Chin.

I pulled Shaky's watch from my apron and showed it to him. "Ten o'clock! Time to get this water on the boil or my day will never end." Mary promised to return when the sun was over the lightning-scarred pine outside my door, though I protested—I could hardly ask her to work when she should be resting that bruise.

Pulling some coals from the stove and putting them into the scuttle, I lighted the wood piled in my tent's front yard. Positioning the cauldron, I went back inside for a bar of soap and my board, thinking that scrub board both a blessing and a curse. Then I had a flash. Since I didn't have Dutch's gun, why not check a bullet from its twin? I didn't for one minute believe that Jake could have been blackmailing Dutch. But Dutch Wilhelm had been near the scene of the crime, and I had to investigate everyone who had the opportunity to put a hole through the back of the livery owner's head.

Pulling the pillow from my bed, I felt for Shaky's pearl-handled revolver, which I hadn't used in weeks. There it was, that reassuring hardness. But when I pulled it out, it wasn't a gun at all but a pot handle! A spare I'd squirreled away. My brow knitted. Where had I hidden the gun? In the bottom of the sugar barrel? No. I felt truly vexed by my housekeeping abilities. What's more, I hadn't time to hunt a gun. Then I remembered—I sometimes hid the revolver under the crate where I stored my chamber pot. The trouble was that I wasn't a very good shot, and the pistol frightened me. It had a powerful kick that almost disjointed the bones in my hand whenever I fired it. Worst of all, the noise more than unnerved me. The truth was, though I was pleased to have the pistol, I dreaded using it.

Tipping the crate on its side, I found the revolver swaddled in a miner's abandoned flannels. Unwrapping the pearl handle, I held the shining silver weapon, thinking it almost too pretty to use. What a tragedy that Dutch had lost the mate, one lone pearl-handled gun would look so forlorn on Shaky's coffin lid. I placed it thus, and it did indeed cry for its twin.

Opening the side arm, I spun the barrel and took out a slug. Remembering how Shaky had once told me he'd won the six-shooters in a game of strip poker, I recalled him quickly adding that gentlemen were always allowed to keep their hats. I hadn't caught his drift until I walked home, my cheeks blushing the color of fire engines.

Idly placing the slug in the hole, my eyes fixed on the damaged hat's crown. My breath stopped. I tried to swallow, but my throat froze. The bullet was a perfect fit.

CHAPTER THIRTEEN

❧

Later that morning

My mind tangled with suspects. As I considered my list of likely candidates, the noise of rushing water failed to drown out the witches' voices screaming inside my head: *My God, you've driven someone to kill Jake Pardee!*

The day turned overly warm for April, and the packed snow began melting at an alarming rate. With every up-and-down stroke against my washboard, I went over the situation again: Either the bullet that killed Jake had been fired from my gun or it had been fired from its twin. That meant someone had borrowed my firearm, then returned it, or Dutch's revolver had been used. Who had unlimited access to my digs? Mary and Chin. When the witches weren't screaming, *What have you done?* their brothers the demons yelled at me to do what any self-respecting Rubyite would do: *Get out of town.*

Neither Mary nor Chin owned a side arm. (This is me, Pearl, seizing control over her own thoughts.) Had Jake badgered my assistants so badly that one of them shot him? Pardee never passed Mary on the street without shouting taunts regarding her mixed-blood parentage. And little leprechaun Chin! Once Jake had bet an argonaut that he couldn't tar Chin's pigtails. When the prospector proved otherwise, Jake bought the entire town drinks. The next morning Chin appeared on Main Street carrying his yoke of water buckets as if nothing had happened, though the burns on his neck turned to scald scars that he carries to this day. Again I found myself wondering, Did it matter who killed Jake Pardee?

Perhaps someone else had borrowed my gun.

What I needed now was a description of the hoofprints at the crime scene so that I could get busy picking up every hoof in town, shod and unshod. And when Doc got back—which had better be soon if he wanted to be able to ford Salmon Creek—I'd start putting together a list of everyone who participated in Jake's freebooting business and their indiscretions, beginning with Doc himself.

No, no, I chided. First have a talk with Dutch. Find out the circumstances concerning the loss of his gun. Perhaps it had fallen into Windy's or Ella's possession.

I sat down on the ground and lay my head against a pitchy stump, listening to laundry snap in the breeze. Soon I'd have a haystack-high pile of ironing. Glancing at the creek, I watched it carry along entire trees as if they were stovepipes. Even if the man with the photographic equipment made the morning steamer up the Okanogan, he'd not be able to cross into Ruby anytime tomorrow. I'd never have a likeness of Shaky.

Then I thought of Nightingale. She could paint his portrait!

The sound of sliding rock startled me. I turned to see a woman with the countenance of a Greek statue descending the ravine. Carolina Bitterroot called a friendly "hello" in her educated accent. "I've got Shaky's teeth," she said, catching her breath.

Carolina had been taken advantage of by Jake. Dare I pick her brain about his death? Be extra discreet, I cautioned myself.

"And I brought us a treat." She held a jar of Mrs. Brokenhorn's cream. From the pocket of her spotless apron she produced a box of Earl Grey tea the likes of which I hadn't seen since I'd left Mrs. Ritters's kitchen. Carolina removed her freshly starched bonnet, its delicate pattern reminding me of Blue Willow china. "Let's fit his new smile, then have a cup. I should hope you're not using creek water to do public laundry," she said once we were inside and had removed the coffin lid.

I stiffened. "It's safe. Chin collected it from an artesian spring."

"Everything *must* be boiled." Her fine features grew long.

I bit my tongue, thinking, This woman just walks into my place of business and hands out instructions as if I had the brains of a grasshopper.

"I nearly stumbled over a gent sprawled in front of the faro parlor. He'd been taken with the sweats." Her voice rose an octave. "We're on the verge of an epidemic!"

"Who?" I hadn't seen anyone ill on the street.

"Forr," she said with a note of sadness.

That surprised me, since I counted Forr among the Rubyites who seldom sampled the water. "I'll have Doc take a look at him just as soon as he gets in."

Her face remained expressionless. I might as well have said nothing at all. Outside, creek boulders clanked together so loudly that (thank goodness for small favors) I couldn't hear the picks and shovels of the men digging Shaky's grave.

Finally she remarked, "His father will be here soon enough." Reading between the lines, I assumed that even in ill health Forr had rebuffed her helping hand.

I heard the noise of boot stomp. Dutch. Undoubtedly he'd come for some potato porridge and his shirts, which—God be praised—were done to perfection. Then it dawned on me: I'd washed nothing for myself to wear to the funeral!

"No soup yet, but—" The schoolmistress cut me off with an offer of tea. How could I ask Dutch about the loss of his gun in front of Carolina?

When Dutch heard the schoolmistress's voice he seemed to halt midstride, then entered cautiously, removing his navy cap. "*Guten Morgan.* Dat *kline* spring has come up something fierce." Nervously, he gripped his trouser legs with his huge hands.

Carolina replied as if she were the hostess, "Remember when the cloudburst washed Ruby off the map in ninety-one? The sky turned to ink, rained bucketfuls, and that creek changed to a battering sea. . . . But *this,*" she said, with a frightened slant to her slate eyes, "if it gets this warm tomorrow, all the snow in the Cascades will melt and run over us."

"Let's not think about it," I said, which was uncharacteristic of me. Wasn't I the one who always worried ahead?

"Earl Grey?" Carolina suggested, whereupon she immediately began reboiling the water just to make sure.

"*Danke, nein.* Better get back to grave digging," Dutch said and hurried away like an animal just let loose from a cage. Odd. Had I ever known him to pass up the opportunity to engage anyone in friendly political rhetoric?

Mrs. Bitterroot fit the mayor's teeth, which certainly improved his expression. The tea's warm cream coated my mouth and throat, soothing my nerves. "Carolina," I said after a silence, "have you ever done something terrible?"

Her spine stiffened. "Whatever do you mean?" I hadn't meant her.

"I think I've done something awful."

Her perfect lineless brow crinkled.

"The ghost writing," I said, unburdening myself. "You probably know that I'm the author. It shook Jake up pretty good and . . . I think he unnerved somebody so much trying to find out who did it, that . . . they shot him."

Carolina took another sip of tea, her expression remaining unchanged. She had to have heard me, and I waited for some reply. She took another sip.

When no response came, I said, "So even though I didn't pull the trigger, it was . . . partially my fault."

She rose, dumped out the tea leaves, went to the kettle, poured hot water, and began rinsing her cup. That's when I realized that she was preparing to leave. Wanting to throw my hands in the air, I thought, I give up. So much for trying to confide in anyone else in this world except Doc Stringfellow.

Finally I muttered, "Thank you for fixing Shaky's smile." I began tending potato starch. She hesitated at the door. Well, I was no one's servant: Open it yourself, my eyes said. Outside, the raging creek sounded like a railroad train that never finished passing.

She fumbled as if searching her apron pocket for something, then straightened her Blue Willow bonnet. "We can't question God's divine plan," she whispered. "Dying was the best thing Jake ever did for the Okanogan." Turning abruptly, she pulled my blanket door aside, and the sharp smell of the pine funeral wreaths stacked outside rushed in. Watching her walk up the ravine, I felt suddenly bleak. I'd just been completely rejected by Mrs. Bitterroot, a woman who, if I wasn't mistaken, was also very much alone.

With so much work, I hadn't time to mope. Taking up my ironing, I pondered the question of Dutch's missing pistol until perspiration dampened my scalp and the weight of my braids began to make my temples throb. I had carried my only chair into the yard as well as two drygoods crates on which to iron. The smell of scorched starch didn't do my headache a bit of good, and I began to feel as if someone had driven a wheel spoke through the back of my neck. All the same, with the use of a hot brick, I created excellent trouser creases—a brick never scorched like a hot iron could.

By afternoon, soapsud clouds drifted in, bringing relief from the heat. When I heard the forlorn call of the steamboat horn, my headache abated. The *Okanogan Belle* left a white-plumed tail where it slowed near Rattlesnake Point, and I imagined men running out of Squawman Bill's saloon to help pull the boat over the riffles.

When I caught sight of Dutch trudging up from the stone orchard, I remembered that I still hadn't freshened a dress to wear to the funeral. If I didn't get busy, I'd look like a ragbag at dear old Shaky's send-off.

"*Danke,*" he said. Accepting a cup of potato starch soup, Dutch drank the almost boiling liquid right down. "Helps *die* throat," he said by way of another thank-you. Dutch grasped his neck. "Vhen Doc gets back, tell him I need somethin' to help me swallow."

"Of course," I assured. Dutch had a wee bit of trouble with the idea of a female nurse and probably had not wanted to discuss his health in front of Carolina. "You'll drop a Union flag by later, won't you?" I ventured. "To cover the foot of the coffin?"

"*Ja.*" He helped himself to seconds. My God, what was I going to use to starch my petticoats? And when Doc got here, he'd want a cup.

I thought a moment and then said, "But it pains me that we can't have both Shaky's pearl-handled pistols on the coffin lid. Do you remember how you lost yours?"

Dutch shook his head. "I have asked and asked, 'Has anyone seen my pearl six-shooter?' Today Herr Sheriff is busy looking for hoofprints of Jake's murderer's horse, so I do not ask. Two veeks ago vhen I started down the vagon road to the steamboat, I had it. Vhen I got to Pard Cummings's, I did not." He shrugged, spreading out his shovel-sized hands palm up. "Vhat is to be done? And Nightingale saw nothing."

My head jerked. "Nightingale?"

"*Ja* sure, she vanted a ride to the ferry for an important package."

Satisfied with two cups of soup, Dutch paid me for his laundry and returned to the cemetery. "Tell the other gents to stop in for their shirts," I called after him.

I went inside and dug my one good dress—my wedding costume—out of a trunk, thinking, Yes, that's it: Nightingale stole the gun and passed it on to Ella. Examining the gown, I racked my brain for motives. Why would Ella have killed Jake? I ran my hands over the dress, smoothing the black skirt and pleated bodice. On our way to the Manhattan registry, Paddy Ryan had asked me if I'd like an outfit to be married in. I had wanted only to get the humiliating event over with as soon as possible. But as we walked from the rooming house where I was holed up, his eyes shimmered while he explained that ours had to look like a proper wedding. The police were out to break the unions, and they'd certainly guess what he was up to if things didn't look up to snuff. I'd agreed. As we entered the courthouse with its choir of pigeons roosting on the brick facade, I'd thought that I'd better get this over with quick, as I was beginning to like Mr. Ryan.

While freshening the gown with mint leaves, I pondered the ways Ella'd profit from Jake's demise. Did she want to take over his gambling interests? I'd have to have a serious talk with Nightingale before sundown and callers arrived. The thought of her life made me shudder. It could have been my life if I hadn't found a way to make a living.

At 3:24 Doc rode up on Tillicum. I didn't give him time to shake the dust from his hat but started in at once, my sentences coming out so fast they ran into each other. "I've got you a boiled shirt for tomorrow, and your white gloves are drying. Doc, I think I've done something terrible. . . . Have you got a description of the hoofprints? Nightingale was with Dutch when he lost his gun. . . . None of the bullets fit, not Ella's or

Charley's or the blacksmith's, I mean. And you should see what Hames did to Mary's eye. But I found a match, bullet to hat hole. It's just that . . . the ghost writing shook Jake up pretty good, and . . . I think he unnerved somebody so much trying to find out who did it, that they . . . I've got to get to the bottom of this, but I'm not sure I want to."

"Hold on, lass. You've got your wagon's running gear on gallop." Doc took off his plug hat, swatting it against the wet leg of his chaps. The lower parts of horse and rider were soaked to the skin from swimming the flooding creek, the upper part covered with so much red dust that they looked as if they'd just left a brickyard.

Despite being trail weary, Doc's sunny temperament seemed to have returned. I sat him down on one of the crates I'd been using as an ironing board, gave him a bowl of potato broth, then led Tillicum to a grassy slope. When I got back, Doc was scraping his spoon against the bottom of the bowl and looking in need of seconds.

"Floodwater's colder than the North Sea in January," he said. His hands were moon white and covered with gooseflesh.

"Did your specs come?" I asked. His eyes were clear, and his pinprick pupils almost back to normal.

"No, but I got something I badly needed for the mail carrier with frostbitten feet, plus a good supply of chlorite of lime."

"Lime purifier? You think the flood could bring cholera?"

"A stitch in time," he said. "It wouldn't hurt to put a drop in your drinking water as an added precaution. Brought some along, and . . ." He reached down and fumbled for something in his saddlebags. "The best medicine . . ."

You'd think that I had no manners at all judging by the way I grabbed the butcher paper and string parcel. "Gingersnaps! My favorite! How did you know?" My mouth watered. "I haven't tasted a spice cookie in more than a year."

"Nor I," he said, "though it's been much longer than that."

We both talked with our mouths full, crunching the hard disks like cows in the corn crib.

"Hames said that the mail carrier has been asking for you. And Dutch wants something for his throat, and someone else needs you to look at his horse."

He nodded, and I wondered why he looked so solemn. There were times when an unexplained sadness filled his eyes, as if he were looking right through me. I always wanted to ask him about it. Instead I said, "Do you think my ghost writing drove Mary or Chin to kill Jake?" A vision of Mary's frail, bird-like body dangling by the neck from a lynch mob's rope flashed before me. My nerves felt like just-lighted candlewicks.

Doc was a pillar of sanity. "The fact that the bullet from your gun fits the hole in the hat isn't definitive," he said. "It could have come from another weapon with the same-size bullet. What we now know is the relative size of the bullet."

"And whose gun it wasn't," I said. "Well, what do I do, get a bullet from every firearm in town?" I could feel the desperation rise in my throat.

"Matching hoofprints is a better idea, though you're one step behind the sheriff. An unshod horse, the right fore having a sheered heel. See if you can discover what horse Ella borrowed from the livery and have a look. By the way, I heard at Pard Cummings's that a federal marshal is definitely on his way, soon as the danger of flooding has past."

I felt the gray walls of a women's prison closing in on me.

"And Dutch told me that the man asking for Pearl O'Sullivan was right here in town at the Gem!" I said, embracing myself with my arms as if I was cold. Trying to stifle a shudder, I took a deep breath. "Something that would help me would be to know everyone Jake was extorting money from and why."

Doc's head sank into his buffalo hump. He put the bowl down. "The man had a sixth sense," he said after a pause. "He could ferret out your most closely guarded secret as quick as the wolves found Shaky's body outside your tent. Like second sight. And," Doc ran his hand across his square jaw, "he employed it to the devil's advantage—"

"You will ask the lads to build a fence around the mayor's grave to keep out the wolves?" I interrupted. My brain was starting to feel like a piece of frayed cloth.

"Don't fret, lass. General Jones is splitting and sharpening pickets." Doc must have been shedding the river's chill, because he'd taken off his green cable knit sweater. I sat poised, ready to take in each of my suspects and their indiscretions.

"Arizona Charley's situation I've already mentioned," he said. "Horse theft."

"How much did Jake get from him?" I asked.

"It wasn't so much in silver." Doc stared into the coals of the campfire and inhaled the sage smoke, which—if it didn't cause your eyes to go red as poker chips—could really clear out your lungs. "That was part of the mon's genius. Jake exchanged his silence for Charley's 'Wanted' posters and 'Reward' handbills."

"Pardee was a bounty hunter?" Behind us a squirrel trilled notes of outrage.

"No, the handbills helped Jake get information on his other 'clients.' A reward was only a one-time payment, but a free-booting affair could go on and on." Doc touched his index finger to his head to imply intelligence.

"Like who?"

"Hames, for one. Was part of a gang who robbed a bank in Pendleton."

I wasn't surprised. "Changed his name to a part of a harness?" I said with a laugh. "Jake must have figured that out right quick."

"Aye, I think the mon's true calling card is Singletree. You see the logical connection."

"Then there was Dutch Wilhelm, a case of a different color."

"Jake blackmailed Dutch?" What could Dutch have possibly done? Then I thought, maybe union organizing like my so-called husband, Paddy Ryan.

"Jake claims to have caught Rinehard Wilhelm in a compromising situation with the assayer in the back of his metallurgy shed."

"When Dutch went there under the pretense of getting some ore assayed but was in the hope of convincing another town merchant to join the strike committee?"

"Exactly. Not that I think for one minute that Dutch is buggered, but it was his word against Jake's. And Jake had quite a mouth."

"Didn't he." I'd one ginger cookie left, and I was savoring it.

"Got Dutch into a stir. Who would take him seriously with such gossip about?"

"Would you like some English tea?" I asked. "Carolina dropped it by when she brought Shaky's teeth."

"Aye, I would, lass," he said, moving his crate away from the fire. "A wee sip would be wonderful."

"What about Carolina and her husband?" I asked. He'd already told me that he didn't know, but it was easier to go over the known again than for me to ask him why he'd succumbed to Jake's extortions. I certainly hadn't forgotten how chilly Doc had turned this morning when I put the question to him.

"Don't know," he said, taking in the aroma of the Earl Grey.

"And I've even a little cream left," I said. The tension felt as thick as axle grease.

"Smells just like me mitter's kitchen when I was a child in Ben Kirk," he said with a faraway look in his walnut eyes.

"And yourself." There, I'd said it—in an even tone as if asking after his health.

"And meself," he said, exhaling the gust of air that is a dying man's last breath. He shut his eyes as if blindness could shield him.

The copper sun beat down now, baking the ground. By

summer it would be hard as a cobbled street. I moved my crate into the shade. Doc remained where he was.

" 'Twas a long time ago," he began, "the year after the War Between the States. Plenty of doctor's work, but no one had legal script, so I headed west. The railroad took me to Nebraska, and from there I joined a train captained by a man named Spence who treated me like a son. Spence had a daughter, Maggie, just eighteen. Maggie became me nurse, and pretty soon things developed and there was a wedding one Sabbath."

I bit into my last ginger cookie, sucking each piece instead of chewing, so that I'd not miss a word of his story.

"Like a wee sprite, my Maggie. Her mother was dead, and her father worried about her something fierce." Doc's brogue deepened.

I shook my head in sympathy. Life on the trail was hard on a woman.

"One redskin in particular stalked the trains. Cut Nose. A terrible-looking mon who wore a hoop skirt he'd taken off a dead woman. After we crossed the Humbolt Sink, there was a bad Indian scare. The train in front of us lost half their stock to theft and had to abandon fifty wagons. They burned 'em together with their belongings so redskins wouldn't get hold of them. That night Maggie spiked a fever. She'd taken sick from alkali water, as had our oxen. I left her in bed piled with quilts and took my guard. Mountain lions screamed, and what we thought were wolves began howling."

"Makes my skin crawl," I said, recalling a night last winter. "A cougar has the eeriest cry, like the dead come to life in the agony of their wounds."

"I say *thought*," Doc continued, "because they could have been savages calling to one another in preparation for a strike. I heard footsteps in the chaparral, so I kneeled, cocking my gun. When I caught a glimpse of a figure in a blanket, I was paralyzed with fear. I took aim. It moved. I fired."

Doc's gaze fell to the ground. " 'Twas Maggie, gone out for her toilet. Dead, shot through the heart." Doc's face crumpled, and I thought he might break down. But after he jabbed a stick into the fire several times as if to breathe new life into the coals, he caught hold of himself. "I near went crazy when I'd seen what I'd done. Her father tried to shoot me, swearing he'd bring me to trial when we got to California. The others decided that it'd be best if I left the train. It would be about a month's walk, if the redskins didn't get me. By traveling off the wagon road and watching like a vulture, I evaded Cut Nose and joined another train bound for Sacramento. I doctored in mining camps, saw my picture on a 'Wanted' poster once or twice, but nothing came of it. It's been years. I thought that was all behind me, except for a haunting memory. Then Jake got hold of an old handbill, and you know the rest."

I protested, "But surely enough time has passed!" Brushing an ant from my skirt, I added, "It was an accident. No jury would ever find you guilty."

"Perhaps, but somehow it seemed easier just to pay the mon off a few dollars here and there," Doc said. "Especially after he broke me glasses and poisoned me horse . . ."

"Good God," I muttered. "It makes me want to feed Jake's body to the wolves."

"Maggie had hair the color of strawberries. I would have strangled her for trotting out to the bushes in bare feet—if she weren't already dead." There was a silence. I felt at a loss for words.

Finally he spoke. "She looked a lot like you, lass."

I took my last sip of tea and picked at the cookie crumbs in my lap. My face hurt. Pressure built behind my eyes. I thought I might cry. "It was the nicest thing for you to bring sweets." I wanted to reach out and take his hand but didn't dare. We'd never touched that way. His loss made my heart ache, and I couldn't help but think of Davy.

"They were her favorite," he replied, turning his large head away from me. For the first time I noticed that his hump didn't sit squarely on his back but to the left, bulging between his neck and shoulder. "I don't think I've eaten one in twenty-seven years."

CHAPTER FOURTEEN

That evening

It was dusk before I headed up to have a serious talk with Nightingale. To the east, the desert sky turned a quiet blue as smoke from an Indian campfire across the valley went up to heaven in an unbroken line.

Were the fairies playing tricks on me, or did the overflow from Salmon River, né Creek, sound less like an avalanche and more like spring runoff? The tear on the bottom of my shoe elongated as I climbed up the ravine, and the sharp loose rocks stabbed my feet. Inside most dwellings on Main Street, a bowl of bear grease with a rag lighted in the center of it was the only light. I thought of Doc up at his surgery preparing tomorrow's eulogy by candle, as there was no minister within a hundred miles. Did I prefer Ecclesiastes? he'd asked before leaving. His dark mood of early morning had faded into history, his sweet self restored to me. Why not a little of Isaiah 43 thrown in, I'd replied.

The hurricane lantern on Ella's veranda blazed like a beacon, guiding the solitary miner to her door. A thousand moths fluttered at the light's glass chimney, their wings casting excited shadows on the hotel's unpainted wall. If there were no "rooms" available, some gents paid for the privilege of sleeping in Ella's yard. I quickened my stride. Mounting the steps, I saw a number of the doves standing in a ring around a cottonwood next to the kitchen. One, a stout girl with hair the color of dried corn husks, was—for reason unbeknownst to me—poking into the lower branches with a stick.

The front door burst open just as I rang the cowbell nailed to the window sash.

"Oh," said Nightingale, "I thought you was Doc." She appeared taller than I remembered, and there was an authority in her voice I hadn't heard before.

"He's home preparing for—"

"Ella's got one of her headaches again," she said. Her limp brown hair was neatly knotted at the nape of her neck, which showed her perfect nose to advantage. Tonight Nightingale looked more like a missionary than a tart.

"Shh," she called in an exaggerated whisper in the direction of the cottonwood. "Get him down from there and in here quick as you can. And then change into your chore clothes— no eye-jabbin' colors. We won't be entertaining tonight."

"Let me try," said the shortest dove as she took hold of the stick.

Nightingale turned to me, smoothing the bib of her apron. "What'ya here for?"

Apparently Ella's legendary hospitality was not going to be extended to me. "I want to have a word with you," I said, trying to figure out what the doves were up to. "About ah, Shaky's wake."

"We're bringin' venison hams," she said. "I told you that." Ice an inch thick coated her voice, and I wondered how I'd ever jockey the conversation around to Dutch's lost pearl-handled revolver and Jake's death.

"Yes, and I'm grateful. I'll be making my fluffiest biscuits all day tomorrow."

"What, none of your famous sockwater soup?" she asked.

I pretended her remark was a joke and laughed. "Couldn't I come in? I've so much on my mind, and I've been standing up ironing all day."

"Suit yourself," she said, reluctantly allowing me to enter. I stepped into the sheeted hall, heading toward the parlor. Nightingale pulled me back.

"We'll go upstairs . . . to my quarters, I guess," she said, but at the same time held aside the curtain to the red room where Ella had received me yesterday.

"Who's there?" Ella sounded as if she were calling from under water.

Slices of light from the beacon shone through the irregular wall chinks. In the dimness I could see the madam lying sprawled on her bed covered up to her neck with a buffalo rug. Holding a damp rag to her forehead, Ella was as pale as a gent's boiled shirt.

"Did you have a good vomit?" Nightingale asked kindly. "It's the laundress. Don't worry, I'll take care of her."

"Tell her I ain't in the mood for hirin' today," Ella snarled. Pressing the rag to her temple, she called, "Lorenzo? Where's my little birdie?"

"They'll have your rooster back in here in a flash," said Nightingale.

Ella groaned and waved Nightingale away with a swat of her corpulent hand.

"It's her worst migraine yet," she said. "I'm worried. Usually she wakes up with a sick headache, empties her stomach until noon, and is fit as a fiddle by the time evening callers start knockin'. Any kind of light causes her pain, even the sight of the girls' gay dresses." Nightingale shook her small head as she guided me down the unlit hall into the kitchen and toward the back lift that was more of a ladder than a stairs.

"See," she said, pausing in the kitchen. On the plank table lay several venison hams, one decorated with a design of the Union flag made with strips of white pork fat, red peppercorns, dried blueberries, and cloves arranged to form the stars and stripes.

"It's beautiful," I said admiringly. And it was.

Nightingale stepped out the back door and called to the doves, "Get that rooster outta that tree and back into Ella's room quick, if you know what's good for you!"

A pile of dirty laundry in the corner next to the washbasin caught my eye. As Nightingale gave further instructions to the doves, I sidled closer, examining the hem of a large purple dress streaked with ochre-colored dirt. So Ella *had* journeyed to Pard Cummings's ferry. But why had she said she'd gone the day Jake was murdered, when she'd actually gone the day before?

Nightingale's upstairs room had sheeted walls and was as narrow as a water closet. A small but fancy coal-oil lantern hung from the ceiling, casting pecan light on likenesses that were pinned from floor to roofline. One rickety chair was pulled up to what looked like a pantry table sawed in half to effect a writing desk. I rushed to sit down. Oh, didn't it feel good to rest my tired arches. Pressing my back into the chair—tonight I could feel every muscle in my body—I studied Nightingale's pen and ink drawing of Cranky Frank and his stage. Next to it was a drawing of Ella in an amethyst dress sitting on her veranda. Perfect likenesses all of them, better than tintypes.

"You *will* do Shaky's portrait?" I asked. "As many as you can? The man with the photographic equipment has no hope of crossing the creek tomorrow." I must have sounded humble, because she nodded her small, pointed chin without hesitation.

"And Doc had an idea . . ."

"He will be up to give Ella something for her head?" she asked insistently.

"If he said he would, he will, of course."

Her eyes hardened as if to say that Doc's appointments were my responsibility.

"He had an idea that you might have some violet scent for the silk flowers Windy gave me for his breast."

"Windy gave *you* flowers?" she asked, her eyes widening.

I ignored her insinuations, hoping to steer clear of the ghost writing and my purported love for Jake Pardee, but the idea of it made the blood rise in my cheeks.

"She gave them to the mayor," I corrected.

Nightingale rolled her eyes. Outside, the voices below the cottonwood turned shrill. Nightingale went to the window and called, "Quiet! You're getting nowhere. There must be a trick to this. Squirrel, go up to the Gem and ask Frank Belknap how he used to get his parrot out of a tree. And don't accept no drinks. Get back here quick as you can, hear?" I detected Ella's inflection in Nightingale's commanding voice.

"I suppose I could give you something," she said, turning toward me. She began rummaging through a crate that served as her bed stand, and I supposed she was looking for the scent. After a moment, however, she drew out a snuff can–shaped contraption that looked like a vise. Going to the oval mirror, which hung next to a likeness of the pig that used to live under Ella's larder, she affixed it—indeed like a vise—to the two sides of the cleft that split her lip and traveled up to her nose.

"What's that?" I asked.

"A Monitor Imperfection Device. I sent all the way to Ohio for it." She returned to the contents of the crate.

I didn't see how it could help and wondered if it might even do her harm by cutting off the circulation, but I didn't say as much. At last she drew out a small glass vial with a painting of a bouquet of violets on its wee black cap.

"You be sure to return this. Shaky gave it to me, so it's special."

I assured her that I would. "Nightingale," I said after an awkward silence, "I'm curious. Is that the package you picked up when Dutch gave you a ride to the ferry?"

"Yes, if it's any of your beeswax," she retorted, reducing her eyes to slits. She lay down on her bed, which was a pile of feed sacks, and adjusted the device.

"It's a shame Dutch lost Shaky's pearl-handled revolver. I would have liked to have had both of them on his coffin for the funeral procession. You wouldn't remember whereabouts he first discovered it missing? So I could go look for it."

"I don't know anything about any damn gun," she said too quickly. After a moment she added, "You're so greedy."

"Greedy?"

"Yeah, Shaky gave you everything, his gun, his Glory Hole, his watch. Now you're in a fix about a little lost revolver."

"It would be nice to have them united again at Shaky's send-off."

"So you come to me to see if I stole it?"

She was quicker than I gave her credit. And even though she was being contrary, I liked her pluck. "I never said that."

I thought it best to change the subject. "Doc says that there's a physician in San Francisco, a surgeon who can mend your palate."

"Is there now? Who do I look like, little Miss Moneybags?"

"Only trying to help," I said, and something about the defeated expression on my tired face must have made her believe me.

"Sorry. So," she said after a pause, "what's the menu for the wake? Venison hams, boiled potatoes, your fluffiest biscuits, cornbread . . ."

"Carolina's making apple conserve out of her dried stores. Dutch is baking pemmican pie, General Jones said he'd fry up some prairie chickens, Chin and Mary are donating dried salmon, jerked venison, and dried huckleberries."

"Who'll eat Injin food?" She sucked in her cheeks in a gesture of skepticism.

"I will," I asserted. "Doc says dried berries are insurance against land scurvy."

"Doc says, Doc says. You think you know everythin'. But you don't know nothin', even about Doc." The mocking returned to her voice.

"Whatever do you mean?"

"Just make sure you wash everythin' good, get the Injin touch off of it."

I gripped a rung of the chair, feeling my knuckles go white. "No, tell me, what don't I know?"

"Nothin' about a gent puttin' his teapot spout into you, even if you are a Missus."

I ignored her. Only in Ruby Camp was being a virgin a black mark on your character. Though her comment made me wonder: Could people tell by looking at me? Was my virtue the one flaw in my disguise as Mrs. Ryan? "What else? For instance?"

"For instance . . . Doc shot his wife."

Good Lord, in the Okanogan gossip flew faster than a cougar sprang on the first lamb of spring. "I'm aware of that," I replied coolly. "Doc hasn't anything to hide."

She expelled a grunt of laughter. "Can't tell you nothin', can I?"

"How do you know about Doc's past?"

"Jake," she said, spitting his name out as if it were an apple pip.

I should have guessed. Abandoning my line of questioning, I continued with the menu. "Bald Barton's making doughnuts if we can find him enough grease that's not rancid."

"We've plenty of lard here," offered Nightingale. "Ella had us render out the butchered pig." Her face cracked, and I thought she might cry. Then she regained herself, "It's stupid to be sentimental about a sow, but she was my pet, did ya know? A lad gave her to me as a tiny piglet. For my birthday."

"That was your sow?" I asked.

She nodded. "I know it's foolish to be so fond of a barnyard animal, but . . . He was a sweet lad, and I don't always get a birthday gift. He went off to the Caribou Mines, sayin' he'd be back. It's been two years. . . . I never had a pet." She frowned so hard I thought that her small face would fall in like a wall. Above us the lantern cut into the night with unusual sharp-ness. One lone moth orbited the glass chimney.

"Not even a kitten when you were a growing up?" I asked, studying the moth. It had furry brown wings and reminded me of a wood nymph butterfly, my da's favorite.

Impatiently, she waved a hand at my question. "Me ma had nine children. I was the oldest. Dad died right after we walked to Portland from Kansas, and ma opened a boarding house to feed us. We lived on potato skins and chicken bone soup." Nightingale stared at the floor looking glum, then studied me watching the moth. After a moment her eyes widened and she asked, "Do you fancy butters?"

"Reminds me of home." Suddenly I longed to tell her about my life, but I didn't dare.

"I saw the most beautiful butterfly collection the other day." Her expression went inward. I thought she'd finally let down her guard and that maybe I could get some answers, but then her brow wrinkled. "But what would *you* care about that?"

No response coming from my lips would be satisfactory and, after an awkward silence, I asked, "So you've had experience running boarding houses?"

"Not really," she answered. "When we'd been in Portland about a year, the assistant preacher at our church spoke for me, and Ma said I'd better marry him. Her constitution was giving out, and she didn't know how she could go on feedin' all us kids. I was fourteen. He was forty, fat, and sweet as shoofly pie when sober, which was only on Sunday. The other days he used to beat me so bad I prayed God I'd die instead of waking up the next morning. One night he accidentally shot himself with the gun he was swatting me with and, pow, I was a widow and not a bit sorry."

"No!" Somehow I'd finally gained her trust and felt a little guilty about having to pump her for information. I couldn't say why, but now that I'd heard her story, I was convinced more than ever that she'd stolen the gun Shaky had given Dutch.

"Know what he did just before he died? He said, 'Gale'—that's my real name, Gale—'go pick me a good strong willow switch.' He was a traveling preacher and sometimes he'd be gone weeks at a time, which was a blessing. I went and picked him a quirt for his horse. But then he commences to beat the living daylights outta me with the switch. 'What'd I do?' I says. And he says, 'Nothin'. This is for what you might do while I'm away.' " Nightingale paused, adjusting the device on her lip. "Makes me shake with anger when I think of it. Though everyone tells me I ought to bury the hatchet and let bygones be bygones. Forgive and forget, you know?"

"Makes my blood run cold just hearing about it," I assured her.

Footsteps pounded on the ladder-stairs, and then the dove with corn husk hair burst into the room. "Frank says he put water on Captain Hook. With wet feathers he couldn't fly, just fell outta the tree." She had eyes that reminded me of cherry stones.

"I knew there had to be trick," said Nightingale, her Sister Superior voice returning. "Squirrel, go fill a pitcher with water and get Mouse or Lark to climb up and pour it down on him. With luck Lorenzo'll fall at your feet. Towel him off and get him back into Ella's room, quick! There'll be hell to pay if anything happens to that rooster."

Squirrel nodded dutifully. Turning to leave, her hips completely filled the doorway.

"Look," I said, finally feeling that I could come to the point.

"To be honest, I need to talk to you about something else as well."

"Do tell." Any feelings of intimacy disappeared, and her surly demeanor returned.

"It's about Jake. If the sheriff can't come up with the murderer and a good case against him, a federal marshal will investigate. No one wants a marshal around, and Doc says he's due any day." Considering her profession, I thought this would arouse her concern. "You hear things. Do you know who might have killed him?"

"Why should I tell you, so you can go collect the reward?" At this she stood up, putting her hands on her narrow hips. She was as thin as a flute.

With all the funeral preparations, I'd completely forgotten about the reward Windy had staked. "You know," I said after a minute, "you don't have to work here. You could come be my assistant. I'll need someone when Mary starts drying fish. I'll pay you one-third of my profits. That's more than fair." I don't know what had gotten into me, but I'd been so struck by Nightingale's capabilities that I felt compelled to help her.

This was met by hysterical laughter. "And have my hands look like yours?"

I glanced down at my lobster claws, Yank and Hank. Shaky'd named my hands after his pack mules—not beautiful, but willing to lay down their lives for him.

"The money's good here, Ella takes care of me like a ma, and the work ain't unpleasant—except when a fellow smells like his trousers need airing or I meet someone who reminds me of my husband like, what's his name, that oiler, Frenchy Pete."

"You shot French Pete?" I was truly astonished.

"It was only a flesh wound. And he shoulda known better than to come back here again, especially when Ella had one of her migraines."

Outside, Lark had climbed into the cottonwood and

dropped both water and pitcher on poor Lorenzo, who lay unconscious on the ground. "Dunderheads," Nightingale screamed through the window. "Get him dry, perky, and into Ella's room soon as you can. And Mouse, change her vomit pan while you're at it.

"*I* ain't afraid of no federal marshal," she said, giving me a sidelong stare that sent a cold shiver from the pit of my stomach down to my toenails. The first thing that flashed through my head was, What does she know about me? The second was that I'd forgotten about Ruby's particular brand of jurisprudence. Here, prostitution wasn't a crime.

Time I stopped testing the waters. "Maybe you can help me set the record straight. Why did Ella go up to Three Devils the morning Jake got murdered, and why did she lie about where she was?"

"Gettin' ice for her headaches, of course," said Nightingale matter-of-factly. She took off the imperfection device and studied it. "Ella's been getting 'em more often lately and loses whole days at a time. Can't remember nothin'. And you knew she'd be afflicted the day after Shaky died, at least you would if you knew her at all." Nightingale gave me a contemptuous look, as if to say I didn't have enough regard for Ella.

I recalled that Dutch had said Ella hadn't recognized him when she'd torn past him, galloping down the steep trail, that she'd had a wild (pained?) look on her face.

"But don't brother yourself about where Ella was or wasn't when Jake got killed. She didn't do it." Nightingale reached into the crate stand and pulled out a tin of horehound candy. "I know who did, and I'm gonna collect the reward." She took a hard sugary drop but didn't offer me one.

"Who?" I asked, watching her suck its bitter minty flavor.

"Same people as killed Shaky Pat McDonald," she said.

I jumped to my feet. "Nightingale! You're the only person other than me who not only doesn't think the mayor died of

natural causes but that Shaky's and Jake's death are connected."
Standing in front of her rigid with excitement, I whispered,
"Who?"

"Your little Injin friends," she said coyly, propping her feet
up on the crate. Her lace-up shoes were new and well polished,
without a single scuff mark.

I stepped back. Foolishly, I'd played right into the hands of
the enemy. An image of Mary Reddawn appeared in front of
me. "What are you talking about?"

"That no-good Poka Mika, of course." She popped another
candy into her mouth.

"But no Indian ever goes up to Three Devils. They think
the Evil Power lives there. And you know that Pokamiakin certainly had nothing to do with Shaky's death." A sinking feeling grew in my stomach. Had Mary lent my gun to her cousin?

"Course he didn't. Some Chinaman gave Shaky typhoid
water or he ate unwashed squaw food. Thanks to you."

Didn't I tell myself that I'd be blamed for the mayor's death?
Then I thought to ask, "How do you know about Pokamiakin,
anyway?"

" 'Cause I was up there and saw him," she said, playing her
trump card.

"What were you doing at Three Devils?"

"Looking for Ella, of course. There was a storm brewing, and
sometimes she don't pay enough attention to the weather. So I
hiked up there to bring her back. That's when I saw him, that
cross-eyed redskin, lurking in the rocks."

Not in those boots she hadn't hiked anywhere. She couldn't
possibly have two pairs of good shoes. Women in these parts
were lucky to have one, and most children went barefoot. "Did
you see Jake?"

"No," she replied flatly. I couldn't tell if she was telling the
truth or not. "And I didn't hear nothin', either. You know how
the wind howls around them peaks. Never even laid eyes on
Ella. Made tracks back here when I saw clouds dark and wide as

the Black Sea churning overhead. Only person I thought about from then on was myself."

"Or Dutch? Did you see him?"

"Only that crazy-eyed Injin," she reiterated.

"Have you told the sheriff yet?" I asked.

"Tried to, but he was busy down at the flood levy. Said he'd stop in tonight."

From the room below us came a barnyard *cock-a-doodle-doo* booming up through the floorboards. Lorenzo again guarded Ella's four-poster. Nightingale went to the doorway, calling down the stairs, "Good work, girls. Now get into the kitchen and get cooking for Shaky's send-off. Mouse, you take a vat of lard up to Bald Barton so he can make doughnuts." She was direct but spoke kindly as a governess to her charges.

"You don't know for a fact that Pokamiakin killed Jake. If the sheriff arrests him, he could get lynched."

"I always put my faith in the good in people," she said in an ironic tone.

Then it dawned on me. She'd stolen Dutch's gun and given it to Ella to shoot Jake. Now she was trying to frame Poka Mika and collect the reward. How could I stop her? I stared morosely at my tattered shoes. "Look," I said, "any of fifty people might have killed him. There's so many unanswered questions about Jake."

"Like what?" she demanded, lying down on her bed. The soft glow of the lantern shone on her face, turning her complexion the texture of cream of wheat.

"Like . . . ah, did you know anything about him having a child?"

"Yeah. He used to talk about sendin' for the kid and bringin' the kid here. But why ask me? He was talkin' to Ella."

"You were eavesdropping?"

"Course not. I'm always hearin' voices. Sometimes I can't decide if they're comin' through the wall or from inside my head."

"But the child never came?"

"Somethin' about him bein' a no-good runaway, despite every advantage."

"Why'd Jake leave the child out of his will?" I moved the chair closer to her bed. She turned her head away from me. My legs were so fatigued from standing all day that the muscles in them jumped like frogs.

"I guess he disinherited him, bein' a ne'er-do-well. How should I know? I can't read minds. It ain't none of my beeswax, anyway." She had replaced the imperfection device, which caused a trail of saliva to run out of her mouth onto the pillow.

Down in the kitchen the doves rattled pans. Someone dropped an armload of wood on the kitchen floor. Ella screamed, "Quiet." Then a hush fell over the boarding house, broken periodically by Ella's groans.

Nightingale said, "She told me it's like someone's blasting gunpowder off over her right eye."

I thought maybe I could flatter Nightingale into tripping herself up. Jake had been blackmailing Ella, and I was desperate to find out why. "You should become a nurse. You'd be good at it," I told her.

"Go on with you," she retorted. "What I always wondered about you is, how come if you're so smart and have had so much book learnin', you ain't a schoolteacher?"

Because, God willing, I was going to be a doctor. And because the State Normal didn't certify girls wanted for grand larceny. The smell of cornbread and cabbage began to waft up from the kitchen. Below, I could hear Ella retching into her vomit pail.

"Ruby already has a very capable schoolmistress," I said.

"Don't it."

I lowered my voice. "Speaking of Carolina, why was Jake blackmailing her?" I'd use Carolina to break the ice, then I'd ask about Ella.

"Miss Goody Two-shoes?" Nightingale sat up, jerking her thin arms forward and smoothing the wrinkles out of her apron. I'd never noticed that she had such a graceful body, like a sculpture of one of the three graces. "He weren't. It was from her husband, Brownie." She relaxed, stretching her legs out and admiring her new boots, which were polished a deep oxblood.

She said, "Got his hands caught in the till. More than once, I hear."

"Embezzling?" I said, taken aback. I didn't for one minute believe her.

"Can't you talk like normal folk? You gotta always talk biggity?" She yawned. A look of bored exasperation fell over her face like a shade drawn over a window.

I had to buy myself time. "I want to strike a bargain with you," I said, realizing she'd never divulge any information about Ella.

"A bargain?" she asked, rising to her feet with renewed interest. We stood facing each other. I was the elder by a few years, but she was a good three inches taller.

"Hold off telling the sheriff about Pokamiakin until after the wake." It was the most serious swap I'd ever made, and I felt my face go rigid as a hanging judge's on sentencing day.

"Why? The sooner he's arrested and convicted, the sooner I get my reward. And then I'll be on the next stage to that surgeon in San Francisco."

I aimed my eyes at her. "Just hold off and I'll give you half interest in the mine Shaky left me."

Her expression told me that her thoughts had come to a screeching halt. "The Glory Hole?"

"The same," I assured.

"You know, you're not so bad," she said, bending over and pulling something heavy and awkward from her crate. It was a pair of lace-up shoes. They were scuffed but hadn't a tear or a hole and the laces were rawhide. "Want these?" she offered in place of handshake. "Your feet look the same size as mine, and them boots of yours is beyond fixing. If you polish these up you won't look a disgrace at the funeral tomorrow."

As if I wasn't humiliated enough, she thrust something else into my apron pocket. "And you can borrow these," she said. "But mind you don't stain them with bear grease."

I looked down, clutching the softest, snow-white pair of kid gloves I'd ever seen.

CHAPTER FIFTEEN

April 20

The funeral procession began in front of the Gem precisely at two o'clock by the deceased's own watch. Pines scented the air, and the sky turned the color of sage. In top hat and tails, Doc led the way down the street, crossing from side to side to avoid wagon-eating potholes. He was followed by a marching band of publicans pumping out strains of Chopin's funeral march on drum, fife, fiddle, harmonica, and several crude instruments I could not name. Behind the musicians was Dutch in his Civil War uniform leading Shaky's favorite pack mule. Then came the hearse driven by General Jones—a carryall pulled by Sheriff Barton's sleek black mare in patent leather harness. Ruby's red fire wagon followed the coffin. Then came Cranky Frank Belknap's stage, the sheriff himself accompanied by the town council, Ella and her girls in a surrey driven by Nightingale, and twenty springboard wagons, one of which bore me and my chair behind scores of miners and cattlemen. Indians led by Pokamiakin brought up the rear. Clad in buckskin and copper bangles, Mary carried a rose branch, alternately holding it like a talisman and then sweeping it through the air.

With so many horses about, I seized the opportunity to study every hoof and hoofprint. As the procession neared South Ruby, Dutch staggered and had to be given a leg up on the mule, riding to the graveyard. With my eyes constantly downcast, my sleuthing was mistaken for grief, and more than one hand was laid on my shoulder in sympathy.

"Don't a marchin' band give a funeral a special air?" said the woman riding next to me. Cranky Frank's wife, a full-figured matron with thin graying hair, had a kindly face as florid as a desert sunset. Mrs. Belknap held her newborn on her lap while two other children each grasped a handful of her skirt.

As the grave site came into view, the sun beat down unusually hard for April. Buzzards perched silently in the lower branches of the cottonwoods. After wagon brakes were locked and horses secured, we gathered our chairs around the gaping hole. I broke down, sobbing so hard that Nightingale had to swat my back so I'd stop choking.

The pallbearers—Dutch, Arizona Charley, the mine foreman Brownie Bitterroot, and Sheriff Barton—unbuckled the harness from the sheriff's black mare, making it into an apparatus in which to lower the casket into the hole, which the children had lined with willow. Carolina placed evergreen wreaths on the pile of black earth. Jones held the antsy hearse mare who shied repeatedly at the hole in the ground. Tossing her fine ebony head, she reared before the African could mollify her with his mournful calming voice. As the mare pawed the air with her forelegs, I studied the underside of her hoofs. Not a single imperfection on either side of the heel on either leg.

Dutch began singing Shaky's praises over the noise of floodwater lapping at the lower graves. "Herr Mine Owner has millions, vhile *die* miners barely earn enough to keep beans in his pot. Zhaky saw this and gave *das* workers of *die* vorld everything he had." Here Dutch's voice halted, and something that sounded like a square-wheeled cart running over a cobbled street came out.

Doc studied the crowd, his large head swiveling on his neckless body as he counted the vast number of lads who'd come from as far away as Salmon City and Nighthawk. "I've not seen so many soldiers since General Baird captured the Rebel guns on Missionary Ridge," he told Dutch and General Jones.

At the sight of the coffin being taken off the wagon, Sheriff Barton's black mare reared over top of the ex-slave who, for some unknown reason, looked suddenly stunned, as if he had completely forgotten he was holding onto a horse at all. Tearing the lines from his hands, the mare streaked off. Regaining his presence of mind as quickly as he'd lost it, Jones chased after her. Doesn't grief take us all out of ourselves? I thought.

Dutch doubled over clutching his left shoulder, claiming heartburn. Mary Reddawn, who stood beside the mound of earth among a group of aboriginals, bent down in sympathy, then began raking the dirt with her rose bramble. Hames rushed from the rows of chair-sitters and took Dutch's corner of the coffin. Mary flinched at the blacksmith's sudden lurch forward. Her blackened eye, while much improved thanks to Chin's herb doctoring, was swollen and had turned the color of calf's liver.

Grabbing the coarse sleeve of his navy blue uniform, I warned Dutch, "Best you get a nap before the festivities tonight."

"The mayor's decline begun the very same way." Carolina held Dutch's wrist, taking his pulse, then lay her marble-white fingers across his brow, feeling for a fever.

"Think I'm comin' down with somethin' myself," said Ella who sat beside me. Her doves gathered on her left, sitting as erect as a choir. Ella, who seemed to have recovered from her migraine, wore the brightest purple dress I'd ever seen. Her lips and cheeks were painted cranberry, and her brow was pebbled with sweat. She told her doves, "We're sure to have a full house tonight with all these gents in town." Ella smiled, rubbing her hands in satisfaction, then hugged her black-fringed shawl to her fleshy body. "Maybe that nice-lookin' fella with the fancy, gold-toothed smile I met at the ferry. Never will forget him."

I cringed. Ella dabbed her cleavage with a tear towel she kept stowed in the deep pocket of her skirt.

"Whole town's coming down with typhoid," said a nervous, skeletal-looking man. The local assayer, who went by the so-briquet Grasshopper Jack, wore a bowler hat cocked over one eye and a perfectly folded white handkerchief in the breast pocket of his black serge suit. A bottle protruded from his hip, and it was from this enclosure that he pulled a rag on which he wiped his nose. "One for show and one for blow," he said in a womanly voice.

From in back of me came a peal of laughter. I wasn't the only one to turn around to see Windy Pardee decked out in the largest flowered hat in the county. She wore a navy dress trimmed with silver braid, her yellow sausage curls expertly coiled under her canopy headgear. Over one arm was hooked a tatted parasol, the other linked into Arizona Charley's when he raced to her side after the coffin was lowered into the three-by-six-foot pit with its lid tight on, affixed forever now over Shaky's sweet face.

When Doc mounted a drygoods crate, all the graveside chatter suddenly ceased. As he cleared his throat my face flushed so hot that I couldn't breathe.

"Patrick McDonald, the Lord hath called thy name. . . ."

The sun felt like a branding iron pressing down on the top of my bonnet. Ella, whose mental faculties must have flown south, mistook me for one of her doves, saying, "There, there, dearie, don't cry. He's gone to his final reward as we all will." She clutched my knee. Her hands had deep dimples where knuckles ought to have been.

Pokamiakin sat silently on the ground next to Blindy and

the Belknap children who had no fear whatsoever of Indians. A white cabbage butterfly flickered near the little Belknap girl, landing on the puffy shoulder of her checked dress. It made me think of myself at that age when my da and I used to hunt butters for his collection. The cabbage fly hovered above one of the Indian's dogs as the skinny mongrel frisked from mourner to mourner smelling every pocket.

Ella swatted him away in disgust. "Why'd they let that cross-eyed redskin come? He's double dangerous. Gets you fixed in one eye while his other's on his next kill."

"When ye passest through waters . . . When thou walkest through fire . . ."

Mary Reddawn began swaying. Her sister, who bore a baby in a cradleboard on her back, moved her arms like a soaring bird caught in a downdraft. A cedar-colored youth pranced in place like a colt. The string of beads on his bare chest rose and fell, making a rattling noise, while the others droned native words I didn't understand. The squaws had high cherubic voices, and I never tired of listening to their a cappella.

"Psaw," said Ella in disgust. "Double psaw. Shell," she said, addressing me, though why she called me Shell, I did not know, "How'd them 'skins get invited?"

My first reaction was annoyance, then the germ of an idea began to mature.

The mine foreman came forward with an assistant and spread straw over the coffin's lid. I noticed that he'd waxed his penknife mustache into two sharp stilettos. His assistant, a youth with a weak chin and rumpled clothes, carried only a few handfuls. Was Shell the name Ella had intended for me should I join her staff?

I had an idea and ran with it. Instead of beating around the bush, I'd put it to Ella: Was Jake blackmailing her, and why? "Doesn't Brownie look spiffy," I began. "That's a spanking new funeral suit and store-bought shirt." I held my breath and took a chance that she thought I was one of her girls, "Mom"—all the doves called Ella, Mom—"why was Jake digging into Brownie's pockets?"

"To everything, a season . . . and a time . . ."

"Didn't like havin' his wages cut when Shaky sold the mine. Ain't no other jobs for a minin' engineer. Which is the trouble with givin' a man book learnin', if ya ask me. If everybody gets book learnin', who's gonna do the work? That's what I wanna know."

"He took the difference outta the till?" Had Nightingale been telling the truth?

"When the mine sold, it was a spoken agreement 'tween Shaky and the new owner that Brownie Bitterroot be kept on as foreman at his same salary. But spoken words don't mean nothing to an Easterner."

"Though Ye walk through the shadow . . ."

She continued, "And you'd think Mr. Mine Owner owed Mr. Mine Foreman more than wages for keeping Forr on what little feed he consents to eat. That boy looks like he needs a few extra slop buckets, don't he?"

"That's Forr?!" I stared at Brownie's assistant. The fire in his lecherous eyes had dimmed, and his once-perfect teeth were chipped. How he had become so transformed? "Has he ever paid our parlor a visit?" I prodded.

"Shell," Ella took a deep breath and dabbed at the drops of sweat on her neck with a grimy shred of towel. "A man can only burn from one fever at a time."

"We commit our brother departed in the sure and certain . . ."

"Don't care what kinda fever," Ella lectured, "lady, gold, or gamblin', men're built differently from gals whose candle has to burn at both ends if she wants to get by."

I felt as if I was leaping off a rock into water. "Was that Jake digging into your pocket, too, Mom?"

Forr paused, his eyes growing unfocused and confused. For an instant I was drenched in pity for Mrs. Ritters's godson. A moment later my expansiveness fell away, and I was washed over by another wave—"Deliver him not into the bitter pains . . ."—of frustration and impatience. Here was Shaky about to be consigned to the ground, and I knew nothing more about his demise this afternoon than I had on the day he died. And hadn't I turned a thousand stones and not gotten much closer to Jake's murderer? Was Ella ever going to answer me?

"Course. Has been for years. Threatened to expose my circus days," she said matter-of-factly. "Said he'd see me shamed and run outta the county."

The natives moved their dancing and swaying behind me, their song ringing out in time to the thud-thunk of hands slapping against a tree trunk. Doc stepped down from his crate and picked up a handful of dirt, salting the grave with it. Others went forward, one at a time, throwing on fistfuls of black soil. Dutch threw on the first shovelful, which, because of the straw, did not, thank the Lord, make that terrible hollow sound of dirt upon a casket lid that will shatter your heart into a million shards once you've heard it.

Arizona Charley returned to his seat behind me, and Cranky Frank went to quiet his children who'd begun to fuss because they weren't permitted to dance with the Indians. I heard a scuffle. Windy let out a little yelp. I could not bring myself to acknowledge what I presumed to be an ensuing argument over her favors by turning around but kept my eyes fixed on the dirt piling up on Shaky's coffin. Had she and her contingent killed Jake, or had Ella?

When the *P. McD.* monogrammed on the coffin's lid was completely obstructed, Doc climbed back up on the crate: "One generation passeth . . ."

Tears welled in my eyes. I almost never prayed, so it must have been Doc's spunk injected into those Bible words that inspired me to ask God for the cheek to put my next question to Ella, "Mom, *what* about your circus life . . . ?" Had she traded in belladonna as carnival folk were known to do, leading too many farm boys to an untimely death?

Just then Dutch walked over and handed me the shovel. I rose, carrying it to the dwindling pile of loose earth that emitted the smell of a newly harrowed cornfield. All that was mortal of our mayor was now delivered to the grass.

Suddenly, the native singing stopped. I turned around, scanning the crowd. A barrel-bodied white man stood amid the Indians. Some of the cedar-skinned youths waved their arms to heaven. One let out a war whoop as the sheriff wrestled the largest red man to the ground. Gents from the back of the funeral party tore off their shadbelly coats, running to assist. The sheriff stood up, pulling the Indian to his feet. Then with a satisfied air, our blacksmith tied Poka Mika's hands behind his back with a piece of harness. The sheriff pushed the shirtless red man forward, commanding, "Walk."

"Blessed are the pure . . ."

As I dropped the shovel and looked to Nightingale, my gaze froze on her, calculating the cost of her betrayal. But she stared back at me equally rage-faced. Rising from her chair, she went for a handful of dirt.

"Damn you for tricking me out of my reward money!" she shrieked, her split lip calling up the image of a rattler's forked tongue. "Damn you!" Then in a high, furious arc, her arm pitched the fetid clods into my face.

CHAPTER SIXTEEN

That night

Spooning food into my mouth, I felt too nervous about what might happen to Pokamiakin to taste the hillside of hasenpfeffer rabbit on my plate. Glancing at Doc, who stood near the Gem's back window, I sent mental teletypes: What do we do? When I thought I might be observed, I gazed out the window where snowy peaks had turned violet and a starlit sky hovered like a canvas ceiling. If Doc noticed me, he didn't let on, so I had no way of knowing if he'd been overtaken by another fit of silence.

Next to me, Mrs. Belknap passed out portions of General Jones's southern fried prairie chicken and her own salt pork pilau while screaming at her little son that she would beat him to a jelly if he didn't stay put under her skirt. Carolina held the new baby for her as Blindy ate a plate of hominy while sitting on a church pew pushed against the wall. Above him hung Shaky's collection of taxidermy art—two cougars, several stags, marmots, and beaver all rendered with a questionable amount of skill. Across the room, above the warped mirror behind the bar, were the birds: swans, eagles, and seagulls. Whenever a miner was down on his luck, Shaky had purchased one of his stuffed peltry for a five-dollar gold plug and drinks all around.

Blindy scooted across the pew, moving closer to where I stood serving potatoes seasoned with bacon fat and onion grass. Frank paused in front of him for a word with Sheriff Barton, and then Doc came over. The Gem was so crowded that there was hardly floor space to stand on or air to breathe. And Brownie Bitterroot wasn't the only one using an upside-down saucepan lid for a plate.

They talked of sluices and flumes, trail races and fifteen-dollars-a-day pay for a ton of ore. Then Frank said to Bald Barton, "Gotta remember to take my picks down to Hames to sharpen," and Sheriff Barton said to Frank, "Blacksmith swears them tracks at the crime scene matched an Injin cayuse, likely Pokamiakin's."

My spine stiffened.

"Point of fact," said Frank, the lines in his deeply creased face setting into canyons, "Arizona Charley heard that Injin threaten Jake's life. On more than one occasion." Frank jutted out his chin shaped like heel of his cowboy boot.

Someone thrust a mess plate in front of me. I spooned a heaping serving of potatoes onto it, then glanced up at the face of the hand that held it. Stifling a gasp, I went as rigid as the plank table. "More," Blackman Forrester, Jr. demanded. After giving him another helping, I stared at the nit sores in his shirt V, bloodied by scratching.

Swallowing a mouthful of air, I took a wild chance, making a pact with myself. If Forr recognized me, I'd leave Ruby to-morrow. Never mind my mineral claims, I'd find some other way to put myself through medical college. Now that Shaky was safely in the ground, I felt exhausted from fading into the shadows for fear Forr would point a finger at me. "Hello," I said. "Fancy meeting you so far from home. Remember me?"

Forr's pin eyes blazed. "Aren't you the laundress down in the ravine?" he said.

"Indeed." Ella was right. Addled by gambling fever. Moving on toward the venison hams, Forr shoved food into his mouth without giving me a second glance. I breathed a sigh of relief.

"Took him in for his own protection," said Cranky Frank, staring across the room at Nightingale whom Ella herded— along with her other doves—back to the boarding house where callers waited. Frank's scowl lines deepened. So many unfamiliar lads had crawled out of the mines. Down the street, the canvas walls of the faro hall bulged.

"Poka Mika won't get out free on bail this time," said Hames, joining the conversation. He tore into a loaf of bread with his tobacco-stained teeth. "No matter how many fancy-ass Spokane Falls lawyers he hires."

When Forr got to the end of the serving table, instead of being sociable, he walked out of the Gem onto the veranda and down the steps as if an invisible fisherman's line pulled him back to the Knights of the Pictured Pasteboards at the gambling tent.

Doc never met my eye and said nothing to Hames or Sheriff Barton. His large, dark pupils darted furtively around the room. Whom was he looking for? His gaze paused for a moment on the Widow Pardee and Arizona Charley seated so close together it would have taken a crowbar to pry them apart. I'd like to give Windy a sharp look myself. She could easily have been the one who framed Pokamiakin. Doc put his plate down in order to massage the tic in his right shoulder. His war wound always pained him when he got anxious. Sometimes after those old injuries flared up, they sealed Doc's lips for days at a time.

Nightingale said her good-byes, and various gents sprang forward kissing her hand. I wanted to square things with her, but if she met my eye at all it was to cut me to the ground. I watched to see if Frank Belknap would follow her.

"Francine, get your hands outta the biscuits 'n' gravy or your pa'll switch you good." Mrs. Belknap's face went the color of a red peony as she made furious gestures with a serving spoon against her daughter's backside. Francine wailed.

"Frank," Mrs. Belknap called after her husband, who was halfway out the door, "come back here'n tell this kid to shush-up before you give her something to cry about."

I ran after Nightingale, hoping to have a private word with her outside.

"You talk like quality," she said, "but when it gets right down to it, you're just a donkey between two bales of hay. I want my reward money *and* my shoes," she jeered.

"Yeah," chimed Squirrel and Mouse, their hands on their hips.

Nightingale pranced off flanked by the other doves, singing, "Wife, she's the curse of my life, I wish I was single again, I wish I was single . . ." over my pleadings, then broke into ringing laughter. Standing on the veranda staring after them, something caught my eye. Under the porch, Mary huddled with her husband. Chin's head was bound with a black scarf, the ties hanging down his back longer than his queue. He "Ollo, ollo'd" me, but Mary remained sullen and downcast.

Nightingale's shrill, "Single girl, goin' where she please; married girl, baby on her knees," overrode Chin's last "Ollo."

Inside, Carolina decreed that the apple fritters, cabbage strudel, and potato candies be brought out and set on the bar. (Land to Goshen, if she hadn't organized the desserts in alphabetical order.) Soon, with only a little lubrication, everyone sang Shaky's praises.

My plate and I stayed out on the porch. The noise of the vexed water and the scrape of gravel against boulder in Salmon Creek grew fainter as the sky darkened to ink. Mary motioned me under the veranda. Though it was a warm evening, she huddled beneath an old buffalo hide. "*Moose-moose* and *sapolil,*" she said, gesturing her stick arm toward the jail, a squat structure on the downhill side of Main.

"Meat and bread for your cousin? Yes, all right. Then I have to figure what to do before the whole village goes on a drunk and . . ."

"*Kah,*" she said, making a sudden gesture across the valley toward the reservation.

I listened, catching the faint strains of native music over the rushing water—a thunder of drums, human voices, and a faint tin-tin of bells.

"What's that?" I asked.

Mary grunted and went mute. A few of the lads came out to listen.

"Ghost Dancin'," said Hames. "I seen 'em do it in the Dakotas when I was Injin fightin' with the Seventh Cavalry. Got somethin' to do with the new moon."

"Damned Messiah craze has got hold of 'em," corrected the sheriff. He held a plate of goose crackling in one hand and a tin cup of bitters in the other.

"Course it has," agreed Hames, his expression crumbling like a rotting jack-o'-lantern. With his putrid mouth, I wondered how Windy could bear to be within a yard of him. Again I considered my case against each of my prime suspects. Had Mrs. Pardee convinced Hames to murder her husband so that she could have Jake's money and Charley's name—staking a reward to cover her tracks, then framing Pokamiakin? Though the boarding house contingent had the lead as far as opportunity and means were concerned, surely Jake couldn't have been extorting more than information from Ella. Who would care that she'd been the fat lady in a circus? Unless . . . unless, as a circus woman, she'd passed secrets from one side to other during the Civil War. Ella hadn't a political turn of mind, however, so I thought it doubtful.

And there was still the mystery of the horse with the flawed hoof. After spending all afternoon looking at hoofprints, I hadn't uncovered a thing. Neither Ella's hack nor Charlie's mount fit the description. Hames, on the other hand, could have borrowed one of the hundreds of horses at his disposal without anyone being the wiser.

"Name your poison 'n' I'll stand another round," sang the assayer, Grasshopper Jack.

"On *das* wagon train there was eight hundred schooners and Zhaky and I vere in *das* very last one," boomed Dutch from inside. His second serving of mountain oysters and a bottle of Doc's Wizard Remedy had restored his voice. "Ve ate all the dust in creation from Fort Leavenworth to South Pass. Today ve did not just bury our mayor, ve buried a piece of Kansas, Nebraska, and Vyoming." Laughter filled the saloon.

"My stars," exclaimed Mrs. Belknap, "the train must have been a mile long."

"Vhen ve saw a dust storm, *der* train captain said, 'Buffalo.' I thought, hostiles. But no. It vas *der* cavalry carrying a black flag. Ve all vondered, what's happened? I'll never forget that spring Lincoln vas shot. Zhaky tore up his shirt so that ve vould have black armbands. *Ja*, and one sourpuss vidow from Atlanta tied a vhite dish rag around her arm. She vas dealt with immediately and didn't put her face out of her vagon for a veek. In the end Zhaky vas the only Yankee she vould speak to."

"What do them Injins think it is? The Second Comin'?" asked Hames, pointing across the valley.

"The comin' of the great Medicine Man of the North," replied Sheriff Barton's self-assured voice. He and the blacksmith stood only a few feet from me, but either they didn't notice or didn't care that I was there. Bald Barton was relatively new in town and had run unopposed for office. He wore the tightest trousers and the highest-heeled boots in the county. No one knew where he'd come from or if he'd had a lick of experience.

"I've heard it called the Porcupine curse," Barton went on.

"Chief Porcupine claims to know a dance that'll bring back the buffalo and return them Injins their lands."

"Should lock up the dancers and their 'Christ,'" said Hames.

"Didn't we just arrest Poka Mika and get a good start on that job?" asked the sheriff.

"If there's any leftovers, could I take the prisoner a plate?" I asked.

Both men turned toward me as if one of the porch posts had spoken. Then simultaneously both heads jerked in the other direction as the iron triangle on the back stoop of Ella's boarding house clanged furiously. An indistinguishable hoot came from one of the hotel's upstairs windows, followed by heated threats, and then two shots.

"What kinda trouble them hens in now?" The sheriff put down his cup and plate, streaking off the steps of the Gem and along the sidewalk. More shots came from an upstairs window, followed by another round of cursing.

By now a crowd had gathered out on the porch of the saloon. From inside came the twang of instruments being tuned— fiddles, bugles, and a sweet accordion.

A hand clamped down on my shoulder, the nails digging in. "You have to do something," whispered an authoritative voice. I looked up and saw Carolina glowering down on me.

"About that Indian. You know what'll happen."

I? I have to do something? She picked a fine time to buddy with me, though I had to admit I swelled with importance. "But what?"

"Has Doc got any ideas?" she asked. We walked back inside and leaned over the desserts. Using a dried gourd as a bowl, she served Blindy a helping of pemmican pie.

I couldn't help but regard this situation with a little contempt. Just as when an expectant mother got herself in a fix and the midwife had to fetch the doctor after hours of fruitless labor (which the midwife should have done in the first place), now that we were really in Hell's Kitchen, Carolina demanded that Doc *do something.*

"I've been trying to get his attention, but . . ."

Dutch told the mourners, "That night Zhaky dreamed he heard *vater.* The next morning at first light ve hiked into a coulee. Did ve find *vater? Nein,* but ve found vet sand, so ve kept going and, *jawohl,* ve find the prettiest *klein* spring! Ve built a signal fire, and the whole train came running—even the tiniest *kinder*—with anything that vould hold *vater,* and ve made a bucket brigade back to where the stock vere corralled."

"Do something! Our sheriff's sure to hand over his jail key to the lynch mob. The only good news is that Jake's not here to organize a justice committee, so things may take a little longer." Carolina's high patrician forehead furrowed into the sable braid coiled around her head. Her mouth was fixed and her fists clenched. "Find Doc. You're his little Highland Mary, you can persuade him to make a plan. I'll do anything to help."

I stiffened at her insinuation. Studying her braid, it reminded me of a snake ready to strike. Then scanning the room for Doc, I saw his stoop-shouldered silhouette.

Carolina's voice flew at me. "Don't stand there like a turnip!"

Her son, who had been listening, parroted her. "Turnip," he said impishly.

She turned on the boy and for a moment I thought she might swat him. "Hush!" Blindy flinched, a look of fright stung his sightless blue eyes.

Carolina turned back toward me and continued. "After my parents came west, they saw all the work that had to be done to rekindle the life of the savages. My mother suffered an unspeakable indecency at the hands of a man who thought Indians an obstacle to civilization and believed they should be removed by whatever means possible. I couldn't live with myself if this camp . . ." Her voice faded like the wick of a snuffed candle trailing away in a wisp of smoke. "I owe it to her memory." She began to shake.

"I'll speak with him this minute," I said, inching toward Doc. I'll make him talk, I thought, I have to.

Prying my way between the funeral suits and full skirts, men in fresh-made chaps stinking of untanned leather and men who already reeked of whiskey, I caught Doc by the coattail. He had just stepped out onto the veranda, where everyone waited to see if more shots would be fired from Ella's boarding house. Conversation ceased and, across the valley, the native drums grew louder. Inside, musicians began sawing their fiddles: "Who's gonna shoe your pretty little foot, who's gonna glove your hand?"

"Doc," I said, "we're needed at Ella's." I amazed even myself at how well I lied.

His head swiveled toward me, "We?" I'd actually gotten him to speak, so I didn't much care what he said, though for an instant I thought he didn't recognize me.

"It's a delicate matter," I told him.

"Turkey in the hay, dance all night and work all day."

Just then Dutch elbowed his way through the mourners, continuing to spin his yarn as he went. He paused and looked down at me, then addressed his audience, "And here is Frau Ryan who has taken a lock of Zhaky's hair to embroider into *ein* keepsake." The crowd burst into war whoops and a thunderclap of applause.

My face must have turned as pale as cottage cheese. How could I have forgotten! Dutch rushed past me, continuing his saga out on the porch.

Doc leaned over, "Don't say anything. There's a cure for this oversight."

Stepping out the back entrance into the dark, I reeled from my stupidity.

"Who's the injured party?" Doc asked, heading for his coat

and bag in Shaky's quarters, which were being used as a cloak-room.

Never before had I made such a stupid blunder. "I don't know that there is one. I had to say something to get you out of there. Doc, what can be done?" The little room was heaped with coats and blankets and sleeping children. Entering it, I could not bear to look at the bed where Shaky had died.

"My hair's not a perfect match, but it's gray. Won't be the first time . . ."

"That's not what I meant." (Was it true? All those locks of hair from the dearly departed kept by a loved one—had they come from someone else?) "Carolina's mortified they'll lynch Pokamiakin before the night's through," I said.

"Aye," said Doc. " 'Tis been eating at me."

"She says we have to do something and that she'll help. I got permission to take the prisoner a plate, so I can get him a message at the same time."

Doc's head settled into the saddle of his buffalo hump. My pulse hammered through my chest, and I perspired so hard I thought my dress would wilt. Doc looked at the situation from one angle, then another. When he got it into focus, I took in his every word: blasting caps and gunpowder placed outside the northeast side of the jail, balanced on a piece of stove wood six inches above the ground where he could get a clear shot at it.

As we returned to the festivities, the accordion started to sing, "And hit em up a tune called Turkey in the Straw." Doc asked me, "Have you seen General Jones?"

"No, why?"

"When Bald Barton's mare broke away from him at the bur-ial, she gave him a good whack on the head with a hind hoof. Wondered if he was all right." That was Doc, always thinking about his flock.

"He must have been here. His fried prairie chicken's on the table. Though, now that you mention it, I haven't seen him all night."

Inside someone tried to organize a Virginia reel. There weren't enough women to go around, so a white armband designated a gent as a lady. And wouldn't you know it, Grasshopper Jack, the assayer, was the first to volunteer for a white streamer to be tied to his biceps.

"I'll fix the prisoner a plate," I told Carolina, who immediately began to fill the lid of a dutch oven with salmon bake and potatoes. "If you could take your son home to bed and bring back a little black powder from the Ruby Mine's stores . . ."

Her eyes turned as cool and hard as creek pebbles. "Are you speaking to me?"

Good God, of course I was. "You said you'd help." I pulled myself up to my full height and spread my feet shoulder's distance apart. "You said you'd do anything. Though I suppose I could go rustle up some blasting caps, but it could take half the night."

"All right," she said, exhaling a long heavy breath. "All right."

"Then you're to accompany me to the jail when I take the prisoner his dinner."

"Why?"

"For the sake of propriety. And because I need a witness. No one would dare doubt your word." I wondered if she had a single friend anywhere.

While she was gone, I went to the bar and, may the Heavenly Father strike me dead, downed a glass of bitters, followed by a thimble or two of tincture to fortify myself and calm my nerves. Ever since my da met his end in the bottom of a bottle, I swore I'd never bend my elbow even once. But here I was, ten years later, in West Babylon, Washington, becoming my father's daughter.

Sitting down on a splintery bench, I sang along with the musicians as they thumped out "Careless Love." Sheriff Barton joined in, playing a banjo. Soon the news flew around the room: He'd taken one of Ella's callers into custody.

"To keep that no-good company," someone said.

"Best way to keep an Injin is in solitary," retorted Hames.

I wondered if the new prisoner was some unfortunate lad who'd either reminded Nightingale of her late husband or who'd accidentally intruded on one of Ella's headaches.

When Carolina returned, she actually wore a smile, or maybe it was the washtub whiskey that helped me see everything in a cheerier light. I figured that she too must have taken a bracing sip. As we waited for the mourners to get good and lubricated, we obliged a gent in a dance or held Mrs. Belknap's baby so that she could have a romp.

"Now you see what a woman can do, outdo the devil and her old man too."

My new boots gave me blisters, so I stood on the sidelines clapping. Carolina took up the comb and tissue while Mrs. Belknap beat rhythm with a mortar and pestle.

I had another little tincture and noticed that Doc was imbibing gin, a never-seen-before sight. By now the sheriff had returned from rechecking his prisoners and was dancing with Windy while Arizona Charley held up the wall, wearing a sour expression. At ten-thirty I caught hold of the back of Carolina's skirt. "We'd better get that poor red man his dinner," I said. We picked up the supper tray and walked out the back entrance.

Immediately, my face and hands were attacked by the first mosquitoes of spring, and I almost dropped the tray. Catching it made my head spin. I had to sit down for a moment on a mounting block.

"Take deep breaths," Carolina instructed, "clears the senses." What little moon shown was bright, and our shadows spread as dark as creosote across the street.

You'd think it was payday the way the sidewalk was cram-jammed with new faces. I leaned back against a hitching post. Mansmells of tobacco and sweat filled my head. Opening my eyes, I looked across Main at a buckskin horse and what struck me as a familiar rider making his way past the Ruby First National. "Who's that?" I called. My fuzzy brain couldn't hang a name on him, though his Gaelic features made me think of home. "It's me husband," I muttered.

"Excuse me?" said Carolina.

"Nothing but blarney." It wasn't me talking, but the drink. As horse and rider were eaten by darkness, I thought, didn't his long legs remind me of the man I married.

Then the idea of witnessing an innocent lynched for a murder I can't solve spurred me to pull my taffy brain together. Taking a firm grip on the supper tray, I rose, striding across the street behind Mrs. Bitterroot. "Why did Brownie leave the festivities so early?" I asked.

She flinched at the bold way I referred to her husband. "Getting the mine books in order," she replied. "Mr. Forrester's due any day and . . ."

The rest faded into the rush of blood in my ears as I remembered that Mr. Forrester might recognize me. Across the valley the Indian drums pounded.

"Don't forget," I whispered to Carolina after we'd headed down alley. "Plant it outside in the northeast corner."

I entered the log jailhouse that contained two iron cages. The roof was low and without a ceiling, and the smell of mice droppings almost made me retch. In one cell lay a man wrapped in a blanket, snoring louder than a horse. Pity his poor wife, I thought. In the other Pokamiakin crouched on the floor, head between his knees, hands crossed over the back of his neck. He moaned in long, even tones, imitating the rush of the river.

"Here's some food," I said. He continued moaning. I wondered if he'd heard me.

"Pokamiakin." In the next cell, the sleeper's snores caught. He thrashed his blankets, then the heavy breathing resumed its rise and fall.

"*Moose-moose*, meat," I said, remembering that a native could seldom be coaxed into a white man's house, to say nothing of being locked in a cage next to a stranger.

I went outside, grabbed a stick, and reached it through the bars. First I poked his thigh, then his chest. Nothing. A gentle tap. A whack. He looked up, startled.

"*Moose-moose*," I said, pointing to the plate I'd put on the gunny sack–covered floor and shoved under the bars. Darkness enveloped me. The only light came from the moon filtering through the open door, as pale and thin as mare's milk.

His bonfire eyes leveled at me without recognition and filled with hate. For a moment I was not at all unhappy about him being on one side of those bars and me on the other. I shuddered. If Mr. Forrester recognized me, it would be me inside that cell.

"When you hear shots, stand as close to the barred door as you can and away from the wall," I told him in a low voice, enunciating each word. Even in the dim light his crossed eyes glowed crimson. Whether he understood me, I couldn't say; he had turned as mute and sullen as Mary Reddawn. When the sleeper in the next cell stirred and muttered something unintelligible, I turned, almost tripped over my own boots, and fled.

Carolina and I reconnoitered in the street. A nod of her shawled head told me that she'd planted the black powder where it would do the most good.

"Pray he doesn't get blown to smithereens," I whispered, noticing that Chin and Mary watched us from under the Gem's veranda. Inside the saloon, raucous laughter and fiddle playing blared. Steam rose from the roof shakes, and I actually thought I saw the building breathe. Wild as the mourners had become, their noise didn't drown out the strains of native music from across the valley. The Indians' drums had grown louder, and I imagined their dancing becoming more frenzied.

Carolina touched my shoulder. "You're trembling."

I nodded, grabbing for breath. She placed one hand over my brow and another on my shoulder. For all her refinements, there was a surprising strength in her palms. I saw that she must be a fine nurse and would be a comfort to anyone ill. If only she weren't so bullheaded, she and Doc would make a perfect team.

"In less than an hour, this will all be in the past," she said in a controlled whisper. "We will never speak of it again."

"Not a word." I held my finger to my lips in a gesture to Chin and Mary.

Slipping through the back door of the Gem, we were met by the acrid smell of outhouse whiskey. The floor shone with tobacco juice and shook in the foot-stomping rhythm of Ruby City's anthem, "My Sweetheart's the Mule in the Mines," punctuated by knee slapping and bottle breaking. "On the bumper I sit, I chew and I spit. All over my sweetheart's behind." Everyone had converted dinnerware to cymbals.

"Ruby's citizenry has lived without the restraints of Sunday school influences for too long," said Carolina, collecting empty pie tins.

The effects of the tincture wore off, and so I had another and then another. Carolina, lost in a flurry of dish stacking, imbibed nothing. When the gents asked that the table be cleared from the dance floor, all hell broke lose. Square dances I'd never heard of were called, words I didn't know the meaning of (and knew better than to ask) employed. Most of the ladies retired to the sidelines while the lads bucked and reared as furiously as unbroken horses. In between dances, they fell into alternating fits of weeping and laughter. We'd gotten the deed done just in time.

"For years ve shared fry pans and blankets," said Dutch, mourning his lost partner.

Mrs. Belknap screamed with outrage when someone used her behind as a drum.

Arizona Charley began a verse of "Vacant Chair." Of course, every so often one of the Union vets would let out a wailing of "Lincoln & Liberty," which was answered by several verses of "Dixie." For such a variegated population, we got on remarkably well—when sober. But it wasn't long before shots began to ring in the streets.

I dove under a pew pushed up against the wall. The room filled with the terrible roar of gunshots and hammer smoke. There is nothing in this world like the smell of lead and black powder, the way it hangs in the air longer and thicker than pipe tobacco. I covered my ears to block the drunken screams and terrified woman shrieks. The Belknap children, who'd been sleeping, began to cry as if they were about to be slaughtered.

Horses unaccustomed to a shootfest pulled down their hitching posts and galloped away. Because every make of firearm has its own special *pop*, I counted shots, trying to ascertain which came from Doc's gun, but gave up when I got past twenty. Then a blast shook the windows, its echo bouncing off the granite ledge above town.

We'd done it! A hole in the north side of the jail. The Gem shook as if an earthquake had struck, the walls shuddering in a multitude of aftershocks. As a final touch, a few minutes later various powder kegs exploded up in the digs—miners who'd already made their way home, thinking our blast part of the send-off. I sidled up as close to the wall as I could get, my back protected by the pew.

The explosions ceased, the fray quelling to gunfire. One lad would blast from the livery end of the town, and another, at the opposite end of Main near Ella's, would answer his shot. In the alley on the other side of the log wall, I heard a dull noise between gunshots, as if something was being dragged along the ground, a heavy sack, a saddle maybe. I heard grunting, and then the dragging noise stopped. A man moaned.

Someone was hit! "Doc!" I called, but was answered with wild laughter and another round of rifle shot. "Someone's hurt!"

One of the mourners fired out the back door, laughing like he was in an asylum. The groaning on the other side of the wall persisted. A bad thought occurred to me: It was Pokami-akin, injured in the blast! When the gunshots thinned to almost nothing, I got up and walked, head down, to the side door. I heard a commotion in the street, loud snarling voices, reminding me of one of Mr. Ritters's Long Island fox hunts, when the hounds had just caught the scent and the huntsmen galloped madly across the cornfields shouting and cracking their whips.

The alley reeked of saltpeter and urine. Slowly, as my eyes grew accustomed to the dark, I made out the shape of a rain barrel. Everywhere broken glass glistened like dew in the moonlight. Carefully, I inched forward. The groaning came from near the veranda where a dark shape lay huddled next to the side of the Gem like a wounded dog trying to right itself after being kicked by a horse. A sweet, salty scent flew into my face, a smell I knew all too well. Blood.

It wasn't Pokamiakin. "Jones! Don't move!" Sweat gleamed on his nut-colored face. "I'll find Doc as quick as I can." The ex-slave held a hand over his right shoulder, and I could see that there was quite a burn hole in his once-white shirt. You'll never make any kind of doctor, I told myself, if you can't even look at a bullet gouge.

"Chin," Jones said. "Get Chin."

"Chin? All right." Make the patient comfortable. Get him what he wants until you find Doc. No, get clean rags for a pressure bandage. Now. There's no time. I ran down the alley, stopping in front of the veranda before going back inside to look for something to use as a dressing. "Chin," I called. "Chin." Huddled under the front steps was a single shape, that of Mary Reddawn. She turned slowly toward me, *"Klatawa."*

"Chin's gone?"

She turned away, staring through the porch slats at the valley below. And that's when I noticed. At first I thought that it was merely the waters of Salmon Creek that had quieted, but no. The Ghost Dance across the river on the reservation had also ceased.

There was only one thing to be done. I pulled up the skirts

of my wedding dress and yanked off my petticoat, tearing it into bandage strips. The frill sewn around the hem could be used as gauze. "Hold on, General," I called, winding the bandage as fast as I could, trying to keep it off the filthy ground. His was a gaping wound and invited infection. Securing the ruffle under my arm, I held the rolled bandage in both hands, ready to bind up his shoulder. Walking back along the wall, I thanked God for the dark—that way I couldn't see the terrible damage so clearly. Stumbling over a bottle, I accidentally dirtied the bandage. Catching my footing, I felt my way along. But when I got to the place I'd left Jones—about three coffin lengths from the Gem's back door—he wasn't there. He was nowhere at all in the alley; gone, utterly and completely gone.

CHAPTER SEVENTEEN

April 21

The next morning I woke up feeling like Pokamiakin's search posse had ridden through my mouth and across my face. Poisoned by drink, I couldn't hold my head upright but went around with a huge pulsing wound-of-a-brain. "God strike me dead if blue ruin ever passes my lips again," I groaned.

Staggering across the room in order to let in the morning air, I was overcome by two thoughts (amazing, actually, that I could hold even a single thought in my damaged brain). The first was that Shaky now slept under the sod without me being able to prove a thing about foul play leading to his demise. The second was, What had happened to Jones? My imagination ran wild. I had looked for him, as best as I could in the dark, for hours before staggering home, but to no avail. Was Jones afraid that if Doc couldn't be found, I would treat him and so he'd fled? Or had he known I'd broken Poka Mika out of jail and dreaded having anything to do with me for fear of being judged an accomplice?

Looking in my shard of a mirror, I saw a redheaded, red-eyed resident of West Babylon, a place where no one would think twice about stringing up an Indian lover from a pine tree. Imagine it! Hanging a woman. Crowds would ride here to witness the sensation. My head throbbed like a blacksmith's hammer beating against an anvil: *Run*, pounded the mallet. I went outside to my little privy and had a good long vomit.

Tillicum nickered for his morning corn. After feeding my poor, neglected pony, all I could manage to do was sit and hold my hands to my temples as if I'd been shot. Run? I couldn't walk upright. And how could I leave before I'd heard from Willamette Institute of Medicine? I'd meant to bound out of bed first thing this morning and begin securing pickets around Shaky's grave. The idea of wolves digging up the poor man's sleeping place made my head hang even lower.

More sharp thoughts stabbed my brain. Shaky's death aside, Jake's murder kept nagging at me. How would Windy have gotten hold of the missing twin revolver? The more I worried, the sicker I felt. And what about the horse with a sheared heel? In a flash it occurred to me: Hames had placed that particular unshod horse at the murder scene. Hames was a suspect. Was evidence he gave reliable?

If only I could step back and see the whole mess with a detached constable's stare. Someone was lying, obviously. Maybe everyone was lying. Maybe it was more than just a simple conspiracy between a widow (who'd not even bothered to make a single pretense of grief) and her husband's cronies. Maybe they were all in this together: Windy, her suitors, and Ella. Or had I taken the wrong turn and embraced a false clue? Something about the loss of the pearl-handled revolver troubled me, though I couldn't say what. The truth was, if my own hide—and Mary's cousin's—wasn't at stake, and if I didn't have such a strong hunch that Jake's murder and Shaky's were connected, I wouldn't care who had avenged themselves on Jake Pardee or what deeper truth they conspired to conceal.

All morning, horsemen trailed past my door either on the way home to their claims in the higher elevations or down into the sage ocean searching for the escaped Indian. The waters of Salmon Creek must have fallen back into their banks, because I could barely hear the rush of the freshet. Mary had never brought wood, nor had Chin delivered water, so I assumed both were lying low. Several bewhiskered, pouchy-eyed gents stopped to ask Doc's whereabouts. As to General Jones's fate, I could only hope that some able-bodied lad had borne him to Doc's surgery and helped clean and suture his wounds. God knows, I'd be no use to anyone today. Putting my head between my knees, I remembered that when Da felt particularly under the weather, my stepmother said that if she could get something bland into his stomach to sop up the poison, he'd be on the mend.

Plunging my hands into this and that pot, I finally found a rockrose root. I made tiny rabbit-teeth marks in the parsnip-colored vegetable, chewing the small pieces a hundred times before swallowing. I thought of brewing coffee, but the fire was dead. I hadn't much kindling and was low on water. I lay on my bed and tried to sleep but could only gaze helplessly at the canvas ceiling, studying the elephant-shaped blobs the waterproofing made in the fabric. How long before the sheriff had me under suspicion?

Then I heard a shod horse approach, and Doc appeared. His eyes were puffy and his pupils tiny as fly specks. After straightening my apron, I fixed a loose coil of hair behind my ear. "Did they find Poka Mika?" I asked, not really wanting to hear the answer. As Doc glanced at my cold stove, I felt more than a pang of guilt that I'd not a sip of potato soup to offer. President Lincoln, Doc's fine black gelding, stood patiently hobbled outside. Somehow Doc had managed to get his mount's missing shoe replaced.

"No and they shan't, lass," he said wearily.

I let out a breath of relief. Doc took a second glance at the cold stove and empty pot. "Probably buried himself in the sand under a saltwort bush. Nay, they shan't find the mon unless they dig up the valley." His eyes asked, Not even hot water for tea?

"I had a drop too much last night," I said by way of apology. "But the mayor would have been proud of that send-off. As for myself, why'd I take that glass of bitters and rum? Pure snake venom. Do you know, I actually thought I saw my husband."

" 'Tis the loneliness of this place," Doc said. Unbuttoning his coat, dust the color of rusty nails rained onto the floor. "A pretty lass like yourself should have a peck of chums and admirers." Doc ran a finger around the neck of his green cable knit sweater. As he did so, I studied the garment for wear, regretting that I still hadn't had the time to darn the elbows. Truly it was one of the handsomest knits I'd ever seen.

"I'm much better at judging horseflesh than people and husbands," I said, shaking my head in the hopes of dispelling past mistakes. "I take after my da in that respect.

"You're sure they won't find Pokamiakin?" I asked, knowing full well he could promise me no such thing.

"Nay, a more cunning creature never lived." Doc chewed his giant thumbnail, then balled his meaty hands and thrust them in his pockets, searching for his soapstone pipe.

"I've never done anything truly wrong before," I said. "What if I'm found out?"

"I'll always vouch for you, lass. The only other living soul to tell on you is Mrs. Bitterroot, and she's as guilty as you are."

"She has the demeanor of a nun. They'd hang it all on me. Especially if they find Pokamiakin and drag it out of him how he managed to escape."

"Unlikely," said Doc. He sat down at the table, lit his pipe, and began tugging on it. Little white plumes sprouted from the bowl. After a brief silence, he said, "And, all things being equal, it would be better that everyone go on thinking Poka Mika was Jake's murderer and leave it at that."

Though pipe smoke usually doesn't have a bad effect on me, I thought my stomach would turn itself inside out. The muscles in the back of my neck tightened, making my head throb so much I imagined that it would split open like a dropped tomato. "It's not that I don't see your point," I said, "but we must clear him, we must get to the bottom of this. If I could only find that missing gun."

" 'Tisn't justice, lass. And don't think I'm saying that it is. 'Tisn't a perfect world. But it may be the only way to keep the lid on a boiling pot."

Doc's pragmatism only made me more determined to put the situation right. As my stepmother used to say, redheads had a stubborn nature, and I was no exception.

I said, "Been several fellas asking for you." The pounding against my temples abated for a moment, and I imagined that the good news about Pokamiakin being still at large made it so.

Doc waved his hand as if to say "psaw," though he never did, being a proper Scotsman. " 'Tis an awkward position that I'm in with those chaps, lass. Most are probably wanting tincture of opium to quell the hunger they acquired from Jake. I've only so much laudanum—it's not easy to come by due to the unreliability of the overland stage. My responsibility's to the sick and wounded."

Didn't I know about the unreliability of the mail stage. Would I ever get my letter? And what about Doc's glasses?

Then I remembered the poor suffering General. "Did you get Jones stitched up?"

Doc's caterpillar brows were a puzzle. "What's this?"

"General Jones, he got hit in the shootfest last night. I found him lying in the alley. He asked me to get Chin for him, but when I got back, he was gone."

Doc bolted to his feet, " 'Tis the first I've heard of it! Poor mon, must've tried to crawl up to his digs." Doc was through the door with such suddenness that his horse took fright and, though hobbled, plunged down the ravine. Loose rock and mud buried poor President Lincoln to his knees, and I feared he would lose another shoe in the commotion.

I'd never seen Doc so determined to be on his way and decided that it was his red-rimmed eyes and day's growth of lead-colored beard, not merely his sudden fit of silence, that made his expression look so fierce. He mounted, taking the uphill fork. Good God, I'd let him get away without a lock of his hair to embroider into Shaky's keepsake.

Cursing my stupidity, I decided I needed some pitcher plant tea. But there was still no sign of Chin. As Doc's horse's footfalls died in the distance, I grabbed a pail and made my way slowly down to Salmon Creek. It was dangerous drinking floodwater, but if I could manage a fire and boiled it a good long time, it would serve my purpose.

The freshet had indeed subsided, and my feet sank in silt. Which made me think: The problem in fording Salmon Creek wouldn't be the cold and the current but my horse miring down in sludge. All the same, a voice in my throbbing head pleaded: *Run. Now.*

Then, as I slowly made my way back, I saw a fast-strutting man headed for my door. Coming down the ravine, he caught a rock in his high-heeled boot and stumbled, his tight trousers straining against his thighs beneath the tie strings of his chaps. I should have known who it was, but, because of his hat, I could not see his bald head. And before I realized that those glistening iron rings hanging from his belt next to his knife sheath were handcuffs, Sheriff Barton hailed me. I froze where I stood, feeling like one of the butterflies my da and I used to collect, my wings pinned to a cold, unyielding wall.

CHAPTER EIGHTEEN

ＨＨad I walked into a trap?

It was a long tramp to the Skookum House, as the jail was called, and I tried everything I could think of to make it longer. When the unpainted buildings on South Main came into view, I stopped to reconsider the sheriff's odd request.

While delivering his message, Sheriff Barton had sung on and on about his qualifications for the office of mayor of Ruby City. Women had the right to vote—in local elections only—and clearly he wanted to harvest every possible ballot.

Listening to the insect hum of his voice, I had stood holding my pail of gritty creek water, unable to take my eyes off the handcuffs jangling from his belt. Freckled with rust, one bracelet connected to the other by a heavy chain of six oblong links.

The sheriff's denim shirt stretched tightly across his swelled chest, and I thought his buttons would burst before he finished. "The chap we took in last night has been crying for a Miss Pearl. I asks him, what business he's got with our laundress? He commenced to laughin' his head off. Swears he knows you. 'Bring me the laundress,' he says. Might ya step in today, ma'am, and put his pesterin' to rest? I'd be obliged."

I nodded, "Certainly." The strength drained from my hands,

and I almost dropped my bucket. "What's he charged with?" I asked in a voice so breathless that I had to repeat myself. The sheriff's campaign smile remained affixed to his pale, angular face. "Indecent liberties," he said flatly. Even through my liquor-poisoned brain I wondered what could constitute an indecent liberty in Ruby. "And passing water with malicious intent," he added, raising an eyebrow to indicate there was more to the story.

"What might his name be?" I finally managed to stutter, keeping my eyes on the rocky soil in front of my door. The ground sparkled with flint.

Sheriff Barton shrugged. "Didn't ask him."

I thought, Mr. Ritters. It had to be.

Watching the sheriff struggle up the ravine, I abandoned the idea of pitcher plant tea. My blood was up and my hangover began to subside. Was the sheriff thickheaded or terribly cunning? Hauling the laundress away wouldn't have been good for his political career. But cajoling me into walking to the Skookum House of my own free will would be quite an accomplishment. Just who waited for me on the other side of those bars?

I was in no hurry to find out.

I put a fresh apron over my tattered dress, then pinned my hair up with two tortoiseshell combs, Davy's last present to me. The very sight of the fleur-de-lis designs carved into them made me want to cry. I always felt like a proper lady wearing them. Which, if I was going to be arrested, would certainly give the right impression.

<hr />

The late-morning light whitened the granite mountains above town, and the glacier atop the highest dome of Three Devils shone like the skull of a huge animal bleaching in the sun. I took the longest route to the Skookum House, heading first to the trading post to purchase some nails for the fence encircling the mayor's grave. Two nickels and a quarter clanked in my pocket against Shaky's gold watch.

Not a soul was on the street. Most, like Doc, came in early this morning from Pokamiakin's search party, got a fresh horse, then went out again. The exception was Pigeon Belcher, the mail carrier who'd just come over the mountains. Pij had suffered terrible frostbite, and Doc had had to amputate several toes, as you might recall. Born clubfooted, Pij walked with one shoe perpendicular to the other, so God knows how he'd plodded through snowdrifts eight feet high carrying his mail pouch without losing his life instead of just a few phalanges. (According to my medical books, that's what fingers and toes were called. Time to start using their proper names, I told myself.) Now, with the help of a cane and a crutch, Pigeon Belcher hobbled along the plank sidewalk, both feet bound in bandages covered by raggedy gunny sacks. When I offered to hold his elbow and steady him along as far as the mercantile, his expression brightened.

"First day up," Belcher said. "My sight's near normal again. Never could run, so I ain't missed my toes." A small man with a gaunt face, his piercing hazel eyes were stained with brown rings from having tea bags affixed to them as a treatment for snow blindness.

"Take it easy," I told him. For a split second I forgot about the stranger at the jail. Pij asked if, after I'd finished at Windy's, I'd help him cross the street to the livery where he bunked. I jumped at the chance to have a look in Jake's office for evidence of freebooting and finally find out why Pardee had been digging into Ella's pockets.

At the trading post, Pij sat on the bench outside while I fished around in the lard pail by the door. Please, I prayed, let there be a letter for me. I pulled out a long envelope. It was fresh and white and had my name on it! But the return address was not that of the medical college. It stated: Charles B. Wolff, Justice of the Peace & Attorney at Law, Ruby City. Why would Arizona Charley be writing to me? Tearing the envelope open, the message was brief: "This is to confirm our meeting of April 22nd at 12:30 P.M. to discuss a personal matter of utmost importance." Tomorrow!

I must have stood there looking dumbfounded because Pij said, "Not bad news, I hope. Jus' remember, I didn't bring that letter. Frank musta brung it on the stage. Stage mail is more likely bad news than mail hauled in over the mountains, point of fact."

"No," I said, "just puzzling." As I stuffed the envelope into my apron pocket, someone rapped on the trading post's tiny window. Looking up I saw Windy's powdered face and a halo of straw-colored curls pressed to the glass.

"Received letters're twenty-five cents," she called in a mocking, childlike voice.

Turning the cold iron doorknob, I entered the mercantile, which reeked with lavender scent. Except for the proprietress, it was completely empty of its usual fellowship. Windy stood behind the counter, wearing a blouse with huge leg-of-mutton sleeves filled out with wadded newspaper. "Most folks pay before they open 'em up," she said, thumbing through a stack of catalogs. "If it's credit ya need, I could give it to ya on this here Never Break Warner Corset." She pointed to a Marshall Field's *Coming Styles*. "White or buff?" She studied me hopefully, whispering, "Twenty cents more for black."

"But the letter wasn't mailed. Charley put it in the pail outside," I protested, ignoring her sales pitch. Why hadn't he called at my door, stating his business? Or spoken to me last night at the wake? Did he have a "Wanted" poster with my picture on it?

"Regulations," she said, pointing to a sign below the counter: "Letters mailed, ten cents; letters received, twenty-five."

"But that's—"

"Regulations," she said, tilting her head as if posing for a photographer.

Begrudgingly, I handed her my quarter.

"If you had a smaller waist, it would call attention away from that nappy hair."

"Actually, it's a pound of eight-penny nails I need today." I felt too nervous to pay her advice (or whatever it was) any mind.

"Unless, of course, you want to look like a tart . . ." She stared heavenward as if to ask for divine intervention.

"They're for the mayor's grave's fence," I said, feeling suddenly battered.

Making a great issue of measuring nails from a keg, she weighed them on the brass balance. When I presented my two nickels, she refused payment, which surprised the tar out of me. "I've still got Mr. Pardee's laundry," I added.

"Shan't be needing it, shall I?" she said and began flipping through a *Harper's Bazaar*. I took note as her eye paused at various traveling costumes.

"Can I give them to a gent who's down on his luck?" I suggested.

Turning to *Peterson's Ladies Magazine*, she yawned, "Fine with me," without the slightest note of sentimentality. If she'd had her husband murdered, then framed Pokamiakin, what else was she capable of?

Back outside, the morning sun had struck the porch, and Pij dozed in the warm palomino rays. A bramble of serviceberries climbing up the side of the wall had burst into flower, and their faint smell calmed me.

I wasn't sure how Pij Belcher had crossed Main without soiling his bandages, but I could see that the only way I'd be able to return him to his bed in the livery was to load him into a wheelbarrow and push him across. Without a horseman anywhere to ferry him over, I reluctantly loaded Pij into the truck, his legs raised like the masts of a frigate. Pij held on to the sides of the wooden barrow, his normal foot pointing straight ahead toward the livery entrance, the clubbed foot pointing back the way we'd come.

"Made it! Where're your quarters?" I asked, placing his crutch under his arm.

"Jake's office," he said. Just as I'd hoped.

Making our way past the cold forge (Hames was out with the search party), to the rear of the building between the actual feed room and the "other" feed room containing the still, I was stunned by Jake's office. Perfectly finished in yellow pine, the walls were lined with framed pictures of horses. Not at all the opium den I thought it would be, filled with pipes and slag and awful brown smoke. Immediately I spied a photograph of a field of horses at Brooklyn Downs. My heart nearly stopped as that tintype took me back a decade. Next to it was a portrait of a bay horse I'd know anywhere—Minstrel's Song. And that groom in a tweed coat and cap holding the rope? Was that my da? A wave of loss and grief washed over me. I stared transfixed for so long that Pij fell trying to heave himself into the bin of flour sacks that had once been Jake's couch.

"Oh, sorry," I said, helping him lie back. I piled sacks beneath his maimed feet so they would be higher than his heart, allowing the surgeries to drain. Didn't Doc tie a bandage well? Horse or human, his bandages stayed put, applying pressure to the wound while allowing air in to promote healing. Would I ever be able to master as much?

Pij closed his tea-stained eyelids.

"I'll stay a minute, till you drop off," I said, all the time staring at Jake's framed photographs. My nostalgia turned to anger. What right did Jake have to put a likeness of my father on his wall? The pictures weren't hung only above his desk but also from floor to ceiling around the neat room. Who would have thought Jake a good housekeeper? A shelf of books along one of the shorter walls contained publications from the Bureau of Indian Affairs. What was this? At the far end sat a framed case covered with a sham.

I meant to look through Pardee's papers but instead pulled the cloth away and nearly let out a gasp. Surely my eyes played tricks on me. Was it possible? My father's butterfly collection! The autumn-colored monarch in the center had a circle of zebra swallowtails framing it—insects gathered from my stepmother's Park Slope garden. All our possessions had been auctioned off when the bank seized our house. But what, I had always wondered, had happened to Da's butterflies? Tears welled in my eyes as I stared transfixed at what had been the one bright spot on the wall of our carriage shed, studying each insect intently: The hairstreak at the top had been caught in a jar by my sister, Mary-Terese. In the corner, the only butterfly the poor dead twins had captured, a silver skipper.

Take it, said the voice. *It's yours by rights, isn't it?* The voice screamed with such intensity that I almost forgot about having a glance through Jake's diaries and accounts.

"Can you sing?" asked Pij sleepily. "I'd love a trail song if you can manage it. 'Camptown Ladies,' " he said, smiling. "It was pure peace lying here and listenin' to them fiddlers up at the Gem last night."

"I wonder if there's a score in this desk," I said, searching through the invoices. "Camptown Races, five miles long, dodah. Camptown butterflies sing this song . . ."

I flipped through one ledger and then another, wondering why Jake had kept my da's things and in such good repair. Indeed, how had he gotten hold of them in the first place? Jake wasn't the sentimental sort. The only souvenir Jake collected was money.

The entire town had filed through this office to pay their respects to Pigeon Belcher, so anyone could have rifled Jake's belongings, and from the looks of things I'd say that's exactly what happened. There were accounts of horses rented, feed purchased—not to mention barrels and barrels of molasses, which told me that Jake had made the rum I'd poisoned myself on last night. I was sure his still was constructed from lead pipe, and now I was living proof that lead caused softening of the brain.

As I studied the names in the account books, my eyes kept straying to the butterfly collection and the picture of Da and Minstrel's Song. Not a mention of Ella or her girls appeared anywhere. When I heard a rush of horses' hooves and excited shouts out in the livery's foyer, I replaced the sham over the case, vowing to come back later and get it.

The office door flew open. Hames stood in front of me, his belly hanging over his silver belt buckle. "What ya doin' here?" he demanded. "Pij, you okay?" Intuiting my snooping, Hames spoke far more solicitously to the mailman than to me. The blacksmith's face was streaked with trail dirt and hung above me like a malevolent moon.

I didn't like the twist of his lips. He took a step closer to me.

"I've got to be getting to the sheriff's," I said, pushing past him. He tried to block my path, but I ducked under his arm and ran into the atrium where the search party was watering their mounts and inspecting hooves for loose shoes.

Hames's wild laughter rang out behind me. "You seen that half-breed friend of yours or the Chink?" he called. "I need water 'n' wood." His heavy body scent followed me into the alley. Bursting into a run, I actually rushed to the Skookum House.

In front of the jail, some lads toed the earth along with Sheriff Barton, who leaned against a hitching rail. Three horses were tied there, and methodically I checked their hoofs, but all were shod and their feet showed no imperfections. I eyed the lawman's assistants who'd been deputized to help with the man-hunt. Did they mean to grab me?

"Searched the ridge down to the steamboat dock," said the

assayer, Grasshopper Jack. Today he looked so thin he almost disappeared around the middle.

"Snowmelt 'n' mud covered all the tracks along the creek, if there were any," said Frank Belknap.

"Glad I can count on your support," said Barton. It seemed the sheriff's major concern over the escape of Poka Mika was that it might have cost him some votes.

"The mine owner ain't gonna like it if he arrives and finds his entire crew out chasin' Injin," retorted Frank.

I walked past them into the jail, trying to act completely at ease, as if I were a perfectly honest citizen.

The Skookum House wasn't much larger than a sweat lodge, and I felt I had to crouch to enter. Today instead of being overwhelmed by the smell of rodent droppings, the aroma of charred cedar ran into my lungs. An entire corner of the squat building had been blown out, rocks and logs piled up to fill the hole. In the cell that remained secure, a man with a mop of brassy hair sat on the floor. His fancy shoes bore deep scuff marks, his tailor-made pants had a gaping tear in one knee. He stirred, combing his forelock with long white fingers—those fingers! Then his handsome chiseled features spoke. "Pearl?" He studied me with nettle green eyes, "Pearl O'Sullivan, is that you?"

The sound of his voice knocked the wind out of me. My dread replaced by surprise, I felt as if I'd just taken a step and found no floor beneath my foot.

"Pearl?" he said my name again, as if it meant riches.

" 'Tis I," I assured, my heart pumping so fiercely that I had to strain my ear to hear.

"Your voice is the same, but I wouldn't have known you."

There he was, not a photograph, but in the flesh, my own dear Davy.

CHAPTER NINETEEN

⟨⟨⟨⟩⟩⟩

In a split second an entire year of my life fell away, and I almost believed we could take up where we'd left off.

I'd never seen Davy in need of a shave or covered with trail dust, which was why I was so surprised when he said, "I knew it was your sweet-as-lilac voice I heard last night. I knew I didn't dream it, but God strike me dead if I'd ever recognize you, just look at yourself. You're a Bowery charwoman. Pearl, how'd you let this happen?"

I nearly burst into tears at the truth of it. My singed hair was a nest of cinder-colored snarls, my dress so patched that I looked like a refugee of the Mexican War.

"Ah, don't cry." He had his fists around the iron bars shaking their welds. "Buck up! What's important is that I've found you. We can be married. You've had a rough time, and it's all my fault. Don't let my desertion come between us. I forgive you your mistake, forgive mine? Please with marzipan on it? The whole mess has eaten my heart for a year, love. Just get me out of here. If we're married, a man can't testify against his wife."

An electric charge ran from my chin down to my knees, and my exhaustion vanished like ice in the washbasin on a spring day. I remembered what it was to long for wedded harmony. Pulling myself together, I palmed my eyes dry. (No wonder Da used to call me Pinky; my eyes must look like radishes.) "But I didn't steal the necklace. How could you think that I did? I never stole anything. Besides, I'm already . . ."

"It doesn't matter," he said in a loud whisper.

The sheriff and his deputies had come to the door, making intimate conversation impossible. I felt frustrated. The delicate features of Davy's Michelangelo face pressed into the bars, which appeared as a grid across his head. I'd never seen his eyes so intense. His red-gold hair was such a pretty color you wanted a gown made that very shade. I longed to bury my head into his chest, breathing his special smell. How could he think I'd stolen that necklace? "Nothing matters," he said, reading my mind. "It's all behind us. . . ."

Grasshopper Jack began yelling so loudly that Davy and I could not hear ourselves think. Whom was he shouting to?

At that second, a portly woman burst in, purpling the jail. Ella looked flushed. Her thin hennaed hair had come unpinned, exposing her bald spot. She glanced at Davy, her gaze passing over him disinterestedly. "You seen Doc?" she asked me, breathless.

"No," I replied. "And what have you charged this man with?" I gestured to Davy.

"Who's he? If you see Doc, tell him he's needed up at my place," she said, turning sideways in order to press herself out the door. I'd never seen so large a person move so furtively, like a bull moose who'd just caught the sent of a cow.

"Get me out of here," pleaded Davy. He sounded weary, as if he might cry.

It hurt to see him in so much pain. "Don't worry. There's not enough in the town coffer to feed prisoners. They won't keep you."

I heard the rush of galloping hooves and the excited voice of a young woman.

"Sheriff?" I asked. "What's this man's bail?"

Barton named an outrageous sum, so I asked again over the

rumbling voices and screaming horses. One of the deputies swore loudly. My shoulders drooped under the weight of the sheriff's reply—all the money I'd saved for medical college.

Davy's wide brow clouded. "Pearl, Pearl," he entreated. "There's rats in here."

I'd forgotten how I'd once been contented just to study his sculpted nose.

Out in the alley the woman's voice grew louder and more excited. Nightingale? What did she say? Something about Dutch? What was the commotion about?

"Anyone got the exact time?" shouted the sheriff. I took out Shaky's watch; it was a little before noon. Nightingale continued her excited chatter. Bursting into the jail, she stood with her hands on her narrow hips, her pale hair pulled into two tight braids, a sprig of serviceberry blossoms in each. Outside the sheriff began striking a rod against a sheet of metal bent into a crude bell, the universal call for assistance.

"That's not your husband finally come for you!?" she asked ruefully, pointing a finger at Davy. A note of laughter escaped her thin rouged lips.

"Harlot," Davy sneered at Nightingale.

"Your kind think all women are harlots," she retorted, narrowing her eyes.

"Nah, no," I replied.

"Reminds me of the gent I married, the one who promised to love and keep me," she scoffed. "Can't countenance a drunk who fancies himself God's gift to women."

"I'll get the bail reduced," I told Davy. "The sheriff's in a bad humor right now."

"Pawn that gold watch," said Davy as hoofbeats pounded through the alleys.

"For the likes of you?" said Nightingale. Distracted, she kept looking out the door. "You've the manners of a swine. I take that back. I once had a pet pig, and she had better manners. I never saw any beast behave the way you did last night." She turned to me, her harelip twisting. "Don't you dare pawn Shaky's watch for the likes of him."

"Licentious bitch," scoffed Davy. "Surely they have laws here about boarding house women keeping their sensuality on a shorter tether."

"You'd feck the wimple off a nun!" Nightingale retorted. "I'll tell you who there ought to be laws about," she said, turning to me. "You, Pearl. Come crawling up to me room like a mouse one day and then try to steal me reward money for capturing that Injin the next. Well, the joke's on you. His people sprung him, and neither of us gets a dime."

"There's no evidence other than circumstantial against Pokamiakin," I told her. I'd no intention of ever parting with Shaky's watch and didn't bother dignifying her accusation with an answer. "If you're looking for Ella, she just left," I added.

"I saw that Injin on the morning of Jake's death up near Three Devils sweeping something off the trail—probably hoofprints, 'cause when he saw me, he fled." She glared at me with a put-that-in-your-pipe-and-smoke-it expression.

"I can't stand this sty another minute," said Davy. "I've done nothing wrong."

"You'd no intention of paying for my services. You're lucky I didn't shoot you dead through the belt buckle," she sneered. "Sheriff," she called through the door, "you can testify as to the state of disarray of my undergarments." Turning back to Davy, she added, "You're nothin' but a common urinater."

My head began pounding with a vengeance, and my stomach felt as if it had filled with quicksand. Something about the white of Davy's fingers made me think of strips of rancid bacon fat. Then I noticed that there was a nick above his right eye, that it wasn't the dark shadow of his brow, but blood caked there.

"I'll get Doc to examine that cut as soon as he gets back," I said.

Nightingale laughed haughtily. "He'll fix you up all right, just like he did Ella's eye. It's your just desserts."

Truly vexed, I turned to her, "What are you talking about? Doc made Ella look like her old self again, attaching the false eye so that it moved like it was real!"

Nightingale folded her hands, pressing the apron ruffles to her chest. "Think you know everything, don't you? Soon as they find him, Doc's going to be plenty busy."

"Why?" I asked. "What's happened? Is someone hurt?" My God, they've caught Pokamiakin. They've shot him. No, it's Jones. The injured Negro had finally been found.

Davy rattled the bars so violently I thought the sod roof would come down. Dust and cakes of mud fell from above, and several of the stones blocking the hole in the wall rolled into the room. "I don't care how much it costs, get me out of here."

My nerves frayed to rags and my temples pulsed so hard my ears began to ring.

"Dutch Wilhelm," she said. "I found him at the bottom of the grade below his claim on my way up to the ice caves."

"Pawn the watch, Pearl," Davy insisted. "We'll get it back when my ship comes in."

"Dutch?" I said to Nightingale. "He must have misjudged his footing last night. He's probably been lying there for hours! How bad is he? Is he conscious?"

"Damn it, Pearl." A surly look crossed Davy's face.

"He's dead," said Nightingale.

CHAPTER TWENTY

Noon the same day

The white sun beat down through the new leaves of the cottonwood with such force that I could almost smell the mud turning into the dust of summer. Pulling my bonnet bill forward so that it shaded my face, I thought my heart would break as I watched the sad procession bearing Dutch down-mountain. More than six feet tall and as broad-shouldered as a horse, it took four strong men and a mule to carry him along Main to the gathering in front of the Skookum House.

"Terrible accident," whined Grasshopper. He embraced himself with his two frail arms, which were covered with a dusting of orange hairs. "Jis' terrible."

"Ain't no accident, if you ask me," said Frank Belknap.

"You think?" questioned Hames. He'd run to the jail still holding the horseshoe he'd been fashioning. "Someone tell Windy to bring a burial cloth."

Arizona Charley and Pardee's widow approached, Charley holding the folded shroud and Windy carrying her tatted parasol. Pigeon Belcher hobbled in back of them. He hadn't covered his bandages with sacking, and I worried that he would dirty his dressings. Pij didn't need mortification to set in on top of everything else.

"I don't believe it," said Charley, his face gone solemn as a vicar's.

The minute I saw the justice of the peace I wanted to ask him about his note and the nature of our appointment tomorrow, but this was not the time or place.

"What'd you-all think?" prodded Hames. Everyone looked at the ground.

Brownie Bitterroot lay the shroud over Dutch, whose ruddy complexion had turned a terrible purplish gray. His eyes were rolled up so that only the whites showed, his limbs contorted, his mouth open like a wound as if he'd died gasping for breath. So gruesome, I had to turn away, wiping a tear from my eye. Looking back, I saw that his clothes were scored by mud as if he'd fallen quite a distance. Shale fell from the cuffs of his overalls when Brownie tucked the shroud under his size-thirteen boots.

"Doc here yet?" someone asked.

"He's hunting General Jones who caught a bullet last night," I said.

"Somebody close Dutch's eyes," said Grasshopper Jack.

I rushed forward, thumbing Dutch's veiny lids down. Reaching into my pocket, I pulled out the two nickels and laid them one on each eye.

"My wife could have a look at him." Brownie pulled at the ends of his mustache.

"Where is she?" I asked.

"Tending a sick Irishman." Brownie shifted his weight from one to the other of his stork legs.

"How do we know someone didn't push him?" asked Hames.

There was a chorus of grumbles.

"He was as pickled as a three-legged chicken in a carnival

jar when he left the wake," said Brownie, speaking rapidly. "Misjudged his footing." Clearly the mine foreman didn't want any trouble with Mr. Forrester about to arrive.

A round of throat clearing and "yes, buts" followed. Inside the jail, Davy rattled the bars, calling for a dipper of water. Everyone's eyes remained fixed on Dutch.

"He's been talking nothing but *strike* ever since we heard the mine owner was comin'. If you want my opinion, he was pushed down that ledge," said Grasshopper. He put his hands on his hips, flaring his long, bony arms like insect wings.

"He had an Irish tongue in his mouth when it came to or-ganizin'," said Frank.

Brownie Bitterroot shrank back into the crowd and stared at his boot tops.

"Tripped on his own bum foot," said Arizona Charley, look-ing at Windy for agreement. Her curls drooped as much as her smile, and it struck me that she showed more grief for the fallen Dutch than for the death of her own husband.

"He's been digging in these treacherous gulches, pick in one hand, pint in the other, for five years and never missed a stride," argued Hames.

"I put my money on him being pushed," said one of the sheriff's new deputies.

"I'm inclined to agree," said Frank, staring through the crowd at Nightingale who leaned against the cottonwood's trunk, sulking about the lost reward money.

"Pushed," shouted several lads, one after another.

Frank said, "It would look real bad if Dutch's strike had any effect. Forrester might just sell out—why bother with a bunch of mountain Molly McGuires? Ruby'd be a ghost town quicker than a flooding creek changes course."

"My money's on 'foul play,' " yelled Grasshopper.

Spirits flamed. Where was Doc? Now that Shaky was gone, he had the only personality strong enough to turn the tide of public opinion. In a minute the scene beneath the cottonwood would change into a gambling ground–cum–courtroom. I didn't like the feel of things. First Shaky, then Jake, and now dear Dutch whose only thought was bettering the lives of working folk.

"Can't a fellow get a dipper of water?" was the litany from inside the jail. Instead of pulling at my heartstrings, Davy's petition made my temples throb and my chest tighten. I kept straining my eyes, looking for Doc to ride into town. Meadowlarks gathered above us in the tree, jabbering in flutelike trills.

Thank God the Gem was closed and tempers couldn't be fueled by drink. On Sunday, public houses were locked up for the morning out of respect; otherwise there was no recognition of the Sabbath whatsoever in Ruby City. But in an hour the saloon doors and faro hall would open. All these grizzled miners would file in and, after several proclamations of "More power to your elbow," begin placing bets on the ruling of this most recent mishap. Was Dutch's death connected to Jake's and Shaky's? Certainly a federal marshal would be summoned with all possible haste. I had to leave. But what about Davy? The only good news was that, for the moment, everyone seemed to have forgotten about hunting for Pokamiakin.

Sheriff Barton's guttural voice called, "There's Doc. We'll get his opinion."

The crowd parted as the physician pressed his way to the center, his face as gray as his whiskers. Doc bent over Dutch for a good long time, turning the patient's neck this way and that, then opening the gaping mouth and pulling out his terribly swollen tongue.

Running his knuckles across his jaw, Doc said in a heavy burr, " 'Tis a suicide."

My breath caught in my throat. The crowd went totally silent.

Cranky Frank spoke first, "What makes you say that?"

"Pearl O'Sullivan, get me out of here," yelled Davy.

My spine stiffened. No one paid Davy any mind. Except for Nightingale.

"I knowed what you done!" she said, calling to me. Her eyes blazed like lanterns with the wicks turned all the way up.

Here it comes, I thought, praying I could faint dead away.

Run, the voice said.

"You jilted him, skipped off, married another gent, and didn't tell him!"

I hoped that my face didn't betray my great relief.

Doc rested his chin in the cup of his fingers. "The mon's been in terrible pain from smoker's throat. Was only a matter of time. Being high on spirits last night, he might have figured what better opportunity to join his partner in a trek to the hereafter."

"Sounds logical," said Arizona Charley. Whether he was a real attorney or not no one knew, but he was acquainted enough with the law to steer his clients clear of its entanglements as well as doing all the legal business of miners regarding the many claim forms that had to be filled out and filed. No one felt eager to disagree with him, still . . .

There were loud mutterings. The little Miner's House of Parliament beneath the cottonwood was not convinced. Nor was I. Poor Doc looked as tired as an ox run four days through the desert. His lids drooped over reddened eyes. Had he ruled Dutch's death a suicide in the hopes of thwarting the mob?

Hames piped up (of course it would be Hames who spoke against Charley), "Jus' last week Dutch was talkin' about all the lumber he had to whipsaw, flumes and sluice boxes he had to make. Don't sound like a man who planned on dyin' to me."

"Just one dipper of water." Davy's plaintive cry pulled me away from Dutch's terrible fate. He sounded like the Davy I used to know, the one who needed my help diagramming sentences and calculating the number of acres in a cornfield. Gulping a mouthful of air, my pulse raced. I wanted to take him in my arms and lose myself in the rhythm of his heart. Certainly if pure water had been anywhere in Ruby I would have brought him a bucketful, but considering its polluted state, Davy was better off going without. Where was Chin? It had not taken him so long yesterday to find good water.

"Don't sound like a fittin' end for an old warhorse like Dutch," agreed Pigeon Belcher. The tea stains around his eyes made him look sorrowful indeed.

Hames concurred, "Hard to believe." Dutch and Hames held politics of different hues—back in the sixties, Dutch had embraced Lincoln from the first day he landed in America. Hames, on the other hand, was born into Southern secessionist stock. Blue or gray, no matter what color your cap, the verdict of suicide was a hard wafer to swallow.

"The mon suffered acute pain day and night," said Doc. Settling on his haunches, he put a sympathetic hand on Dutch's shoulder. "He couldn't sleep nights, and no remedy brought him relief. Now he's at peace." Doc closed his weary eyes as if in prayer.

None of us had but an inkling of Dutch's torturous pain. Just last night he'd been singing Shaky's praises without a grimace. I could tell that Hames felt as guilty as I did.

"Will there be an autopsy?" I asked as I folded the shroud back and crossed Dutch's shovel-sized hands over his chest.

The crowd made muttering noises.

"Aye," agreed Doc, "if it'll put your mind to rest. But this is a suicide. I'll stake my professional career on it."

Bending over Dutch, I caught the rancid smell of vomit. Why would a man who'd thrown himself down a cliff have vomited? Perhaps he'd lost his balance in the throes of being ill. Or an assailant, seeing Dutch in a vulnerable position, had taken full advantage.

"Frank," Doc said, turning to our expressman, "when's the next stage due?"

"Tomorrow before dark," Frank replied.

"Let's get him up to the ice caves until then," said Doc. "I'm expecting a new set of instruments along with a supply of hartshorn and hopefully my new pair of specs."

Amen to that. But wouldn't it be better to autopsy Dutch right now while the evidence was fresh? Look what had happened when we waited to autopsy Shaky.

"Doc?" I whispered, then felt unable to press my opinion on him, not with the entire town looking on. Instead, I stammered, "Did you find the General?"

Doc shook his head. "Not a sign of him, lass."

A terrible rattling came from inside the little jail, and I thought every stone would roll out of the gaping hole blasted in its corner. "I demand justice," shouted Davy. "Pearl, have you pawned that watch yet?"

"Can't you make that oiler shut up?" said Nightingale, turning to me. "I've got to hand it to you, Pearl Ryan, I never had you fixed for a girl with a husband *and* a beau. And I don't blame you for hiding out from that one."

My face must have turned as crimson as rose hip jelly.

"I bet your old man was the boneless type," she went on. Thank God no one paid our womantalk any mind.

Hames and several other men bent over, preparing to lift Dutch onto the litter that would bear him to the ice cave where he would join Jake's body.

Then I had a thought. "Shouldn't I go up to his digs, Doc?"

"Whatever for, lass?"

"To look for a note, a good-bye. Something to prove suicide."

"You bring it straight to me," said the sheriff as I turned to fetch Tillicum.

Nightingale called, "I know what you're all about. You're goin' up there to look for a will, 'cause you think you'll be mentioned in it. Suicide note my foot. You think you're goin' to become an heiress for the second time in a week!"

For a moment I felt as if I were back in the employ of Mrs. Ritters—the other servants used to jeer at me in the same tone. I was so used to it that I almost laughed.

"Better let the pleats out of your bonnet, before your head gets too big for it."

Striding as fast as I could away from Nightingale's theorizing, the boy who said he was my Davy rattled the cage bars. "Pearl, Pearl," he called. As my name rang into the trees, it sounded more like a profanity than a plea.

CHAPTER TWENTY-ONE

An hour later

Tillicum's roan shoulders struggled up the rocky trail, his nose bent almost to the ground. Leaning over the saddle horn, I balanced my upper body along my cayuse's neck, then let the reins go slack, giving him his head as he pivoted around the switchbacks.

Imagine, Davy Witherup had followed me here. I had so many fantasies going on inside my head that at first I'd thought I'd invented him. As I'd stood facing him in the dark, bad-smelling jail, I'd thought, It's not Davy but a paper cutout with the bone and sinew missing. Still, there was enough of him there to make my blood pulse like a rising river. The flesh of my wrist where Davy's fingers had caressed me burned with anticipation, and I knew that I would always carry the memory of his touch.

Why had he waited an entire year to come after me?

A certain numbness crept into my soul. Whether it was from the death of Dutch or the shock of seeing Davy, I couldn't say. And why had my heart turned to mush just because Davy had visited Ella's hotel and gotten himself in a fix? Isn't real love supposed to forgive anything? If the truth were told, my cayuse's liquid brown eyes melted my heart more than Davy's, which had not been the case one short year ago.

I headed up the long climb cut into the side of Badger Slide. As Tillicum stepped gingerly along the loose rock, I tried not to think that at any moment both of us could be carried down-mountain by a wave of falling shale. Staring at my polished toes positioned in my stirrups, I gave thanks for the gift of Nightingale's boots, forgiving her behavior—though the thought of her and Davy together in her narrow room made my stomach twist. I wondered, Had he touched her the same way he'd touched me?

I pulled Tillicum to a halt, letting him have a short breather, then put my heels into his warm flanks to encourage him on. My head began to throb again, the pain jabbing into the back of my eyes every time Tillicum's hoof struck a rock. Though my little horse was doing all the pulling, I began feeling more and more exhausted. Back at my Laundry by the Lake, the washing was piling up. Tomorrow there'd be Dutch's autopsy. I hadn't yet found a good piece of oak for Shaky's marker, much less carved it. And Davy. How to get him out of jail? And what would I do with him when I did?

Suddenly, far below me came a buckaroo call, followed by a thundering of hooves and a series of shots. A faint blue trail of gun smoke drifted along the banks of Salmon Creek. Pokami-akin's search posse had gone out again.

Trudging on through piles of discarded ore, called "grizzly", I reconsidered the suspects in Jake's murder, trying without success to connect either Windy and her contingent or Ella and hers to Dutch's demise. Contemplating other Rubyites, I stopped at Carolina and Brownie Bitterroot. Brownie had acted awfully uncomfortable when Dutch was brought in this morning. I remembered that when Jake was murdered, Carolina had been off delivering a baby. But whose? Doc had delivered Mrs. Belknap. What other mother was expecting? None that I knew of. And today when Dutch met his end, Carolina had suddenly been called away to nurse a sick Irishman no one had ever laid eyes on. I wondered about her absences at these strategic times. Point of fact, Dutch Wilhelm's strike would make Brownie Bitterroot look bad to Mr. Forrester. Who else would benefit by Dutch's death? The Bitterroots had certainly benefited from Jake's death: no more blackmail payments. Still, Brownie and Carolina hardly seemed the murdering sort. Still . . . murder would explain why Carolina was so eager—no, so adamant—about springing Poka Mika from the Skookum House. She wasn't the type to stand by while an innocent man got hanged. And, unlike most everyone else in town, she seemed certain sure of Pokamiakin's innocence.

The stovepipe and corrugated iron roof of Dutch's digs came into view. I spied a black-and-white cat sitting in the open doorway. Sluice boxes, which looked like the makings of a child's coffin, littered the yard. Tillicum whinnied to a long-eared mule tethered nearby. The cat's and mule's heads jerked toward me, thinking I was their master. An arrow pierced my heart when I saw the disappointment in that mule's face.

Looking up at the shaft openings, my gaze traveled to a gravel slide, at the bottom of which Nightingale said she'd found Dutch's body. Again I considered my list of suspects: Ella and her contingent, Windy and hers. Nightingale had been near the scene of Jake's killing, and she had also been the one who found Dutch. But what motive could she possibly have had for killing the old socialist? Something nagged at the back of my brain. Why hadn't Ella recognized Davy? Obviously he had been the gent she'd met at the ferry, the one she'd never forget. Did she live in an opium fog, or was forgetfulness a cover-up for some larger plot that I'd completely overlooked?

Just then the mule—whose name was Engels—burst into sorrowful brays. Dismounting, I went inside the cabin. When I lit the lamp, everything seemed to be in order. Dutch had insulated his walls with leather-bound books. I pulled down a volume of Sir Thomas More's *Utopia,* then a volume of the *Communist Manifesto* and *Das Kapital* as well as a biography of Robert Owen. Most were printed in High German so ornate that I had trouble recognizing the letters of the alphabet.

Several books on the Civil War caught my eye. One contained a map, which I unfolded across the bed. It looked like a campaign souvenir with various battles circled: Antietam, Perryville (here it was noted in ink that had faded to gray: "McClellan surrenders to Burnside"). There was a dark blue circle around Missionary Ridge. As I undid the map all the way so that I could refold it properly, a thin, square piece of metal fell to the floor. Holding it up to the lamp, I saw a tintype, very old, one of the first: a picture of a line of men in uniform in front of a background of tents. All wore Union hats and had long bayonets hanging at their sides. Several stood on crutches; one— did he have any legs?—was supported by the men on either side of him. Three black men hovered on the right-hand edge of the tin print, one with his arm in a sling; on the left of the portrait stood a boxy little man with a large head. He wore a Union uniform but had no bayonet. Over his head was a dot of fresh blue surveyor's chalk. I looked for Dutch, but the portrait must have been thirty years old and I didn't see anyone who resembled him, except perhaps a large, broad-faced man with one foot bandaged. Turning the daguerreotype over, I made out the words "Missionary Ridge" scratched across the back.

Replacing everything, I began searching for a note. On the washstand sat a clean china plate, one tin cup, and a half-empty bottle of Doc's Wizard Remedy next to an unopened bottle of the same elixir. A pair of snowshoes hung over the door. Dutch had grown up in the Alps and was one of the few miners who didn't winter in town.

Not a straw out of place, not even an empty whiskey bottle on the floor, though there were several in a crate outside where the cat slept. If Dutch had left a note, it was gone now. Nothing under any pot. I checked his tools, a row of picks and shovels lined up against the wall. His traps were neatly stacked. Like most who didn't draw wages from the Ruby Mine or have the financial backing of relatives, Dutch grubstaked his claim by selling pelts at the trading post.

With the lamp casting a happy light on the mud-chinked walls, it was hard to believe he wasn't just gone for the day. I sat down in a chair with a seat made of woven rawhide strips, having a little rest in the hope of shaking off the remains of my hangover. The sound of an approaching rider startled me awake. Karl Marx, the black-and-white cat, jumped to attention, and the mule brayed. I peeked out the window. A woman on a chestnut horse with a well-brushed tail came over the rise.

Carolina! The nurse-schoolteacher rode straight up to the door as if she belonged here. "Hello," I called, walking into the yard.

She rode astride, not sidesaddle as most women in her station might have done, and sat perfectly erect atop her lovely mare. A faint smile flickered across her perfect bow of a mouth. "You shouldn't get too near me," she called. "I might be contagious."

I stopped dead in my tracks. What's this? I looked at her questioningly.

"I'm thinking of bringing a patient here," she said, her face expressionless.

"Who?" I asked.

She either ignored me or misheard me. "I'm not exactly sure what ails him," she said, "but this would be a good place for a quarantine."

Someone dropped icicles down the back of my dress. "Cholera?" the word caught in my throat. I don't know how I knew to ask—maybe I'd make a good doctress after all.

"I can't say," she answered.

Can't or won't? I wanted to demand but didn't.

I started to reach for her horse's bridle, so as to hold the mare steady while she dismounted, but Carolina stopped me. "Please, no closer. I'd feel terrible if . . ."

"You've heard about Dutch, then?"

She bit her lip. "If only I'd known last night that I'd never see him again . . ."

"What should I do?"

"Leave," she answered. Then, as if she were having second thoughts, she asked, "What are you doing here?"

"Looking for a . . . a suicide note." I didn't for one minute believe that Dutch had killed himself and waited for a hint of a reaction from her. I should have known better.

There was a long pause. "If I bring my patient here, I'll be able to look after things and feed the mule." She acted as if I hadn't spoken.

My fists tightened. She'd heard perfectly well what I'd said, yet she denied me a glimmer of a response. What power this haughty woman had over me. My face burned as if I'd fallen into a patch of nettles. Count to ten before you speak, I told myself and in the end said nothing at all. I wanted her approval and her friendship, so I did as I was told, hoping she would warm to me. She never did, and I never learned. I bid her a curt good-bye and mounted Tillicum, cursing my docility.

All the way down Badger Slide, I berated myself for my timidity. Why hadn't I had more of a look around? What was she really doing there? Hunting for something? Maybe I had Carolina figured all wrong. Maybe she *was* the murdering kind. Where was her "patient," anyway? Dare I go up and check him out tomorrow, risking cholera? No, I dared not, and that was her ace in the hole. Oh, how I hated it when I felt outsmarted.

Traveling down-mountain proved almost as difficult for Tillicum as the exhausting climb up. I put my weight in the stirrups and sat back in the saddle, holding on tightly to the reins to help balance him. With every step I pondered it: no note and no will. Surely Doc would think about changing his ruling on Dutch's death or at least come up and look for a suicide letter himself, quarantine or no. If this newcomer's illness was that serious, surely he should be seen by a physician. The health of the entire camp could be at stake.

I came down off the steep decent and rounded Lone Pine Turn. There, next to Doorknob Rock, a native woman stood bending over the trail, studying the horse droppings made, no doubt, by Carolina's mare.

"Mary Reddawn!" I called, elated. Was it she or just wishful thinking? Yes, it was her little sparrow face and thin shoulders wrapped in an army blanket painted with tar.

"My stars, am I glad to see you. Where have you been?"

She stood motionless, obviously startled. Whom did she expect, if not me? She held something to her chest under her blanket, a gathering basket made of spruce root. She glanced up at me sidelong, not unlike a just-beaten child. How it stung my soul when she looked at me like that. Stop acting that way, I wanted to say, and then felt sadder still, because those had been Dutch's words.

"Where have you been? I need firewood. The river's receded and there's stagnation everywhere; all water has to be boiled. But," I faltered, "I figured you were lying low, because . . . of your cousin."

"Visiting gathering grounds," she said, sweeping her arm across the uphill side of the trail. I glanced at the ancient pines. Their bark looked like reptile hide. Sap the color of bee pollen ran down the trunks the way wax ran down a candle. So this was where Mary collected the pine pitch she made into a poultice, remedying colds and weak lungs. She also mixed it in with a bag of hot sand to treat earaches. An old Indian cure or something she'd learned from Chin? All I could say was that it had worked on that terrible earache I'd had last winter when Doc was bedridden by a mule kick.

"Mary, listen, don't worry about your cousin." I glanced over my shoulder. Why? Who was there to hear me? "They'll never find him. I have to ask you something. Nightingale says she saw him near where Jake was killed at about the same time. First she told me he was hiding in the bushes, then she said he was wiping something off the trail. She thinks it was hoofprints. Of course she was mistaken, but . . ."

"Pokamiakin there." She said matter-of-factly. "Jake die. So cousin sweep trail." She spoke as if this was the logical thing to do after a shooting. And maybe for an Indian it was.

At first I said nothing. She was a straightforward person, and I'd never known her to lie, but I did not understand this new complication and wasn't sure I wanted to.

She sucked her lower lip into her mouth, so I decided it best to change the subject. "I'm in dire need of water," I told her. "Has Chin found a good spring? There's a newcomer in the jail who's not used to drinking from creeks." Somehow I couldn't bring myself to tell her the newcomer was Davy, though she knew all about my love match gone wrong. She'd even given me a charm, which she said was strong enough that, if I ate it, he would feel the effects thousands of miles away. I think it was pulverized robin heart and beaver testes, but couldn't be sure—Indians are very guarded about their medicine bundles. It had had a dreadful taste, though I'd eaten it to please her.

Mary wasn't listening to me but surveying her trees as if they were ponies in need of grooming. No white person ever stared at trees with such affection.

"Do you know where Chin is?" I prompted

"*Ipsoot*," she said. I could barely hear her. A flock of Canadian geese flew overhead. Their loud chatter seemed to speak their Chinook name, *Kalakala*, and their wings made a singing noise the way a broom does brushing through the air just before it hits the rug you're trying to beat the dust from.

"Hiding? But why?"

"*Chickamin*." Mary's gaze rested on a lightning-scarred pine tree. Lightning Power was stronger than animal power, so she believed this conifer had special healing qualities.

"Money? You mean the China tax?" There was a special five-dollar-a-year tax levied on Chinese miners in these parts. It was called an "immigrant tax," though it did not apply to the Irish, German, or French. I didn't understand it myself but thought it stemmed from the fact the Chinese were buying up worked-out claims and reaping profits from them. No one in Ruby had ever enforced it, if you can believe that (though it might have something to do with rumors of the Chinese grinding their stilettos for the heart of the elected officials who passed that law). We had only one Chinaman, and he wasn't a miner anymore—and where would we be if Chin didn't bring us fresh water every day?

"No *chickamin*," Mary said, pulling her robes over her head and clasping them with her clawed fingers at the V in her neck. "I bring you wood tomorrow, you pay?"

"Of course," I said. "I always pay you. What's the matter? Why do you need money? They've never collected that tax."

Her blanket fell over her shoulders, and she unclasped her hand in order to untie a small buckskin bag fastened to her belt. "You give this to General Jones?" she asked, handing me the herb pouch. "From Chin."

"Do you know where Jones is?" I asked.

"Doc got him."

"No, Mary, that's the trouble. Doc can't find him." I leaned down over Tillicum's shoulder and looked imploringly into her dark, leathery face. Her cheekbones were as high as these Cascade peaks, and her nose bore a certain amount of pride in its sharpness. "Do you know where Jones is?"

To my surprise she reached up and snatched back the medicine bag. "*Kla-how-ya*," good-bye, she said and sprang through the pines toward the Lightning Power Tree. Scurrying up the side of the mountain, she ran close to the ground like a forest creature, her moccasins never sliding backward on the slick, pine needle–strewn floor. When she disappeared from view, the sun fell behind her gathering ground. The late-day light leaked through the evergreen fringe, turning the wild the color of blood oranges.

CHAPTER TWENTY-TWO

Riding into Ruby, I headed for Doc's surgery at the north end of town. Studying the log building's square glass windows set like two vacant eyes on either side of the door, I knew before I tried the latch that it would be locked. Still out looking for General Jones, I told Tillicum.

Reining my horse down Pipe Stem Alley, I located the sheriff in front of the jail and told him I'd found no note at Dutch's digs. Saddling a fresh mount, he was about to rejoin the search posse. Barton tightened his saddle cinch and checked his cache of ammunition. "If you see Doc, could you tell him?" I asked, lowering my voice.

"What say?" asked Bald Barton, putting a finger to his ear to clear it. "Shootfest last night blew out my hearing."

I repeated the request, still speaking in a hushed tone because I didn't want Davy to know I was nearby. The sheriff mounted, tipped his hat, slapped his horse's flanks with the ends of his rawhide reins, and galloped down to Salmon Creek. The sun had fallen well behind Three Devils, and a sudden sharp chill in the air made me shiver.

Back at the Laundry by the Lake, a huge load of wash had piled up on my porch. Tethering Tillicum near my door so he could be protected from the wind, I fed him, then cranked up my stove. I had some pine sticks and a few blocks of cedar, but the pine was too pitchy and cedar burned too hot. What I needed was Mary's perfect wood.

Washing the trail dust from my hands, I opened my last tin of sardines, kept for when I was too weary to cook. I ate the wee oily fish bones and all, then drank the juice. When my spirits revived I boiled a kettle of water, starting one pot of potato starch for clothes and another for soup—should a hungry client stop by in the morning. My heart sank. It wouldn't be Shaky or Dutch knocking at my door. The fabric of our village had changed forever with two of its most redeeming citizens having crossed the Great Divide.

Blowing out the lamp, I went to bed early, but my sleep was made fitful by troubled thoughts and the howling of wolves. Getting up to poke the fire, my breath came white in the faint moon glow seeping through the tent canvas. I sat next to the orange gleam of the stove, toasting my stockinged feet and pondering: So Pokamiakin *had* been at the scene of Jake's death, removing hoofprints from the trail. Maybe he did kill Jake—who could blame him? Guilty or not, should the Indian buck with Rabid Coyote Power be caught, he'd never get a fair trial in Ruby City.

Though I still had a vested interest in who killed Jake Pardee, what I really wanted to know was how he had gotten hold of my father's things and why he had kept them. Had he gone to the sheriff's auction when our carriage house and its contents were sold? If he'd had the money to buy our belongings, why hadn't he paid my father his share of the profits from the sale of Minstrel's Song or helped him to get out of the workhouse?

The night turned fiercely cold, and the howling grew louder. The wolves must have been hungry, because I heard them padding around my door and imagined their sinewy gray bodies and long pink tongues. My house had no near neighbors, so I was a perfect target for the *leloo*, as Mary called the wolves.

Something about their dung-colored eyes reminded me of Jake. I heard the *leloo* brushing against the piano crate and feared for my little horse. For once no one in town was shooting, making the wolves bolder. "Never thought I'd wish rifle volley would go on all night," I said, thinking aloud. Then I began to hope that just one lad would abandon the all-night search for Pokami-akin, oil his elbow at the Gem, and start firing into the night. I kept going to the window, pulling the sheepskin aside, and glancing out. Tillicum stood with one hind leg cocked, ready to strike should a wolf come too near. If he broke into a nervous sweat, he'd surely take a chill.

Clearing a corner of my tent of laundry, I brought him in-side. With the stove at one end turned down to a low glow and his body at the other, I wouldn't have to worry about my wash basin icing over. I put on a wool sleeping cap—you'd think it was the middle of winter—then lay down, pulling the blankets over my head.

Davy's face kept flashing in front of me. I recalled the two of us lying in the summer bracken. The memory of his fingers stroking my arm was as fresh as if our holiday at the Ritterses' Long Island estate had happened yesterday. Moving my hands across my shoulders, I mimicked the way he'd caressed me. My breath came in little fits and starts as I imagined myself sitting on Lucifer's golden throne. How was it that Davy could still make my body sing, but not my heart? I wasn't looking forward to tomorrow. The problem of bigamy aside, how would I ex-plain to him that, until I'd sorted out my heart, marriage was out of the question?

Before confronting Davy, I'd keep my mysterious appoint-ment with the justice of the peace. "A personal matter of ut-most importance," Charley's note had read. Which meant, I supposed, that his business with me had nothing to do with my mineral claims—or did it? Maybe the town attorney had some-thing he wanted to tell me concerning Jake's death. Or was he on to me about Mrs. Ritters's necklace?

Just past midnight the *leloo* must have found something to occupy them, because their ghoulish wailing abated. I would have slept the sleep of the dearly departed if it weren't for Tillicum's snoring. I remember my da used to come home from night watch at Brooklyn Downs stables dead on his feet. The loud breathing of thirty horses at rest wouldn't let even the deaf sleep in peace.

I rose at first light and ate the lone sardine left in the tin for my breakfast. But as I licked the can, a black thought stuck its talons into me. I flew from the house, past Tillicum whom I'd put outside, down the ravine to South Ruby where my worst fears were realized. The damn wolves had knocked down the temporary fence and dug up Shaky's grave down to the coffin!

Wavy claw marks scarred the lid, but otherwise His Honor slept undisturbed. I ran home, grabbed a shovel, and feverishly threw the dirt back over him, tears running down my cheeks. Not enough hours in the day, I told myself. It had been too dark last night—and I was feeling too low—to finish the fence. That and the ill fate of cold weather had almost been the mayor's undoing.

The needed pickets were close at hand, so work went rapidly. When I finished just before noon, it looked like the tiniest garden fence. By then the sun was a white poker chip. I wiped the sweat from my brow and walked back to my laundry to wash and change my apron for my appointment with Charley. Putting on my good bonnet, I pinned up my hair as best I could with Davy's tortoiseshell combs, reminding me . . .

When visiting him today, I'd speak plainly and directly, saying that I thought he'd forsaken me. For an entire year I had been heading down a singular trail and felt unsettled changing paths. Of course I was omitting the most important things: that I was uncertain of my heart and that I was already married. How would he react? Imagining his head hanging, his face clouded with a downcast expression, I felt even more guilty.

Before putting on the white gloves Nightingale had lent

me, I spit-shined my shoes with lampblack and dabbed a drop of extract of vanilla behind my ears.

Arriving at the office of the justice of the peace, I knocked on the plank door. A gray horse tied out front blinked at me, then resumed dozing in the sun. When no one answered, I rapped again. Then, pushing against the door, I was surprised to find it barred. Glancing in the window I saw a "Closed" sign. Odd, I thought. I stared at the horse swatting a fly with his tail. When he kicked at his belly with his right rear hoof, the underside of his foot caught my eye. I went out into the street to investigate. The gelding was newly shod, and on his right hind hoof, the inside bulb of the heel was sheared, so that his foot looked slightly lopsided and almost cleft when viewed from the back.

That's it, that's the horse! Couldn't a right hind be mistaken for a right front? A horse put more weight on his front legs and so the prints of the forefeet were stronger than the hoofprints of the rear. But an error was possible. Only an Indian could really tell a hind hoofprint from a front on an unshod horse, but—because they were Indians—they were seldom consulted in matters pertaining to law, or anything else.

I paced up and down the plank sidewalk in front of Charley's, waiting for him to return, waiting also for the horse's owner to claim him. When I tired of pacing, I leaned against the wall. After another half hour I slumped to a sitting position. Up the street the assayer, Grasshopper Jack, walked out of the Gem and headed toward me.

"Seen Charley?" I asked.

"No, ma'am. Maybe out lookin' for that Injin." He paused, listing to one side, his smile showing a gap in the front of his elongated teeth. "I'd be with 'em, but my horse came up with girth gall."

"Whose lovely gelding is that?" I asked, pointing to the gray. "Gray horses seldom have such plush tails." I hoped that my attempt at small talk would disarm him.

"Forr's, I believe," he replied. His bourbon breath had to be at least a hundred proof.

Forr's? I studied the gelding's right hind hoof, making a mental picture of it. "Why's he tied in front of Charley's?"

"The boys hitched him here so Junior wouldn't loose him in a gamble. Lost three good horses already, and Jake's not around to keep him in supply. We felt kinda sorry for the little city slicker, and we was tired of riding him double on our mounts. Out of sight, out of mind, that's our theory."

Watching the assayer swing his hips as he sauntered toward the faro hall, I wondered if Forr had always been several beads shy of a necklace.

No use holding up the wall waiting for Charley, who'd obviously stood me up. With a sigh and a last glance at Forr's gray gelding, I headed to the Skookum House, dreading the walk. As the jail came into view, I saw Nightingale trudging up from the creek carrying a gunny sack filled with driftwood for Ella's stove. She stared at her feet as she walked and was so engrossed in thought that she didn't notice me. Despite everything, I liked her spunk. I'd been wrong about her being slow-witted. She had a good head on her shoulders. I wished that she would cotton to me, just a little, then wondered what on earth could have made her expression so sober.

Studying her slim figure climbing the trail, I took a long breath, exhaling slowly. It was the same old game I'd played with the other servants in the Ritters household, hoping that they'd like me, just a little, not minding their jeering so much, because, after all, it was a kind of friendship, wasn't it? At least in Ruby I'd felt welcome by Doc and Shaky Pat, not merely of use but (dare I say it?) indispensable from time to time— though, oddly enough, not by any member of the female persuasion. How I missed our late mayor. Jabbing my boot toe into the ground, I vowed, yet again, to get to the bottom of his death.

Pausing outside the jail, I studied the bark peeling from the logs and the grains of sand in the chinks. The building's corners were dovetailed, and bright moss grew at the joists. Finally, I pushed my bonnet back, opened the door, and plunged into the dusky, bad-smelling room. When I'd been in the Ritterses' employ, Davy was the only member of the staff to take me up. Now his kindness weighed heavily on me.

He sprang to his feet from where he crouched on the floor of his cell, upsetting his mess plate, which crashed against the bars. "Get the money, love?" His face broke into a smile that lit the room. "I thought you'd never come. Have trouble pawning the watch?"

"Ah . . . no, I haven't the money." I could not meet his eye, so I stared at the mother-of-pearl buttons on his poplin shirt, longing to lay my head on his chest.

Davy's brow creased. "Pearl, sweetness, please, I'm on my knees. I can't stand this privy another hour." To my ear, his eastern accent sounded both foreign and familiar.

He grasped hold of the bars. Placing my hands over his, my flesh turned to candle wax. "I'll help you, don't fret. But I could never pawn the watch. It's a keepsake."

His eyes burned holes in my cheeks. "Well, just when the hell am I gonna get out of here?" He kicked at a rock. The laces of his boots had come untied, and I had to fight the urge to reach down and do them up before he tripped.

"Don't worry, you'll be out before you know it. But . . . I must tell you, the truth is . . . The reason I need time is that . . . that I'm not free to wed. Not at the moment." I lifted my eyes to his, but when I saw the fire in them, my gaze skittered away like a frightened quail looking for somewhere to hide.

"What?" He grasped the metal bars so hard that his fingers turned white.

"I married. I had to. I needed money to get out of New York and come west. I'm Mrs. Paddy Ryan, in name only—"

"You're *what?*"

I felt a spray of saliva. His sharp tongue nailed me to the wall like a hatchet.

"It's not like you think. I'm not ruined."

"Not ruined? Just look at you. Who'd take you on to scrub their back step?" His words cut into my soul. How did he expect me to survive? My face must have flushed bright pink because I could feel it burn. He paused, breathed in a long sip of rank air, and unfurled his brow. "Pearly, come on, stop joshing. I've come three thousand miles after you. Are you going to break my heart?"

"I don't know why you've come here, but I don't believe that it was just because of me." My determination surprised me as much as it surprised Davy.

"You *will* marry me," he interrupted. His long elegant fingers reached through the bars and grabbed at my bodice.

"I cannot! That's what I'm trying to tell you."

"I'll turn you in," he said, fixing his hard eyes on me.

"But I'm innocent," I shouted, feeling a combination of frustration and outrage.

"Who'd believe you?"

"Then so be it," I said, finally. "Turn me in. I'm tired of running." If the jail bars hadn't been there, I would have kicked him like a horse kicking at a fly.

"Those combs," he said, studying my hair. "Where'd you ever get such finery? Those are my mother's. You stole them!" His mouth twisted into a lariat about to be thrown at a calf at branding time.

"You gave me these!" I gasped. "For my birthday. Don't you remember?"

He shot me a peeved look. "Stop lying, Pearly. No one would blame you for pocketing them. My mother disapproved of us, and you wanted to get back at her. She was never kind to you, and it always made me feel the worse." His gaze fell to the floor.

As his eyes began to water, my temper blew the lid off the boiling pot. "You *gave* them to me!"

"Get me out of here," he said, pressing himself against the cage wall. "Now!"

"I will, I . . ." I came closer to touch his arm in a feeble gesture of conciliation. Don't let your temper get the best of you, I told myself; don't say something you'll regret. But how could he not remember about the combs?

Eely fingers grabbed my apron just below where it tied around my neck. "It was you," he whispered. "You were the person who came in here the night before last to feed the Indian. I knew I recognized your voice. That's how I knew you were in this town. I heard you give him instructions about the black powder and staying clear of the northeast corner. You get me out of here, Pearl O'Sullivan, or so help me I'll tell everyone that you blasted him out of here, and you'll end up in jail right along with me."

CHAPTER TWENTY-THREE

Four P.M.

Riding through the pines, Tillicum and I leaped Torment Creek, then galloped up the trail into Brushy Gulch. My heart beat as loudly as the little freshet crashing over the rocks, and there was a fire in my stomach, which had nowhere to go.

Though the late-afternoon sun shone, I thought I heard the hideous concert of wolves begin just below timberline. Tillicum's nostrils flared. And though his barrel heaved with exertion, his heart beat as strong and deep as a river. Surely they'll lynch me for helping Pokamiakin escape, I thought. "Lynch her, lynch her," rang every crow call.

Nothing could save me. I was sure of it. And the only place I could go and sort things out was my claim, the Last Chance Mine. But the moment I turned into Saddle Coulee, I knew something was wrong. Not *wrong*, exactly, but out of place, though I couldn't say what. The alpine basin was vacant of trees except for one old wind-topped conifer and a couple of scrub pines. In front of the mine entrance, piles of grizzly stood like grave mounds. The wooden flumes I shared with the lads who prospected nearby stood atop insect-leg supports, zigzagging down the narrow canyon to sluices where we washed and then sorted our ore. Here and there barrels filled with rainwater gleamed beneath a cloud-dappled sky while heaps of debris called "tailings" made ridges between them. Not another soul anywhere. Still, I sensed a new presence, as did Tillicum, who stood dead still in the trail, staring at the blind end of the gulch where, behind the entrance to the Last Chance, a rock wall rose to heaven. A few stones rolled down the steep bank, though no one had trod there. Other than the music of a small stream, there wasn't a sound.

I dismounted in front of a hole blasted into the slate cliff. A lintel supported by two immense posts kept the mine entrance clear, and an actual piece of milled lumber served as a walkway into the opening. Inside, rows of apple crates were the perfect cupboards. My pick, shovel, buckets, fry pan, and kettle lay unmolested.

Hobbling Tillicum and walking into the mine, I thought for a minute that I smelled the freshness of mint, but I must have been mistaken. It vanished the moment I struck a match against the cave wall, lighting the hurricane lamp. Sitting down on a log, I sank my chin into the cradle of my hands, trying to think my predicament through. Helping Davy seemed the wrong thing to do, but his rageful, contorted expression and threats terrified me so much that I was afraid not to. My hands still shook from our encounter. Surely I must flee, but where? Foolishly, I hadn't dug up the baking soda cans full of money buried in my garden. I'd have to go back for them. But by then Davy would have realized I wasn't coming to bail him out and made good on his threat.

I started pacing, my boots making eerie echoes that bounced off the cave walls. Becoming accustomed to the dark, I decided it best to put out the lamp and not advertise my whereabouts. But as I reached up to unhook the lantern from where its handle fastened to a ceiling beam, something way back in the tunnel caught my eye. A metallic flash, a silver ribbon . . . A knife? Scissors? Had I left them there? Had someone spent the night, butchered a deer, and forgotten his cleaver? There was no evidence of such.

I felt my way along the wall toward where I'd seen the glimmer, then stopped dead. I heard the noise of air moving. Breathing. I heard breathing. A bear? Bears came out of hibernation a month ago. The breathing or whatever it was stopped, but I walked no farther. Should I get the lamp? Afraid to turn my back, I reached down, picked up a handful of earth, and threw it into the tunnel. Some of it landed on the dirt floor—the wooden walkway ended but a few feet from the entrance—and some of it landed on what sounded like canvas (a tarp? a jacket?) about twenty feet farther down.

"Who's there?" I tried to sound authoritative but failed miserably when my voice cracked. Something stirred. "Who?"

No response.

I took a small step forward.

First I saw the oily skin of his forehead, then a yellow moon moved toward me. The tip of the silver knife fastened to his black sash of a belt pointed toward the ground.

"Ollo?"

"Chin!" My knees buckled with relief. "Chin, you scared the life out of me!" I said, walking backward toward the entrance of the shaft. But Chin lingered, reluctant to come into the light. "Why are you hiding? They've never enforced that immigrant tax. Why are you so afraid? If you don't have five dollars, we can take up a collection. Everyone's in dire need of good water, there's rumors of cholera . . ."

His face held its blank expression, though I thought I saw his lips quiver. His eyes said, You'd never understand. He hung back in the shadows, holding out a drawstring bag about the size of a goat udder. "Take to Jones."

"But Doc never found General Jones," I told him, exasperated. I don't know why, but tears suddenly began forming in my eyes, and I felt I would burst out crying.

"Glory Hole," he said with a stern expression. His cheeks were streaked with clay, and the dirt I had thrown at him lay on the shoulders of his black tunic. Instead of wearing shoes, his feet were bound in rags crisscrossed with leather thongs.

Getting hold of my composure, I asked, "He's in Shaky's mine?" I took the bag.

"Tea," he said. "Strong. Every hourah."

"Come with me?" I asked. But he shook his head furiously and cowered into the darkness. I bit my thumbnail down to the quick. "Okay."

"Hot tea," he said, "hot, hot."

"Chin, if you talk to anyone, please don't tell that you've seen me." I didn't know where he'd go next, but I knew he wouldn't be here if I came back.

"Ollo," he replied, by which I knew he meant yes.

I caught Tillicum, pushed the silver bit between his teeth, then mounted, heading out of Saddle Coulee. The Glory Hole lay two gulches to the north.

As I came to the mouth of the canyon, my cayuse planted his feet in a sudden halt. He snorted, snaking his neck and tossing his head. I looked around: Here, riding in, I had sensed an odd presence. I studied the lightning scars on the trunk of the wind-topped pine. Then staring up through the dead branches and lacy new growth, I saw what had startled my horse: a canoe in a tree.

Carved from a cottonwood, it had a blunt sturgeon-nose bow. Animals had been sculpted into the sides: A beaver, an otter, and several leaping salmon were painted black and red with copper-green eyes. Leaning back in the saddle for a better view, I saw that the boat was heaped with hides, telling me an Indian had been buried up there. Whose grave, I wondered? The Indian boy who'd been hanged just before my arrival in Ruby?

The thought of a lynching made me shake, and I spurred Tillicum on down the trail through the rabbit grass, rocks, and red vine.

It took me an hour to reach Glory Hole Gulch due to mudslide. The sun had set, and the evening chill stung my cheeks. Shaky's claim (I couldn't get used to the fact that it belonged to me) looked like the Last Chance, only the main entrance was as tall as a house. Two smaller entrances sat on either side, and some wee caves adorned the same ledge. In front of the shaft's opening stood a lean-to kitchen, home to a rusted stove.

I thought it best not to call out. I had no idea why Jones was hiding or what he was afraid of. What had prompted him and Chin and Mary to act like injured animals, taking to the thicket to lick their wounds or die? I walked a good fifty feet into the tunnel and found no evidence of the ex-slave. Nor had I seen any blood outside the entrance. Stupid me, it would have been licked clean by wolves or coyotes by now.

An icy chill crossed my brow—had wolves . . . ?

Searching one spur, I found nothing; ditto with the other. I lost patience as the sky darkened. Then it occurred to me to check one of the false starts nearby, a hole in the side of the ridge where the quartz hadn't shown any promise. Walking toward the nearest child-sized cave, my breath caught in my throat. If I hadn't known what to look for I would have thought he was a pile of leaves. There Jones lay, fretting and in terrible pain. His spidery body gave off the acrid smell of stale sweat.

I ran back to the main shaft, got a lantern, and returned, kneeling next to him. His eyes stared at me unseeing, though he must have sensed me there, because he reached out. My heart sank when I felt his cold fingers. How could I hope to make him drink Chin's tea? It might go into his lungs and not his stomach, killing him for sure. Someone, Chin, I guessed, had put his jacket on backward to cover the wound, and it was with great difficulty that I got it off and had a look at the damage.

The bullet had gone deep into the shoulder, chipping the

bone, but it had been well cleaned, the flesh sewn back over it with horsehair and then a dressing of cattail fluff applied, held in by the backward jacket. I was sorry I'd undone the bandage, but at least I knew his injury wasn't septic—though his pale clammy skin and delirium told me deep shock had set in. The heat emitted by his forehead and the coolness of his hand made me lose heart. First, I elevated the patient's feet, keeping a careful watch that his wound did not begin to bleed. Then I wound a rag around his head as a nightcap.

Fearing all was lost, I filled the old stove with wood—a rats' nest littered the woodbox and had to be cleared away, but never mind (it was empty of little critters and made good kindling)—then ran with a bucket to the spring.

It was the Napoleon of cookstoves, and the kettle boiled in no time. I steeped the tea in a separate pot and unearthed a cup stashed with some flatware and staples in an old steamer trunk behind the woodbox. I don't know what was in that potion, but it stank to blazes. Examining it, I discerned strips of willow bark and bits of what I thought was tansy root. The rest? Pieces of insect—probably cricket—eggshell, and (dare I say it?) ground mourning dove tongue. While the concoction brewed, I made some flat bread out of the flour in the metal trunk. I found a small crock of honey—Shaky's favorite sweet. My idea was to interest General Jones in a bite of food, bringing him back to full consciousness so that he could sip the tea.

His neck could not support his head, and his eyes had rolled back, his tongue lolling out, so it was with immense difficulty that I got food into his mouth. First I chewed it, then cradled his head, placing little bits on the back of his tongue. His head reminded me of a coconut, and his nappy hair was softer than the steel wool I had always supposed it to be. It was long and damp and stuck out from his head in spikes, poor man. I began to piece together the nature of his mistrust: Whenever an Indian was lynched (or about to be), the ex-slaves and Chinese labor shivered in their shoes for fear they'd be next. Sad to say, their fears were well founded. And so Jones, in his shock and delirium, had fled; Chin had become acutely afraid of the immigrant tax; and Mary decided it best to lay low.

Miraculously, within an hour Jones regained partial consciousness. The tea was well brewed by then, and I spooned it into his mouth. It was getting on into evening, and outside the cave the black heavens were spotted with porcelain stars. The ridge of glacier peaks shone bone white behind the coulee, like the vertebrae of a dead horse. Wrapping myself in a blanket, I sucked in the thin crisp air scented with snowmelt.

I sat on the cave floor next to Jones, my back against the jabbing rock wall as he rallied between delirium and occasional moments of comprehension, though clearly, like Shaky just before he died, his mind traveled into the past. Which gave me pause. I considered the deaths of Shaky, Jake, and Dutch. Now Jones was in grave condition. Was there any connection among the four men?

Jones whimpered. I should have forgotten my troubles and ridden down to the village after Doc, but I feared my patient might not make it through the night. By the time I returned with help, the wolves might have found him. It would weigh heavily on my soul if I left him and he died alone.

A long, low moan fell out of Jones's dry lips. "Massa, don't," he said, "we house boys. We given to ya for a wedding present. We don't know where we'd be going. We scared of them Delta rice fields, lotta folks die there. We never see mammy again. What we do? We ain't never stole nothin'. My brotha, he never kill no one, no matter what Sonny says."

Jones's entire body shook, and I didn't know if it was from the wound or the memory. "Not one of my people ever been sold. We handed down father to son. It smell in this shed. What that white boy say: Line up and go one at a time outside onna stage? Bossman weigh us, measure our tallness, how long our arm. 'Show your hands,' Bossman say. 'How much you give?' Bossman ask de audience. Look like a lake of white faces. Red-shirt scream, 'Hundred dollar.' My neck shackle too tight. This chain heavy. I'm a houseboy, not a field slave. Why you do me this way? I got a blood sore from my ankle chain. Bossman say he afraid we all run away. White folks always sayin' that. Tall-hat scream, 'Two hundred dollar.' Bossman pound his hammer onna table. I do that with a hammer, I get put in a cellar. 'Four hundred dollar,' Whitegloves say. Yellow-haired boy with no front teeth prods me with a broom handle. 'Next,' he say. But I ain't listenin'. I lookin' at Mr. Whitegloves takin' my brotha away."

At this Jones's head fell forward, and he collapsed in deep sleep. I took his bony hand, which had become slightly warmer, the fingertips no longer ice-cold.

Dozing for a few minutes, I shook myself awake, then nodded off again. The next thing I knew it was first light and Jones rested peacefully. Then I noticed the fresh blood stains on his jacket. His wound had started bleeding again, and I knew that if he was to be saved I'd have to put my troubles aside and bring help by noon.

Before leaving, I brewed more of Chin's healing tea, making a bowl of flour mush and honey for myself. I found some potatoes and sliced them raw into a bowl of vinegar for Jones to eat if he regained consciousness—vinegar was a vital ingredient to the regeneration of blood. Salt. I forgot the salt—a body couldn't make new blood without it.

Putting the bowl of vinegar potatoes beside him, I said, "General, I'm going to get help, Doc or Mrs. Bitterroot. You suck on these chips if you get a yen for solid food."

To my surprise he opened his eyes, then began flailing his arms like a bird shot from flight. "No Miss Lady, not Dockta Strong!" He collapsed into a fit of groaning.

"Doc Stringfellow," I corrected, tears returning to my eyes. Exhausted, I'd come to the end of my tether. "Doc or Carolina will make you better," I promised, realizing that he'd returned to the nightmare of the slave auction.

Then, despite my fatigue, it came to me, the connection among the four men. Jones, Shaky, Dutch, and Jake were all Civil War vets. Each had fought for the Union. Could the murderer be a secessionist bearing an old grudge? My shoulders slumped, and I shook my head. It seemed like such a long shot.

CHAPTER TWENTY-FOUR

April 23

Galloping Tillicum into Ruby City, I found the streets teaming with wagons, the sidewalks jammed with armies of prospectors. Not only had the posse come back for refreshment at the Gem, but a stagecoach of miners who'd wintered in Seattle had arrived. And I counted five gents who walked in over the mountains, their faces blackened with charcoal and bacon fat to stave off the effects of snow blindness.

Only nine A.M. by Shaky's watch, and already the sun shone so brightly that the storefronts had their striped awnings rolled down for the first time this year. The sky was scoured of clouds, and a breeze bore the smell of sagebud. I studied a crowd in front of the faro tent, a gathering so large that some lads sat on their horses at the hitching post while being dealt in in a hand of poker. The pot lay just inside the doorway next to Forr. And though the betting raged with increasing fierceness, Forr snoozed behind his cards. The ten-dollar limit jumped to twenty. Players were going out and going broke, but Forr dozed on, occasionally nodding awake, his lids crawling up his glassy eyes like harness blinders.

Doc wasn't at his surgery. It was more convenient for him to pay calls on the sick than have them brought to his door, which might worsen their condition. I reined Tillicum south along Main, searching the street for a familiar face.

"Hello, Pearly," someone shouted, raising a crutch in the manner of a salutation.

"Pij! You're out without your bandages! Have you seen Doc? It's an emergency."

"Waitin' on him myself," yelled Pij. "Been by the trading post?" he asked. "Saw a letter for ya there yesterday." The mail carrier hobbled along, his clubfoot tracking at right angles to his good leg.

Medical college! If I hadn't been so exhausted and my mind so preoccupied, my heart would have jumped the track. I reined Tillicum toward the livery, asking everyone I met if they'd seen Doc, and when no one had, I began asking after Carolina. Riding up to the office of the justice of the peace, I noted that the "Closed" sign still hung in his window. Again I pondered Arizona Charley's request for an audience with me. When I went across the street to Windy's trading post, I saw that it too was closed and that the lard pail, which contained mail, had been put inside. When I rattled the doorknob, I found the door bolted tight as a whiskey keg. Staring through the little window, I saw not a soul.

I'd never known the trading post to be shut except for Sunday morning when Windy took her bath. And only Windy Pardee would advertise her toilet hours. Was she unwell? Typhoid, maybe even cholera? Or . . . had she and Charley fled the territory?

Retracing my steps along the muddy street past freight wagons of miners' gear and provisions, I rode toward Pipe Stem Alley to the sheriff's, fearing all the way that Davy had betrayed me. If I had that letter, I could run. Was I a fool to ride right up to his wild anger and accusations? But I had to find Sheriff Barton. I couldn't let poor General Jones down, and no one had seen Doc or Carolina anywhere.

With the arrival of at least fifty new miners and the impending visit of the mine owner the very next afternoon, town sentiment began to shift. After two days of searching for Poka Mika, the posse was losing heart and eager to get back to their digs before one of these *cheechakoes* jumped their claims. And if Mr. Forrester was about to set foot in Ruby, I'd better make myself scarce for fear of being recognized.

When I arrived at the Skookum House, Sheriff Barton was holding court right in the middle of the trail. I braced myself, trying to read something in the lawman's gestures that would tell me if he knew I'd helped blast Pokamiakin out of jail. Don't shrink back, I told myself. Act normal. Barton talked as if he held a buggy whip in one hand and a ballot box in the other. I'd never seen the man from whom he was trying to extract a vote, and he must have thought me rude. It should have dawned on me that something was wrong. Not a single one of the sheriff's new deputies was there reoutfitting his horse.

"Have you seen Doc?" I asked without dismounting (all the better to make a quick getaway). "I've found Jones. He's up at—"

"Doc's with Hames, takin' Charley to the ice caves." The sheriff didn't meet my eye but went on telling the buck-toothed newcomer about his mayoral qualifications.

My heel was poised, ready to spur Tillicum into a gallop, "Excuse me?"

"Found shot to death in the back of his office yesterday afternoon. Windy did, I mean. Was a gun next to him. Don't know if he drawed and fired to defend himself or with suicidal intent." My eyes must have bugged out of my head, because the next thing the sheriff said was, "Thought you knew." He turned to the stranger. "By the way, this here is Pearl, our laundress. Pearl, what're the chances of gettin' a clean shirt by mornin'?" Barton removed his Stetson and combed his dark hair over his bad spot.

"Of course," I lied. Charley? Charley'd been shot?

Now I knew there was a conspiracy afoot, but what? Charley'd been too young to fight in the War Between the States, which crippled my theory about the recent loss of life and health of four—no, five—of Ruby's most prominent citizens as having something to do with the victims all being Union vets. Unless Charley was the exception. Or Charley's death was totally unrelated to the others. Although . . . my memory seemed to rub against some story about military intrigue, one that involved Arizona Charley. But what?

All I could say was, "Suicide? Two in two days' time? Is that possible?"

The sheriff shrugged. He stood so straight that I knew he'd once been a soldier. "A disappointment of the heart." He lowered his voice.

"Windy accepted a proposal from Hames?" I said incredulously.

The sheriff laughed, making some excuse about not knowing the affairs of hens.

An autopsy would certainly tell the tale: suicide or murder. But now Doc had two bodies to examine. Where would he get the time, and why was he dragging his feet about autopsying Dutch? Shaking my head, I thought, If only I could find a common thread among all five men, then maybe I'd find my killer.

"Have you seen Nurse Bitterroot?" My breath came hard and fast, and I could feel my cheeks color, burning as if I'd been out bonnetless in the sun all day. My hands could barely hold the reins. Calm down, I told myself, don't act like you're afraid; he'll mistake it for guilt. Then it occurred to me: Charley must have been dead inside his office when I arrived for my noon appointment. Had that been why he'd been shot? Because of what he was going to tell me? Worse, now I'd never find out why he wanted to see me.

The sheriff shook his angular head, his beard shaved with such vigor that his face was chapped a painful shade of rose. "Nope, but Brownie's at the house. Just saw him."

"What about Jones? What shall I do?"

A woe-is-me expression came over Barton's face. "Got my hands full," he said, turning back to the startled stranger. "I could get you some men, maybe in an hour," the sheriff reconsidered.

"An hour? He could die." Was the sheriff even talking to me?

"He's a tough old nigger," Barton said. "He'll be all right."

"Let me see if I can get help before then." I thought, if it were your horse, Sheriff Barton, you wouldn't let him suffer for a half a minute let alone an hour. I galloped up the trail without asking about Davy.

The Bitterroot house was on the wagon road to the Ruby Mine. It had a white fence around the kitchen garden and a well, the only private watering hole in town. The porch was swept clean as the sky, and the lace-trimmed windows shone spotless.

When I rapped on the door, Brownie answered immediately. He wore a boiled shirt and a black tie; his trousers had perfect creases. For a minute I thought the city fathers had scheduled Dutch's funeral without consulting me, but then I remembered Mr. Forrester's arrival. The mine foreman peered out the door with apprehension, then took a sigh of relief.

"Is Carolina in?" I asked.

"She's nursing a patient up at Dutch's old digs," he said, pulling the door open but not asking me to enter. Though his demeanor was on the stiff side by Ruby's standards, he was less formidable than his wife. Peeking into the parlor, I saw Blindy sitting silently at the table, a slate, some chalk, and a ruler beside him. I knew the drill: One parent held the ruler across the slate and the little boy would attempt to write his name on it, trying to judge with unseeing eyes the distance between his let-ters. His large script was jagged and unruly, and I always found his lessons painful to watch.

"I need her," I said. "Doc's gone and I've found General Jones up at Shaky's mine. He's hurt real bad. There's no infec-tion yet, but the bleeding hasn't quite stopped and—"

As their Swiss cuckoo clock began to strike ten, Brownie closed the door behind him so that his son wouldn't hear me. Something about the way he twirled the ends of his mustache told me he'd like to get me off his porch as soon as possible. "She might be contagious," he said. His eyes and hair were mud brown, which gave his face a sallow look. "Maybe get one of Ella's girls to help you."

"But he needs *professional* help. I'm scared he'll die. He needs attention before mortification sets in. . . ."

"She should be back by noon. I'll tell her," he replied.

"But Doc will probably be back by then. Isn't there some way—" I heard the slate crash to the floor, followed by Blindy's frustrated whimpers.

"Excuse me," Brownie's face clouded as he dismissed me, closing the door.

I stood on the porch for a moment wondering whatever had given me the idea that the Bitterroots would be kindred spirits. To them I was just the laundress. Beyond my ability to iron a shirt, they didn't value me in the slightest.

Despite the misunderstanding about the necklace, for the first time since I'd come to Ruby I deeply missed Mrs. Ritters. I could see her as clearly as yesterday, lounging in her canopy bed beneath a satin comforter as she pushed praline truffles between her pulpy lips, quoting aphorisms between candies. (Did she ever offer me one? I don't remember that she did. They were bad for my teeth and dentists were expensive, especially for someone in my situation.) "Don't let the servants make mince-meat out of you, Pearl," she said, unwrapping a sweet from its colored foil. The servants had been taunting me, and she handed me a kerchief to dry my eyes. "Rise above it. You're made of better stuff than they are. Remember: Sow in tears, reap in joy. You'll grow up just fine and make something of yourself." She'd probably added a few words about staying away from the groundskeeper's dreadful son, Davy Witherup, but I hadn't listened. It made me sad now to think that I was all grown up and still making a mess out of my life. I thought of Davy, and my heart filled with lead. Mounting Tillicum and pointing his head in the direction of Little Ella's, I decided I'd sown in tears just about long enough.

This time when I knocked at Ella's, Nightingale answered with a welcome and (was I mistaken?) a relieved expression. "You look like a horse run thirty miles, then put in a stall caked with sweat," she said. She wore faded brown calico and a starched apron and might have passed as a young wife if I didn't know otherwise. "If you're so good at nursing," she said, "I could use a hand." By this time I'd grown accustomed to her abrasiveness.

"Oh, dear, I'm afraid I've come to ask you the same. What's the matter?"

Just then wild laughter rang out from the street. Below the boarding house veranda, a group of greenhorns enjoyed a bottle of Ruby's choicest bourbon, the brew Jake used to manufacture in seconds from alcohol, water, and burnt sugar—never mind the still. "Days of old, days of gold, days of forty-nine," they sang in a harmony that only intoxication before noon could render. Out of the corner of my eye I saw Mrs. Belknap with her new baby crossing the street to avoid them.

"Cats in a feed tub," said Nightingale, nodding at the Johnny-come-latelies. Turning back to me, her voice cracked, and I thought she would burst into tears. "The girls've come down with quinsy," she said fretfully. "At least, I hope it's quinsy and not diphtheria. Can you tell the difference? Please come look at 'em. I'd truly be obliged."

My heart went out to her. "Yes, maybe for a minute, but I've got trouble. I found General Jones. He's hurt real bad. Doc's taken Charley to the ice caves and—"

"Charley! I don't wanna hear another word about it. Shaky, Dutch, Charley—I ain't countin' Jake—and now I've got a house full of invalids. I'm about run off my feet. Plus," she said, making a wide gesture with her arms toward the singing green-horns, "look at all the new business that's just come in on the stage.

"This way," she said, closing the door behind me.

Had she heard me tell her about Jones?

"Sheriff told me he thought Charley might have shot him-self, because Windy'd jilted him. Do you believe that?" I asked.

Nightingale shook her head.

"Tell me, did Windy really take up with Hames?"

"Psaw," said Nightingale. "Double psaw. The night before Charley died, she'd taken a pint with the sheriff up at the Gem. From the way Barton's talkin' now, you'd think he and Windy was engaged." She rolled her hazel eyes and dismissed Windy's flirtations with the wave of her hand.

I laughed, "Sounds like a dime novel someone used to paper the privy."

She led me to Ella's room, where the corpulent woman lay on the floor in such a deep slumber I wondered if she might be unconsciousness. Wrapped in a bad-smelling buffalo robe, Ella's hair fell across her white face. She'd removed her false eye, and it stared out from a shot glass of vodka set on a nail keg next to her bed.

"If you could help me get her up on to the mattress," said Nightingale. "She's not as bad off as the others. She's just got a weak constitution, even for a woman. One little malady and she can't lift a finger. But Squirrel . . ." Tears appeared in Nightingale's eyes. "Squirrel's sunset red with fever."

Ella stirred. "Lorenzo? Where's my little birdie?" she grumbled.

"Your rooster's here," Nightingale assured. The red-and-black cock was nowhere in sight, though a faint odor of chicken dander still hung in the air. Tenderly, Nightingale put her small hand to Ella's brow.

"If I die, I wanna be buried with that bird," the matron said, then closed her good eye and turned her head away from us.

Nightingale took hold of Ella's black-stockinged feet. I straddled the shoulder end, supporting Ella's immense head as I tried to get a firm grip on her upper body. It took all our might to hoist her like a bale of wet wool up on the bed. Then, simultaneously, both of us buckled to the floor. Ella began snoring loudly. Her glass eye stared down at us.

"Why did she take it out?" I asked, offering Nightingale a hand up.

"Pains her," said Nightingale. "It's an odd thing, but even after Doc took her eye, it pained her, even when it was gone." She slapped her seat, dusting herself off.

"*Doc* removed her eye?" I asked, surprised. "I didn't know that."

"Went septic," said Nightingale. "He said the infection would spread to the other eye. Said it had to come out."

"Good God!" Right then I vowed that if I ever got through medical school, I'd try to better the lot of the mining town doctor.

As we tiptoed out of Ella's parlor, I grasped a strained muscle in my back. "How much does she weigh?" I asked, guessing three hundred pounds. "She must have been a popular circus fat lady."

"Fat lady? She weren't never a fat lady," retorted Nightingale as we walked down the sheeted hall through the kitchen to the back stairs. "She had a 'her 'n' him love act.' I can't remember the exact name."

"Her 'n' him? Free love? Like Victoria Woodhull the famous suffragette?"

"Huh? Naw. I saw Ella's old circus poster for it once, "Him 'n' Aphrodite . . ."

I stopped dead in my tracks. "Hermaphrodite?"

"That's it," she said, obviously without comprehension.

My God! No wonder Jake was blackmailing her. For a moment I felt as if someone had socked me in the stomach, then, regaining myself, remembered why I'd come here in the first place. "Is there any way you could help me with Jones?" I asked.

"You come upstairs and look at the girls and tell me whatcha think," she said. "If it's your opinion that I can leave 'em, I'll go. Jones is tough as a mule. Dutch once told me that durin' the war, Jones was supposed to have his arm amputated. That ol' slave got so frightened about his limb bein' buried in the cold, dark ground that he runned away. And as you can see, both he and his arm survived."

"But that was years ago when he was young, and this is a shoulder wound," I said, becoming impatient. "It's still bleeding, and he's like a house burning down with fever."

Seized by a sudden inspiration, I said, "Nightingale, you hear a lot of local talk. Do you know why Charley wanted to see me yesterday?" Had Charley known about Ella? Had Ella murdered the town lawyer as well?

"I might," she said, cocking her head, "and I might not."

"You *do* know!" I countered excitedly. I ran ahead so that I could look her squarely in the face.

Her hazel eyes narrowed. "Like I said, maybe I do and maybe I don't." Her rabbit lip twitched. Was she mocking me? "I can't give away all my secrets, now can I?"

"What if I paid you?"

"Go on with ya. What do you take me for?"

"Why not? You sold information to Jake."

"It got him outta here fast, before he upset Ella," she said. "When he died, I swore off peddlin' people's secrets. Made a firm pledge to the Holy Virgin."

"Just tell me one thing," I insisted. "Did it have to do with Jake's murder?"

She looked utterly surprised. "Course not."

"Then . . . then did it have to do with that boy the sheriff's holding, Davy?"

"That boneless gent?" A wry expression came over her thin face and colorless lips. After a moment she said, "Yes, I suppose you could say he brought on this trouble."

My heart fell through me to my feet. So Charley had known about Mrs. Ritters's necklace and the warrants issued against me. He'd probably come across a sketch of me on a "Wanted" poster. But why had he requested an appointment? Blackmail? I hadn't any money that he knew of, and he didn't seem like an extortionist. Then I began to worry. Had he told anyone? Windy, did she know?

"Tell me more?" I pleaded.

She moved her tiny fingers across her mouth in a buttoning gesture. "My lips are sealed," she said. "Besides, he's dead. What does it matter?" She shook her head. "Poor Charley, another fallen Yank," she said glumly.

Startled, I asked, "Yankee? Do you mean that literally?"

"*Literally?* You and your book-learnin' talk," she scoffed.

"Charley was too young to have been in the War Between the States," I prodded.

"A lot you know," she retorted. "By age ten Charley was Grant's drummer boy at Cold Harbor. If you'd spent time in Ella's parlor, you'd have known all about it."

"That's it! That's the missing link," I cried.

"That's what?" she demanded. "You know, Pearl, you could be a nice person, if you'd stop actin' too big for your bloomers."

I waved her comment away, motioning for her to hurry along. Shaky, Jake, Dutch, Jones, Charley—every one of them had been a Union veteran. But *what* about being a Union veteran? I threw my hands into the air in frustration. Had Ella killed all of them? Why? She hadn't a political bone in her body. Or did she? Just as one piece of the puzzle fell into place, several others turned askew.

Upstairs, I found Squirrel and Mouse and all the doves red with fever, their bodies covered with perspiration. Mouse asked to be helped to the chamber pot, others pleaded for ice. There was a bowl of cold water and a sea sponge, and as I picked up the sponge to mop Squirrel's brow, I had to ask, "Where'd you get this water?"

Nightingale broke down. "I've been up since dawn," she cried. "I musta carted ten buckets of water down from the ice caves. I don't know how that Chinaman did it, but I sure know why he quit. I've been cursin' him 'cause he didn't wait until tomorrow."

"I'm almost positive it's not diphtheria," I said. "Diphtheria leaves a terrible stench. All the necrocity in the throat."

"What? Please," she said wrinkling her brow, "don't wax biggity on me now."

"My diagnosis is scarlet fever. The important thing is to keep their temperatures under control with dandelion tea. You don't want the fever weakening their hearts. Keep their heads raised so that their ears don't go fudgy. My sister lost part of her hearing that way. And gargle every hour with a tincture of salt water and peroxide, if you have it."

"Thanks," she nodded. "Do you think I dare leave 'em?"

I didn't, and reluctantly I told her so. "I saw Mrs. Belknap outside earlier. Maybe she can help me," I remarked resignedly.

"She's been skirting the house all mornin' looking for her husband. Tell her Frank's not here, will ya?" Nightingale asked in an embarrassed voice.

I nodded, gave her a friendly pat on the shoulder, and said I'd see myself to the door. Passing Ella's room, I thought, a hermaphrodite? Hard to believe, though it made sense. That *was* the one thing that might get her run out of Ruby. And it would explain her mannish bald spot and the way I'd seen her dash from the jailhouse—her muscles flexed with strength as if she had a stallion's serum running through her veins.

"Wait," Nightingale called after me. "Will you be layin' Dutch out?"

"I expect so," I said. The thought of it made me feel down-hearted and weary.

She pressed something toward me wrapped in a piece of flannel blanket. "I think it'd be lovely if he was buried with this."

Whatever it was was stone-heavy. Pulling the bunting away, my breath stopped in my windpipe. I'd recognize that long silver muzzle, gleaming barrel, and mother-of-pearl grip anywhere. "The missing revolver!" I said. "Where'd . . . ?"

"Dutch gave it to me." She spoke rapidly as if her sentence was all one word.

"But why didn't you tell me?" Had Ella used this gun to shoot Jake—and maybe Charlie and the General as well? Again I wondered why. Nothing made sense.

Nighingale's gaze dropped to the floor. "It's the only truly nice thing I own," she said in a voice as high and forlorn as a mosquito's whine. "And since Dutch had already toldja he'd lost it, I figured he didn't want ya to know. . ."

Fitting my hand around the grip, I tried to cock the hammer, but it was stuck, frozen as February. The gun hadn't been fired in at least half a year.

Finally, when I found my voice, I said, "I think he would've wanted you to keep it." As I pressed the revolver into her hands, her sorrowful expression changed to that of a child who'd been reunited with a favorite doll. "It seems to need a good oiling," I added. "You might take it apart and soak it in bear grease." Another red herring? I asked myself. Yesterday I'd been sure that Dutch's gun had been used to kill Jake and would lead me to the killer.

"Don't forget to tell Frank's wife he ain't here," she said, her eyes sparkling like two rain barrels after a downpour.

I nodded, unlatching the door, thinking, Hurry, get back to Jones.

But when I got down the porch steps and into the alley, Mrs. Belknap—and my last hope for getting help for the General—had vanished.

CHAPTER TWENTY-FIVE

There was only one thing to do: dress the General's wounds myself and then head up to the ice caves for Doc. If I hadn't been bursting to tell him the startling news about Ella, I'd have felt like a lantern that was about to flicker out. My little horse had a perky walk as long as we headed in the direction of home, but once past my laundry his steps grew heavy, his head hanging below his chest.

I gazed over my shoulder at the mountain of wash heaped in front of my door. Not a second to spare even for a bowl of soup or a change of clothes. Oh, and didn't I crave a bath! *No time, no time,* said the squeak in my saddle, though I did rest at the bottom of the ravine and let my cayuse have a drink.

Climbing back up to Shaky's mine seemed to take a fortnight. Coming into the coulee, I turned along the mouth of Glory Hole Gulch at the old lightning-scarred pine. Two strides down the fork in the trail, and my horse came to a dead stop. Glancing up at the sturgeon-nosed canoe at the top of the tree (how had they gotten the mortuary craft up there?), I dug my heels into Tillicum's sides, urging him on to the mine entrance. But no matter how hard I kicked, his hooves remained planted.

"Come on!" Reluctantly, Tillicum stepped off the trail, one ear cocked at the gnarled trunk, the other pinned back on his neck in agitation. Then he scooted forward as if chased by dogs, and we were on our way. Fifteen more minutes to Jones. What if the General had died? What if, when I undid his dressing, the wound had mortified? I couldn't bear the sight of such damage to the flesh. What a weak-stomached doctress I'd make. I'd no grit and would have given almost anything to be somewhere else.

What made me turn and glance back over my shoulder, I shall never know. As I did so, Tillicum halted and bent his neck as if to mimic me. There beneath the old tree stood a buckskin-clad, wild-eyed Siwash.

"Pokamiakin!" No sooner had I uttered Rabid Coyote's name than I realized where he'd been hiding. In the mortuary canoe! For two days the posse had combed sage and riverbank tules looking for their fugitive, and here I'd passed by him two, three times without even sensing a presence—though my little horse certainly guessed he was there.

Tillicum snorted, then pawed the ground, and finally, recognizing the scent of the hand who had raised him, stood quietly as the red-eyed native approached.

It sounded like the stupidest thing, but all I could say was, "They're after you."

Laughing, Pokamiakin's jagged teeth parted in the manner of a wolf snarl. His crossed eyes flashed beneath his dark, hooded brow. He was shirtless, his black braid hanging down his back almost to the tops of his buckskin trousers.

"Listen, I don't expect you to help a Boston man, but Jones—the black white man who works at the livery—is up at Shaky's mine in one of those false starts there," I said with a gesture of my hand. "He's hurt bad and . . . Do you know about these things? Could you help me? Please?"

Pokamiakin stood ten feet from me, his muscular arms crossed in front of him. He had the heaviest brow I'd ever seen on a man, and it protruded over his raven nose like the bill of a cap. He remained utterly calm and seemed totally unafraid

even though rifle volley echoed through the lower coulees—
bullets meant for him. The mention of Jones caused his brow to
rise. Rumor had it that when the ex-slave arrived in Okanogan
country, Pokamiakin had been so curious about Jones's color
that he'd captured the General, hauled him down to the creek,
and tried to scrub the black from his face.

"Mary, Chin *kloshe nanitch*," he said, taking several steps
forward and reaching out to pet Tillicum's nose. With his fingers spread, his hands resembled palm fronds—there was something spindly and, at the same time, hugely strong about them.

"Mary and Chin are nursing him?"

He gave a slight nod.

"*Mahsie Tyee*." Thank God. "It's none of my business," I
continued, "and you don't have to answer . . ." Could he understand my English? I thought that he could. "When Jake
Pardee was *mamaloosed,* were you there?"

I didn't expect him to reply, but he did. "*Nowitka*." Yes, he
said raising his brow.

It wasn't the answer I'd hoped for. "Nightingale told the
sheriff you were trying to sweep tracks from the wagon road."

"*Halo*." No, he said emphatically, shaking his head, then
repeated himself adding a bemused laugh. I couldn't tell if he
was staring at me or at Tillicum. The gaze of one reddened eye
shot off toward the pine tree while the other drifted along the
trail.

"Nightingale said she saw you sweeping the wagon road
with a stick."

At this he opened his mouth to the sky and laughed.
"*Mamook huyhuy tzum*."

"Making the marks change? Altering the hoof prints?
Why?" My breath stopped. An ashy taste filled my mouth. It
came to me in a flash what he'd done: made the prints look as
if another horse had made them. "Whose horse made those
tracks?"

One crimson eye jumped to the top of the old pine while

the other darted over the jagged Western horizon. "Tillicum," he said, pointing a finger at me.

The reins fell from my hands and, if they had not been knotted at the ends, would have fallen to the ground. My mouth filled with soot and deep waters came up into my soul. Only one person could have been there that day on my horse. And that same person could have easily taken Shaky's pearl-handled revolver from my digs, shot Jake with it, and then re-placed the weapon without arousing my slightest suspicion.

"Doc?" I whispered. "Impossible."

CHAPTER TWENTY-SIX

Was it possible?

As I rode up gulch to the mine in Glory Ridge, my heart pounded so hard it shook my entire body. It didn't bother me so much that Doc might have murdered Jake—as you know, I could have strangled Pardee bare-handed myself. What pierced my soul was that Doc asked me to investigate. Why? Because he was an honest, conscience-stricken man who could not bear the weight of it until he was found out? Was Doc really that complicated? Suddenly I didn't know the man at all. My mind went into a tumult. Though my heart beat like the hooves of a pony frightened by lightning clap, I felt my face steel itself. Each time Tillicum's hoof struck a stone in the trail, I felt as if I too had turned to the ice and rock of the mountain's sheer face.

When I got to Shaky's silver mine, I thought it deserted. Not a bird sang, the quiet so pervasive that I could hear his watch ticking in my apron pocket. But at the mouth of the false start where I'd left Jones, I found Mary and Chin hovering over the patient.

"*Alah! Mika chako,*" said Mary in her small sparrowlike voice.

"Yes, here I am." My words hardly expressed how glad I was to see her.

"Stick-skin tea," Chin said, spooning a cup of bark broth into Jones's mouth.

Mary made sweeping motions across Jones's chest with a wild rose bramble in the hope of keeping his spirit on our side of the Great Divide and the spirits of the dead on the other. Chin put down the teacup and spoon, went to the stove, took two rocks the size of chicken eggs out from under it, then held the smooth white stones to either side of the patient's face, moving them from forehead to jaw. Jones looked much improved. Instead of a sooty gray, his complexion had returned to its usual nut color.

"Do you know the song of this herb?" Mary asked me, gesturing to the bramble she'd been brushing across Jones's chest.

"No," I said.

Mary sang, "Good grass, good leaves," her words for "rosebush." Laying the briar down, she drew a buckskin bag from inside her robe, displaying her healing charms.

I studied the beaver tooth but did not touch it, since my fingers would cause it to lose its powers. Chin leaned down and put one hooded eye to a blue bird's egg. "Hen berry," he said, then looked at the two small yellow feathers and a mourning dove foot. Replacing the charms, Mary gently shook the medicine bag over Jones's wound.

Ask her about Doc, ask her, the voice screamed, but I didn't know how to begin. "You've got some new trinkets?" I remarked as I took Jones's pulse. His forehead no longer felt clammy, and although his temperature was elevated, it was probably more from his flesh being torn than from infection.

"New, but not new," she said, rubbing her charm bag. "I put them in jar, plant jar in anthill." Her fingers made the crawling motions of an insect. "Purified," she said. "Better than fire." The aboriginals held with the idea that if you put your charms and medicine bundles in an anthill for several months, their powers would be rejuvenated.

Chin pressed a warm white stone on either side of Jones's cheek. The rocks seemed to soothe him, as if his body's tension was drawn out by the limestone. The patient's shoulders drooped in a more comfortable sleep. Every so often Jones smacked his lips, and Chin would pull the patient's mouth to one side and empty a spoonful of "stick-skin" broth between his lips.

Suddenly, Jones's eyes popped open and he coughed up a swallow of tea.

"What do dreams say?" Mary asked him. Jones refused to speak Chinook, so Mary was forced to communicate with him in English. "Dreamspeak?" she asked.

The General's spider-thin neck tried to raise his head but could not. Somewhere Chin had found a straw-filled pillow, which he plumped behind the patient's head.

"Spirit don't flee," said Chin, pulling on Jones's arm. The African's tattered coat was made from blue worsted wool, an aged remnant from his Civil War days.

"He was about to be sold at a slave auction when I left him this morning," I said. "General?" I bent down close to his left ear. "Can you hear us?"

"Lieutenant Dockta Strong?" he asked.

"There's no Doctor Strong here," I told him.

"Don' let Lieutenant Dockta Strong take my arm off," he said, trying to raise himself up on his elbows. Jones looked imploringly at Chin.

"No, no," said Chin, drawing his balled fists up into the sleeves of his tunic.

Ask her, ask Mary about Doc, goaded the voice.

Mary began fanning Jones with the rose bramble with one hand, rummaging in a hemp bag strapped to her waist with the other. Drawing out a strip of groundhog fat, she slid it eagerly into her mouth like a noodle, then offered me one. I shook my head. If there was one thing I will never learn to abide, it's groundhog in any form. Mary gave Chin a strip (my God, it smelled rancid!). His face glowed as he chewed it like gum.

"No one here cut off your arm," said Chin, speaking better English than I thought possible. Sly fox, I bet he spoke French and several other languages as well.

"Dutch, don't let him do it," pleaded Jones. His head fell back. I had no idea from what part of his brain he was speaking.

The three of us looked at one another. "He doesn't know Dutch is dead," I said.

"Don't tell," said Mary, a finger pressed to her weather-cracked lips in a shushing gesture. Chin and I nodded in agreement.

"Mary, there's something I have to ask you about," I said.

Jones spoke but did not try to raise his head. "Lieutenant Dockta Strong get fifty dolla every time he cut off an arm. Keeps all them feet 'n' hands inna bucket, takes 'em to quartermaster end o' the day for his pay."

I shivered. Was that how battle surgeons had been paid, by the amputation? I seemed to remember my da telling me a similar grisly story about his soldiering days.

Jones's head fell to the side. Chin repositioned the pillow. Its mattress tick covering was stained with drool and specks of dried blood. When the patient fell into deep slumber, Chin continued to press the warm stones against his neck. Mary and I walked over to the stove and fumbled through the stores in search of food.

The cornmeal was infested with weevils, but we cooked it all the same, the little bugs appearing as caraway. Stirring the mash, I rehearsed my question to Mary but could not speak it. Chin broke his vigil over the General and went looking for hen berries but found none. Finally we sat down on the ground next to Jones and ate the gone-off-tasting grits by covering them with honey, hoping the pungent smell of raw sugar would bring Jones to and enliven his appetite.

Holding the warm bowl in my hands, I turned to Mary. "You knew Doc killed Jake, didn't you?"

"Yes," she said. I knew she was telling the truth. Contrary to popular belief, Indians didn't lie any more than whites, probably less. Though they often tried to give the answer you wanted to hear—but who wasn't guilty of that transgression?

Chin nodded in agreement and continued moving the stones over Jones's body. What could have driven Doc to such violence?

Just then Jones's torso shot up so suddenly that the stones fell from Chin's hands and rolled across the floor of the cave. "No," screamed Jones. His eyes hardened into two balls of tar and fixed on another world.

"Lieutenant Dockta Strong, no! Hide me, Dutch, like you done the otha boys, please, Massa. Lieutenant Dockta Stringfellow a horse dockta, only know to do one thing to a man." With this the patient fell forward onto his wound, forcing feathers of cattail dressing out of the confines of his jacket, the bloodied fluff scattering over our laps. Chin tried to cushion his fall, then righted him, helping Jones back to a supine position. But he must have passed out from the pain. Chin reapplied the stones, and soon Jones breathed more easily. If he could just take a few bites of food, we'd know he was on the mend.

"He called Doctor Strong Doc Stringfellow!" I blurted out. I felt my brow furrow into lines deep enough to leave permanent slashes across my face. It wasn't possible. I groped for explanations. "No wonder Jones is afraid of modern medicine. He associates white doctors with war wounds. . . ." My voice trailed away.

Neither of my companions met my eye. Mary studied the ground while Chin traced with his index finger the faint gray lines that ribboned one of the warming stones. Now I understood why Mary and Chin vanished whenever Doc came to my tent.

Though the late-day sun shone on the granite outcroppings,

a chill came over me, penetrating to my marrow. My hands turned as pale and bloodless as clay. I thought not just of Jake, but of Dutch and Charley, and God forbid, even Shaky Pat McDonald. Recalling my inspection of Dutch's digs, I remembered his books, the map of Civil War campaigns, and the tintype of the wounded soldiers at Missionary Ridge: The corporal with the injured foot was probably Dutch. There were three ex-slaves on the right-hand side—the one with his arm in a sling must have been Jones. And on the other side, the boxy, big-headed man with a dot of fresh blue surveyor's chalk marked over his head . . .

Doc.

At Shaky's funeral, hadn't Doc made an offhanded remark about not seeing so many soldiers since the Union captured Missionary Ridge? Dutch had doubled over from heartburn. Jones had appeared suddenly stunned, forgetting he was holding onto the sheriff's black mare. The horse had reared up and torn the lines from his hands. At the time I'd thought the ex-slave had been so grief-stricken that he'd forgotten what he was doing.

I did not look at either of my friends as I spoke but at the white intersecting lines of buzzard quartz in the cave wall. "They're the same person, Lieutenant Dr. Strong and Doc Stringfellow."

The silence felt as cold and overpowering as a river of snowmelt. Mary turned sideways, her tule-thin body becoming even narrower, her expression pensive. Chin's face crumbled into a frown. Neither uttered a breath of a denial. Staring out the entrance of the cave into the searing daylight, I thought I might be standing at the mouth of hell.

CHAPTER TWENTY-SEVEN

April 24

I passed a sleepless night on the cave floor, during which time my thoughts raged like wild horses. *Flee,* shrieked the voice. *Now! No use in sorting this out. You may not live long enough to stand trial for stealing the necklace.*

At first light, Mary shook me awake. It seemed I'd only shut my eyes and situated my hips on the damp floor. By the trill in Chin's "Ollo," I knew Jones had stopped getting worse. Indeed, the patient held his head up and asked for, "Water, please Massa." When I pinched the skin on his arm, the flesh felt supple, not dry and limp.

"With you two nursing him, he'll be out of danger in a day's time." They nodded in agreement. Mary sat down next to Jones, whittling stove kindling with a pocketknife. As Chin felt the patient's forehead, I saw a prideful smile flicker across his face.

Exhausted, frightened, and confused, I mounted Tillicum and rode back into town. Every clomp of my horse's hooves asked, *What to do?* As milky fog shrouded the pines, the jaybird's shrill cry screamed, *Flee, flee*. But my heart told me, Have faith, find Doc, he'll put this straight. What hard evidence did I have against him? First, his horse (rather my horse, which he had borrowed) was at the scene of Jake's murder. Second, he could have easily used the pearl-handled gun Shaky had given me. But how could he have been in two places at once? He was delivering Mrs. Belknap's baby at the time. Besides, what motive could he have had for murdering Jake? Certainly not in an argument over a horse. Doc wasn't a hothead. And why would he have killed Dutch or Charley? Surely he hadn't shot the General. Undoubtedly, Jones got in the way of a stray bullet during the shootfest. I didn't want to think about Shaky's death. And if Doc Stringfellow was really Surgeon Strong of Missionary Ridge, a veterinary who got paid by the amputation . . . well, that would explain why he never performed autopsies and why he had me sewing up wounds. *Circumstantial, circumstantial,* bleated the crows. As I myself had remarked many times, Doc truly had broken his glasses, the replacements having never arrived. Only one thing was certain: I had to find him and get to the truth.

Carefully, Tillicum negotiated the hairpin turns into Saddle Coulee. As black thoughts flew through my brain, dampening my spirits, my kindly horse turned his head, eyeing me from time to time, as if checking on how his load was coming along.

Nearing town, the trail widened into a wagon road where ruts were hub deep. Sun flooded the sage valley, burning away the fog. Descending Ruby Grade, I encountered battalions of prospectors tramping up to the mines. Most newcomers wore braces and shirts with all their buttons sewn on. One fellow with my same kinky carrot hair waved. The others burned so fiercely from gold fever that I appeared invisible as I passed, my surefooted pony hurrying toward Doc's surgery.

Leaping from Tillicum's back, my feet stung as I hit the ground. I tried the door. Not only was it locked, it was bolted from both top and bottom of the frame to protect Doc's stores of laudanum. When I had tried the door yesterday, it was only locked, not bolted.

"Doc?" I called at the window. "Are you home? It's me, Pearl." All I heard were hollow settling noises the doorstep boards made when I stepped there.

Scanning the street for Doc's silhouette, I saw three men riding out of town, one on each side of a familiar figure. Without taking stock of my actions, I yanked my bonnet down over my face and fled behind the surgery, peering around the corner of the building at the middle horseman.

Davy Witherup.

What had he told the sheriff about me? As Davy rode past I saw that his wrists were bound behind him, his legs strapped to the fenders of the saddle. Two sheriff's deputies appeared to be escorting him to another jail. Had he babbled about me helping blast Pokamiakin out of jail or mentioned those New York warrants?

What was going on? Taking indecent liberties at a bawdy house didn't warrant such treatment. Davy must have gotten himself in trouble in some other camp, and now the sheriff was trading him for an incarcerated Rubyite—a grand gesture sure to propel Sheriff Barton into the mayorship. I watched the three men's backs as they rode away, taking the east fork toward Pard Cummings's ferry. Davy's head gleamed like a copper kettle. It stung my heart the way things had turned out. Silly Mrs. Ritters had been right: He was a rake. To think I'd once staked my future on him. My former employer's voice screamed at me from out of the past: *stupid girl!*

When they were out of sight, I mounted my horse and hurried through town, asking everybody I met if he or she'd seen Doc. Grasshopper Jack slouched in the doorway of his assayer's hut, the sun speckling his face with a thousand tiny strawberry-seed freckles.

"Seen Doc?" I asked.

His contralto rang into the street. "He's been out pressing palms all mornin'."

I didn't understand and didn't quite catch the explanation. "Doc's runnin' against the sheriff for mayor," repeated Grasshopper. "Didn't ya know?" He gestured toward the "Soles Saved Here/Souls Saved Here" sign above Sheriff Barton's shoemaker shop across the street.

Dumbfounded, I replied, "It's the first I've heard."

What did this mean? Was it just the natural course of events? After a moment's thought, I landed on a plan. I'd go home as if I had no suspicions or evidence whatsoever, warm up my potato chowder, and wait for Doc to come knocking at my door. After he was comfortable and fed, I'd lay all my cards on the table. Why had he murdered Jake? Why hadn't he told me? Was he Doctor Strong who'd served at Missionary Ridge? Then the voice took over my thoughts and began yelling: *Run, now, while you still can!*

On my way past the Gem I remembered the letter, that envelope addressed to me that Pigeon Belcher told me about yesterday. I yanked Tillicum's reins so sharply, steering him down the short cut through Cottonwood Alley, that his eye whites flashed and he turned to look at me. "Sorry," I said, attributing this sudden breach in horsemanship to being on pins and needles with regard to every aspect of my life.

Even before I rode up to Windy's trading post, I could see that her door was still locked, with no lard pail of mail outside. No one at the livery knew when the mercantile would open up again. But Hames knew all about my letter.

He was shoeing a team of bays about to be dispatched to fetch Mr. Forrester from the steamer. "A post for you?" he said, angling his face up at me. "Saw it myself.

"Don't know when she'll open up again," he added, his mouth full of nails. Hames did not look at all displeased that Windy was in mourning over our late justice of the peace. With his sweetheart's husband out of the way, as well as Charley, the field had narrowed, and he was hoping at long last to claim her attentions. Or so I assumed.

"Next mail stage ain't due till the end of the week," he said. "Ain't nobody goin' to be interested in getting into the lard pail until new mail comes. Yours was the only unclaimed envelope."

"Has Doc been around to visit Pij?" I asked as casually as I could manage.

Hames waved my question away. "Been after me to reset them shoes on that black gelding of his, President Whoever."

"Lincoln," I added.

"I knowed, I knowed, but I ain't sayin' it, it's a dirty word." He screwed up his face, determined never to let anyone forget he was a Southern secessionist.

"But you just put on a new front shoe for him. . . ."

"Me? Did no such thing." Hames filed the side of a number-seven shoe, then took it to the anvil, beating nail holes into it with a hammer and punch. "No. Such. Thing."

Perhaps someone else had replaced the shoe. But there wasn't another blacksmith in camp. So President Lincoln hadn't lost a shoe, was that it? But why had Doc borrowed Tillicum after he left Shaky's watchers to go and deliver Mrs. Belknap? I felt the blood drain from my face. Had Doc set me up? It would be my horse's hoofprints that would be found at the scene of Jake's murder.

"Do you have the key?" I pleaded. "To the trading post?" Hames had been Jake's right-hand man and knew how to get into that building.

The farrier gave me a vexed look. "Who'd write somethin' important to you?"

"Do you?"

"I might," he smiled, and not unkindly, either. I could see he was in high spirits. "You go git the sheriff. If he gives me his okay, I'll see what I can do."

Obviously he had no idea that Sheriff Barton was his new rival for Windy Pardee's affections, but that was none of my business. Then my suspicions ran wild: Did Hames know something I didn't and was surreptitiously luring me into the sheriff's custody? Again I worried if Davy had betrayed my secret.

What could I do but reluctantly agree. Plodding up the steep alley, I felt suddenly famished and thought my mount in the same condition. Turning down a line of privies, I found the sheriff in the jailer's hut, tacking up handbills in the fashion of wallpaper. A dry goods crate of "Wanted" posters had been dumped on the floor, and I couldn't help but notice how their whiteness enlivened the dank little building.

"No, I ain't seen Doc," he said mockingly even before I opened my mouth. Barton was chewing tobacco and spat a wad of yellow saliva out the opening cut into the wall.

I shook my head to imply that it wasn't Doc I wanted.

"The prisoner?" he asked, shoving a hand into the pocket of his skintight trousers and fishing out a tin of Bull Durham.

I said, "No, that's not what . . . I saw him being escorted to . . ." I stared at the handbills, wondering if there was a sketch of me in that mountain of a pile.

"Wanted for theft," said Barton with pride. "Found out about him about here." He gestured to the middle of the stack with the toe of his high-heeled boot. "Hauled these and two other boxes down from the Charley's law office. Some go back years. "The kid swears he's innocent, of course." He spat at the word "innocent."

"Davy? Theft of what?" I asked, "Where?" I began taking quick shallow breaths like a woman in childbirth.

"East. New York, maybe. New Somewheres. Do ya think I'll get my name in the Seattle papers?" he asked, his brows rising into his high forehead.

My throat froze shut. I couldn't force a single word from my lips. I wanted to hear what it was Davy had stolen. Though I knew immediately, I just couldn't speak the word.

"Takes them newspapers a month to get here," Barton added. "One loud-mouthed fancy-ass dude, that one," he said of Davy. "Let not the foot of arrogance come against the Lord," the sheriff quoted, then spat yellow rain out the window again. He began shuffling through another handful of "Wanted" posters and bounty hunter notices, reading from them aloud. "1874, Train Robbery . . .

"Said his mother would hire him a Spokane Falls lawyer and that he had somethin' of mighty big import to me."

Kneeling down, pretending to inspect a handbill, my knees gave way and I plummeted like a duck shot from the sky. My God, I could guess what. If Davy even hinted that I'd helped blast Pokamiakin out of jail. . . . *Run, now,* screamed the voice. *Don't even take a saddlebag. Just go!*

"Say's he'll talk only to a federal marshal."

"Is the marshal's deputy meeting him at Pard Cummings's ferry?" My stomach swarmed with biting insects.

"Naw," spat Barton. "Too important. Takin' him all the way to Spokane. Diamonds," he added. "It's sure to get into the papers."

My hands and feet felt leaden, and I was overcome with the sensation of having taken root where I knelt on the floor. Mrs. Ritters's necklace. *He* had taken the diamonds—and let me take the blame!

"People hire you to write letters?" he asked, apropos of nothing. "Them Injins?"

"Yes," I said, breathlessly. "Letters, valentines . . . When my wash business is off." I tried to act normal but spoke as if I was being chased by wild cattle.

My mind raced, remembering the day Davy and I had gone to look for wedding bands in Manhattan's diamond district. Had looking for a ring just been an excuse for making a deal with a nefarious jeweler? I shuffled through the "Wanted" bills, feeling so distraught that the words and pictures all blurred into a haze.

"Then you can read?"

Davy stole Mrs. Ritters's necklace, I said over and over to myself. But surely the other servants must have suspected.

"Oh yes. And write . . ." I faltered, not wanting to remind him about the ghost writing—though it seemed that it, along with Jake's and even the mayor's death, was a thing of the past.

Had Davy ever loved me, or had he meant to use me from the very start? Stupid fool, what a stupid fool I'd been. Nightingale was right. The only person Davy fancied *was* himself. I felt so angry that I had to restrain myself from tearing the "Wanted" posters to shreds.

"Town needs a clerk. If'n I get elected—"

The noise of pistol fire up at the Gem cut him off. Five quick shots were immediately answered by a volley of rifle blasts from the faro hall.

"Some greenhorn's in too high a spirits," said the sheriff, rushing away so fast I thought he would sideswipe a matronly woman making her way down the plank walk. "Can't have Forr get himself shot the day before his daddy arrives."

Mrs. Belknap pressed the new baby to her chest, balancing herself precariously on the narrow walkway, her full skirts dipping into the mud as the sheriff squeezed past her. I watched as Bald Barton streaked up the alley without a horse, thankful that he hadn't borrowed mine. But the letter! I needed it before I could flee.

"Heard you was looking for me," Mrs. Belknap said, peering into the jailer's hut. Her round, pleasant face flushed the color of winesap apples.

Was I? Suddenly I couldn't remember anything. Sitting on the floor amid piles of paper, I must have looked perplexed, because she added, "Yesterday." The black-haired baby arched its body, producing a wild cry that rattled the rafters of the sod-roofed hut.

"Oh! To help me with Jones. I think he's going to pull through." Enmeshed in my own troubles, I'd forgotten about the General.

A bad thought struck me: If Davy stole the diamonds and let me take the blame, what was to prevent him from continuing to point the finger at me despite the "Wanted" poster, in addition to telling the marshal I'd helped a suspected murderer (who just happened to be an Indian) escape custody? And Doc. With such a dark cloud over his head, I certainly couldn't count on him to vouch for me.

No matter how lovingly Mrs. Belknap patted the baby's back, he screamed all the more shrilly. "Seen Frank?" she asked, all traces of a smile dissolved from her face.

I suspected that Frank was either with Nightingale or out on a binge. "No," I replied. "I can't remember when I last saw him. Must have been two days ago when they . . . brought Dutch in." The baby gasped for air between screams.

We exchanged sad looks concerning the demise of dear old Dutch Wilhelm. Then the baby began howling like a prairie dog on the eve of a full moon.

"Better get him up to Carolina," she said, kissing his little head. "He's fussin' more than a wee one his age should."

"Who delivered him?" I suddenly thought to ask.

"Why, Mrs. Bitterroot," she said. "Delivered me my last three since I come to Ruby." She raised her plump hand in a good-bye.

My heart seized up inside my chest. Frantically I tore through piles of posters, the dust working its way into my lungs. I sneezed, my eyes watering. Finally a yellowed, odd-sized handbill caught my eye. Below a sketch of an egg-headed man with broad shoulders and no neck, read, "Wanted: for the murder of his wife, Mary Spence Strong while heading west out of Fort Badger . . ."

I felt I'd been stricken with typhoid. Even the release I should have felt at not being accused of the theft of Mrs. Ritters's necklace didn't buoy me up. Folding the poster and putting it my apron pocket, I ran toward my horse, desperate to get out of town.

CHAPTER TWENTY-EIGHT

I was breathing so fast and hard that I thought I might faint. Loosening my apron strings and unbuttoning my collar gave little relief. And since I'd galloped poor, tired Tillicum all the way to my Laundry by the Lake, it wasn't only me gasping for air.

The tonnage of wash piled on my porch was indescribable. If it had been all heaped together in one haystack it would have climbed higher than the tallest pitch of my tent's roof. But I couldn't concern myself with that now. If I hurried I would be able to catch the *Okanogan Belle* on her next departure.

Up mountain, the Ruby mine went into full swing, and the noise of blasting powder raged louder than battle. I supposed that the foreman knew what he was doing, but I wondered if the shifting ledges wouldn't bring about an avalanche. On top of everything else, I worried that a slide might trap Mary, Chin, and Jones.

Sustenance, I told myself, collapsing at the kitchen table. All there was to eat was cold potato soup, the taste of which had not passed my lips since I'd lived in the carriage house in Brooklyn. As I considered a bowl of cold porridge and all the unpleasant memories it conjured up, the day's revelations came down on me like a landslide of laundry waiting for my scrub board.

I had an excuse for being taken in by Davy: Love was blind. But Doc? How could I have misjudged him by such a wide margin? My predicament had me so unnerved that every powder blast made me leap half out of my skin. Which might have been a good thing, actually. If I hadn't been so jumpy, I might have just laid my head down and bawled myself into oblivion. Pulling the "Wanted" poster from my pocket, I unfolded it on the table, smoothing the wrinkles as I would a shirt before ironing it.

The handbill was yellowed and dog-eared, the print harder to read for all the creases. Still, the message was clear. A Union Army veteran named Strong who impersonated a doctor allegedly killed his wife, Mary Spence, on a wagon train heading west. Not, as Doc had told me, in a tragic case of mistaken identity, but because she had left him, returning to her father's wagon after her husband beat her nearly to death in a jealous rage. The culprit's description matched Doc right down to the war wound in his right shoulder.

I sighed, covering the handbill with my outstretched hand. Hard to believe, even with the poster right in front of me.

I still didn't know why Doc killed Jake, but undoubtedly he'd lured Dutch to his death because he feared that the old socialist would expose him as the Butcher of Missionary Ridge. Which was why it had probably been Doc who tried to kill Jones in the shootfest following Pokamiakin's escape. What about Charley? Had Doc gunned him down as well? Why had Charley made an appointment (by post of all things) to see me? To show me this poster? Had I told Doc about Charley's odd request? For the life of me, I couldn't remember. I recalled Nightingale's comment that the appointment had something to do with Davy, but now that Charley was dead, it didn't matter anymore. . . . Is that what she'd said? If Charley's request to see me had something to do with a jewel theft, it would certainly continue to matter. What had Charley had in mind? Too tired and hungry for rational thought, I still couldn't stop trying to fit the pieces together. What did my appointment with Charley have to do with Davy? Why wouldn't she tell me straight out?

And what about Doc helping Poka Mika get out of the Skookum House? A candidate for the perfect crime: laying blame on an Indian who would never be found. This, after Doc had put me up to investigating Jake's death to clear myself—and him, since he knew I'd never see the truth. And with Pokamiakin gunned down by a posse or forever a fugitive, the truth would never come out in a trial, because there'd never be one.

But I had seen the truth, and instead of setting me free, it made me want to give up and die. I held my head and rocked in the stick-back chair. Had it been Doc and not Jake who'd poisoned Shaky? A sudden thought made my spine go rigid as a divining rod: Would Doc kill me? I began to tremble all over and broke out into a sweat. I'd have to prevent him from realizing that I knew. . . .

It was only my word against Doc's. Everyone else who knew the truth was dead—except for Mary, Chin, the General, and Pokamiakin. And who would believe a squaw, a Chinaman, an ex-slave, a cross-eyed Indian, or a laundress?

I stood up, pulling myself together. Mightn't I appeal to Carolina for help? Surely as a trained nurse she must suspect Doc's fraudulence. But Mrs. Bitterroot had never shown me anything more than a condescending kindness and a lukewarm shoulder. Her husband wouldn't want any trouble in camp. I could imagine airing my complaint to them and having the Bitterroots stare blankly out the window. Finally one of them might comment that the maple was coming into bud as if I hadn't even spoken.

No use, I told myself, filling my saddlebags and knapsack with blankets and clean clothes. Picking up a spade (and looking over my shoulder for fear Doc might appear before I could flee) I went into the garden. Near where I'd planted my second row of beets last spring, I dug up the baking powder tins of money. Dashing back inside, I distributed all I had in the world to my left shoe, the hem of my skirt, my bonnet crown, and my bodice sleeves. Then, standing in front of my stove, feeling ten pounds heavier, I took a cup and filled it with cold potato gruel that had been meant to be laundry starch.

Even the smell of it made me feel unwell. I recalled the very hour I'd last tasted the stuff, a leafless November Sunday in Brooklyn. Sitting around the breakfast table in the carriage house with the family, my sister Mary-Terese and I fought over who would get the chair nearest the fire. My stepmother settled our hash by putting one of the little boys' highchairs there on account of his croup. She'd been up all night with the wee one's coughing, and bruised half circles roosted under her eyes. Just when the little boy went into such a fit of foghorning that we thought he'd have to be taken out of his chair and whacked on the back, Da came limping through the front door.

"Eat your breakfast," Mum told us and spoke not one word to Da. He looked rumpled and dragged one leg as if he'd been kicked by a horse. His violin-shaped face seemed oddly lop-sided, like Mum's mouth had been when she'd had her teeth drawn out.

There was no salt or sugar or milk, and so we spooned bland-tasting potato gruel slowly into our mouths, trying to avoid the black flecks from the scalded pot's bottom.

As Mary-Terese and I dueled with our spoons like bayo-nets, Da took his head in his hands and said to please stop or our noise would be the death of him. Mum lifted her arm to give us each a chop, when there was a rap at the door. On our doorstep stood the largest policeman I'd ever seen. Dressed in navy, his beard blazed the same brass color as his buttons. I stared so hard that I almost overlooked the rodent-faced little man behind him. He wore a shabby suit and carried a black satchel.

"Good mornin', misses," the copper said, giving us a half

smile. Holding out a long piece of sky-blue paper folded into quarters, he reached over our heads, handing it out to my stepmother, who burst into tears and called to Da to come quick.

"You'll have to vacate," the policeman said. "The bank's locksmith's here to change the key."

Mum began to wail, "But where will we go?"

"Effie, Effie," said Da, "ask the constable in for a stout."

"A stout?" she cried. "Stout's what's got us in this fix."

Da called to me. "Pinky, go to the Downs and fetch your Uncle Jake Pardee. He'll get us out of this brine."

I stared questioningly at Da, but he'd covered his eyes with his hands. Was he raving? Mr. Pardee wasn't my uncle. Indeed, Mum forbade him to ever enter our house.

"Go on with ya, Pinky," Dad prodded, "before the constable finishes his glass."

Running all the way, I found Mr. Pardee in the turf master's shed engaged in a game of poker. He had a meaty pink face and hair so blond it appeared white. I explained why I'd come and what I wanted, and he came straightaway, I'll give him that. Pardee wore high black boots that laced in the curve where his leg joined his foot. As I jogged alongside him, I measured myself against those immense boots, which came up to my waist. They'd been polished to a mirror shine, and when I leaned over I could see my reflection in the broad top of his foot just like I could in a pond.

When we got to the carriage house in Flatbush—our lungs near bursting—the door stood ajar. On the table lay our spoons and the blue bowls half filled with potato gruel, but everyone, including the constable and the locksmith, was gone. The grand mahogany phaeton looked strangely forlorn. Perplexed, I remember Jake raking his hands through his hair. In the end he and his black boots walked me back to the Downs, to Da's employer, Mr. Ritters, the racetrack owner.

You know the rest of the story. I was put into service and never saw any of my family alive again. And I hadn't the stomach for potato soup from that day to this, no matter how long I'd gone without food. But now I'd fallen into dire straits, the potato broth my only hope for the strength I'd need to survive.

For years I'd pondered the question: Why had Da picked me to go and not Mary-T or Mum or one of the little boys? And how did he know that telling me to fetch my Uncle Jake Pardee would save me from the workhouse?

I sighed. No one to help me now. Crumpling up the dog-eared "Wanted" poster with Doc's likeness on it, I chucked it into the fire, watching it catch and burn. As I reluctantly pressed the cup of potato soup to my lips, my mouth filled with the taste of grief.

CHAPTER TWENTY-NINE

It was late afternoon before I crossed Salmon Creek and hit the rocky trail along the left bank, riding east. The trunks of shoreline willows were stained by silt. Flood debris hung from their limbs. Even the base of the basalt columns that marked the entry to the tablelands had been grayed by the rising water just like a bathtub ring.

I'd no choice but to flee Ruby. Still, it tore me apart to leave without my letter. My heart ached, and I wanted to ride backward until the tent village nestled in the piney ledge was out of sight. Then, passing the tallest of the rock pillars, I remembered that Lot's wife turned to stone for one last look at Sodom, and I cast not another backward glance. Spurring Tillicum on, I tried to stop thinking about all the unfinished business I'd left behind and the fact that Doc might be following me. Not the Doctor Stringfellow I'd known for the last year, but another who'd seized control of my friend and mentor, a complete stranger who terrified me. Slapping Tillicum on the neck with the end of the reins, we broke into a gallop.

At the wagon road, I struck out toward the ferry. As the foot of the mountains curved gently down to the town of Okanogan and the river of the same name, rolling meadows dotted with haystacks came into view. Groundhogs the color of potato skins scurried into the chaparral, their dangerous holes everywhere. I feared Tillicum might put a hoof in one and break a leg. Then I remembered that he was a cayuse, not a white man's horse, and possessed greater endurance and cunning.

At Spring Coulee the fading sky turned as blue as Chinese silk, but the air held its warmth, making the larks chatter happily well into dusk. As I approached the log frame of the North Star School, I caught sight of a hastily lettered handbill nailed to the door. My breath stopped, my heart flying into my throat. "Doc Stringfellow for Mayor, Ruby City," it read. How long ago had he been on this trail posting signs? Half a day? An hour? I reined Tillicum sharply to the right, heading back to the creek where I wouldn't be seen.

I made camp in a stand of greasewood at the mouth of a cave, afraid even to venture out for a drink of water. Unsaddling Tillicum, I hobbled him and let him go in a narrow strip of bottom land. No one would think it odd that an Indian pony grazed there.

At dark I took the tin cup from my saddlebags, hooked it on the end of a stick, and dipped the stick into the creek. My first sip screamed, "Typhoid." Crawling deep into the cave—animals slept there; the bones of their prey lay everywhere—I gathered driftwood and built a small fire, thus purifying the water and enabling myself to keep warm and cook some ash cakes out of the cornmeal and flour I'd brought. Since the smoke seemed to be exiting through a crack in the cave's ceiling, I hoped my fire wouldn't give my whereabouts away, leading Doc to my hiding place. Would he shoot me in cold blood? Or would he try to make it look like an accidental drowning or suicide as he'd done with Dutch? My teeth began to chatter so violently that my jaw ached.

Staring into embers the color of orange zinnias, I pulled my shawl around my shoulders, embracing myself. Small blue flames danced on the cedar log, and I stared into the fire, hypnotized. Even Mary and Chin had suspected Doc's disguise.

Why hadn't I? Was I destined to go through life so easily taken in? The trouble was, a part of me still couldn't believe it. Not having Doc in my life was like having my house burn down. Rolling myself up in my blankets, I used my saddle as a pillow, but sleep would not come. My thoughts screamed at me like gulls: Perhaps I hadn't the intellect to become a doctor. Again I remembered the letter waiting for me at the trading post, wondering if I would ever know its contents. My head jerked upright at another pressing thought: I hadn't carved Shaky's headstone. I couldn't live with myself if I left Mayor Shaky Pat to sleep forever in an unmarked grave. Settling back, I listened to the crickets, trying to make their music into a tune. Didn't Chin say that with crickets came luck?

Just after the waxing moon set behind the white peaks of Three Devils and before the first streak of dawn splashed across the riverbank, I threw a driftwood stump on the fire and crept out to Salmon Creek. Stripping off my clothes, I plunged in, the cold water nearly halting the blood in my veins. Carefully, I scrubbed myself with the creek sand, letting the current tickle the roots of my hair. I hadn't had a bath since Shaky's funeral, and despite the paralyzing cold, I felt refreshed. Drying myself with pine boughs before the fire, I skeined my hair back into a bun and took a hot cup of pine needle tea.

Approaching the outskirts of Okanogan City, sun filled the valley with honey-colored light, and I could hear the *click-click* of grasshoppers in the sage beside the road. It was coming on rattlesnake season, and reptile skins decorated the shanties of bachelors and squawmen. Log huts gave way to houses, until finally, I jogged along a street of whitewashed bungalows with neat gardens and picket fences. All roads led to Pard Cummings's ferry, but I had a sad piece of business to transact before I boarded. Heading north on a street that paralleled the banks of the Okanogan, I cantered away from the steamer dock toward the Indian side of town.

"Tillicum," I sang, staring teary-eyed at my cayuses's red

roan mane, which fell on both sides of his neck. Would I ever forget the slant of his furry ears or the kind expression in his eye? I was going to have to part with my best and only friend, and it tore my heart up worse than being betrayed by Davy or deceived by Doc. Would I ever touch Tillicum's velvety muzzle again?

Passing the gristmill, I trotted toward a boatyard filled with Indian canoes. The road narrowed, and suddenly log and plank warehouses gave way to Indian teepees. Tears streamed down my face. I felt at cross-purposes, always glancing over my shoulder, afraid Doc was following me. But didn't a little piece of my heart want Doc to come after me and plead my forgiveness, say there'd been a terrible misunderstanding, and promise to make everything right?

No. I had to get away.

Still, I was in no hurry to say good-bye to my faithful mount. Since I hadn't the heart to sell him, I planned to try to give him back to Pokamiakin. But if Davy could make his accusations stick and I was charged with consorting with an aboriginal, being seen in the Siwash part of town wouldn't do my case a lick of good.

Many of the inhabitants looked to be of mixed blood, the men dressing in buckaroo chaps and beaded gauntlets. The women still wore buckskin and cooked in outdoor cauldrons like my laundry tub. The odor of fish broth curled into my nose. Oddly enough, if given the choice, the residents of Indian Town preferred to live in teepees rather than houses. The air in white men's homes had deadly power, and they blamed this evil for the ravages of measles and white plague that spirited away many a native child.

I stopped in front of a large teepee that had at least twenty poles lashed at the top of it. Fish stew boiled on the campfire. Next to it, an old woman with a pendulous lower lip sat on a crate, sewing with a porcupine needle. As a baby slept in a hammock strung between the teepee and a jack pine, a younger woman singed the hair from a newly killed groundhog. Pearls of perspiration from the heat of the fire dewed her forehead. Before looking up at me, she dipped a sheep's horn spoon into the pot, took up some broth, then dripped it into the side of the baby's mouth.

"*Kla-how-ya,*" said the younger, who recognized me. The unseeing eyes of the aged woman stared straight ahead as if in a trance. Stitch, cross, stitch. She embroidered a buckskin shirt, feeling her way across the front of the garment. According to Doc, blindness was common among Siwash, due to chronic pinkeye brought on by campfire smoke—hydrochlorate of cocaine their only relief. Doc said, Doc said, there I went again. How would I ever get him out of my head? He'd been my beacon, and now . . .

"Hello," I gestured, addressing Mary's sister. She did not smile, as was the Indian way, but offered me a spoonful of soup. How wonderful to be welcomed at someone's door. Even though it was a communal spoon just used to scrape some awful-smelling groundhog fat into the pot, I accepted as I felt suddenly starved. Unlike Carolina and Nightingale, Mary's sister's face appeared open and inviting. Swallowing the thin liquid, I chewed a morsel of salmon skin. Digging into my pocket, I pulled out a dime, but she turned her little cricket face away. Most Indians did not understand the white man's concept of "restaurant." Charging for food went against their grain. I took another sip and another. The tot cried for more *liplip muckamuck,* so I gave the spoon back to his mother.

The old woman continued to sew. I'd never seen even a sighted woman embroider so well. Occasionally she held the shirt up two inches in front of her face, the morning sun shining into it.

"I've got to leave town," I told Mary's sister. "Your cousin, Pokamiakin, swapped me this pony for sewing him a suit of clothes, and I want to give him back."

Mary's sister eyed me suspiciously. What white person ever gave anything away?

My voice cracked and tears sprouted in my eyes. "I'm in deep trouble," I said. "Trouble" was such a common word among the natives that it was the same in both English and Chinook, so I knew she understood me.

"*Ikta mika ticky?*" what to do? she asked in a whisper.

"I want you to take this pony to the river after the steamboat leaves and let him swim across and join his herd. You know where Pokamiakin used to cross his cayuses, a mile north of here, where the water spreads out wide and the current slows? There."

She nodded, spooning soup into the tot's mouth. He had fat red fingers and grasped the spoon in frustration, wanting to feed himself.

"If I don't come back," I said, "give *tenas* the saddle," I gestured to the child. "And please," I begged in a whisper, "tell no one you've seen me. No one."

Even the grandmother nodded knowingly. With that I put my arms around my pony's muscular neck for the last time, kissing him, the coarse hairs of his long fire-colored mane cutting into my lips. While I removed my blanket roll and saddlebags, he stood stoically as was the habit of the people who had raised him. I handed the reins to Mary's sister. "*Mahsie,*" thank you, I said. Hoisting my gear over my back, I turned and walked with as long a stride as I could manage toward the steamboat dock.

Behind me I heard a plaintive nicker followed by a loud whinny. Salt tears blurred my vision and stung my face. Soon all I could hear were my own sobs and the sucking sound of mud as I headed for the white part of town.

CHAPTER THIRTY

April 25

Pard Cummings was called "Pard" because he called everyone he met "Pardner" and then sold them a horse or tent or wagon or whatever they needed. He traded in most anything, or did, until he got hold of his ferry. That's when he built a wharf in front of his livery–cum–drygoods store and painted "Steamer Stops Here" on the downriver side of his weathered building. The ferry looked like a raft attached to a cable rigged with ropes and pulleys. Powered by the force of the current, it looked dangerous in the extreme, so most paid an Indian two bits to row them across the river in a canoe.

When I arrived at the depot, the *Okanogan Belle* had already docked. A plank stretched from the beach to the lower deck, and guide ropes had been tied to the trunks of two cottonwoods. A crowd pressed around the plank but was held back by a steward on horseback. I judged there to be at least fifty passengers waiting to board, a good thing, as I could easily lose myself among them. Dusty homesteaders, threadbare sheepherders, a tall, lean man who looked like a traveling minister, several blackgowns, as Mary called priests, and wagonloads of cargo, including I don't know how many barrels of whiskey, which the Indians followed with their dark, expressionless eyes.

Tears stained my face while perspiration—brought on by the exertion of running with my bundle of blankets and saddlebags—stained my dress. Before entering the depot, I took a handkerchief from my apron pocket and tried to tidy my face, then swabbed my boots, cleaning them of mud. I always carried two hankies ("One for show and one for blow," as the old folks say). So when I walked in to purchase a ticket, I had a fresh white handkerchief tucked into the sleeve of my dress, hoping to appear as if I'd just stepped off a stagecoach and not like a woman on the lam.

"One billet for Portland," I told the ticket agent. Portland was the opposite direction from where Davy was going and only fifty miles north of the medical college.

Pard, a small, gopher-faced man, lay behind the counter on a heap of flour sacks with a quilt over him. "Sold out," he said, lifting his head to appraise me, then letting it fall back onto the sugar sack he used for a pillow. Pard suffered from dizzy spells caused by a fall from a horse and found life more agreeable from the supine position. He sold hardware, ammunition, and dry goods. Boxes were stacked everywhere, even in front of the window. I remembered that once Windy Pardee had remarked on this, saying what a pity that the largest mercantile in Okanogan County didn't have a "dressed" window. If she'd had that window in her millinery shop, it would have a dressed window of which the town would be proud. I tell you this because the horse Pard fell from was one he traded with Windy's late husband, Jake, a trick horse Jake sold more times than anyone could count. It was a palomino, lovely to behold, but no one could ride it, though some, not knowing its history, would have given their eyeteeth to own it. The fall ended Pard Cummings's career as a liveryman and horse trader, enabling Jake to step in and monopolize land transportation in this part of the world.

"Please," I told him, "I've got to get to Portland. I've a sick relative."

"They all say that," Pard replied, reaching between one of the fifty-pound sacks and pulling out a bottle. Uncorking the top, he took a swig and replaced it. Pushing a pair of wire-rimmed glasses onto his face, he looked fixedly at me. "Aren't you that scrappy little laundress from up Ruby way?"

Damn—I almost said aloud—now he'd be sure to remember me if Doc came in pursuit. "No, sir. I'm one of Ella's girls." Whatever possessed me, I cannot imagine.

He peered at me as if I were a fly under a microscope. "You don't say."

"The name's Shell." I tried to look coy.

Pard lay back as if exhausted. "Our only professional woman left last fall," he said, shaking his head. He had tiny brown eyes and a remarkably pointed nose and chin. "A bad sign for a town," he added resignedly, then rolled over on his side. "Ah, Ruby City," he added, "a wide-open little village, free of Sunday school influences."

"You're right," I said. "I did fib. It's not my relative who's sick, it's Nightingale's. Her mother, very ill, and Nightingale's got her hands full with a house full of sick doves and can't leave."

He took off his spectacles, wiping the lenses on the corner of the frayed quilt.

"I'll pay double," I said, rummaging in my apron pocket. I certainly didn't want him to see me take money out of my shoe or from the hem of my dress.

"Go, get on," he said, handing me a red, second-class billet.

"How much?" I asked, wanting to know the fare so that I could twice it.

"On the house. Won't be boarding for an hour. Some dignitary just come in and has to have a nap 'fore he gets off the boat and don't want to be disturbed."

Thanking him profusely, and adding a flourish of, "If you ever get to Ruby, you just ask for Shell," I dashed from the depot to the line of passengers. So much for the fringe benefits of being a virtuous woman. No one had ever first denied me something at any price and then given it to me free. Not a bad disguise, if I did say so myself.

The crowd pushed toward the narrow gangplank. A steward mounted on a rawboned horse with "U.S. Cavalry" branded on his neck tried to drive us back. The steward wore a wide sombrero and carried a black bullwhip, which he lashed over our heads as he shouted violent language. When the *thunk* of a paddle against the stern of an Indian canoe circling the steamer caused the steward's horse to shy, the cavalry gelding reared uncontrollably, tossing his rider onto the beach. With that the crowd pushed onto the plank, and we began to board.

The *Okanogan Belle* was an aging riverboat with a stern wheel—a "wet-behinder," Shaky had called it—and a huge donkey engine with a ravenous appetite for wood. Piles of fuel cut into two-foot lengths lay stacked on shore and were due to be loaded by Indian power. I made my way up the plank and then to the upper deck, clutching at the rickety railing that had once been painted white. An ear-damaging whistle blew from one of the black smokestacks above me, followed by a belch of dark smoke, the craft shuddering so convulsively I thought she would come apart. Cinders rained down on us. Someone must have had his head singed because I smelled the terrible odor of burning hair. The crowd of passengers was so dense that I was pressed first to the rail, then, when I tried to find a seat inside the second-class galley, into the door of the stairwell. The narrow stairs were dark as a cellar. At the bottom, I found the halls through the first-class compartments deserted, so I sat in a fireman's alcove, waiting for my heart to cease pounding. Good disguise or no, you've become an inveterate liar, I chided.

The door of the cabin opposite rattled, noises of discord coming from within. I heard a trunk scrape across the floor. "Get it unlocked and get me another pair," came a man's impatient voice. Inside my head a bell chimed, and Mrs. Ritters's drawing room with its red fleur-de-lis wallpaper flashed in front of me. The impatient voice had the accent of an educated New Yorker who might have frequented the Ritterses' dinner table.

Above, footsteps pounded on the ceiling. I fumbled with my bundles, pulling out one of the ash cakes I'd cooked the previous night. The dank alcove smelled of mold. Instead of my little horse's warm shoulder next to me, I leaned against the chilly iron of the steamer's starboard side. The doughy cake gave me a moment's comfort, but the cold, rigid metal against my back brought on despondency. What chance did I have of the U.S. marshal believing me? It struck me that I'd spent the last year of my life hunting Doc for this or that patient and now I might spend the rest of it looking over my shoulder and running from him. The muscles in my arms jumped. Doc wasn't going to make things right. If that were his intention, he would have found me by now. Wouldn't he? My heart sank. I had to admit it: Doc's morose fits of silence had finally overwhelmed all the good in him.

Waiting was agony. All I wanted was for the ship to be on her way. Staring out the porthole, I watched a crew of shirtless mixed-blood Indians lugging wood on board, wheeling it up the gangplank by the barrow load or carrying it on their backs in large, filthy tarps. The whistle blew, followed by black smoke and a spray of falling cinders the color of a million scarlet poppies.

Just then the door of the cabin opposite me burst open, and a well-dressed man with hair that rippled across his head like gray lake water darted into the aisle, looking anxiously in both directions. "Are you . . . ?" he asked, directing an inaudible question at me. He held onto the door handle with the whitest, most perfect hands I'd ever seen on a man, prompting me to wonder just what kind of work he did.

"Beg pardon?"

"Are you for hire, by chance?"

My God, news traveled fast. "I'm a laundress, thank you." I didn't even try to hide my indignation.

"Are you for hire?" he repeated. "I need some sewing. That is, my employer does."

"If that's what you're truly about, I'll be glad to oblige." I thought, all the better to sit in a first-class cabin and not be seen. And maybe pick up a half-dollar as well. I figured that his employer must be the dignitary whom Pard Cummings had told me about.

With a sweep of his arm, he motioned me through the door, then reached down to help with my saddlebags. Educated *and* a gentleman—he wasn't from these parts.

Once inside the spacious quarters furnished with two berths, two chairs, a desk, and innumerable pieces of leather luggage with brass fittings, I got the shock of my life. In front of me stood a man in braces, wearing nothing but a white shirt, white drawers, and a pair of scotch plaid socks that came up his stout hairy legs almost to his knees. Which wasn't what gave me a start. That face: I'd have known his florid jowls and handlebar mustache anywhere.

"Mr. Forrester!"

The graying, well spoken man—the mine owner's secretary I presumed—dropped a pair of men's pants torn up the backside into my hands. Mr. Forrester, who was in a state of distress before I blurted out his name, turned the fuchsia of an Okanogan sunburn.

"I, I . . ." he stammered, obviously unable to place my face.

"It's Pearl, sir, Mrs. Ritters's companion." He looked utterly baffled. His secretary, whom he addressed as Hopkins, handed me a needle and thread. I sat down immediately without waiting to be invited to do so, examined the damage, then threaded the needle.

"From New York City, sir. I was with the Ritterses for ten years. . . ."

"Yes, yes, of course, I remember you," he said, though I wasn't sure that he did. His bulging hazel eyes weren't focused at me but looked inward, as if searching his memory for a Pearl.

"At the Fifth Avenue address, sir, after her son died . . ."

"I do remember," he said, "rest assured. It's just that . . ." He sat down, crossing his legs in a gentlemanly fashion, becoming perfectly cordial, as if we were about to take tea. In fact, Hopkins brought us two crystal tumblers of chilled water, which tasted sweet and refreshing. I thought, How wonderful to be free of having to boil and strain your drinking water. What utter extravagance. I took it as a sign that my fortunes were about to change.

Basting the rip, I saw that the trousers were made of quality gray worsted the likes of which I hadn't seen in Ruby, and it was a pleasure to hold such exquisite cloth.

"Did you know . . ." he said, then stopped midsentence, taking a long sip of water.

"I left the East a bit unexpectedly," I said by way of an apology, hoping not to jar his memory enough so that he'd remember the unpleasantness about the diamonds.

Both Mr. Forrester's heavy face and Hopkins's narrow one looked on almost helplessly as I stitched. They bore expressions of relief as well as gratitude, and it crossed my mind that perhaps they could help me with my troubles.

"How is Mrs. Ritters?" I asked. "She *was* kind to me." I meant it sincerely and even shocked myself at how instantaneously I fell into a servile mentality, always polite and grateful to my betters.

"Terrible," said Mr. Forrester in a voice that turned suddenly severe. He took another long sip of water.

A thousand thoughts ran through my mind. She'd broken a hip, or an accident had befallen Mr. Ritters at the racecourse. "What bad news," I said. "Is it her sugar fits?"

"The fact is, she's dead."

"Dead?" I felt so stunned that I pricked my finger and had to press it into my mouth for fear of bleeding on the seat of the mine owner's pants. "She was healthy as a horse. . . ." I regretted the simile the minute it fell out of my mouth.

"Malta fever," he said. "Last fall. Slipped away almost overnight. Terrible shock. Just terrible. At the end, it was as if her joints were on fire, and we all prayed. . . ." He sat back in his chair as if exhausted. "Surely you were informed."

Shaking my head, I didn't know what to say. All this time I'd been thinking of my employer as alive, feeling badly that I hadn't written, and here she'd been dead for months. "Does Forr know?" I asked stupidly, unable to think of anything else to say.

At this Mr. Forrester rose to his feet and practically yanked his trousers away from me before I could knot the thread. Hopkins's brow furrowed. "Your apoplexy, sir," he said, "remember . . ." And then I saw why we'd been brought glasses of water. Hopkins produced a vial of pills, presenting his employer several that he counted into his hand.

"My son . . ." said Mr. Forrester after swallowing the tablets. He balled a fist, slamming it into his palm several times. "My son." Pulling on his trousers without apology to me, he turned to his secretary. "Let's stop loitering here, Hopkins, and get off this boat. We've business to attend to." Hopkins took a cigar from a traveling humidor that he carried in his leather valise, cut the cigar's tip, then offered it to Mr. Forrester, who gummed it vigorously. "My son," he said again. "I'll tell you one thing. I'd like to hang the man who turned him into an opium fiend." His face had gone white and was contorted with rage. He spoke not so much to me or Hopkins but to the walls and air, to someone neither of us could see.

I hung my head, nodding not just in agreement but at the sudden clarity of the situation. Surely I'd guessed at Forr's condition. After a moment of silence, Hopkins stepped out into the hall and called for a porter. I wondered if he knew that, other than the Indian carriers, there was no such thing. I thought of Jake, the opium—or "flying horse" as it was called in the Okanogan—dealer, remembering his hat and the hole made by the bullet that had killed him.

"He's already dead," I said, looking Mr. Forrester straight in the eye.

Mr. Forrester's drooping jowls shook, and he stared at me with the intensity of a boxer dog. "The local doctor is dead?" he demanded, stepping out the door and walking hurriedly in the direction of the gangplank.

Maybe it was because the mine owner's dentures were studded with gold that made me think I heard his words clatter to the floor. At first I wanted to bend down, collect them, and stuff them back in his mouth, but I was so seized up with fright that I couldn't move or utter a sound. By the time I'd gotten hold of myself and thought to explain my troubles, asking Mr. Forrester if I could count on him to be my witness, the mine owner and his secretary had disappeared up the stairwell.

CHAPTER THIRTY-ONE

I felt as if I'd turned to stone.

After what seemed like an hour, I got up and walked trance-like onto the stern deck. Though shoved and elbowed, I felt it not very keenly but as if through a fog; and, despite the open air, I was short of breath. Finally making my way to the rail, I stared into the corrugated water as it ripped over treacherous boulders, then swung into an eddy.

The memory of something Chin and Mary had said after Jake's death called to me. The three of us had been sitting in front of the trading post, staring across the street at the lads milling around the livery. *"Kalakala kuitan,"* flying horse, Chin had said. *"Moosum nanaitch kuitan,"* dream horse, Mary added. Later it had dawned on me that those weren't just Siwash words for "the hereafter," but for "opium," and I realized that Jake had been the local opium tradesman. Now it came on me: The men outside the livery weren't mourning Jake but waiting for the other flying-horse trader: Doc Stringfellow.

As the puzzle pieces fell into place, things started making sense—horrible, terrible sense. Doc and Jake hadn't had an argument over a four-legged horse. They'd been vying for territory. Doc's Chocolated Cure contained more than cocoa, spirits of bourbon, and a pinch of hydrochlorate of cocaine. I suddenly saw how insidiously he lured unsuspecting clients into a greater and more expensive need. But unlike shrewd Jake, who never partook of a swallow of euphoric medication, Doc had become trapped in his own snare. The pinprick eyes, dark moods, and fits of silence. Undoubtedly his chewing tobacco hid any stench of the opium pipe that might have lingered about him. And the choking brown smoke? We had seldom practiced at his surgery. Now I understood why.

Would it be far afield to surmise he'd begun his descent innocently enough by trying to stave off the chronic pain of his wounded shoulder? No, I thought not. Then, shaking my head, I saw another truth. That Mary and Chin had suspected—or even known of—Doc's weakness all along. They disliked Jake (who didn't?), but when Doc came around, they utterly disappeared, and not just because they were afraid of white medicine. And Jones. The day that he and Dutch had brought Shaky's coffin to my laundry, I recalled how the ex-slave had sulked, even been rude to Doc. Afraid to be under the same roof as a corpse, I'd thought, but now I saw that Jones too had known. How had I been so blind? I considered myself an insightful person, a watchtower. How had I been fooled so? Suddenly I felt overcome by fury not just at Doc but also at myself.

The *Okanogan Belle*'s whistle blew. At this a wild cheer went up from the passengers on deck. The huge, many-tiered craft floated slowly downriver amid a rain of cinders and a fog of black smoke. The smell of the river and the spray from the turning paddlewheel mixed with that of falling soot. In the bowels of the *Okanogan Belle*, the donkey engine chugged, panting and gasping as the boat gained speed, lurching forward not unlike a locomotive, though with fewer belches to the mile.

I heard a commotion portside. A sheepherder with long gray hair pointed to a drover driving his stock across the river.

The horses swam the fastest, their heads well out of the water, while the cattle swam low in the current, just their nostrils and horns showing as they churned the river to a malt brown.

Someone on the starboard side began shouting, "Lookie there." As I jockeyed for a better view, a cloud of dust appeared to chase the steamer. Pressing myself to the rail, I saw its source: three or four horsemen riding at a dead gallop along the wagon road that followed the river. The *Okanogan Belle* went to Portland only once a week. If you missed the boat, you'd be in sore straits, as it was an arduous trek over the Cascades.

"They're tryin' to catch us," a youth with a pocked face yelled. Immediately the sheepherders took bets as to whether this would be accomplished.

The dust cloud grew larger. As the horseman gained and then lost distance rounding Rattlesnake Point, their speed didn't diminish. Awfully fierce riding for a missed passenger, I thought, becoming even more ill at ease.

Turning away from the crowd, I descended the rabbit-hole stairwell to the first-class compartments. What had been Mr. Forrester's cabin was unlocked, so I entered and sat down between the desk and private water closet. My chest heaved. Surely anyone who walked down the hall would hear me panting. But when I tried to breathe with my mouth closed, my heart beat into my ears so fiercely I felt faint. How far to the next town? An hour by boat to Coulee City and the confluence of the Okanogan and Columbia? No one could ride that hard that long. All I had to do was sit it out here. And if the horsemen did board and search for me, then I'd hide in the water closet.

Pressing my chin into my palm, I began plotting a strategy. I knew what opium could do to moral fiber—fray it away like a pack of mice eating upholstery. Hadn't Da brought home terrible stories from the racecourse about grooms who'd gone the route of lotus-eaters? I was treading on mush ice. Not only would Doc deny anything I told a federal marshal, but he'd kill me as easily as he'd shoot a snake, without a second thought. *Steel your heart,* said the voice. *Don't be a fool, it's your life or his.* Intellectually I saw the truth, but my inner being could not give up even the tiniest glimmer of hope that Doc would appear and make everything right.

Just then I heard footsteps and the chatter of women. Darting into the water closet, I clicked the sliding door shut as they entered Mr. Forrester's cabin. Listening to their skirts sweeping the floor, I heard them set down their carpetbags. The cabin door opened again, and the heavy, booted steps of a man entered. "Buckaroos are chasin' our boat, Mum," said a boyish voice on the verge of changing to that of a deep-throated male's. "Can I stay up and watch?"

"All right, St. John, all right," replied a tired-sounding woman. "Stay near your pa and don't get too close to the rail or the stern wheel, hear? Be a good boy."

The smell of stale urine made my stomach queasy. My God, I couldn't ride all the way to Portland next to a chamber pot! Besides, I was sure to be discovered when nature called to one of the ladies.

Suddenly exhausted by my plight, I wondered why I always behaved like the hunted. Up until the day I helped blow up the Skookum House in Ruby City, I hadn't done a single lawless thing in my life, yet I'd spent an entire year running like a criminal. Pressing my face into the paneling, hoping to smell cedar instead of toilet vapors, I decided: This is it. I can't go on.

What pushed me over the edge? That letter waiting for me in Windy's lard pail. If I never went back to get it, I'd never find out if I'd been accepted to medical college.

The women, who seemed to be two matronly sisters traveling with missionary intent, began unwrapping what sounded like the paper parcels of their midday meal. With a sudden inspiration, I began walking my fingernails along the wall and floor of the urinal. Outside, the paper smoothing abruptly stopped. I made more scurrying noises and then puckered my lips, emitting squeaking sounds. I heard one of the sisters catch her breath. The other jumped. They gathered up their lunch parcels and carpetbags in a terrible hurry, leaving after only the briefest discussion of the question: rats or mice?

Walking out of the closet, I made a pact with myself: stop running, stop hiding. And don't let your heart do your thinking. I swallowed the words as if they were medicine. And yes, I would stand up to Doc even if it meant my life. It was a wide world. Someone had to listen and believe me. Not everyone was powered by liquor and opium and greed. I owed it to the memory of Mrs. Ritters who, while a silly woman, had high hopes for me. It never occurred to me before, but it was because of her—and maybe a little of my da thrown in—that I believed things were possible. If I'd never met Mrs. Ritters, would I have ever dreamed of medical school?

The new Pearl sat in the first-class cabin in Mr. Forrester's chair until the *Okanogan Belle* docked at Coulee City, a town on a treeless, mosquito-infested sand bar, which consisted of a drygoods store, a livery, six liquor emporiums, and a Spanish dance hall with rooms to let upstairs. I ate my last ash cake and must have been able to think better on a full stomach, because it came to me that if I returned to Ruby, surely Mr. Forrester would stand behind me about Doc. Surely. At that revelation, the weight of the world fell from my shoulders. I felt a head taller and in charge of my fate.

Above me the ceiling rattled. Outside on the forward deck came the banging of a hundred feet as passengers prepared to depart or change seating arrangements to make way for newcomers. A steward went from deck to forward watch, calling out the stop, departure time, and destinations.

Tired and feeling sleepy, my eyelids drooped. Just when I'd decided to stretch out for some much-needed sleep, a steward came banging down the stairs calling not a departure time but (did my ears deceive me?), "Mrs. Ryan, is there a Mrs. Ryan on board?" he asked in a shrill nasal voice. "Important message ashore for a Mrs. Ryan."

My temples pulsed. Breaking into a prickly heat, I felt worry lines cut my brow.

My cabin door opened unceremoniously, and a wan-faced steward poked his head in, "Mrs. Ryan? Is there a Mrs. Ryan here?" he asked hopefully. It was the first-class cabin, which is, I presumed, what accounted for his extreme politeness.

"The name is Shell," I answered in the sweetest tone I could muster. I wasn't about to be tricked by Doc's scheme. An important message ashore? I'm sure that there was and that it was printed on a lead ball lodged in a gun barrel, possibly the same pearl-handled revolver Doc had "borrowed" from my digs to kill Jake. My blood boiled, and I felt only slightly relieved when the steward nodded, closed the door, and walked on down the hall, calling out for Mrs. Ryan.

I got up and paced the cabin floor. When I felt the stern began to drift and heard the twang of the lines being untied from the wharf, I decided to go up on deck. Concealing myself in the crowd, I hoped to get a look at whoever it was on shore wanting me off this boat. There had been several horsemen racing after the ferry, not just one. Who was in league with Doc? That's what I wanted to know.

Outside on the lower tier, I stood behind the wide skirts of a schoolteacher holding a satchel of primers in one hand, her other pulling down her bonnet bill against the brilliant afternoon sun. Searching the sand bar, I saw all manner of men: miners, professional cardplayers, a handful of Indians, and a broad-shouldered farm girl with a belly as large as a watermelon. But no Doc.

The steamer veered to avoid the rapids, which marked the beginning of the Okanogan's entrance to the Columbia, a vast corridor of deep green water a quarter mile wide that rolled west with solemn, menacing urgency. Then something caught my eye, or rather, my ear: the plaintive neighs of a horse. The crew stoked the engine with more and more wood in order to propel the *Okanogan Belle* safely over the turbulent confluence. A burst of red cinders hailed down on us, and everyone ran for cover, except me. I pressed myself to the railing, craning my neck, then ran back along the starboard side to the stern deck. That whinny had to have come from an Indian pony. The natives taught their horses to "speak" to them in short low nickers.

On shore watering their lathered mounts in the river south of the dock—it couldn't be! Carolina Bitterroot on her chestnut mare and a sapling-thin girl who looked like Nightingale on a horse from the Ruby Livery? Behind the two women rode a squaw on a bobtailed pony alongside a little horse, which at first I thought was a foal. . . .

Tillicum!

"Captain Hanson, wait," I screamed to the boat pilot. "I want to get off. I'm Mrs. Ryan. Wait!" But the barrel-chested Swede couldn't hear me over the ship's whistle.

People turned their heads, casting curious looks. My voice came out like an angry wind, "Wait!" And for a moment it did seem that the boat stopped moving.

The men around me moved away. One asked, "Drunk or daft?"

A sheepman made a wager out of the question. Two sour-faced ladies, whom I imagined had been the matrons who invaded my cabin, looked at me sternly, then averted their gaze the way they probably did with a cripple or a drooling idiot.

"Wait!" But it was no use. The boat paused only to reposition itself among the rapids. Frantically I waved my arms toward the three women on shore. Did they see me?

I knew what I had to do. Running to the farthermost point of the stern deck on the bottom tier, I tried to judge at what point I'd be safe from the paddlewheel and its crushing effects. The wheel blew a fine mist and in it shone a rainbow.

The voice screamed, *Now!* Climbing the railing, I hurled myself off the boat. Aiming for the colored arch, I leaped to a fixed point in the boulder-shadow below.

CHAPTER THIRTY-TWO

April 29, four days later

I thought you was a come-opened suitcase someone chucked over the side to lighten the steamer's load," said Nightingale, picking up the scrub board. "When you hit the water, I saw it was a person, a child is what I thought. I figured you was dead." Nightingale raked a pair of denim trousers over the board. Then with an angry, hurt expression, she put a hand to the cleft in her lip and asked, "Do you think Ella shoulda chucked me out like that?"

"Certainly not. You were her mainstay," I said, surveying the geography of laundry. It was early morning, and our shadows stretched across the piles of kindling Mary had brought before dawn. My laundry cauldron spat boiling water into the fire, the smoke filling the day with the odor of burning cottonwood.

"She loved that rooster to distraction, and when she found out it'd died—Lorenzo musta been ten years old; how long can a chicken live?—it was all my damned fault. Chucked me out.

Me, nearly run outta shoe leather haulin' water, tryin' to feed and nurse! No time to tend a *bird*. And I'm still not sure that Squirrel'll get her hearing back. Her throat got so swollen it closed off her ears."

"You did the best you could," I said, hoping to placate her. Nightingale still hadn't the slightest notion of what a hermaphrodite was, so I didn't mention my theory that the stallion serum in Ella's blood mixed with her mare cycles, causing dementia.

Contemplating a pair of four-pound woolen blankets, I wondered if I could find a line strong enough to hang them from. "We'll save these for the cold water vat," I said, glancing over my shoulder. A stand of brush across the ravine jangled. My breath knotted in my chest. Nightingale put the washboard down, nervously grinding her teeth. I felt almost too spent to be jumpy about Doc coming back and giving me a taste of his own special brand of gunpowder.

"False alarm," she said. "It ain't Mr. Stringfellow lurkin' in the scrub ready to slaughter us like sheep." Nightingale took a long exhale and stared at Tillicum itching his tail on a tree trunk. "It's just your cayuse. How long you gonna worry about Doc stalkin' your every move?"

I shrugged. No one had seen or heard of him in days. At the moment my biggest fear was the sheriff knocking at my door on business—the escape of Pokamiakin. Ruby's mayoral election, however, seemed to be eating up all his time. And, sad to say, I still hoped the real Doc would reappear and explain away the sadist, though by this time I knew it would never be. All I could say was, thank goodness I had Nightingale's help. I'd been laid so low by the entire episode that I could barely lift a single piece of laundry.

Nightingale had been bunking with me since the four of us got back from the riverboat. After they fished me out of the drink, we spent the night in Coulee City at the Hotel Spanish

Dance Hall, where we were three crammed in a bed, with Mary on a pallet. Then in the middle of the night some gent knocked on the door, saying he'd been rented floor space in our room!

"Can you believe it? All this time Injin Mary could talk!" said Nightingale.

I raised my brow in mock astonishment. "I think that until I get my pluck back, ironing's going to be unheard of." It amazed me how well Nightingale and I worked together. How long, I wondered, until the honeymoon was over?

"You're the boss," she said with a shrug of her narrow shoulders and a cynical laugh. "Know what Carolina calls Mary Reddawn? Mary Smart Eyes. Said it didn't surprise her none, that story Mary came running to us with while we was tryin' to move the invalid out of Dutch's digs. Kept cryin', 'Skookum Doc, Skookum Doc,' 'n' wavin' her arms. Me, I had Doc figured. Course, Carolina and I nearly dropped that poor ailing gent off his litter when we heard her talkin' like a magpie."

"You knew he wasn't a real doctor?" I asked, feeling the sting of my stupidity.

"Only 'cause he did amputations so well. That's a sure sign. I mean, the only way he could cure somethin' was to cut it off. So he had a lot of practice and got real good at it."

"I hardly knew him to do so many," I said.

"Before you come to help stitch people up, he sure did. And Ella's eye? I don't think he needed to take it from her—time woulda cured it, if you ask me. Some of his other patients looked like they only had flesh wounds that a bandage mighta fixed."

I stared at the flint-speckled ground, toeing a stone. No wonder Doc had to straddle all his patients while I sewed them up. He'd sold all his morphia or used it in his concoctions. For a moment rage replaced my exhaustion, as if I'd taken a tonic.

"Anyway," Nightingale continued, "Mary gallops up Badger Slide to Dutch's digs, crying that you'd gone and Doc was gonna kill you and Chin was hidin' Jones from him and on and on in Injin jammer. . . . I said to Carolina, 'She's just an ol' copper-skinned drunk. Got into some Sanford's Jamaica Ginger and it unparalyzed her tongue.' Then Mary started wavin' a rose briar, sayin' that you'd run away in fright and we had to go bring you back so that the spirit world people wouldn't snatch your soul away."

I felt deeply touched by Mary's loyalty. Ever since Shaky'd died she'd been terrified that his soul would come back and drag me across the Great Divide. Now I understood why: She feared Doc would do me harm, just as he'd done to his patients, not to mention Jake and Dutch and probably Charley. I recalled the day I'd gone to look for a suicide note at Dutch's cabin and encountered Mary on my way back down the trail. How I had startled her! At the time I'd thought it peculiar that a white person should startle an Indian. Now it made sense. What had made her skittish wasn't my presence but my identity. It was Carolina she'd been waiting for. Mary'd probably been trailing Mrs. Bitterroot for a week, hoping to find just the right time to talk to her.

Something thrashed in the sage behind my tent—probably just a prairie chicken. Nightingale craned her neck, peering into the thicket. Even she feared Doc.

"Carolina's patient . . ." Nightingale again took up the miracle of Mary's sudden gift of speech.

"Didn't he have cholera?" I asked, feeling my surge of energy ebb.

"Just a bad case of ague. Jittered with shivers one minute, taken with sweats the next. Weak as a noodle." Nightingale examined a pair of mud-caked trousers, pulling a handful of nails from the pockets. "Don't think I'd be much at nursin'. I figured that, him being Irish, it was just the drink. You know how them micks get."

I was about to tell her that I thought she'd make a good

nurse, but I couldn't let the dig go by. "I'm Irish," I said. Taking over the scrub board, I dragged a flannel shirt across the metal ridges, scraping the skin from my knuckles.

"Go on," she said, shaking out a bedroll. "If you're Irish, why don't you talk like it?" She flung one of the woolen blankets over a lower branch of the old pine and began swatting it with a broom.

"So how come you want to work for me and not Carolina?" I asked. "You told me yourself you wouldn't have charwoman hands." Nightingale's fingers were as flawless as a china figurine's.

"Too bossy. I couldn't countenance her for more than a day's time. She's a friend to a friend in need, I give her that. Took me in immediately when Ella put me out, but on the day to day . . ." We exchanged knowing looks. "Besides, she'd always be throwing my past up in my face—every time a gent smiled at me."

"Which gent?" I joshed. "Frank?"

She looked downcast, and I regretted my teasing. "He's good to me, but he already has too many rows to hoe."

We'll see, I thought, unconvinced that she'd given him up.

"I done this likeness of Blindy to pass the time, and when I showed it to Carolina, she had all kinds of spiteful words about it. Too much shading here, not enough color there. 'At cemetery school we were taught never to undertake a study head-on, at cemetery school we were taught. . . .' "

"Seminary," I corrected.

"That's what I said. Almost put me off doin' a likeness ever again." Nightingale glared at me, then continued. "You look like you been stricken with influenza. Maybe you should set a spell," she added kindly. "Just don't forget you promised to teach me my letters better than I know 'em already. And if you get to be a doctor, you'll help me to fix my face." She paused, studying a loose button on a work shirt. "Anytime you want a likeness of somethin,' I'll be glad to draw it for ya."

I nodded, then felt in my apron pocket for the letter Pigeon

Belcher brought to me yesterday morning. "What's left of my feet stay warmer when I walk some," he'd said. I had smiled broadly to hide my thoughts: Had he really needed to lose those toes? My fingers pulsed with anger.

As I watched Nightingale wring out the shirts, then put them in a bucket, taking them down to the ravine for a rinse, I thought of the sharp black writing on clean white vellum, a blue seal at the top of the letter: Williamette Institute of Medicine. It wasn't an acceptance exactly. But, in exchange for tuition and fees, I could attend lectures, standing-room permitting, and if, at the end of the year, I scored within the top ten percent of the class on my final examination, I would be reevaluated for admission. Before I'd even finished reading the letter, my mind had turned into an abacus. If I sold the Last Chance Mine and the Glory Hole to Mr. Forrester, there'd be enough of a grubstake for a year of studies. Riding to the Willamette Valley would take me a month's time, so summer would find me packing my saddlebags and heading south. The scent of pine filled my lungs with the smell of destiny, and I gulped air at the thought of the possibilities that lay before me.

My head began to spin, and I had to sit down on a stump to catch my breath. The sun rose higher like a single white coal shrouded in a haze of gray ash.

Trudging back up from the ravine, her skirt and apron tucked into the tops of her boots, Nightingale carried a load of red flannel shirts wrung into coils like intestines on butchering day. "Almost time to get the smudge pot out," she said, moving a hand in front of her face to free her vision of insects. Unpleasant as it was, smoke was the only thing that drove mosquitoes away.

"Tonight, will you help me carve on Shaky's headboard?" I asked. "I've got it all done, except the 'R.I.P.' "

"Yeah," she replied. She shook each shirt out in preparation for hanging the garments. " 'Rest in Peace,' " she said, spelling it out. "I can do those letters."

"Didn't you have any schooling?" I asked.

"No," she said, "none. I learned myself to read all on my own."

"How?" Examining the tear in the knee of a union suit, I said a silent thank-you to Mrs. Ritters for seeing that I got my lessons.

"From the food tins in my ma's boarding house kitchen. *p* for peaches, *s* for salted cod. I never heard tell of the letter *z* until I saw 'zinc' on a gunny sack at the blacksmith's. You'd think I'd discovered gold, finding a new letter was so excitin'.

"Ya know . . ." Her voice broke off. She had clothespins in her mouth, so it was hard for me to understand her. "There're those chaps up at the ice caves needin' a burial."

"Poor old Dutch and Charley . . ." My voice cracked. Had Charley been killed on my account? Because Doc thought he was going to tell me about the "Wanted" poster? My appointment with the justice of the peace remained a mystery. I'd queried Nightingale about it more than once since she'd come to bunk with me, and all she said was, "You'll see," then smiled like a bobcat who'd just eaten your last venison ham.

"And Jake," she added. "His burial's long overdue."

"Jake," I said, my shoulders drooping, though not for long because we both doubled over in a giggle fit at the irony of it. Oh, it was bliss to have a chum.

"The humble laundress and her assistant are the only ones seein' him safely under the sod." Nightingale pinned a shirt to the line and watched the breeze billow it out like a sail. "Puttin' a body underground's a terrible lot of work," she continued. "With the excitement around Mr. Forrester and election speeches at the Gem every night, who's gonna dig the graves? Both of us are fresh outta steam."

"We could get the new 'flying horse' trader," I said with a half smile.

"Don't know that there is one," she replied. "Now that Doc's disappeared, the lads are havin' to go to Canada for their balsam." She paused, removing the clothespins from her mouth. "That invalid easterner I helped bring down from Dutch's is a gravedigger by trade," she said with a coy smile. "And he's not bad looking for a . . ." she stopped herself, "a foreigner." She had a peculiar grin.

"Your new beau?" I asked. No wonder she'd vexed Carolina.

Nightingale shook out a pair of big-bottomed trousers with such violence I thought she'd do them damage. "I'm offa men. Always get mixed up with the wrong one. Like I have a sign on me sayin', 'Trigger-tempered lads, this girl's for you.' "

"You? What about me? How could I have been taken in so?"

"Since you come, hardly anybody lost an arm or even a finger," she said kindly.

I'd gone inside, fetching us jerked beef and an apple bought in Coulee City. As I cut and pared the winesap, something caught my eye. On the floor next to my bed sat a box the size of a wagon seat covered with a sham. Pulling the cloth away, my mouth felt like a barn door falling open. My da's butterfly collection!

"Nightingale," I shouted, flying out into the yard, "where'd this come from?"

"Don't you like it?" she asked, first looking expectant, then hurt, even a little frightened. "You once told me you fancied butters, and I wanted to give ya somethin' . . ."

"Where'd you get it?"

"Hames gave it to me." She stood with the laundry pile between us in case she might have to ward off my attack. "Belonged to Jake."

"Thank you," I said, trying to appear calm, even gracious. Had Hames truly given it to her, or had she stolen it? I'd definitely have to keep an eye on this girl.

Regarding with suspicion the intensity of my surprised expression, she rushed to explain herself. " 'Member you kept asking about Jake's child? Well, he was savin' it for the kid. Got it off a trash heap when the child's people were put outta their digs and sent to the poorhouse. I thought it would please you," she said sulkily. Then she screwed up her face. "You're a hard body to figure, Pearl Ryan."

I felt stunned. I was the child Jake had told Ella about?

"It does make me happy," I assured her. My voice vanished, and my words came out in whispers. "I can't tell you . . . Thank you." So that's how Jake had gotten a hold of my da's treasures. Again I wondered why Jake had held onto them all this time.

Nightingale looked dubious. Keeping an arm's distance away from me, we ate in silence. As I bit into the first fresh fruit I'd eaten in months (it had been fresh last fall, anyway; now it was terribly withered), I figured I could find it somewhere in my heart to give Jake a decent burial. Hard as it was for me, I had to concede that he had a kind bone somewhere. Had he guessed at my true identity? I held the apple in my mouth a long time before I swallowed, sucking its comforting perfume. Let the dead rest, I told myself. I didn't really want to know.

Chewing tough victuals did not bring out the more pleasant side of Nightingale's features, not with her palate in the condition it was. The first thing I'd do at medical college would be to look into rectifying deformities like hers and Pigeon Belcher's.

After a while I asked, "Where do you think Doc disappeared to?"

"Gone to some railroad camp," she said. "Lots of call for amputations in the railroad business. You'd have plenty of morphia on hand. No one would question it. I'd bet Canada, less likely to run into Civil War vets up there. When word got out here that he was the Butcher of Missionary Ridge . . . Well, he's lucky he slipped out of Ruby before he got dragged through the streets. And you can say amen to that. Probably swapped his horse and his name as soon as he crossed the reservation."

Would I be looking over my shoulder all my life, wondering if Doc was going to come after me? He'd killed his wife for deserting him, and sometimes, I thought, he had confused me with her, which made me even more nervous. After all, I'd deserted him as well. With this revelation, all sentimentality evaporated. Now I felt only a vague grief—and more than some anger—over the loss of something I'd never really had.

"You shoulda been there when Sheriff Barton come to talk to Carolina," she said.

We'd finished our lunch, and crows suddenly appeared perching on the ridgepole of my tent.

"He said he'd had a bad report from Doc on you. That it was you who'd busted Poka Mika outta jail and did Carolina know where you was. Well, she looked down that stovepipe nose of hers and told the sheriff that she did not give credence to false testimony and that she did not know where you was—this is just after we found out Mary could talk and we was wondering what to do: come after you or let you run. 'Who's an unreliable witness?' asks the sheriff. And Carolina says that Doc had been a contract doctor in the war, didn't have a medical certificate from nowhere except a veterinary school, and was a danger, if not a public nuisance. Well, a smile spreads across Barton's face like a flash flood. 'Sorry to bother you, ma'am,' he says and tipped his Stetson, strutting away like he'd already won the election."

Just then I heard the rocks along the short cut to my digs begin to slide down into the ravine. Coming along the trail was a dark-haired young man with a gaunt face, a gold tooth on the side of his smile, and eyes so hollow they looked like they'd been blackened in a fight. He had a wobbly gait, as if his knees were gelatin, and steadied himself with a pine branch cane. Even though the day had become warm, he wore a coat with the fur collar turned up. "More laundry," I said tiredly, though relieved.

Nightingale stood, shielding her eyes from the sun with a graceful motion of her hand. "It's the new gravedigger." She smiled so that her small white teeth shone between the slit in her lip. Usually when she grinned, she held her hand in front of her mouth, so I'd never seen how gaping her deformity. Which was not my first thought. What flashed through my head was, Good God, men flock to her like bears to a honey tree.

"He's got no knapsack, he's not bringing any wash," I thought aloud. "Wonder what he's up to." As if I didn't know.

"Probably wants to hit you under the nose with his mouth," laughed Nightingale. Her hazel eyes were on fire with excitement. "He tracked you here from New York. That's what Arizona Charley wanted to tell you, that he was on his way." Her voice was high-pitched and shrill. "Don't you recognize your own husband?"

CHAPTER THIRTY-THREE

An hour later

We headed up Main Street's boardwalk. You can't imagine the gawking or the number of lads hiding behind buildings peeping back at us. What whispering. There was a great wind of, "He's finally come for her. Well, I'll be . . . Musta broken Doc's heart. No wonder he closed up surgery and left without a word." And society accuses women of being gossips and bearers of tales!

Taller than I remembered and thin as a pencil, Paddy's illness had changed him considerably. "Think you can make it as far as the Gem?" I asked. His larkspur-blue eyes peered out at me from under a hood of molasses-colored hair. He was attractive enough, especially when he cocked his head to one side like a bird as he glanced at the gents holding up doorways pretending they were checking on the color of the sky.

"I'm slow yet, but I'll get there," he said resolutely, though his voice sounded like a breeze caught in a coulee.

I had to laugh. It was like vaudeville: All these lads trying not to stare but clearly staring as if their eyes were nails and I a magnet, their whispers not quite drowned out in tobacco chew and foot stomp. They never guessed why Mr. Paddy Ryan had really come for his wife. One reason was that he'd caught gold fever—not to mention the beguiling idea of free land. If the lads had guessed at his ultimate motive, however, tongues would have wagged the dog clear around the chicken house.

We paused for him to catch his breath in front of the sheriff's shoemaker shop beneath the "Soles Saved Here/Souls Saved Here" sign, its broken hinge making a lonesome whine in the warm Chinook wind. All these rough, denim-clad gents thought they were watching our blessed reunion, imagining that they heard an exchange of long-awaited words of endearment. So just what did Mr. Ryan say to his dearly beloved?

"Pearl, ma'am," he said, catching his breath, "I've come to secure a divorce."

So that was why Charley posted me a letter instead of delivering his message in person. He knew Mr. Ryan's business and wanted to keep everything professional.

His chest heaving, Paddy leaned against the post that held up the green-and-white-striped awning in front of Grasshopper Jack's assaying shed. When he'd asked me to have a pint with him at the Gem, it just didn't feel right, but he was so adamant, so happy to see me. He was a kind soul, I could see it in his face. Though sunken, there was a babylike softness about his cheeks and mouth. So I'd agreed. How could I do otherwise? Nightingale had already fetched my bonnet and good apron, tied me up, and pushed us both along the trail. In the end, all the attention buoyed my spirits, making me feel like a new person.

"Miss Bridget McGregor of County Cork," he replied when I asked the name of his sweetheart.

"She's not in this country yet?" To tell you the truth, I'd half expected Nightingale's name to fall out of his mouth.

"She canna leave her old mother," he said, lapsing for the

first time into dialect. Otherwise I'd been impressed at his perfect English.

"I see." No wonder he'd come west after the lure of a homestead and a fortune in the mines. He'd have two women to support.

We passed the pine tree latrine in the vacant lot next the faro hall where, because of rising temperatures, both of us held our noses with one hand and swatted flies away with the other. The situation sent us into a fit of titters that seemed to dispel all awkwardness. Walking up the rough-cut steps onto the veranda of the Gem, we were delighted to get away from the smells of the street.

Inside, after my vision adjusted to the tobacco air, I glanced at Shaky's taxidermy collection, trying not to feel sad. I hadn't been here since the wake, and now without the mayor's and Dutch's lively voices, the atmosphere felt incomplete. Something, which my heart had once rejected, flashed through my mind. Just before Shaky began to sink like a stone, Doc prescribed more of his Liver Purger and Wizard Remedy. While treating the mayor's illness, Doc must have learned just how much morphia it took to poison a man so that it looked like death from what ailed him and not from opium.

Closing my eyes against this revelation, another piece fell into place. As Doc and I readied ourselves to perform Shaky's autopsy, Doc had given me a swig of one of his remedies. It had to have been a calculatedly powerful dose, because, I remembered now, I'd fallen instantly into a strange, deep sleep. While I dozed, Doc undoubtedly took the opportunity to go outside, making it look as if wolves had eaten the mayor's organs. That way, I'd never know that lead hadn't killed him and that opium had.

Lifting the beer glass to my lips, I stared down at the cedar slab table, studying the initials carved into it. And what about Arizona Charley? Doc hadn't had time to poison him. Pigeon

Belcher probably inadvertently told Doc about the letter Charley wrote to me, and no doubt Doc suspected the worst: that our justice of the peace had recognized him in an old "Wanted" poster and was going to tell me about it.

We sat in a corner, and even newcomers who knew nothing about me stole a glance. Street noise filtered through the wall chinks, mingling with the clanking of glasses being rinsed in a tub by the bartender. If it weren't for the red glow of his cigar, which marked the spot where his mouth must be, I wouldn't have known he was there at all—the air was that thick and the light from the shuttered windows that frail. As the door swung open and closed, the noise of marching feet followed patrons inside. The sudden jumping activity on North Main undoubtedly concerned Mr. Forrester's tour of the village.

"You needn't have come all this way," I said, then thought to ask Paddy how he knew where to find me.

"You talked about nothing but Okanogan Country all the way to the registry. I almost asked if I could come with you. Tell me, did you ever find Mr. Pardee?"

My God, Mr. Ryan was as sharp as an awl. "Old water under the bridge," I said. "And don't you have a memory as keen as a bush rabbit is quick."

He actually blushed, then went on to say that he'd begun having sweats and chills and feared it was the onset of white plague. He'd heard that the northwestern desert was good for weak lungs and hoped that the climate here might cure him.

"When I got off the ferry and looked up valley," he said, "I could see a hundred miles into Canada. Not a renderer's stack or foundry in any direction. And every chap so friendly. One jolly tart with hair the color of beet soup wanted to bring me home with her, no charge," he added, lowering his voice and widening his eyes.

"Ella!" I said too loudly even for the Gem. "*You* were the

gent with manners that our bawdy house matron met at the ferry, the one she'd never forget!" No wonder Ella hadn't recognized Davy. She'd never laid eyes on him before.

"Couldn't breathe during a New York summer. Glad I've come," he said again.

I wasn't sure what he meant. "Quinine's good for what ails you," I told him. Believe it or not, I began to regret not ordering one of Windy's hats—a straw trimmed in blue cornflowers that, as she said, would show my hair and skin to best advantage.

"You're a nurse?" he asked solicitously.

I told him I'd mopped a few brows and stitched up a few flesh wounds, then—he was easy to talk to—jabbered on too long about my plans and the letter from Williamette Institute of Medicine, which I would have shown him if it weren't for the faint light.

Someone slapped a deck of cards down on the table next to us, and then four gents in beaded gauntlets and Spanish boots began a hand of stud poker. One was a mixed-blood wearing the biggest plug hat and silver belt buckle I'd ever seen. He must have been wealthy, because copperskins were seldom so welcomed in Ruby.

"I've no hold on you," I assured him. "We can ride to Okanogan City whenever you like and draw up divorce papers. We've no attorney here anymore." He said nothing, so to fill in the space I asked, "When does your sweetheart arrive?"

"When I send the fare. I've got her and her mother's saved. But now there's her just-widowed sister and yearling niece." His watery eyes were as serious as if he were filing a mineral claim and trying to read the fine print.

"You're paying for all of them?" Judging by his clothes— custom made—he'd done well for himself. But he was such a soft touch that I feared some Rubyite would soon relieve him of his exquisite green coat with the beaver collar as well as his wallet.

He nodded. "I'm figuring I'll buy a claim down on the flat-lands by the river near the stage road where I can hang out my shingle."

A gravedigger advertising, that was one on me. "And what would this sign say?"

"I've a degree in bookkeeping and clerking from Trinity College, Dublin," he said with pride, though without even a tinge of arrogance.

I should have known from his hands that he'd not wielded a shovel all his life. "But I thought . . . Nightingale told me . . ."

"Ah, that." He waved as if to shoo away a fly. "Was the only work I could get when I landed. The New York law firms aren't fond of Irish. Well, it's not the firms—it's their clients they say would object. I found out pretty quick that it's not first rate to hire micks. I'd met a chap on the boat whose cousin . . ."

"I see."

"There's plenty of call for that kind of work. And I felt at home, all the auld boyos were from South Dublin. If the police tried to get their paws on one of us, the others would come to the rescue. Was how I got in with a union gang."

"And union troubles," I added. "I feel badly that you've spent your money to find me. Truly, I would have . . ."

"When I saw the advertisement, I knew I had to put it to you face to face, if nothing else but to thank you. Really, I've al-ways been obliged to you, ma'am."

"What advertisement?" I asked, then leaned over and whis-pered, "You must call me Pearl or the gossip will never stop. And besides, you paid me for my trouble. That's how I got here. . . ."

"In the *New York Daily News* last autumn. 'Reward,' it said. Anyone who had knowledge of your whereabouts was to call at a Fifth Avenue address."

"The Ritterses?" I asked but was interrupted by street noise.

From outside came a series of hoots, followed by at least five pair of horses galloping up the grade, going so fast it was a wonder the mire didn't suck the iron shoes off their feet. It had to be Cranky Frank with the payroll.

"Is there always so much excitement here?" Paddy asked. "The night I rode in, it reminded me of when Princess Alexandra visited the lowlands—so many guns popping."

"Shaky's wake!" I said, feeling my eyes widen. "Did you ride through town on a buckskin mare?"

"Yes," he said, "more than a week ago. So sick I could barely stay in the saddle."

"Then it *was* you I saw and not the drink playing with my brain!" We laughed and touched glasses, and I tried to act gay, as he seemed so eager to please me. "But why did Mr. Ritters advertise for information about me?"

The swinging doors creaked open, and Windy Pardee and the sheriff entered, ordering a pint each. Barton stood while Windy sat on one of the pews. "All there is to do now is go out and open a millinery store," said Windy. She wore a cartwheel hat completely covered in dried everlastings the color of egg yolk. "I'll need at least three girls. It takes two days to shirr enough chiffon for a lady's hat."

For a moment Paddy sat transfixed by Windy's spectacular apparel. Then he said, "Yes, your employer. I went there out of curiosity, mostly; it wasn't the reward. I wondered why someone would want so much to find you, not that. . . ."

"I know what you mean," I said, trying to hurry his story. Rifle volley exploded below the Skookum House, answered by gunfire near Ella's. Only ten minutes past two in the afternoon—no telling what kind of a night this was going to be. Luckily I had a gent to see me home. Odd how at ease I felt with Paddy, as if he were kin. Then I began to worry about Chin who was still nursing Jones and Mary who was out wooding. I felt the reassuring hardness of Shaky's revolver through my apron pocket.

"Skilled hat trimmers fetch ten dollars a week," Windy told Sheriff Barton.

Paddy cleared his throat and took a long swallow. "Mr. Ritters placed the ad," he said, "because his wife had passed on and there was a legacy left for you."

"For me?" It felt as if the feeble-legged chair I sat in might give way. "Mrs. Ritters left *me* money?" So she really *was* fond of me. Perhaps she had even loved me. I felt a tear well in the corner of my eye. Then another shadow fell over my thoughts. No doubt my good fortune had helped persuade Davy to try to find me.

"Not exactly," he went on, holding his glass next to his face. "Say, didn't they write to you? I told them your whereabouts, and they said they'd send a messenger."

Davy, I thought. Before Mr. Ritters realized that it was Davy who stole the diamonds. No wonder my former fiancé was so intent on marriage. If we'd married, Davy would have my money—or whatever this legacy was—and I wouldn't be able to testify against him regarding the necklace. I clenched my jaw, trying to swallow my anger.

Paddy ran his fingers through his unruly hair. He had the white hands of a scholar, but he had bitten every one of his nails down to the quick. "The money was saved over the years, sent to Mrs. Ritters for your education and board. Instead she put it away for you."

"My board? I worked for my keep. And Mrs. Ritters paid for the servants' children's tutors."

"So the mister said. His wife put your wages aside also. They paid you double."

"They did?" I was overcome for a moment, then asked, "Who sent my board?"

Next to us the card game was heating up. "I'll raise you ten blankets, ten guns, and ten fathoms of tobacco," said the mixed-blood.

At this point Cranky Frank Belknap burst through the doors. All heads turned in his direction. Even Windy stopped talking.

THE PEARL OF RUBY CITY

"It was on the headlines of the papers in Walla Walla," said Frank. Probably a hanging, I thought, as he passed the newspaper around. My stomach twisted—had Doc been lynched?

"That friend of your father's sent it every month," Paddy Ryan said.

"What friend of Da's?"

"Ten charges of powder, some knives, and ten shirts," said the mixed-blood.

"Your Mr. Pardee," said Paddy.

Cranky Frank opened his mail bag, pulled out a parcel the size of a matchbox, walked over, and laid it on the table in front of me. "Could ya pass this along?" he asked.

My face clouded. I gave him a nod.

"Couldn't give away ten charges for six bits now," said Frank, who was looking on at the game. "Raise him some ponies," he encouraged one of the white men.

"Mr. Pardee?" Had I heard correctly? Outside more guns went off, followed by the hollow sound of gummed miners' boots running along the boardwalk. "Mr. Pardee sent *money* for my keep and schooling?" Was that possible? Jake was the tightest man I'd ever met. Money was sacred to him. Money, according to his creed, was something to be kept and never spent. But he must have had a conscience after all. Perhaps he felt terrible about how things ended with Da and wanted to make amends.

I turned the brown parcel over, examining the jute string and address label: "Doctor Angus Stringfellow," it read. For a moment my hand shook.

"They weren't the kindest words that Mr. Ritters had for your da," Paddy said, hanging his head a little.

"I shan't take the money," I replied. "I've got property of my own now." I felt my hackles go up and my brow prickle. "My da was a faithful servant to Mr. Ritters and the Downs." I shook the wee box. It had a soft rattle.

"It was your father's habit of bending the auld elbow so

often as to put his family at risk that Mr. Ritters was referring to. He never said that Seamus O'Sullivan wasn't as charming as any man who touched the blarney stone."

"I don't care to hear any more about it," I replied, toying with the parcel.

Don't ask what possessed me, but I ripped open the package. Inside was an oblong case, very much like the one that held Mrs. Ritter's diamonds. But when I opened it up, what did I find? The spectacles Doc had been waiting on for nearly a year.

"Do you wear glasses?" asked Paddy kindly. "My ma does and my sister."

I put them up to my face, hooking the metal wires behind each ear. They were the strongest reading glasses, and I wondered how Doc could have seen a thing, being so farsighted. I studied my hand, staring at the orange hairs on my arm. There were two red dots on my wrist, and even in such bad light I saw that in the center of each were bore holes a bedbug had left, totally indiscernible with the naked eye.

"Very becoming," said Paddy. "Like Princess Alexandra."

I tossed my head. Oh, he's a flatterer, I thought, taking a swig of bitters. But wearing the glasses did make me feel dignified.

As Frank walked past me, I pulled on his sleeve. "What is it? What's the excitement?" All this commotion was over more than a hanging—it reminded me of the stories of the day Lincoln had been shot.

"The danged bill Congress just passed," Frank said, spitting saliva.

My face was a question mark. I took off the glasses and replaced them in their case, thinking that they could certainly be of use to me in my doctoring. But why should a congressional act affect the townsfolk? The last time anyone in Ruby had given a belch about Congress was when Washington Territory had acquired statehood, which had serious bearing on what was (and what was not) considered a felony—as if anyone would ever be found guilty by a jury of his peers in this town.

"The new gold standard," Frank explained, jutting out his boot-heel chin. "Congress just voted it in."

"But this is a silver town," I said, still perplexed. "What does it matter to us?"

"Yeah, we're silver miners," said Frank, whose leathery skin hung in creases over his stubbled jaw. "And the silver market's just gone bust! Only gold is legal tender for payin' debts." His mouth was shaped like an upside-down horseshoe with all the luck running out of it. "Mineral claims in these hills ain't worth the paper they're drawn on."

For a moment I stared past Frank, transfixed by wafts of cigar smoke, feeling like I'd just taken a heart-stopping fall from a horse. Time froze in that otherworldly moment between the second I toppled from the saddle and the instant I hit the ground.

CHAPTER THIRTY-FOUR

Dusk, the same day

Lacking the mental energy to face Nightingale, I'd bid Paddy good-bye after he insisted on seeing me most of the way home—though not before I'd promised to give him a tour of my mineral claims the following morning. Why he wanted such, I couldn't imagine. As of now the Last Chance and the Glory Hole were of almost no value.

Feeling for the safety of the six-shooter in my apron pocket, I trudged off to find a private place to mull things over. As I sat on a driftwood stump at the end of a row of privies below the Skookum House, the hoopla in the streets rose to an angry octave interrupted by gunshot interrogation marks: *What, what, what* was I going to do? Which was somehow easier to think about than my da's failures. The misty ghost of Jake Pardee crawled up the back of my neck, making me shiver. Essence of outhouse mingled with that of black powder, causing my gut to twist. Bending over in a fit of stomach cramps, I noticed the door of the privy closest to me crack open. No one had gone or come during the hour I'd been sitting there. The slivery, split rail door opened a foot, and then a set of white fingers bent around the frame, holding it ajar. Had someone been spying on me?

I thought not and, because I wasn't up for even the briefest encounter, I crouched down behind the stump, hoping to be left in peace with the terrible truth: How was it that Jake Pardee had provided more for me than my own father? I pressed my forehead into the log's peeling bark, trying to hold back the tears. Whoever it was in the outhouse closed the door almost soundlessly and began padding away toward the next latrine. Peering over the log, I couldn't see anything but the elbow and cuff of a green wool sweater.

My breath caught in my throat. I'd know that garment anywhere. I'd darned it a hundred times, making sure I perfectly matched the stitching and color of yarn to the cable knit. Doc's Shetland pullover!

The voice screamed: *Now! Shoot him in the back, and you'll never have to glance over your shoulder in fear again. It would look like the accident he perpetrated on the others—Dutch, Jones, Charley. That's justice, isn't it? No one would pin it on you.* For a moment, paralyzing indecision jolted me like a sunrise crashing down on a winter white valley bringing on snow blindness.

Digging my fingers into the grip of the revolver, I crept in the manner of Mary Reddawn from behind the log. Hiding in back of the privy Doc had just exited, I watched as he made his way past the next latrine down to the creek and the safety of the shadows of the bathhouse. More rifle volley erupted on Lower Main. The voice screamed, *Shoot the vermin!* Wasn't Ruby City's creed do unto others before they do onto you?

No, that's not justice; he'd never know what hit him. Hadn't Jake known who'd helped him meet his maker? Much as I hated to admit it, didn't I owe something to Mr. Pardee? For a moment I thought myself the kind of moral coward who would have gladly shot Doc in the back, but . . .

But what?

Suddenly I wanted to have the power over Doc's life that for an entire year he had had over mine. I wanted him to see me holding that gun at his heart, the way he'd aimed his angry eyes at me. The way he'd aimed a pistol at Jake, Jones, and most likely Dutch. And I certainly owed it to Shaky to bring Doc to his knees.

Doc tiptoed around the east side of the bathhouse. Tying up my skirt, I ran soundlessly from the back of the privy to the near side of the stack-wood building where Doc hid. I imagined he was waiting until dark to sneak up to his surgery or to a grub tent. Who would have thought of looking for him in a stand of latrines?

Then I heard the splashing of water. Rushing forward, I saw Doc bolt through the creek, making for the wagon road away from town. Pulling the gun from my apron, I held it in front of me, with both hands steadying the firearm. My entire body quaked. When Doc bent down to splash the day's grime from his face, I ran to the water's edge. He wasn't ten feet from me.

As I flexed my finger, the noise of the hammer cocking took up all the space inside my head. His back was to me. "Doc," I called in a voice so firm I surprised myself.

He straightened, then spun around, facing me. For an instant our eyes locked. Gravity tried to pull the gun to the ground, but I held it firm. He must not have recognized me at first, because for the instant my eyes hooked into his, his face took on a bewildered expression. Then he leaped backward in the water, yelling, "Pearly!" as if he'd just seen a ghost.

You mean the Pearly Gates, my trigger finger pulsed. I spoke not one word, waiting to see what he'd say. Would he explain himself, plead for his life? My eyes bore holes into his grizzled cheeks. Fright deepened the furrows in his brow.

"You wouldn't shoot an unarmed mon, would ye?" he asked plaintively.

Was he unarmed? I saw no weapon, but . . . Maybe that was how he tricked the others. "You did," I countered.

Doc flinched.

"Would you have shot me, too?" Venom laced my words.

Doc's jowls drooped. "Pearly, please, I was a good man once." He looked tired and spent.

Yes, I lamented, he had been a good man. But then I thought, no. Now he's just using me again the way he used me all along. "When was that, Doc? If you can be honest with me." His deceptions stung my heart like carbolic acid and I prayed he'd tell me the truth, just once.

"Get hold of your senses, lass. Another wrong won't put this right." He stared into the water, chewing his lower lip.

As the sun fell behind Three Devils peaks, the mountains turned a dusty purple and the treetops flamed yellow. A wind picked up, bending the creek willows. It gusted so fiercely that I made an adjustment for the bullet's trajectory.

When Doc saw my gun move, he did the most extraordinary thing. He ducked inside his sweater, pulling the garment up over his head, hiding his face. It was as if he'd just leaped down a rabbit hole, denying me the satisfaction of watching him meet his fate. He hadn't even the gumption to look me in the eye or give me a hair's breadth of an explanation. I was so angry that it felt as if I had a ten-pound weight tied to my trigger finger.

"Damn you!" I shrieked but could not pull the lever. Not because of my abundance of moral fiber but because of that cursed sweater. I'd spent hours mending it, preserving its loveliness. It was the only thing Doc had of his mother's handiwork. I'd seen what a gunshot could do to clothing. Sometimes there was nothing but a broken stitch to mark where the bullet entered the chest. But the exit hole! A burned crater as broad as the back of the garment and almost impossible to repair. I couldn't bring myself to destroy it.

"You won't get away from me," I commanded. "Take that sweater off, or I'll come do it myself."

He didn't move. Not a twitch.

Well, two could play at this game. I was prepared to stand my ground on the creek bank until evening stole every particle of the amethyst light. Doc was the one calf-deep in creek water and in danger of cramping from the ice melt.

"Pearl?" a man's voice called from the alley. "Pearl, is that you?"

"Yes," I shouted, but as I turned, glancing over my shoulder at a familiar figure, my aim migrated to the left. Doc saw his chance, pulled his head out of the sweater, and sprang for the other side of Salmon Creek.

"Been looking for you for an hour," Paddy shouted. "Forgot to ask if you needed help digging those chaps' graves . . ."

I fired, aiming at Doc's buttocks, but missed. In the instant it took me to correct my aim, then cock and fire again, Doc was gone. The last rays of sun disappeared. Bleak, smoke-colored clouds washed over me following Doc down the wagon road.

"What's going on?" Paddy asked, grabbing me by the upper arm. "That fella troubling you? See here, this time you let me take you to your door."

"Just a little accident," I said, breathless, staring after Doc.

"Didn't look like any accident," he replied, following my gaze. "Looked like that gent almost got his justice." Mr. Ryan's shock of raven hair hung down over his eyes thick as a horse's forelock, his gaunt face suddenly enlivened.

" 'Twas an accident that I missed, but a mercy," I muttered.

My shooting arm dropped to my side, grazing the sleeve of

Paddy's coat. I took a long, deep sigh. For a moment I felt over-come with the sensation that Mr. Ryan was a tree against which I might lean. "Sometimes," I stammered, "maybe even an acci-dental mercy is more important than justice." Lightly, my hand touched the spectacle case in my pocket.

CHAPTER THIRTY-FIVE

May 1

The sun hung above Paddy, Nightingale, Mary, Chin, and me like a brass plate. Loosening my shawl, I already felt as if I was wearing two layers of dust. From the wagon road above the stone orchard came the drone of cart-creak punctuated by the snap of goad stick and whiplash. A hundred voices mingled together, and occasionally one rose above the others, calling out a good-bye or a where-ya-bound-fur? or some other such signature. "See you in the Oro Fino," roared Frank Belknap's baritone.

When Paddy finished outlining the graves with a trowel, Nightingale and I turned the sod next to Shaky's resting place. Near us three white-shrouded bodies lay waiting. The mud had dried to a fine powder, dusting their final bedclothes.

Shaky's plot with its little fence and headboard was complete. As we dug the new graves, our backs bending and arms stretching like the tugs on a harness, Paddy set the point of his whittling knife to three little crosses that Mary had made. Slowly, his blade spelled out *Wilhelm, Charley, Jake* across the top limb of the crucifixes. Mary and Chin watched each name appear as if it were a duckling hatching out of an egg. Wiping the sweat from his brow, Chin adjusted his scull cap. He and his wife gave off a peculiar odor, having rubbed themselves in valerian stinkroot to repel snakes. Usually Mary wore no jewelry with her cavalry blanket and buckskin shirt, but today a string of violet seed beads dyed with sage flowers graced her thin neck. Her clothes must have weighed as much as she did, and I wondered how she could wear such heavy robes even on the hottest days without steaming herself to death.

"Why wouldn't ya take the money?" Nightingale held her nose whenever Chin got within a yard of her. "Pride comes before the fall, that's what I always say. Washington, Hamilton, 'n' Jackson—they were Jake's dearest friends, and he wanted you to have 'em."

"It's how he got his cache that troubles me," I said, leaning on my shovel.

"How does anyone get money?" she retorted. "With Jake dollars were a weakness like drink or opium. If he knew someone had a silver plug, he'd spend all day tryin' to figure how he could spirit it out of their pocket and into his."

I shrugged, then looked along Salmon Creek as it downrushed through the coulee to the Jordan-like Okanogan. Today the river that divided east from west was a green serpent twisting through the narrow valley.

"It musta near killed Jake to send money for your board every month. Like takin' a bite of flesh from his own body."

I had to agree with her on that point. My nose prickled, and I sneezed, my lungs not having quite adjusted to the smell of stinkroot.

"At least you'd do something good with it."

Putting my foot on the top of the spade, I pushed down, cutting into the sod. "My poke's big enough to grubstake a year of medical studies, if you'll keep house for me and be my assistant like you offered."

"I offered and I will. Mind you, stick to your part of the bargain and help me fix my what'd-ya-call-it? Palate. And for God's sake, take the money."

"It's a nice place, the medical college—on the Willamette River below the falls a days' walk south of Portland. Farmland, green as Ireland, I'm told, and filled with mist."

"Too close to my old ma and her boarding house," Nightingale scoffed. "She disapproves of my life—letting my husband die and then turnin' professional."

"But he tried to kill you!" Out of the corner of my eye I could see Paddy trying not to appear interested in our gossip but with an ear cocked in our direction all the same.

"Windy and her hat shop will inherit Jake's money, if you don't take it."

"No," I corrected. "Jake sent the money to Mrs. Ritters. Her godson Forr is her heir."

Nightingale threw me an exasperated look.

Paddy put down his knife, asking, "What were Wilhelm's dates?" He was a good sport to help lay to rest three men he'd never known and for no pay. Mr. Ryan stood at least a foot taller than I did, and those larkspur eyes lit up his entire face, despite the burgundy-colored shadows beneath them. The stout timbre of his voice told me that he was finally on the mend.

"I can tell you each man's death day, that's all," I answered. "And each served in the Union Army, so if there's some way you can mark their crosses . . ."

"I drove him to it," Nightingale said.

"Your husband shooting himself?"

"Me old ma said so."

Stooping down, I ran my fingers through a shovelful of dirt. It felt cool as spring water and smelled like snowmelt. "When we get set up," I told her, "we'll invite your mother over and show her what a pretty daughter she has. A pretty daughter following in Florence Nightingale's footsteps—your namesake, did you ever think of that?"

"My given name's Gale, remember?" she said. "Named for my pa—I was supposed to be a boy, a gypsy saw it in the coffee grounds." She blushed and for the first time looked meek and filled with childlike impishness. "Take the money," she repeated.

"I might," I said.

Mary glanced furtively at the traffic up on the road, her licorice-drop eyes afire. Then her gaze fell to the ground. It was bad luck to touch the backs of travelers with your stare. I suspected that the bad luck she hoped to avert was the possibility that the Rubyites might decide not to leave after all.

I told Paddy, "When we're through here, we can ride to Okanogan City and make out those papers." I wasn't sure I wanted a divorce. I rather liked being called Mrs. Ryan, though it wasn't fair to keep him from his sweetheart.

Up on the road I heard Windy's voice ring out above the clomping of a two-horse team, the last to leave Jake's livery. Sitting beside the sheriff, who drove a surrey, Windy wore a leghorn hat sporting two ties knotted under her chin. Hames rode alongside, leading a pack mule weighed down with blacksmith's gear.

"Hey, Windy," screamed Nightingale, "Pearl wants her reward. The thousand dollars you put up for information leading to the murderer of your husband."

"Save your breath," I told her. "The reward already rode out of town. It was Forr's money, and he's gone."

Windy's surrey stopped but only to move to the side of the trail as a dray struggled up the rutted lane toward the center of town, bucking the flow of traffic out of Ruby. It was a homesteader eager to salvage lumber from the now-abandoned buildings. Milled lumber was in short supply in these parts, and word of the closing of the Ruby Mine and the departure of the Forresters had traveled faster than a timber wolf strikes.

We'd been digging for more than an hour when Paddy took a turn. Too weak to stand for very long, he sat down and began working on the second grave with the spade. He seemed in no hurry to finish the task.

We paused, leaning against our shovels, listening to the boards being pried from Ella's veranda. In the distance, the *ping-ping* of wooden pegs falling on the plank walk below the bawdy house sounded exactly like grasshoppers swarming in the sage. "Thought I just heard the locusts that drove my people out of Kansas," said Nightingale.

"I'm not so sure about drawing up those papers," said Paddy. He tapped the fresh earth nervously with his index finger, pursing his lips. I thought they looked a little fuller today and with more color—the same dusty pink as a rockrose.

"Definitely on the mend," I whispered to Nightingale. Studying him as he sat digging with a trowel, I imagined that his old mother must miss her silk-voiced son.

"Suit yourself," I told him. "We're leaving for the Willamette Valley in the morning." I averted my eyes, pretending to check on my horse. Tillicum was tethered to the same willow as Paddy's sturdy buckskin mare. In the sun, her flanks shined the color of a barley field, her mane and tail dark as carbon. "Come along if you like."

"Where're they all goin'?" asked Nightingale. Shading her eyes, she stared through the road dust at the Bitterroots' Studebaker wagon. The runners of a rocking chair stuck out over the sideboards. Mrs. Brokenhorn trotted along, tied to the back.

"According to Pigeon Belcher they're headed for the Sweetwater north of Boise Basin," I said, casting a side glance at Mr. Ryan.

A motion of Chin's arms told me it was time for him and Mary to spell us. He took my shovel and Mary took Nightingale's, jabbing the newly sharpened blade down into the loose rock below the weave of sod. Even though he wore rags on his feet and she wore soft-soled moccasins, they dug as if shod in heavy boots. Occasionally, Mary glimpsed at the passing emigrants through her fringe of dark hair. Chin picked up a pebble, tossing it at his wife's feet. It was their way of flirting. Soon this ridge and the Siwash's sacred herb grounds would be restored to them, rattlesnakes and all. It gave new meaning to the meek who shall inherit the earth.

"Nightingale?" I asked. "Before we leave, could you draw me a likeness of the mayor's grave?" I studied Shaky's resting place, then looked across the ravine at my tent and piano crate, committing the landscape to memory.

She nodded. "Oh," she said, her jaw falling open, "I almost forgot. Do you think we could bury these next to Shaky's grave?" She thrust a hand into her apron pocket and produced a pair of gold and ivory false teeth.

"Shaky's missing dentures! Where'd you . . . ?"

"Swiped 'em," she replied in a perfectly even voice.

"You stole the mayor's teeth!" My God, what kind of a person had I chummed with?

"No, no," she said in a how-stupid-can-you-get tone. "I don't know who took them out of poor ol' Mr. Shaky Pat's mouth. I stole 'em from Carolina. Forr won 'em in a card game. He brung 'em up to show her. But I figured they ought to be buried with their rightful owner."

I stammered, "I think that's exactly what we should do." I took out Doc's spectacles, which I kept in my apron pocket with Shaky's watch, and examined the dental plates. Each hand-carved tooth was exquisitely sculpted. Some of the teeth had even been placed askew, so as to appear authentic.

"You look like a real doctor in them specs," said Nightingale as I replaced the glasses in their case.

I couldn't help smiling. I was beginning to feel like one.

Paddy pretended to occupy himself with the grave markers.

Stealing a glance at me and then gazing out over the valley tracing the loops of the Okanogan with his whittling knife, he asked, "What was the name of that river you're bound for?"

"The Willamette," I told him, stepping into the first grave. It was now too deep to haul up any more dirt from the side. But just as I did so, Paddy reached his hand down and pulled me back up. I didn't know he had that kind of strength in him and stared at his bony, thick-jointed wrist in amazement. His face was so gaunt I could see the hinge of his cheekbone and jaw, though a day of grave digging had put wild strawberries on his cheeks. As he gripped my hand, I marveled at the softness of his flesh.

"I might do just that, come along and keep you company," he said. There was a pleading light in his eyes that cut straight to my heart.

I thought of asking, But what about your sweetheart? Then I decided not to. Putting on my new spectacles and adjusting them to fit the bridge of my nose, I gazed down at the Okanogan, feeling a sudden inner peace. Turning to Paddy, I met his magnified eyes head-on, studying the gold flecks in his watery irises.

"You know what the old-timers say," I told him. "Any river might be Jordan."